love sex
& secrets

love sex & secrets

Re'Telle Lee

LOVE SEX & SECRETS

iUniverse books may be ordered through booksellers or by contacting:

iUniverse
1663 Liberty Drive
Bloomington, IN 47403
www.iuniverse.com
844-349-9409

Because of the dynamic nature of the Internet, any web addresses or links contained in this book may have changed since publication and may no longer be valid. The views expressed in this work are solely those of the author and do not necessarily reflect the views of the publisher, and the publisher hereby disclaims any responsibility for them.

Any people depicted in stock imagery provided by Getty Images are models, and such images are being used for illustrative purposes only.
Certain stock imagery © Getty Images.

ISBN: 978-1-6632-6437-4 (sc)
ISBN: 978-1-6632-6438-1 (e)

Library of Congress Control Number: 2024913283

Print information available on the last page.

iUniverse rev. date: 07/24/2024

prologue

I don't wanna sound lame or make you think I'm insane. But I say what's on my mind and I don't think about it again. Who am I? What's my name? It's for me to know and you to find out. Now pick a spot get comfy and sit, but make sure you got time for this. Cause what I gotta say you gon wanna hear. I have to take you back, all the way back, to the very beginning. Listen carefully and picture this!

February 4, 2005

As I pull into the gas station, bumpin' Beyoncé, jammin' and looking sexy as hell! I throw my car into park. I turn off the engine and hop out. With my MasterCard in hand, I swipe and then I hear, *"Excuse me, but can I say that you just took my breath away!"*

Before turning around, I roll my eyes and I think *YEAH NIGGA PLEASE!* But as I spin around, I meet his gaze. My eyeballs stretch, I lick my lips and think, damn! Brother man is fine.

He walks over to me and says, *"Now that I've caught my breath allow me to introduce myself."*

He licks his lips as he speaks to me, but all I can hear is gibberish.

I blink my eyes and with a confused look on my face, I say, *"Excuse me!"*

He smiles and says, *"Hello beautiful, I'm Rodney! And you are?"*

I smile back and say, *"Hey"* and I introduce myself.

He responds with, *"Well it's nice to meet you. I would love to get to know you better!"*

With slight arrogance I say, *"Oh really! And how do you plan to do this?"*

"Well if you would give me your number I would like to start there."

I smile again and say, *"No."* His face cracks, his smile leaves and he looks totally embarrassed.

He stammers out, *"W w w well sorry to have bothered you!"*

I stand smiling as he says this and I say, *"Don't give up so easily! I'll take yours."*

February 6, 2005

After a few days, I call him. He picks up after a few rings. In a very deep sexy voice, he says, *"Hello!"*

"Hi is this Rodney?"

"Yes, and I know who you are! Your call is the only one I was waiting for. I'm glad to finally hear from you!"

We stay on the phone and get to know each other. He is twenty-five years old and he stands at 6'2". He has a bald head that makes you just want to rub and lick it. His eyes are hazel brown and his lips are full and thick. He has a very thick full beard and mustache. In each of his ears, he wears a diamond stud. In his mouth he wears a gold diamond grill. His complexion is a light caramel hue. He is a father to a three-year-old daughter. He lives alone and he works as a longshoreman. Yes, Damn! Ain't he fine?

As I learn about him, I like what I hear. He's smart, educated and he seems to have a good head on his shoulders. I decide to give him a try. We agree to meet up and go out on a date.

February 1, 2009

For the question burning in your skull! Who am I? I think it's time you found out. But just a lil' bit though. My name is Tasha, but you can call me DIVA! I'm an African American female. I work in a doctor's office, and I'm pre-med. I don't have any kids. But hopefully one day.

I am very voluptuous with DD breast and a big round butt. Most men would describe me as thick. My milkshake does bring all the boys to the yard. And yes, it is better than yours! My measurements are 36, 26, 42. I have long thick kinky black hair down to my back. My skin is as smooth as milk chocolate. My eyes are light brown and beneath them sit's a round button nose and sexy plump pouty lips. I stand at 5'5".

chapter 1

Old Flames

May 30, 2005

**In life, one should never have any regrets. Whether it's love,
education, work or with family. Live your life to the fullest.
After all you only get one life. There are no do overs.**

I decided to take summer courses to get some experience. I'm sitting up in my bed with my laptop on my lap. I've done enough studying for today. I need a break before I fry my brain. I get on the internet and log into social media.

I look at the top of the screen and I have a friend request. I click the link and low and behold, I see it's from my high school love. It's Walt. Along with his friend request, he includes a message:

> **WaltDaGreatPerry:** *Damn Ra'Quel, you look good as hell. How you doing sweetheart? I miss you.*

Ra'Quel is my first name. Only my close family and friends know this and of course Walt. He's always called me by my first name and he is the only one that I allow to do it. I can't help, but to smile. I've missed Walt too. I couldn't give him what he wanted at that time. I had to let him go. But that's another story for another time. I accept his friend request and he is currently online.

He sends me another message and asks for my number. Shortly after I hit enter to submit my number, my phone rings.

When I answer the phone, I hear, *"Hey Sweetheart, what's up?"*

"Hey, not too much. Just been studying and working. You?"

"Same here. You miss me? Have you been thinking about me at all?"

"Yeah, I do miss you."

"I wanna see you."

"You are hundreds of miles away."

"Not really. I decided to come home this summer."

"Really?"

"Yeah. When can I see you sweety?"

"I'm seeing someone."

"And. We're old friends. We got some catching up to do. And like I said, I miss you."

"You don't have a girlfriend back in California?"

"Nope. Not since you broke my heart."

"I did not break your heart."

"Yeah you did. I haven't been able to put it back together again. When can I see you? Maybe you can mend my broken heart."

Wow. He really isn't taking no for an answer. Rodney and I went out a few times. He hasn't staked his claim or nothing. Hell, it's been over three months and he hasn't made a move. We're together every weekend and frequently during the week. As far as I'm concerned, he's seeing other women. I know how to play the game. Either play or get played. For now, I'll play.

"What about this weekend?"

"What about now?"

"No, I'm already in bed. I have class in the morning and work."

He starts laughing, *"Well, I don't mind."*

"Very funny. I bet you don't."

"Ok. What day this weekend?"

I already have a date with Rodney on Saturday, so that won't do. *"How about Friday evening?"*

"What time? Name the place."

"How about eight? You staying at your parent's house? How are they doing?"

"Eight is good. Yeah, I'm staying with them while I'm home and they are doing good. Where you wanna meet?"

"I can meet you at your parent's."

"Nope. I wanna spend time with you. Not you, me and my parents. You know they love you and they gonna monopolize your time."

I smile. *"You know I love them too. Well, you name the place."*

"We can meet at our spot."

"Ok, I'll see you there at eight. I'm going to bed now."

"Ok sweetie, goodnight."

June 3, 2005

It's finally Friday. I'm getting ready to go see Walt. I get all dressed up. I put on a sexy chocolate dress that hugs me in all of the right places. It's sleeveless and low cut to show some cleavage. It's fairly short; about mid-thigh is where the hem stops. I accessorize with some gold jewelry and open toe stilettos. I look very sexy.

I arrive at the rendezvous location and I spot Walt waiting for me. It's the Battery. It's a harbor where couples go to spend time together. Some get a little too freaky, but hey that's none of my business. You can walk around the harbor or just sit on the benches and listen to the water and feel the breeze. It's pretty romantic, if you like that kind of thing. Walt and I spent a lot of time here together.

When I arrive, I spot Walt from a distance. He looks exactly the same just sexier and bigger, in all the right ways. He is about 5'11" and around 205 pounds. He's put on some weight or rather muscle since I've seen him last. It looks good on him. Really damn good. He is very stocky, an all-around thick man. He has the build you would expect to see from a football player. He has a sexy brown sugar complexion. His hair is jet black. He has a Caesar cut with waves that will make you drown in them.

"I see you're fashionably late."

I smile, *"Of course."*

"I brought these for you." He hands me a bouquet of roses.

"Thank you. That's very sweet." He walks with me and I put the roses in my car.

"Can I get a hug or something?"

"Of course, you can."

He pulls me towards him and wraps me in his arms. I put my arms around his neck and we just stand there for a while, silently, while he holds me. It feels good to be in his arms again. Once we finally pull apart, we begin walking and talking.

"Damn Ra'Quel. You look good."

"Thank you. So do you. I see California is treating you good."

"Yeah, I guess. It would be better if you were there with me though."

"I'm sorry. I just couldn't go again. The timing was all wrong."

"I know it was. And I don't want to bring up any of that pain from back then, but I miss you sweetheart. We was pose to be at least engaged by now."

I smile at the thought. *"Yeah. Life is funny."*

"I still want to be with you."

"We already talked about that. I'm still not interested in anything long distance right now. And I'm seeing someone, remember?"

"Well I don't see him here. Besides you saying you seeing someone, not that you have a man. Two completely different things. He hasn't made it clear to you what he wants?"

"It's a little complicated. We started off being friends and now we're trying something different."

"We started off as friends too. All the way back to middle school, but I already knew what I wanted. I still know what I want. I want you to marry me."

I burst out laughing, *"Now that's funny. Stop playing. You play too much."* Once I control my laughter, I look at his face, then into his eyes; he isn't laughing. He is serious.

"I'm not playing." He gets down on his knees and pulls out a ring. *"Ra'Quel, will you marry me? I'll move back to South Carolina. Whatever you want."*

"Walt baby, I can't do that. I'm not ready to get married. You can't leave school because of me. It would be the biggest regret of your life. Please get up off the ground."

"The biggest regret of my life is that I didn't stay here with you. Now you're dating other people and I'm still in love with you." He begins to get up. *"As far as school is concerned, I might leave anyway. I have some recruiters looking at me. I may go pro."*

"Please don't drop out of school to go pro."

"Why not? There is nothing holding me there."

"You need to finish school and get your degree. So, when your ball playing years are over, you will have something to fall back on. I know you have what it takes to be a pro baller, but keep your options open."

"You were my something to fall back on. I haven't made up my mind yet about going pro, but I'm really considering it."

"Please take my advice. Don't do it. You are a great football player. That life will always be there for you."

"Not always. I'm in my prime now. I'm at my best. I'm gonna think on it. There is nothing holding me back. You won't marry me. I may as well live out my life."

"If the timing was right, I would marry you. But I'm not at a place in my life, where I'm ready to be someone's wife."

I'm unsure as to why, but he begins to smile. *"That's why I love you so much. I tell you I'm thinking of going pro and I want to marry you. You say finish school and that you can't marry me because you're not ready. You love me, for me Ra'Quel. Not for my potential earning ability."*

"You're right Walt. I do love you for you. You are easy to love. You are a good person. You won't be single for long."

"I'm single by choice. Those women in California look at me and they see dollar signs. I can't recognize the real from the fake. But with you I know it's real. Those women out there, would say go pro, get that money. They would just be along for the ride. But if something were to happen, I get injured or some shit. Then I can't play ball anymore. They would be gone. On to the next one. But not you. That's why I love you so much."

"You're not gonna make this easy, are you?"

"Hell no. It's a war. I've lost some and won some battles. Now I'm trying to win the war."

"Cute. That's very funny."

"I'm serious. Love is a war. Do you know I've had this ring since back in high school? I was gonna pop the question on graduation night, but you had other plans."

I really begin to feel bad. I had no clue he was thinking like this back then. I wonder if he'd had asked what I would have said. *"Walt I'm sorry. I didn't know you felt this way."*

"You knew that I loved you."

"Yes, but I didn't know what you were planning. Why didn't you ask me then?"

"Would it have made a difference? How could you know? Right after we graduated, I came looking for you. I ditched my family, to find my girl. I wanted to celebrate with you. I called you and you didn't answer. I went to your house and no one was home."

I really feel like crap hearing this. I do regret how I ended things with him. Not moving to California with him set my life on a completely different path. I let him continue to talk.

"I never found you. All summer I kept trying. I went by your house again, you weren't there. Eventually, I found out you didn't live there anymore. You moved and changed your number. I couldn't reach you. If it weren't for social media, I still wouldn't have been able to find you."

"I really don't know if it would have made a difference. I was in a different place then. I loved you, but I wasn't giving you the love that you deserved. I was in a dark and broken place. I thought I was holding you back. I wasn't ready to love you as you loved me. So, I had to let you go. I'm sorry I hurt you. I never meant to do that. I felt like letting you go then would give you a chance to be with someone who could love you like you deserved. I thought it was best to just cut ties because it wasn't fair to you to put your life on hold for me."

"It didn't because I never stopped loving you. And two years later, you're still not ready? I'm still in love with you."

"I will always love you. You are my first love. The first man to teach me about love. But, I'm not ready for what you want right now. I'm not ready to be a wife. I have so many years of school left and that's my focus."

We're standing on the pier and he has his arms wrapped around me, *"I want to make love to you Ra'Quel."*

I can't believe what I'm hearing. *"How about this, in eight years at our first high school reunion, we can reevaluate our situations. If we're both single, we can give it a try."*

"I still want to make love to you tonight."

"I guess we'll see about that in eight years at the reunion."

"Damn. Eight years is a long time. Can I at least kiss those pretty lips? I've missed them so much."

I flash him a smile. Actually, I'm blushing. *"Yeah you can."*

I spin around to face him. He pulls me closer into his arms, places his hands on my booty and squeezes. He gently kisses my lips. His lips are so soft. He slides his tongue into my mouth and I slide mine into his. He has long ago, mastered the art of kissing with tongue. He starts kissing and sucking on my neck. We're interrupted when his cell phone goes off.

He pulls back from me. *"Damn."* He looks at the display and hit's the ignore button, *"That's Alex, I told him I was seeing you tonight and that I'd holla at him later."*

"How is that nut doing?"

"He's good, still fool as ever. But enough about him. I'm gonna be waiting to see you in eight years, with this ring."

We begin walking back to my car. *"You will probably be married before then. Just make sure you don't give her this ring. That's a little tacky."*

He starts laughing. *"Naw I wouldn't do that. But it don't really matter. Cause I'm not gonna be married. I'm waiting for you."*

"That's if you're single. Just because you're not married it doesn't mean that you are single."

"I'll get single. Hopefully you'll be single too. But I don't know if that's likely, cause you fine as hell. You bout something and I know your future is bright. I expect you to shine like the star that you are. But if you aren't, I will do whatever I have to, to help you get single."

"Only time will tell."

He takes my hand and he walks me back to my car. *"Yeah it will. I don't want this night to end yet. Can I feed you?"*

I smile at him. In spite of my memories. I don't want the night to end either. I feel some regret for how I ended things with Walt. It wasn't right and he still cares for me and is understanding. What the hell was I thinking letting him go. I shake the thoughts off. Our lives are on different paths now. That's on me. I do regret my decision to let him go then.

As much as I want to be selfish, throw caution to the wind and say forget Rodney I want you Walt. I don't want to make a decision now that will hold him back or hinder him. I love him too much for that. I want him to be as great as he can be. If I tell him I want to get with him he'd leave school. I don't want to be the cause of that. I'll just enjoy the night and the time I have with him.

"I could eat."

We make it to my car and he opens my door. We discuss where we'd like to dine and he follows behind me in his car. Dinner with him feels like old times. We didn't miss a beat. Falling back in with him would be so easy. But not fair to him. I have to do the mature thing. I sure as hell don't want to though.

After an amazing dinner, he walks me to my car again. He opens the door and our eyes meet. I feel his hands pulling me towards him. I feel his breath warm across my face. I smell the fresh mint scent of his breath. Our eyes meet in a heartfelt gaze. I'm hoping he can't see the pain in my eyes. The pain I feel because I know I have to let go of him. But I don't want to. He tilts my chin up towards him as he's staring into my eyes.

"What's wrong?"

"Nothing."

"Naw. It's something. Tell me. What's on your mind?"

"It's nothing Walt. It's just nice to be here with you."

"I know you. I know it's something more than that. I won't push it though. Tell me when you're ready."

"Ok."

I want to tell him I love him. I've missed him. But I can't. He pulls me closer to him and I know what's coming next. I know I shouldn't, but I want to so badly. He places his lips to mines and begins kissing my lips. He slides his tongue in my mouth and I slide mines in his.

I hadn't noticed until now, how much I've been missing his lips. He's always been a great kisser. He has the perfect lips. He definitely knows what to do with his tongue. We are stuck in a lip lock together for a while. We finally come up for air.

"Can I come back to your place tonight?"

"I don't think that would be a great idea."

"Why not? You can trust me."

"Oh, I do trust you. It's me that I don't trust."

I lean in and kiss his lips again. Passionately, as I slide my tongue back into his mouth. I realize that my feelings for him never died. They were lying dormant. Now they have come to the surface.

"See I can't trust myself."

He starts laughing. *"Well I don't mind it at all."* He licks his lips. He's so close to me that he licks mine as well. He flashes me a smile. *"Damn girl, I want you. I want you bad."*

"That's why you can't come over. You're a bad boy."

"You like me bad. Especially back when we were together. If I remember correctly, you were a bad girl. Let's be real you were no angel."

I start laughing. *"Yes, I was."*

"Everyone thought you were. But I know the truth. You are a freak."

"Whatever."

He still has me wrapped in his arms. *"When can I see you again?"*

I can't continue to see him and allow him to move on. Or to allow myself to move on. It's not fair for me to keep him in love with me knowing I can't be with him without him sacrificing his life for me. Especially when I know I want him. I want him in every way.

"In eight years."

"Hell no, that's not soon enough. Me, Alex and the rest of the crew been talking about getting together. You know Alex still wants Kenya."

I let out a laugh. *"Of course, he does. Well let me know when ya'll getting together and I'll tell Kenya."*

"Ok beautiful." He kisses me once again before I get in the car.

When I get back home late Friday night, I have to take another shower. I have to be honest with myself. He has me hot and bothered. I'm a little moist. He does something to me. I had a really good time with him. I hope that I am single in eight years. If I am, it will be so on. I head to my bathroom and run the water for a shower.

While standing in front of my mirror, I begin getting undressed. I lean in closely to see if what I think I see is right. When I lean in, I see a big hickey on my neck. That's not good. Rodney will not be ok with that. We're not official or anything, but I know it's going to be a problem.

chapter 2

New Love

June 4, 2005

New relationships can be tricky. When do you know that he is all in? When does that moment occur when he says, to himself, that's it, I'm done looking? I found the one. Some men make the assumption that we as women know this, but unless they tell us we really don't know.

I spend my Saturday morning in bed studying. It isn't until after 4pm that I decide to get out of bed. Rodney gets to my house a little past 7:30 for our date. I open the door and he greets me with a kiss.

"*Hey beautiful.*"

"*Hey. Come on in.*"

When he steps inside the first thing, he notices is the roses from Walt on the fireplace mantel. He walks over to them. It's almost as if he's looking for a card or something.

"*Where the hell these come from Tasha?*"

"*From a friend.*"

"*What friend?*"

"*An old friend from high school.*"

"*Really now?*"

"*Yes. It's not that important. Can we leave now?*"

"*You say that because it's you. If this were me in this situation, it would be a big damn deal.*"

"*Do you wanna argue or do you wanna go out?*"

He rolls his eyes. "*Alight Tasha.*"

After dinner and dancing we go back to my place for a little quality time. We are sitting on the sofa hugged up together. Before we went out, I put some makeup over Walt's hickey. Periodically throughout the night, I've been checking my neck to make sure it stayed covered.

Since I got back home, I hadn't checked it. Somehow it must have rubbed off. I feel him rubbing the makeup from my neck.

"What the hell is this?"

He gets up to turn the lights up. I thought dimming them would help with the concealment of the hickey. I was so wrong.

"What's what?"

"What the hell is this damn hickey doing on your neck?"

"It's nothing."

"You got a hickey on your neck and I sure as hell didn't put it there. That's something. I want the truth."

"You have the truth, kind of. It's from an ex-boyfriend that came into town and he asked to see me."

"And you went? That's some bullshit."

"No, it isn't. We were friends before we started dating. When he moved to go off to school, I broke up with him. And quite frankly, he's single and so am I." Like I said I know how to play the game.

He looks at me as if he's stunned. *"What the hell you mean so are you? Did you fuck him?"*

"You haven't committed to me. As far as I know, you're still dating other people. Until a man tells me he wants to be with me and only me, I assume that he isn't with me and only me. Once he makes this known, I'm with him and only him."

"You said all that bullshit. But you didn't answer my damn question. Did you fuck him?"

"Hell no. I'm not a ho."

"You just let him put his lips and hands all over you."

"You don't know what happened, you weren't there."

"I didn't need to be there. I know that when I'm kissing you, my lips and my hands are all over you. I wouldn't expect him to do anything different."

"Rodney we aren't in a relationship."

"How did he get back in contact with you?"

"He found me online."

"Of course, he did. He needs to be deleted right now."

"What? That's ridiculous."

"Hell, no it's not. I want him deleted now Tasha."

"No Rodney. I'm still single you don't have a right to tell me who I can and can't be friends with. Last time I checked, when you introduce me to someone, it's as your friend. You are the one with the commitment issues, not me. You've been running away from committing to me. As long as we are 'friends' I can go out with other guys. You don't like it, change it."

"Ok. I'm sick of this shit. You need me to make it official that your ass is off the market. I'll do that. Your ass is off the fucking market. But you are going to delete his ass off tonight." He grabs my laptop and passes it to me. *"Here, delete him."*

I grab it from him and log into my account. I don't really want to delete Walt, but I think that I've already stuck my foot in my mouth.

"Don't you think that's a little premature, perhaps?"

"Hell no. He's an ex. Ya'll don't have kids together, therefore he don't need to contact you. Why'd you break up with him for anyway?"

"I had a lot of personal things going on. He went off to school and I stayed here to be close to my family."

As if he really doesn't give a damn, he says, *"Oh alight. Now delete the mother fucker."*

I stand looking at Walt's profile picture one last time. I've asked Rodney to step up and he has. Now it's my turn. There's no turning back. I select the link that says "Friends" and I watch it change to Add Friend.

I look up to Rodney and say, *"It's done."*

He gestures for me to hand him my phone.

"You don't trust me?"

"Do you have something to hide?"

I roll my eyes and pass the phone to him. He takes the phone and he is looking through it. He scrolls through my contacts and deletes Walt's number. Then passes the phone back to me.

"We good now?"

"That's the same thing I want to ask you. You understand we together now? No more damn dates with no other niggas."

"Yes Rodney, I got it."

September 2, 2005

It's been about three months since Rodney made me un-friend Walt and he and I jumped into a relationship. Rodney and I have now known each other for seven months. Since becoming official, he wined me and dined me. We love to go out and we party and club together.

After I first deleted Walt he called me several times, but I wouldn't answer. Since I committed to Rodney, I promised to cut all communication with Walt. Needless to say, that meeting with Walt, Alex, Kenya and I never happened. Or rather it happened just without me.

I wanted to explain things to Walt myself, but I knew Rodney would be pissed. Seeing Walt isn't good for my relationship with Rodney. I'm a faithful type of woman and I want to keep it that way. With Walt I tend to lose my head a little.

Kenya had the tea about Walt. Right after the meeting a few months ago she stopped by my house. She told me Walt was upset that I stopped taking his calls. Or rather he was furious. Kenya is my girl, she defended me and explained for me. After that meeting Walt started calling me again. I ignored the first few calls. He stayed persistent. Eventually, I broke and answered. I felt like I owed him that. Especially with our history.

I explained my disappearing and that I was in a relationship. He didn't care. He asked me out anyway. I told him that I couldn't go out with him. He kept trying anyway, but I just ignored him. I knew if I kept talking to Walt, I'd cheat on Rodney with him. After all Walt is my first love. Although it was just puppy love, it still counts. When summer ended, I heard he went back to school in California. I hope he is doing well though. I still think about him from time to time.

Rodney and I have a lot of chemistry and we spend a lot of time together. He is more than just my man; he is my friend. That's the type of relationship, we've built and I love it. I have met his family and his daughter and we all get along. We have a lot of dates in which his daughter is with us. I've found myself diving headfirst into step mommy roll with her. I didn't think I was ready, but with her, it's easy. She's a sweetheart and so easy to love.

Hell, I've even met his daughter's mother, Whitney. She seems to be ok. They're co-parenting and she's in a relationship with someone else. She ain't checking for Rodney. Long as it stays that way, we'll be good. Everything is great!

Until…Of course there's an until…There's always an until! Or I wouldn't have a story to tell.

chapter 3

A Four Letter Lie

December 2, 2005

**I LOVE YOU! It is supposed to be the sweetest phrase that can come
from someone. But what happens when they don't show it?**

Rodney and I have been officially dating for six months and we've known each other for
ten. During our relationship, we haven't had sex. I know, that's long as hell. I've been making
him wait for it. Although, I have let him go down on me. I've even let him touch and play with
it. I haven't gone all the way with him yet. Hell, he was begging to kiss it, who am I to say no.
He does it very well.

I can tell that he is sexually frustrated. I never made any promises to return the favor.
He loves me and I know he is tired of waiting. I may give in to him soon. I don't want to feel
pressured. I want to do it when I am ready. I am just not there yet. We are already having
some little problems in our relationship here and there. He's been somewhat secretive lately
which makes me think something is up. Which is making me even more reluctant to have
sex with him.

While sitting on my couch in my pajamas studying, my doorbell rings. I head to the door
and look through the peek hole. Its Rodney. I invite him in, we sit on the couch together and
talk a bit about our day. I am not super engaged in conversation with him because I am still
trying to study.

I hear him talking to me, but I kind of tuned him out a bit. He pulls me out of my studies
when he pulls me close to him. He begins kissing me. His lips feel nice. He softly and gently
kisses me. He smells so good. His Burberry cologne flows into my nose. He catches my bottom
lip in between his. Then he begins sucking.

We share a passionate moment. As I attempt to resume studying, he slides his hands up the top of my pajamas. He makes his way to my breast and grabs them. I push his hands away. I already know where his mind is headed.

"Stop Rodney!"

"Stop? Why I gotta stop? You always do this shit!"

His phone rings, he pulls away from me. Then he checks the caller id and he does the unthinkable. He gets up from the chair and walks off to answer his phone. To myself I wonder, *why the hell can't he answer his phone in front of me?* I do, what any other woman in my situation would do, I proceed to follow him. When he hears me coming, he ends the conversation and hangs up the phone.

"Who the hell were you talking to?"

"My homeboy! What you checking up on me now?"

"Hell Yeah! Why couldn't you talk in front of me? You got something you need to hide?"

"Shit Tasha don't start! Damn."

"Start what Rodney? Let me see your phone!"

"No!"

"What you hiding then?"

"Can we just go back and chill on the couch. Come on let's go sit down."

He grabs my arm and pulls me back to the couch. He sits next to me and tries kissing up on me again.

"Move Rodney!"

"Damn baby! I've been knowing you for a while now. We done been together for six months. Six damn months and you acting like I am a stranger. How much longer do I gotta wait before I can make love to my woman?"

Furious and upset. I look at him and yell, *"Fore as long as I say!"*

He raises his voice back and says, *"Well when you gon be ready? Huh? It's been six months and you still ain't ready. I can kiss your pussy and lick it, but the moment I talk about giving you the dick then you wanna run. But when that mother fucker Walter came into town, you didn't have no damn reservations. He could put his hands and his mouth wherever he wanted to."*

I roll my eyes, *"If sex is all you want from me then you need to go someplace else and get it!"*

"Maybe I will."

He grabs his keys and storms out of the house. I stay on the couch in shock. No, that nigga did not just up and leave? I need somebody to pinch me. I do love him, but I am not ready to go there with him. A cell phone rings and I notice that Rodney left his phone. I guess it must of fell out his pocket. I pick it up and look at the caller ID. It says Melissa. I push the send button.

"Hello!"

"Who is this?"

"This is Tasha and how do you know Rodney?"

"We been kicking it for a while. Why? How you know him? What you doing with his phone?"

I'm livid. *"Wow! Really? I am his girlfriend. He just left my house. How long ya'll been kicking it?"*

"He ain't tell me he had a girl. We been hanging together for a couple of months now."

"Well he does have a girl. And it's me."

"Well why is he on the way to my place?"

I am pissed. I'm seeing red and in disbelief. Here goes his secret. I knew he was hiding something and here it goes. No woman wants to hear this. Her man being unfaithful. Talking to the other woman. *"Imma kill him, I scream! Where do you live?"*

"Why?"

"Look I don't have a beef, with you, Melissa. But I wanna confront his lying cheating ass."

"How do I know your ass ain't crazy?"

"I guess you don't know and you don't owe me anything, but he's been playing both of us. As a woman of my word all I can say to you is I guarantee you we don't have an issue. My issue is with the man I've been dating and who was supposed to be committed to me."

"Ok, girl. Long as we don't got no problems, we cool. Cause I'm too grown to be fighting over some nigga."

"So, the hell am I. I just want to bust his ass and see what he got to say for himself."

"Ok then Tasha let's do this."

She gives me her address and I hang up the phone. During our conversation, I was changing my clothes and getting dressed. I get in my car and I head over to Melissa's.

My phone rings and it's Rodney calling from his work cell phone. I don't answer it, instead I ignore his call and send him to voicemail. He leaves me a message, but I don't check it. I arrive at Melissa's apartment and I actually beat Rodney there. I park my car a few buildings over and walk back to her building. Melissa and I begin to talk some more and compare notes. We are both on some grown woman shit. Not the petty bullshit. Shortly after, the doorbell rings and she walks over to answer it, as I hide in the kitchen. She invites him inside then locks the door as he enters and sits on the couch.

He says, *"Hey baby!"*

"Don't hand me that shit! Who the hell is Tasha?"

"Who? I don't know any Tameka baby! Why you so far away? Why don't you come over and sit on Daddy's lap?"

"You know damn well I didn't say Tameka. I said Tasha. She answered your cell phone when I called you back!"

He scratches his head, trying to sound like he had an ah ha moment. *"Oh Tasha? Yeah, I know her. Baby that's my cousin. I left my phone at her house. I went back to get it and she had already left, that's what took me so long to get here."*

"Oh yeah Rodney?"

I can't believe what I am hearing standing in the kitchen. How could he hurt me like this? I am pissed. I am anxious to run out the kitchen and beat his ass. I've never felt this type of hurt before.

Melissa has her back towards him. He stands and walks over to her and puts his arms around her waist.

"Yeah baby. You know you the only one for me!"

I quietly step into the room from the kitchen. I can't wait any longer. I sneak up behind him and slap him on the back of the neck.

He yells, *"What the fuck?"* He spins around to see who has hit him. He sees me.

"I'm yo cousin Rodney? You bastard!"

"Baby, baby, baby. It's not what it looks like. I love you."

Melissa is just standing listening. I scream, *"Oh yeah Rodney? You not lying to me and screwing another woman? What, is Melissa your cousin too?"*

Melissa looks him up and down shaking her head and says, *"I knew you wasn't nothing, but a dog. Get the hell out of my house man."*

I say, *"Exactly! Lose my fucking number and forget you ever knew me. Thank you, Melissa, for being honest."* I leave and he comes running out behind me.

"Baby, please wait?"

"You are as good as dead to me mother fucker!" I open my car door and he grabs my arm.

"Baby please, I'm sorry! But it's been six months and we haven't made love! How long do you expect me to wait?"

"That's all this is about? Sex? You know what, you are full of shit. Because if you loved me, you would have continued to wait. But no, you wanna go fuck somebody else. You don't love me! You don't even know what love is!"

"How can I make this right?"

I snatch my arm from his grasp. *"You can't."* I throw his cell phone at him, then I get in my car and I drive off. I see him in my rearview mirror looking stupid and staring at me heading down the street.

December 6, 2006

A few days have passed and Rodney has continued to try to contact me. He leaves me voicemails and sends me text messages. Always apologizing and begging me to take him back. He has sent dozens of roses to my home and my job. But I am not feeling it. I throw away everything. I'm sitting at home relaxing on the couch when my doorbell rings. I look out the window and see Rodney. I sigh and walk to the door and open it.

"What you want Rodney?"

"Baby I want you. It was only one-time wit that girl. I don't love her. I don't care about her. It was just sex."

"One time? That's another damn lie. Stop fucking lying."

He looks like a deer in headlights. I guess he thought I didn't know. Melissa told me it was many times. Well over three months.

"You right Tasha. I'm wrong baby. I love you so much. I made a mistake with her. I am sorry."

"Yeah you are sorry Rodney, now get your sorry ass off my porch!"

"Baby? Please let me come in. I want to fix this. I'll do whatever it takes. Baby please."

He leans forward to attempt to grab me. When he does, I slam the door in his face and lock it. He stands on the porch for a few seconds longer. I look out the window and he looks like he wants to knock again. He doesn't, he just leaves. I lean against the door and exhale.

He almost had me, but I don't want to play the fool again. I still love him. How do you turn that off? Like an idiot he did cheat. What's to stop him from doing it again if I did take him back? I slide against the door down to the floor. I begin to sob. Damn love hurts!

December 23, 2005

Some weeks have gone by and I miss Rodney like crazy. I miss snuggling up to him and kissing his soft sexy lips. I miss being in his arms, being held and smelling his Burberry cologne. This is the man I've spent all of my free time with for the last six months. I even pushed Walt away for him. Why did he have to dog me out? My doorbell rings and I go to the door and I see my cousin Diamond.

"Hey girl! What's up? I know you not still hung up on Rodney's lying cheating ass. Fuck him!"

"I know, but I miss him! And it's almost Christmas. Now I have to be alone and lonely for the holiday. I even have his Christmas gift here sitting under my tree. What the hell am I supposed to do with this?"

"Oh, none of that. You are never alone sugar cause you always have me. Let's take his gift back to the store and buy you something nice with the money. To continue to take your mind off things, let's go clubbin'!" She starts dancing with silly moves that are sure to make me laugh. I can't help, but to crack a smile. *"Tonight, is the annual Christmas party at our favorite club."*

"Who wants to go through the hassle of taking back a gift that they've wrapped for the one they love. And clubbing, nah, I don't really feel like it."

"Come on girl. It will be fun. Get your mind off that dog. Dance. Get your drink on." She heads over to the tree and picks up Rodney's already wrapped gift, *"And don't worry about taking his gift back. I will do it for you just get me the receipt."*

After finding the receipt, I cave in and I get dressed. We go to the club and I begin having a good time. We dance most of the night and I am buzzed. As I am dancing with some guy, I hear, *"Excuse me! May I cut in?"* It's Rodney.

"No."

"Please baby!"

I sigh and like a punk, I say, *"Okay. One minute."*

Diamond walks over and says, *"Oh hell no Rodney. Leave my cousin the fuck alone."*

Rodney doesn't respond to her, instead he looks at me pleadingly.

"Diamond it's ok. I got this."

Diamond stands glaring at him. She looks to me for reassurance and I give it to her. He grabs me by the hand and we walk off the dance floor to a table.

"I miss you so much baby. Why you in here dancing with that buster instead of with me?"

"What do you want?"

"You know what I want! Damn baby I want you! Only you."

"You had me and only me. But I obviously wasn't enough for you! So, you got with Melissa too."

"What I did was wrong, I admit that. And I am sorry! Damned sorry. But I can't take it back. I would if I could."

"You already said all this Rodney."

"I know. And I mean it. I love you baby. All I need is one more chance."

"I can't."

"Yes you can."

"Sorry Rodney."

"I am not gonna stop til I get you back. You are the woman for me."

"But you're not the man for me. The man for me would know how to keep his dick in his pants."

I walk away leaving him standing alone. I have to let him go. I don't want to get dogged out again.

chapter 4

The Day My Heart Broke

December 30, 2005

There are times in your life, in which things do not always go according to plan. But you have to find the strength to continue to go on. Especially when you want to throw in the towel.

I head out to the grocery store to pick up a few things. I hear my named called and I spin around to see who it is. When I see her, I'm thinking *Oh my gosh!* Its Walt's mom. We meet each other in an embrace.

"Don't you look beautiful Tasha. How are you doing sweetheart?"

"Thank you. I'm doing well Mrs. Perry. How are you?"

"I'm doing wonderful. It is great to see you. Walt and his dad are around here somewhere."

Before I can respond, I see her husband coming down the aisle with Walt trailing behind him. Walt's dad is fine. He always has been. He is aging like a fine wine. Walt looks exactly like his dad. With his dad's genes Walt is going to be a very fine old man one day. When his dad sees me his face lights up and he walks over to hug me.

"Hey Tasha!"

"Hello Mr. Perry," I say with a smile.

When Walt sees me, he is standoff-ish. I don't like it, but hell I understand. *"Hey Walt."*

He looks at me with disappointment on his face. He looks anguished at seeing me. I get it, but it still hurts. I've hurt him and that is the last thing that I ever wanted to do. Part of me wants to run into his arms, but his reaction to me is so cold. I can't expect that after I blew him off for Rodney, that he'd still be waiting for me. I'm sure he has moved on. He is fine as hell and a football phenomenon. A lot of women always wanted to get with him. He had eyes for only me then and never gave anyone else a chance.

"Hi Tasha," he says very dryly.

Mrs. Perry says, *"We'll give you a chance to catch up. It was so good to see you Tasha. You should come over for dinner tonight or soon if you're not too busy."*

"That would be really nice. Thank you."

"You're welcomed anytime." Walt looks at his mom agitated. She smiles at him before walking off with his dad.

"How are you doing Walt? You look good."

"I am good. Ra'Quel, I can't stand here and pretend like we are on good terms. It was good to see you, but I don't think it's a good idea for you to come over for dinner."

Damn. He stunned the hell out of me with that. He's never done me like this before. I can't help but feeling like I deserve it. *"I see. Well I guess I won't then. Please give your mom my apologies. It was nice to see you."*

I turn to walk away. I guess he's had enough. I understand. As much as his rejection hurts, I get it. I still love him, but sometimes love isn't enough. Being with him reminds me of my parents and its why I pushed him away. Walt and I spent so much time together at each other's houses and with our parents. Our parents even became friends. He and I dated for nearly six years. It started in middle school.

My parents loved him and wanted him for a son in law. That says a lot because my dad was very protective, but he loved Walt for me. That meant everything in the world to me knowing I had their blessings to be with him. Seeing Walt is bittersweet though. It feels good because I still love him.

However, it brings back bad memories. Memories that haunt me and I wish I could forget. I know it's not fair to him. He didn't cause or bring about the memories, but somehow, they've attached themselves to him. He reminds me so much of the saddest time in my life. He also reminds me of my dad. He was and still is the same type of loving man my dad was.

I don't know why, but I want to cry as I walk away. Many emotions come over me. We were friends first. It started in sixth grade. We hung out and spent a lot of time together. Then gradually things changed. I realized that I liked him as more than a friend. He was fine and so very sweet, yet humble. You would expect him to be a jerk because he was so attractive. However, he was the exact opposite. His looks first attracted me to him, but his personality attracted my heart. Then I found out, he liked me too.

By the time we were in seventh grade, we started dating. Secretively because my daddy wasn't having it. To our parents, we were just friends. I wasn't allowed to have a boyfriend yet. However, he asked me out to the school dance. My sister and mom talked my Dad into letting me go. So, I accepted his invitation. By the ninth grade, surprisingly my dad eased up and gave me permission to date Walt. He really liked him. We stayed together throughout high school.

I begin to wipe away the tears. I think he's moved on. Deep down, I know that's good for him. I can't give him what he wants. Hell, I've never even been honest with him about why I pushed him away. Initially, I think I feared losing him after everything that happened. Thinking about it now, I realize how dumb that sounds. I'll chalk it up to not being in my right mind. Now I just want to forget the hurt so not being with him makes forgetting easier.

April 22, 2006

About four months have come and gone. Rodney has finally decided to leave me alone. During those first two months, I went on a few dead-end dates with a lot of idiots and losers. I have just about given up on love. I keep meeting trifling men who just want to get in my pants. I can't blame them too much. I am sexy as hell. Don't judge me. If you don't think highly of you, who will? That being said, I am the bomb.

For the last two months I took a break from dating. I really buckled down during the months. I was studying for my admissions to medical school test. I spent my days and nights focused on work, school and myself. I can't lie though, those two months have been lonely. I want someone in my life.

Now I'm ready to meet someone new. I took my test a few days ago and I have to wait to get my score. I studied really hard and I feel good about the test. Hopefully my grade reflects so.

Like any other weekend, I decide to stay in on a stormy Saturday night. My love life is nonexistent. I have some male friends, but they are just that, friends. I would never go there with any of them. They have all tried and failed.

It is storming outside and my satellite dish is unable to pick up a signal. Then of all things, my power goes out. I make my way to the kitchen and get a flashlight. Then I light some candles. I lay on the couch bored out of my mind. I begin thinking and my mind runs on my past. The official worst day of my life.

2002-2003

It was on a Monday about four years ago. I was only sixteen and I can remember it like it was yesterday. I was excited on this Monday. Last weekend was homecoming and I won. Yes, I was crowned homecoming queen. I'd been ecstatic since. This upcoming weekend is prom. I'm in the running for that too. Homecoming Queen and Prom Queen two very nice titles to have. I'm so super excited. My life is great. I'm dating the captain of the football team, Walter, but everyone calls him Walt.

We've booked a room for prom night and I plan to give him my virginity. We've done a lot of the touching and feeling stuff. Me on him and him on me. A few weeks back I did let him eat the kitty. We've done that numerous times since then. That's as far as it has gone so far. I've promised the kitty to him and the time is almost near. I'm going to give him my all. And some head too.

I think he deserves it. It's his turn. I am so excited and so totally nervous. I love him and I just want the night to be special. We are going to lose our virginity together. It's the sweetest thing.

Imagine my surprise, while I'm sitting in History class, not really paying attention. I'm thinking about my most recent victory, the next victory that I am aiming for and going to prom with my baby. Then over the P.A. System I hear the principal call me to the office. To myself I'm thinking, well I didn't do anything. My grades are good, I don't have any disciplinary issues, what's this all about? My teacher excuses me and I head to the principal's office.

When I walk inside, I find Carmen and Ron, my sister and brother. I'm not sure why they are here, but I guess I'm going to find out.

"Hey ya'll, what's up? What ya'll doin' here?"

Carmen looks at Ron with sadness in her face. I see tears welling up in her eyes. I look to Ron's face, if only to find some type of comfort. I find none. Ron's face displays the same sadness that I see in Carmen's.

Unsure of what's going on, I say, *"What's wrong guys? What is it?"*

Neither of them responds. Millions of things run through my head. But I wasn't prepared for what they had to tell me. They walk over to me and embrace me in a hug. I hug them back, but I still don't know what brings them such sadness. Ron has just gotten married and is expecting his first child. Carmen has been married for four years, she has a son and she is expecting her second child. I am the baby of the family and I always use it to my advantage.

"We have something to tell you," Carmen finally musters out.

I can see the sadness in their faces, and I don't like where this is going. *"Earlier this morning, Mom and Dad were in a terrible car accident. They were hit by a drunk driver."*

"What," I yell out? I can't believe it. I am in shock. *"Well, where are they? What hospital are they in? Let's go see them."* I begin walking towards the door. They don't follow me. *"What's the matter ya'll? Let's go!"*

Carmen doesn't say anything. Ron steps in and speaks, *"Baby they didn't make it. Mom died instantly and Dad died this afternoon."*

My legs feel like spaghetti. I feel like I am going to pass out. They have both gathered around me and they are holding me. The tears begin to swell up in my eyes. I understand it now. Their tears suddenly make sense. I feel like I can't breathe. I understand why I could find no solace when I looked in their eyes. I've always thought my parents were invincible. Never in a million years did I think I'd be here.

I am an orphan. I have no parents. They'll never see me graduate high school, college or get married. My daddy won't walk me down the aisle on my wedding day. They won't be there when I have my first baby. My baby will never get to know their maternal grandparents. They won't get to see me get all dolled up to go to prom. Hell, I'm not going now anyway, after all of this. I feel like I've been robbed. My life will never be the same.

For a long while, I shut down. I don't want to do anything. I express myself through my writing. I've always enjoyed writing and I use my poetry as an outlet. My sister adopts me legally and I live with her. We put our family home up for rent, until we decide what to do with it. The drunk driver that killed my parents was drinking on the job. Our family lawyer sues the driver and the company he works for. We win the lawsuit, but no amount of money can bring my parents back.

Walt tries to be there for me, but I push him away. He tries to get close to me, but I won't let him. He tells me he loves me and I don't really care. It's like the harder he tries, the more I resist him. He hangs in there with me anyway. He backs off some to give me my space. School gets out for summer and he is going out of state to a football camp all summer.

He calls me and writes me and sometimes I answer and write back, but I don't treat him the way he deserves. When school gets back in, it's our senior year and I'm still withdrawn from him. I treat him more like a friend than a boyfriend. I know he wants to be close to me and that he wants intimacy, but I'm just not interested. I tell him that he should move on and see other people.

After some time, he does. Around the beginning of the second semester of our senior year, he is single again and I'm still single. I haven't been interested in dating. Somehow, somewhere, we spark things back up and we get back together. Things go well for us and I'm trying to move on in my life. When it's the anniversary of my parent's death, we hit a roadblock and I shut back down.

Through it all, he still stays with me. He is still there for me. I love him for it. However, as the end of the school year approaches, I begin to pull away from him. He is going off to school to the University of Southern California. He has a scholarship for football and I don't want to do the long-distance thing.

I need some time to heal and get my life on track. I call things quits with him, against his will. I never really gave him a choice. He heads off to CSU and I stay in South Carolina and go to school here. He tries to stay in contact with me, but I don't contact him back. I break all ties with him. Eventually he has no way to contact me. I moved and my cell number has changed. I even cancelled my email and chat accounts. I just wanted to break all ties.

April 22, 2006

I hate thinking back to this moment because whenever I do, it brings me to tears. From time, to time, I wonder about Walt. I haven't seen or heard from him since I ran into him and his parents at the grocery store. I wonder how he is doing. Did he dropout and go to the NFL, but I never look into it. I hope he does make it if or when he decides to go. I'm sure he will make it; he was All-American.

I wonder what things would have been like if I had gone with him. He asked me to and I refused. I had a scholarship to USC also. That was our original dream. We'd graduate high school, go to USC together, he'd turn pro after graduating and I would go to med school near whatever team he was drafted too. My preference was in Florida, but for him I would have settled for wherever he was. Eventually, we would marry and have three kids and the white picket fence. I was supposed to be Mrs. Walter Perry. Boy does life throw curve balls.

Now I'm all grown up. I've become an independent woman. I live on my own. Living alone can be lonely and it's times like this, when I wish I wasn't so alone. I wish I was with him; the white picket fence and three kids sound really nice right now. Mrs. Walter Perry.

My power is still out and I've shed some tears. In my feelings, I pick up a pen and begin to write. I have this thought that runs through my mind. From this thought I write.

Heartless

The day you left
And went away
Was the day
My heart fell prey
To hurt
Pain
Anger and anguish
My heart broke
On this day
To lose my first
True loves
Not able to say
One last I love you
No longer able
To get a hug or a kiss
But left
With a picture
Of you in caskets
No life in you
No warmth
Just bodies
That once housed you
Your spirits gone
Up to the heavens
Leaving behind your little girl
Who just wasn't ready
To lose her parents
With no forewarning
Of the tragedy her life would become
Not knowing
That as I headed off to school
It would be the first of mourning
And the last morning
That I'd see you
With life and breath
Still in you
When you left
The biggest piece of my heart
Left with you
Leaving a hole
That was once filled
By you

I put all of my feelings and emotions into my writing. Tears have been flowing from my eyes. I don't wanna cry anymore. I don't want to think about the past or the hurt from my past. I wipe my face and try to clear my mind. Instead of wallowing in my hurt, anger and pain; I search in the dark and find my phone.

chapter 5

First Time

April 23, 2006

Stepping out of the box and trying new things can be really hard.

It is now after midnight and I'm still in the dark. This storm still has not calmed down. Sounds like it's going to be a long one. With my phone in hand, I get on the internet. Thank God it is fully charged. I find a chatting app and I decide to install it. Once it installs, I begin touring the app. It's somewhat of a dating website. I upload my picture and begin checking out the people on the site.

I meet different men online and chat with them throughout the stormy night. In complete boredom, I find a little fun. I go through and meet a lot of men, but none catch my eye. Then I stop at the picture of this handsome guy. He is currently online. I click on his profile and stroll through his pictures.

From what I can see, he has long thick black hair down to his back, which he wears cornrowed. He is a light caramel complexion with nice thick lips. His eyes have a light brown hue. I decide to read his profile to find out a little more about him.

> **Skilled_Baller –** *I see you sexy ladies.*
>
> **About Me***: 19 years old - 5' 11"- From Chucktown – Let's talk – I don't bite.*

While I am reading his profile, he sends me a message.

Skilled_Baller: *Damn baby. I wanna know you. How you doing?*

I laugh when I see his message.

ChocolateGoddess: *I'm good...how are you?*

Skilled_Baller: *I'm good now that I'm talking to you. Tell me about you. What's your name?*

ChocolateGoddess: *My name is Tasha...I am 5'5"... I live alone...I don't have any kids...Currently in college...I am single...How about you?*

Skilled_Baller: *I'm Malcolm. It's complicated. I'm in an on again off again thing with my son's mom.*

ChocolateGoddess: *Doesn't sound complicated to me. Either you wanna be with her or you don't.*

Skilled_Baller: *I don't. I know she ain't the one. I'm still searching. I'm trying to be with you though.*

ChocolateGoddess: *I don't date guys with wives or girlfriends.*

Skilled_Baller: *She ain't my girl. You really ain't gon give me a chance? You profile say you from Chucktown too. We don't live too far apart. Give a brother a chance.*

ChocolateGoddess: *I don't know about this. If she ain't your girl, she is your something.*

Skilled_Baller: *Yep my son's mother.*

ChocolateGoddess: *Yep and your lover. I bet ya'll live together.*

He goes quiet for a little while. The fact that he lives in South Carolina is great. However, this girlfriend and a one-year-old son thing sounds like a whole lot of drama. I don't know if I am up for this mess. Chatting with him is keeping me from the boredom of being in the dark with nothing else to do. I scroll through the site some more while I wait for his response.

I've gotten several messages from some other guys, but based on either their pictures or their profiles I am not interested. Maybe I scared Malcolm off. Oh well. I am about ready to call it a night, when I get another message from him.

Skilled_Baller: *Yeah we live together. But I ain't try to hide nothin' from you. I been honest with you from the jump.*

He has been upfront with me it seems. Which I do respect. However, that doesn't mean I'm gone to ignore that he's with someone and be a side piece. I'll never be that. At least not intentionally. I make him wait a while before I respond.

ChocolateGoddess: *Ok. Well I'm tired and I'm going to sleep.*

Skilled_Baller: *Can I get yo number? Can we stay in touch?*

ChocolateGoddess: *Yeah that's fine.*

We end our conversation with a promise to keep in touch and an exchange of phone numbers. Still without power I blow out the candles and drift off to sleep on the couch.

May 9, 2006

Malcom and I have continued to talk over the past few weeks. Our conversations have remained very surfaced. Nothing too deep has been discussed and I'm ok with it. I don't see Malcolm as my soulmate. Hell, I don't even see him as my boyfriend. Just a little fun. He's been trying to get me to go out with him and I keep avoiding it. I think we should be just friends since he has a girlfriend. However, I know that is not what he wants.

I'm at home relaxing when my phone rings. I look at the caller ID and see it is Malcolm. I answer the phone warmly.

"Hey."

"What's up gorgeous?"

We chat for a bit. Per usual nothing deep. We catch up a bit and talk about our days for a while. Out of the blue he completely changes the subject.

"It's been over a week since I've gotten some."

I don't know why he thought I needed to know his girlfriend hasn't been giving it up lately. Obviously, he is looking for sex. For some reason I continue to talk to him anyway. Let's chalk it up to boredom. I don't even give him a response. The phone is silent for a little while.

"How many men have you had sex with?"

I know I have somewhat of a secret to tell. My biggest secret, what I am hiding, I am a twenty-year-old virgin; soon to be twenty-one. Yes, virgin. I never got the chance to give it up to Walt. I really wanted to. I was head over heels in love with him. I hadn't been in love with a man like that since.

I did love Rodney, but I didn't trust him. Apparently, it was for good reason. I had gotten so use to not giving it up, it just kind of got easy. In my mind, I ponder telling him. He's not my man, but I don't want to lie. Rodney never knew this and he cheated on me anyway. What will his reaction be? I am not sure, but almost certain I don't want to find out.

After thinking, I finally answer his question. I respond and say, *"Zero!"*

After a very long pause, Malcolm responds to what I've said in total shock. He is only nineteen years old and more experienced than me.

He says, *"Damn! Really? Well I wouldn't mind showing you some tricks."*

"Yeah I bet. Why am I not surprised?"

We continue to talk about a little this and that. Nothing too deep. He asks me for a picture of myself and I send it to him.

"Damn girl! It's something about you that drives me crazy. I wanna see you."

"I don't think your girl would like that."

"We can't be friends?"

"I doubt it. But we will see about that."

"Damn. Why not?"

"Let's just take it day by day."

"Ok cool."

We continue to talk to one another. I have been browsing the dating website on my laptop while talking to Malcolm on the phone. I discover another man that has caught my eye.

chapter 6
Cyber Search

May 10, 2006

**Online dating has become a new thing of today's society.
How do you know when someone is lying?**

When I first see a picture of this new man my first thought is that he is gorgeous. I feel a tingle at the sight of him. As I gaze at his photo I begin to smile. He has a very sexy light brown sugar complexion. His hair is black and curly. He wears it in a tapered cut, almost like a curly low fade. He has very full thick lips and a nice mustache with long sideburns that connect to his beard and a full goatee. Beneath his beard I can see a very sexy set of dimples. He has light green sleepy eyes. I also notice that he has tattoos. From his pictures I can see that he has several. He is wearing shirts so I don't know how many he has, but I sure hope I get to find out one day.

After seeing all of his photos, I decide to read his profile. It reads:

> **VirgoKing – *Lookin' for a beautiful woman I can grow wit.***
>
> **About Me***: I'm 24 years old from Harlem, New York. Harlem stand up. I'm 6' 6" and 243lbs pure muscle and freaky. I love sports. Giants and Lakers all day. Hoping to meet that special someone. If you wanna know more hit me up.*

After reading his profile I decide to send him a message. I see he is online and I want to know more about him.

> *ChocolateGoddess:* Hey Handsome! My name is Tasha...I am 5'5"...I live alone...I don't have any kids...I am a Junior in college studying pre-med and psychology and minoring in business...I am single...How about you?

It isn't very long before he responds back.

> *VirgoKing:* What's up Beautiful! You definitely have me intrigued. I love a woman wit beauty and brains. And I love chocolate. Well about me I am Adontis. I live alone got 1 brother 1 sister. I'm the oldest. No kids yet, but definitely one day. In the process of opening my own urban clothing store. I am very single, maybe you'll come change that though ma. I love to go out, workout, play ball and travel. I will try almost anything once.

No kids, that's a shocker. But it's not a bad thing. I don't necessarily want to be a mom right now. I'm not against it or anything, but I prefer someone without kids. Someone I can start a family with.

> *ChocolateGoddess:* Maybe, I will go ahead and change that. Are you ready for that? You may just get a chocolate high. By the way, you have beautiful eyes. I'm sure you hear that all of the time. Where you get them eyes from handsome?

> *VirgoKing:* I was born ready. That's my type of high. Thank you, your eyes are beautiful too, as you are. But to answer your question, I'm not too sure where I get these eyes from. I'm a melting pot so to speak. I'm part Black, Indian, Italian and Spanish. Where you get your eyes from?

I love his confidence. He really seems like someone worth getting to know. Of course, I know this is online, but I am willing to see it through and see what happens.

ChocolateGoddess: *You born ready, huh? Ok time will tell. Thank you. You're not the only one intrigued. Tell me more about your ethnicity. Which parent gave you what heritage? And to answer your question, like the song says, I get it from my mama.*

VirgoKing: *Yep I was. Yeah it will, you just be ready. We on the same page. My moms Italian n Black. Her dad Italian n Black and her moms Black. My pops Black, Spanish n Indian. His pops Black n Spanish n his moms black n Indian. I bet you do get it from yo mama. I look forwarded to one day getting to meet the beauty that created you.*

ChocolateGoddess: *Aye papi, I see. Your parents beautifully crafted you. Tell me why are you still single?*

VirgoKing: *Papi? Ok mami. Don't start nothing. Te hare llamarme papi! I'll tell you, but first I noticed you quickly changed the subject. Am I missing something? You gon keep me hidden from the family. You got a secret husband or something?*

ChocolateGoddess: *Maybe you will maybe you won't. I guess time will tell that too. No secret husband. What subject did I change?*

I know exactly what he means, but who wants to start off getting to know someone by telling him, you lost your parents. That's not the best conversation starter.

VirgoKing: *You ain't told me nothing about yo parents. Why is that ma?*

ChocolateGoddess: *Well I wasn't going to bring it up. My parents died when I was 16. It was a really bad car accident. I don't like to talk about it, you know. But they were married for over 20 years before they died. And if they were here, the only way you'd be able to get close to me would be through them. Now its just me, my sis, bro, their spouses and kids.*

VirgoKing: *Damn ma. I'm sorry to hear. I shouldn't of pressed you on it.*

ChocolateGoddess: *It's ok. If this goes somewhere, you'd have to find out eventually right. Might as well get it out and in the open.*

VirgoKing: *I see this going somewhere. I hope you do too. To answer yo question, I'm single cause I haven't met anyone that makes me not want to be single, until now that is. So I been actively looking. Hopefully my search can stop here.*

ChocolateGoddess: *Time will tell.*

VirgoKing: *That's yo favorite thing to say. But you right. Time will tell. When yo birthday?*

ChocolateGoddess: *July 15th. When is yours.*

VirgoKing: *Oh, you a cancer. September 7th.*

ChocolateGoddess: *Yes VirgoKing. Is that a problem?*

> *VirgoKing:* Naw ma. I'm just trying to get to know you.

We both like what we hear and continue to message each other. I really like him. I like the way he thinks. This online dating thing is new to me, but I'm willing to go on the ride to see where it takes me. After all, what do I have to lose? After messaging for a short while, we decide to exchange numbers.

We text each other and talk for hours learning about one another. I find out that he is smart as hell. He graduated high school at sixteen. Then he went off to college. He majored in business. He also played basketball while in college. He was going to go pro, but he tore his ACL the year he was going to enter the draft. He finished college instead while he recovered. He has since recovered, but decided not to enter the NBA again. He loves the game, but he had other passions he wanted to explore.

Instead he went and got his masters degree. Brother is book smart and street smart. Which I find to be very sexy. He tells me more about his store and it's name. The name is Fresh. I think that it's kind of dope. Malcolm is still in the picture. I think he is a nice guy, but him having a girlfriend is a major problem. I know it won't go anywhere. I see him fading away more and more. I see a text come across my phone.

> **Malcolm:** She ain't giving me none and I'm horny and want some. I need some its's been over a week.

Before texting back, I laugh out loud.

> **Tasha:** You keep saying this. Who you want some from?

> **Malcolm:** You!

When I read his response, I burst out laughing again.

> **Tasha:** Ain't that what your girl for?

> **Malcolm:** I don't want her. I want you!

> **Tasha:** Whatever. That's not gonna happen.

Several minutes have passed and he hasn't responded. I figure, he must be upset, but I could care less. I text him one last time to ensure him this conversation is over.

> **Tasha:** *Goodnight.*

After getting ready for bed, I slip in and begin to think about Adontis.

chapter 7

Two at a Time

July 14, 2006

**Living the single life leaves room to date and
meet men. No strings attached.**

Over the past few months, I've been continually checking for my MCAT score. Impatiently waiting to see how I did. A few days ago, I got my results. Not only did I pass, but I got a tremendously high score. I scored in the top percentile with a five hundred and sixteen. I absolutely went out and celebrated with my family and friends. My next steps will be to apply to medical school. I have my eyes on Florida for med school. Jacksonville, here I come.

Adontis and I have moved from messaging to texting to talking on the phone. We actually talk more than we text. We usually only text if I am at work or in class. The first time I heard his voice oh Lord, it did something to me. His voice is deep and debonair. Also very distinguished and sexy. I love to listen to him speak. Each time we learn more about one another and I am interested in him. We share intimate secrets and details and I decide that I should tell him that I am a virgin.

While we are on the phone I kind of blurt it out. I don't give him an introduction or ease him into it. I decide to just rip off the band aid.

"I think you ought to know, I'm a virgin."

The line goes completely silent. I don't know what to think at this point. He and I have shared a lot so naturally I thought he should know this. I am feeling him and I think he is feeling me.

"Adontis are you still there?"

"Yeah I'm here. Damn, you for real ma?"

"Yeah."

"Damn that's sexy. I like that."

"Really?"

"Yeah."

"That doesn't scare you off?"

"Naw. I like you and I'm enjoying getting to know you. It would only scare me off if I had bad intentions for you. I got the best of intentions for you ma."

Hearing this makes me smile. I really hope he is who he has presented himself to be. From what I know of him, I can see myself with him.

"Ok."

He asks me, *"Why are you a virgin? It's obvious that you are gorgeous. You can have any man you would like."*

I go into the story of my plans with my then boyfriend, Walt, to lose my virginity. *"The weekend before I planned to lose my virginity, my parents died. After they died, I never went to prom that year. As the years passed, it just got easier and easier. Since then the time just never seemed right. I have been saving myself for the right man. I haven't met a man that I've been ready to make love to since. But with the right man, I will."*

"Damn, that's deep. I wish I had the words to say to make you feel better."

"Thank you."

"But I hear ya! Hopefully I can be that man."

"Well only time will tell. I guess we will see."

"Your favorite phrase to say. We will see shorty."

"Let's change the subject, I don't want to talk about sad times."

"Ok ma."

We continue to converse and he tells me that he wants to visit me, but it won't be for a little while. Until then he wants to continue to get to know me. I tell him that I would like that. We continue to talk and communicate with one another. Out of the blue, Adontis ask me a question.

"Are you talking to any other men online?"

I hesitate at first, then for some bizarre reason, I tell him about Malcolm.

"Yeah. There is this guy Malcolm that I talk to online."

"Damn shorty. Real talk?"

"Yeah."

"I ain't gon lie. I don't like that, but I guess ain't shit I can do about it right now. I like that you ain't lie though."

I can tell he isn't happy about what he hears. However, I wanted to be honest with him. That's why I told the truth. If this is going to be something, I want it to be based on the truth.

"Alight. Which one of us do you like better? Tell the truth."

"I always do. Honestly, you!"

"Ok ma. That's good. I'm feeling you. I don't mind a little competition."

"Well you should know I'm feeling you too. You don't need to worry about him."

"I ain't worried. You dealing with a man here ma."

"I've noticed."

"Once I get you that motherfucker got to go."

"That won't be a problem."

I like that he is planning to be with me. I wish he didn't live so far away. As I am talking to Adontis, I receive a text from Malcolm.

> **Malcolm:** *Hey gorgeous. You been on my mind.*

I don't really have a response because Adontis is on my mind. I really haven't thought about Malcolm in days.

> **Tasha:** *Really?*

Adontis and I continue to talk.

> **Malcolm:** *Yes really! When you gon let me take you on a date?*

> **Tasha:** *Early August!*

> **Malcolm:** *Damn. I got to wait til August?*

> **Tasha:** *Yes I'm about to take a trip. That's when I'll be back.*

> **Malcolm:** *Alight. How about August 4th?*

> **Tasha:** *It's a date.*

> **Malcolm:** *Alight. Good.*

The entire time I am texting Malcolm, I am on the phone with Adontis. However, I don't tell Adontis about the date. He said he didn't mind a little competition and I've already told him too much. I wonder to myself why did I agree to a date with Malcolm. I come second to none and I'm into Adontis.

I guess it is because you can't really trust and believe what these men tell you online. Hell, you can't really trust what they tell you face to face either. Adontis could be married. In the back of my head, I don't think I'll ever meet him. I know he says he is coming, but people lie.

That's why I agreed to go out with Malcolm. He is accessible. I'm lonely and I miss the touch, the scent and the company of a man. I need to be held. Is Malcolm that man? Absolutely not. He is here now and Adontis is hundreds of miles away. I need to see that Adontis is more than talk before I let my heart get involved. I won't put all of my eggs in one basket.

July 15, 2006

My date with Malcolm isn't until next month because today is my birthday. Adontis has scored some brownie points. We've only been talking for a little while and he sent me roses for my birthday. It was very sweet. It tells me he does listen. He sent my favorite flower and he remembered the date all on his own. Maybe his interest is real.

I open the card and it reads:

> I hope you have a very happy birthday with a day just as beautiful as you my queen. As always I'm thinking of you. Have a safe and happy trip.
>
> Adontis

I call him and thank him for my flowers. We chat for a bit about our days and other miscellaneous things. Damn. I like him.

I am ready to turn up and turn out. Its summertime and my girls and I will be heading to sunny Cancun for two weeks. We fly out tomorrow and we will be back on the thirty-first. Tonight, I will be having a nice dinner with my family and close friends. Let's face it, this girl is now twenty-one. School has been stressful as hell. I've aced my classes, now I deserve a little party time. I'm ready to get my drink on. I'm single as hell. I don't kiss and tell and I know the boys will be flirty as well.

It will be five of us ladies going. Kenya, Diamond, Janet, Rita and me. I am the youngest of the crew meaning now we all can drink, legally that is. Kenya is my best friend. She moved upstate for college. We don't get to see each other as often as we'd like, but we keep in touch all of the time. She and I have been through the good and the bad times. We've been best friends since elementary school. A long-time built friendship. If I ever call her, I know she'd be there. I would do the same for her.

Diamond is my cousin and numero uno. She is my other bestie. Our bond is forever. Don't get me wrong she drives me crazy and I her. I know she'll always go through the trenches with me. We hang and party together all of the time.

Janet and Rita are best friends. Their bond is unbreakable, they are much like Kenya and me. The biggest difference is that they live close together. So, close they are roommates.

My girls and I have agreed that what happens in Cancun, must stay in Cancun. We are taking this trip to our graves. Sorry not sorry.

chapter 8

Single to Mingle

August 4, 2006

The best time of a person's life. Having no one to answer to and being able to date whomever. You gotta shop around.

Cancun was the greatest time of my life. What I can say is there was no drama. We all got along well. No one was lost, kidnapped or sex trafficked. I'm thankful we had a safe trip there and back. I did keep up with Adontis while I was gone. I'm still enjoying getting to know him. I made time for him, while on my trip.

My date with Malcolm is today. I feel nervous and I'm kind of second guessing myself. After all, he does have a girlfriend. Maybe I shouldn't go with him. It doesn't take much before I convince myself to keep the date. I just wanna have fun. I'm tired of the stress of dating. School starts back soon and it's my senior year. You only live once. I tell myself it is just dinner. I'm not going to have sex with him or anything. I will go out with him and then I'll make up my mind if I'm interested. Plus, all work and no play make me sad and bitter.

I get off of work and rush through traffic. Our date is in three hours. I get through the rush hour traffic, get home and get into the tub. When I step out the bathroom, my phone rings. On the caller ID display, I see Adontis' name. I ponder answering it and decide to let it go to voicemail. We usually are on the phone for hours at a time. I don't have that kind of time right now. Hopefully he will leave a message.

After I finish getting dressed, I head out the door. As I open the door, I see Carmen proceeding up the walkway.

"Where you going?"

My sister is nosy as hell. I love her with all my heart, but she is the nosiest person I've ever met. Hell, she is nosy about anyone's business. My business is just dessert to her.

"Out! I don't have time to talk. What you doin' here?"

"Well I just came by to see you. But I guess I should have called first! Where the hell are you going?" She is looking me up and down.

I smile and say, *"Yes you should have. But it's ok. I gotta go though. I will call you when I get back in."*

She hasn't moved out of my way. *"Back from where?"*

"Since you must know nosy, I have a date. And you are gonna make me late."

"A date with who?"

"Can I tell you about it, after I get back."

"No. I need to know you are safe and he ain't crazy."

"He is not crazy Carmen."

"I don't know that."

I start laughing, she is really making me late. *"I'll text you his name, number and a picture, how about that?"*

"Ok sis. Send it now."

"Ok." I send Carmen a text.

"Oohh he's cute."

"Yeah."

"Ok, I'll let you go."

We hug and she gets back in her car and pulls out my driveway.

"Love you sis. Don't forget to call me when you get back home."

"I won't. Love you too."

I get in my car and head to the restaurant. I text Malcolm and let him know I am running a few minutes behind. I arrive at the restaurant, walk in and the first person I see is Malcolm. He is every bit as sexy as in his pictures. He stands when he sees me.

"Damn you're gorgeous! That's why I want you."

I chuckle. He is funny to me. I don't understand how he can want me and he has a whole girlfriend. I'm not about to be anyone's concubine. At least I'll have some fun stories to tell my grandkids one day. We exchange hellos and a hug. Then we walk over to the hostess stand and get seated.

Our date starts off very well. Light conversation with a little bit of catching up. He asks how my trip was and I keep it very vague. Malcolm's phone rings. He checks it and then ignores the call. His phone rings two more times and he silences the ringer then the last time he turns his phone off.

"Your girl looking for you huh?"

By the look on his face, I know I am right. But he responds with, *"Nah, that's my home boys."*

I don't buy it, but I don't mention it again. Hell, my bullshit detector is working just find tonight. However, it doesn't really matter. I've already decided that this will be my first and last date with him. I need a man. Not a little boy. He needs to focus on his girl and kid. If he doesn't wanna be with her, he needs to tell her.

We go on to finish the rest of our date and as dinner ends, Malcolm says, *"I'm feeling you. You gonna give me a chance?"*

I decide to BS him back. Why the hell not. I might as well entertain myself. *"I like you too."*

"What's the problem then, boo?"

"Your girlfriend is the problem!" Then we engage in a heated discussion.

He looks at me and says, *"Yeah I got a girl, but you knew this and still agreed to go out with me."*

That's the little boy stuff I'm talking about. He thinks because I agreed to go out with him that this is going somewhere. Like in seeing him I had a dummy attack and decided to be a side piece. Never that. Man, I was bored.

"Yeah, I did. Obviously, that was my mistake."

I get up from the table with my purse and keys in hand. Then I head for the door. He throws some money on the table to cover the bill and tip and he runs out after me.

When he catches up to me, he says, *"Tasha what you want from me?"*

"Nothing", I say. I begin to open my car door and he closes it.

"Can't we finish talking?"

"What is there left to talk about? You got a girl. You can't have your cake and eat it too!"

Jokingly, Malcom says, *"But isn't that the point of cake?"*

He caught me off guard with that. I kind of want to laugh, but I'm not going to entertain him. I just beam at him with my evil eye.

"Seriously, yeah I got a girl. But I won't break up with her until I find the right one."

"Yeah that's the problem. That is such a cop out. Grow up. If you don't want her then don't string her along. Stop going out with other women when you still with her. I can't be with you in anyway as long as you with her."

"Is that an ultimatum?"

"No, it's good-bye Malcolm. You are not for me and I most certainly am not for you."

I get into my car, crank it up and drive away. On my way home, I call Carmen. I fill her in on my dead-end date. Let's be real. Did I even have a choice? This nosy heifer was ready to get the details. We talk for my entire drive home. I pull into my driveway with Carmen still on the phone. I walk into my house and we talk for a while longer. After we get off the phone, I notice I have a voicemail. I get cleaned up and slip into my jammies. I get snuggled up in my bed. Then I call and check my messages.

I hear, *"Hey ma, What up? I been thinking bout you all day, I just called to see how you doin. Hit me back when you get this."* Hearing Adontis' voice sends chills up my spine. I notice I have another message and I listen to it.

It says, *"I hear you was on a date tonight. Did you tuck junior in too? When you gonna come around and know I am the one for you? Stop cruising nurseries. Holla."* It was Rodney. Damn is he keeping tabs on me? That's crazy. Whatever forget him. Back to Adontis.

August 5, 2006

It's a little after midnight and I don't wanna call him because it is late. But I really want to talk to him. I contemplate calling him and decide to do so. Ring. Ring. Ring. No answer just voicemail. I leave him a voicemail.

"Hey baby. Sorry I missed your call. You have been on my mind also. Hit me up when you get this."

When I finally go to bed, I have Malcolm and Rodney off my mind.

chapter 9

Reality or Fantasy

August 5, 2006

Sometimes you can allow yourself to become entangled in a false reality. Open your eyes and see what is really going on.

While at the library, the next day, Malcolm calls me and I send him to voicemail. He doesn't leave one. He just sends a text.

> **Malcolm:** *Can we please talk? Please? I like you and I want a chance with you.*

I don't text him back. Apparently, he hasn't realized that I'm done with him. Adontis is where I want to be. We talk just about every day throughout the day. The days we don't talk or video chat we communicate via text. Later I receive a text from Adontis. He tells me he is sorry he missed my call. He has been busy with getting Fresh together. He will give me a call tonight after he gets off work.

I've been home for a few hours. I am relaxing, but I'm also a little tired. I am laying on my couch watching Lifetime and my phone goes off. Unfortunately, I left it in the kitchen. I start not to get up, but I go to answer it anyway. The caller ID says Adontis. I quickly try to wake myself up and be alert. I push the send button.

In a very sexy voice, I say, *"Hello."*

"What it do shorty? What you doin?"

"Hey. Just relaxin'."

"Well how was your day?"

"It was aight. I got everything with my fall classes situated and all of my books. That was my main goal for today. How was your day? How is Fresh coming along?"

"My day was good. Fresh is doing great. It will be opening up soon."

"Congratulations. That's what's up. When am I gonna see you? You find out when you can come down yet?"

"Yeah that's why I called you last night. I will be down there on January fifth to see you."

"Oh my gosh! That is so long."

"You saying you can't wait to see me?"

I laugh. "I can wait to meet you; I just don't want to."

He laughs. "Uh huh. Your ass spoiled huh?"

"I can be. Is that a problem for you?"

"Nah, I plan to continue to spoil you shorty."

"That's my type of man."

"I bet."

"Seriously, why is the wait so long?"

"Spoiled ass."

I burst out laughing. "And! We already established that."

He laughs, "You right ma. We did."

"So why am I waiting so long to meet you?"

"I wanna have Fresh up, running and in a good place before I leave. By then it will be close to the holidays. I figure we can both spend that time with our families. After that I want your time."

"Ok, I hear you."

"I'm serious shorty."

I smile and say, "Okay, I'll be patient and I'll wait. I look forward to spending some time with you."

"I can't wait to spend time with you too. And I ain't going nowhere. Ain't nothing changing, I'm staying in contact with you."

"You better."

He chuckles, "Yes ma'am."

We continue to talk for a while longer and it is getting late. I tell Adontis that I am sleepy. He tells me to get some rest and go to sleep, he will talk to me tomorrow.

chapter 10

Trust

January 2, 2007

Letting your guard down and putting faith in someone is a scary thing to do. How do you believe that everything someone says to you is true?

Several months have passed and it is days until Adontis' arrival. We have continued to talk throughout the months on a daily basis. Malcolm has continually unsuccessfully tried to contact me and has finally given up. I've spent the last few days shopping and getting prepared for Adontis' arrival. I'm excited for the day to get here. I am also nervous. I've never done anything like this before. It's a little scary.

However, over the last eight months I've really gotten to get to know him. I believe that he is the man that he's been showing me over the months. After all he is coming down to meet me. He's walking the walk. I'm from the show me state and he's doing just that. He is showing me that he is serious by coming here.

I trust him enough to let him come to my house and that's scary. I trust he is a good man. Just in case he isn't, I've told Kenya and Diamond all about him. They have pictures, his name and all the details about him. I have to text them both when he gets here and several hours later to insure them that I am ok. Whoo pray for me.

January 5, 2007

Today is finally the day. Adontis calls me and tells me he is a few hours away and he will call me if he gets lost. A few hours pass and I don't hear from him. I sit nervously waiting for my doorbell to ring. My stomach has been in knots all day. I didn't get any sleep last night, anxiously awaiting today. Another half hour passes and still no Adontis. By this time, I am walking the room pacing.

I begin to question myself. Is he standing me up? Maybe I should have never agreed to this. Maybe he is just all talk. Hell, I can't take the thoughts running through my mind anymore. I am tired of my mind wondering. I contemplate calling him and I decide to do so. As I pick up the phone, my doorbell rings.

Hearing the doorbell, I instantly begin to feel nervous and excited at the same time. I walk to the front door and I am shaking. I stop and tell myself to get it together. The doorbell rings again. I look through the peep hole. It is Adontis. He looks exactly like his pictures, but even better.

He is standing wearing a big smile while holding a gorgeous bouquet of long stem red roses. I take a deep breath; exhale and I send a group text to Diamond and Kenya.

> *Tasha:* Ya'll he is finally here. Damn he fine as hell and looks just like his picture.

I put my phone on silent, then slide it in my back pocket, then I open the door. He is very handsome. His body is right. God crafted him in all the right ways. In his pictures and on video chat he was fine, but seeing him in person is everything. This man looks like he was tailor made for me. I've never felt this much attraction to any one man.

He says, *"Hello, Shorty. Damn you are beautiful. How are you doing?"*

I bite my bottom lip in excitement. *"Hey. I am good. Very excited to finally see you."*

"Please don't do that ma."

"Do what?"

"Don't bite your lip like that. I can't take that?"

I'm blushing. *"Really?"*

"Hell yes. That's sexy as shit. I shouldn't even be telling you this, but that turns me on. Now ain't the time for that."

I burst out laughing. *"Ok. That's good to know. I will definitely make a mental note of that."*

He laughs, *"Naw ma. Forget I said that."*

"Too late!"

He smirks as I invite him inside. He hands the roses to me. *"For the very beautiful lady."*

"They are beautiful. Thank you." I accept the roses and after smelling them, I place them on the fireplace.

I spin back around to face him wearing a huge smile. *"Can I have a hug,"* he asks?

"Of course, you can." I walk over to him.

He grabs me by the waist and hugs me. I knew he said he was 6'6", but dudes lie about their height all the time. Daddy wasn't lying. I might need a step stool. Naw, I think I'd rather climb. I laugh inside as I think this.

He says, *"Damn ma you smell good. I could just eat you! I am glad to finally be able to hold you in my arms. And I don't want to let go."*

"Well you don't have to." We continue to embrace one another and I ask, *"Are you hungry?"*
"Starving. You cooked for me?"
While wearing a smile, *"Yes, I did."*
I escort him to sit in the dining room. I head to the kitchen to warm the food. While in the kitchen I look at my phone and Diamond and Kenya have been blowing it up.

> *Kenya:* Bitchhhhhhhhh! Yes!!!!!

> *Diamond:* He a man of his word.

> *Kenya:* What is going on? Tell me more! He ain't crazy or nothing right?

> *Diamond:* T you good?

> *Kenya:* Say something Tasha.

> *Diamond:* You starting to make us worry.

It's almost comical, but I know my girls just want to make sure that I am ok. I have to ease their minds.

> *Tasha:* Sorry ladies. Yes I'm good.

> *Diamond:* About damn time you respond. I just pulled into your driveway. Don't worry I'm not coming in.

> *Kenya:* Damn Tasha. I'm in the car too.

> *Tasha:* My bad we just getting acquainted. I'm in the kitchen warming dinner and he is in the dinning room. And no Kenya he doesn't seem crazy.

> *Kenya:* *Ok well I'm headed back home. Keep us posted.*

> *Diamond:* *I'm back home. Well enjoy your man.*

> *Tasha:* *I will. And he's not my man.*

Dinner is warmed. I slip my phone back into my pocket. It's show time. I enter the dining room with our meals and we have a candle lit dinner with nice conversation. We both take in the moment. Finally meeting after all of this time seems surreal. After dinner is finished, I clear the table.

"Beauty, brains and she cooks. That was delicious. I have to hold on to you."

He has me blushing. *"Thank you. Would you like some dessert?"*

"Only if you are on the menu!"

I blush and laugh. *"No silly, but I made your favorite."*

"Well in that case, yes I would love some."

We finish dessert and move to the living room to talk and watch TV. For the very first time we kiss. I can't resist his thick sexy lips against mines. The more we talk, the more comfortable I feel with him and the more we keep kissing. I've never felt so comfortable, so quickly, with any man before.

I excuse myself and head to the restroom, I have to let them know things are still good. I unlock my phone and these heifers have still been texting me. They been talking a lot of shit.

> *Diamond:* *He drove all the way from New York. That mother fucker is your man. He is all we've been hearing about for the last eight months.*

> *Kenya:* *Exactly D. Stop lying to yourself Tasha. You gon let him wax that ass girl?*

> *Kenya:* *Oh shit D. She ain't respond yet. Maybe he is waxing that ass.*

> *Diamond:* *Damn I sure hope so. It's about time my cousin get some. Shit.*

> **Kenya:** *If her ass walking funny then we know what's up.*

> **Diamond:** *I'm gon let you know if she is when I see her.*

> **Tasha:** *Really this what ya'll doing?*

> **Kenya:** *Damn. You pose to be letting him wax it.*

> **Diamond:** *Exactly. You ain't got all that ass for nothing back it up on that man. His ass will be sprung.*

I am laughing my ass off at them. They get on my nerves, but they my girls.

> **Tasha:** *I hate ya'll! He is not waxing anything. We just talking and spending time. Now I'm going back to him. I'll check in with ya'll later.*

I put my phone back in my pocket and head out the bathroom. My girls are really a mess. When I return, Adontis ask to use the restroom. I escort him to the restroom and relax on the couch until he returns. When he returns, we talk for a while longer until we both fall asleep snuggled on the couch.

January 6, 2007

Early the next morning I awake in his arms and smile. Careful not to wake him, I wiggle from his arms and head to the restroom to freshen up. Of course, I also check my phone.

> **Kenya:** *Alight. I'm done tripping. 😊 I guess you really like him then. He is who he said he was so far right? Enjoy him. I can't wait to get the details later. My man just walked in and time for me to put him to bed. Kisses. Talk to ya'll tomorrow.*

> *Diamond:* Goodnight. Have fun T.

> *Tasha:* Good morning. Oooh Kenya you so nasty. Yes he seems to be. Just wanted to check in and let ya'll know I'm still good.

When I walk back into the living room Adontis is walking into the house with his luggage in hand. He heads to the restroom to freshen up and comes out without a shirt on. I didn't know he was hiding all of that under his shirt. He has a washboard six pack. Nice muscular arms that are covered in tattoos. I knew he had tattoos, but I wasn't expecting this much. He has tattooed sleeves on both arms and a few on his chest and back. It looks good on him. Hell I'm turned on by them. He has a very nice stature. From the way he is wearing his pants, I see he didn't skip out on leg day either.

I smile at him and say, *"Damn!"*

He doesn't say a word, he just smiles back at me. He knows his ass is fine. I give him a tour of my home and it ends with my bedroom. We sit on the bed and discuss our plans for the day. I put on some music and we decide to go to dinner and a movie. We begin playing around and he starts to tickle me. I beg for mercy, but he keeps going a little longer. He ends up on top of me while I am laying on my back.

As I am loudly giggling uncontrollably, I muster out, *"Stop please, I give up. You win!"*

He smiles in victory and then he kisses me. He begins to feel on my breast and I like it. I don't want it to go there yet, but I don't want to stop him. His hands are soft and he has a very gentle touch. We continue to kiss and I move his hand and he moves it back. This time he goes into my shirt. I move his hand again and I pull back from kissing him.

"I am not ready," I state.

He looks at me and kisses me softly and says, *"Ok. I respect that."* We continue to lay in the bed, cuddled together, laughing and talking. Ding Dong! Ding Dong! Ding Dong! He looks at me, *"You expecting company?"*

My forehead wrinkles as I try to think, who in the hell that could be. *"No. Not at all."*

We get up and walk downstairs to the front door. I look through the peep hole and see: Carmen, her husband, Frank and their three kids; Ron, Kia, his wife, and their two kids. Carmen and Frank have all boys. They are seven, three and one. Ron and Kia have all girls. They are four and one.

Adontis says, *"Well who is it?"*

I just shake my head. I can't believe they are here. Why? It's so early. I look over at Adontis and say, *"It's my brother, sister and their families."*

He laughs and moves over to me wrapping me tenderly in his arms. He kisses me on the back of my neck while holding me.

"Well do they know that I am here? It looks like it's time for me to meet the family."

"*No, but they will in a few seconds.*" He goes to put on a shirt. Ding Dong. Ding Dong. Ding Dong!

Kia yells out, "*Open the door Tasha! Damn it's cold!*"

Adontis returns with a shirt on and sits on the couch. I open the door and say, "*What do ya'll want? Ya'll phone broke?*"

Ron looks at me, pushes me out the way and walks into the house like he owns the place. My nieces and nephews hug and kiss me. Everyone else is looking at me fussing for taking so long to answer the door. Therefore, they don't notice Adontis when they first step into the family room.

Frank and Ron sit on the sofa and that's when they notice him. They both look at me, while pointing at Adontis and ask, "*Who the hell is this?*"

Adontis stands up and I say, "*This is my friend Adontis.*" Kia and Carmen look at me with a surprised look on their faces. I introduce Adontis to everyone while my family gives him a stare down.

Carmen says, "*We need to talk.*" She and Kia pull me to my bedroom.

I look over to Adontis as I'm being pulled upstairs, "*I'm so sorry! I'll be right back.*"

He just nods an ok.

Carmen asks, "*Where did you-*" Before she can finish Kia jumps in.

"*Fuck that. He spent the night? Did you finally get some?*"

I look at both of them in complete frustration. Hell, I just met the man last night they didn't need to meet him yet. I don't even know if it is going to go anywhere. The chances are probably really damn slim now.

"*Not that it is any of your business, but I will tell you anyway. Listen carefully cause I will not repeat myself. I met him on the internet we have been talking for about eight months. He came down from New York yesterday to visit me. He stayed here; we fell asleep on the couch. Nothing happened! Now get your men and children and leave!*"

Kia and Carmen look at each other and Carmen says, "*She must think she grown.*"

"*I am, now out of my room.*"

We return to the living room where we find Ron and Frank grilling Adontis. I tell them to stop and I tell them who he is and how we met.

"*What are ya'll doing here?*"

Kia laughs, "*Damn he got you that open you forgot it is your turn to host breakfast? Damn I guess so! We do this every first Saturday.*"

I sigh, "*Damn I did forget.*"

I try to get Adontis away from my brothers, but they aren't having it. "*Excuse me guys, can I borrow Adontis for a minute?*"

"*Naw Tasha,*" go on Ron says as he gestures for me to leave.

Adontis looks cool as a cucumber. "*No Ron. Adontis!*"

"*I'm good ma,*" Adontis says.

"*Yeah he good ma,*" Frank says as he mocks Adontis.

I don't want to leave him with them. It is way too early for them to be all up in his business. I don't want them to run him off shit. I look at Adontis again for reassurance. He smiles and gives it to me.

"You can go ahead with your sisters ma."

"Ok," I say reluctantly.

My sisters and I head to the kitchen and get to cooking. I send the kids in the room to watch cartoons while Ron and Frank talk with Adontis.

Kia says, *"Damn Tasha, Honey is fine! If you not going to test drive him, can I?"*

Carmen laughs out loud. *"Kia girl you are fool!"*

"Ha ha ha. Kia, don't lose your life. Messing with that one you just might."

"He is fine, but damn Kia she gonna kill you. You got kids to take care of."

Kia laughs. *"I know right. Imma have to leave him alone."*

"That's right Bitches!" We all laugh and finish cooking.

Carmen looks at Kia and says, *"So I guess somebody is really over Rodney."*

"Yeah, I guess so," Kia replies.

"I am over him and it feels good. After all he fucked up. Not me."

Breakfast is ready so we begin fixing plates for the men and children. The children dine at the table in the kitchen and the rest of us dine in the dining room. We have a really nice spread for breakfast. French toast, grits, bacon, sausage, eggs, hash browns and biscuits. Breakfast is delicious.

Over breakfast my sisters join in and help with grilling Adontis. All I do is roll my eyes. I wasn't ready for them to meet him. Hell, I just met him. I certainly don't want them to run him off. This is just too early for him to be meeting my family. I don't want him to get the wrong idea. I don't want him to feel set up or put on the spot. Adontis allows them to ask him all the questions they want.

He remains calm and cool through it all. He doesn't seem bothered. He answers each question appropriately and seems to be winning them over. Even Ron. He is especially hard on any man I date. After all I am his baby sister. After we all eat, we sit on the couch and watch a movie.

To my surprise Adontis pulls me onto his lap. I don't say anything I just lay back and relax on him. When I look over, I see that Frank is sitting up on the couch sleeping. Ron and Kia look at him and start laughing.

Ron looks at Carmen and says, *"Damn, Carmen your man would fall asleep on a picket fence. Just like a newborn after he eats, he falls asleep. What's his schedule? Eat, sleep and shit? Carmen that's a shame. You still breastfeeding too?"*

"Shut the hell up Ron. Leave my man alone. He works hard."

"Obviously, he sleeps even harder."

We all sit, listen and laugh. Frank wakes up and notices everyone staring at him. He has drool coming down his chin. He wipes his face off. *"What? What ya'll looking at?"* We all burst out laughing again.

The movie ends and we all chat a little bit. The guys are chatting while I'm catching up with the ladies. After a few moments of silence, I am ready for everyone to leave.

"Ok it has been fun, but we have plans and we need to get ready."

My brother looks at me. *"Damn you sending us home?"*

"I don't care where ya'll go, but you gotta get up outta here bro."

"Damn sis, that's cold."

"I still love you though."

They gather their families and we say our goodbyes. Ron shakes Adontis hand. Hell, I think they may have bonded. They all finally go out the door and I am happy to be alone with Adontis again. I lock the door and lean against it.

"Well I wasn't expecting for you to meet my family so soon or like that."

He mutters out, *"It's okay."*

"What's wrong?"

"It's not important."

"If it's on your mind, it's important. Tell me what's the matter?" I walk over to him and sit next to him. *"What's the problem?"*

He stands up and walks a few steps away from me. He looks over at me and begins talking. *"Well, honestly. I thought we were more than friends. But that's how you introduced me. I didn't travel here for a friend. I can make friends in New York. Do you want this?"*

I look at him and I am in total shock. I never saw that one coming. I turned Walt down because I didn't want anything long distance, now I'm contemplating it anyway.

"I didn't know you felt that way. I like you a lot and I didn't know you were interested in a relationship already. I am cool with that. But answer this for me can you handle a long distantance relationship? Can you be faithful to me? Can I trust you? How can this work?"

He looks at me as he listens intently. *"I like you a lot and I think we can have more. You smart, sexy, outgoing and beautiful. Shorty you the whole package. Why wouldn't I want to be with you? I can handle a long distantance relationship. Can you? Is this what you want? I can be faithful and I can be trusted. If we both willing to try this can work. Would you be willing to visit me sometimes? I'll get your plane tickets to New York. Would you come?"*

I sit quietly thinking to myself. I ask myself some questions: Now that I have met him, is he what I want? Yes. Do I want to live without seeing, kissing, hugging or talking to him again? No. Would I have any regrets if I didn't pursue a relationship with him? Hell yes. I still have regrets from Walt. I don't want to have anymore. I have one life to live and I want to live it to the fullest.

As I am thinking all of this I hear, *"Earth to Tasha."*

I look at him and stand up. I walk up to him. *"I was just thinking and yes I want this. I want you."*

He pulls me in towards him and kisses me. *"Will you come visit me in New York shorty?"*

I look him deep into his eyes. *"Papi, whenever you want me, I'm there."*

"Keep on calling me papi. I'm gon show you why I'm daddy."

I burst out laughing. I can't lie I want him to show me.

He smiles, *"I ain't playin with you ma."*

"I know. Are you gon tell me what you and my brothers were talking about earlier?"

"Naw."

"Why not? I want to know."

"You don't need to know. That's man stuff."

"I do need to know. You really not gon tell me?"

"No shorty."

We relax on the couch for a while snuggled together and talk about our relationship. We share what we expect from each other. Communication and faithfulness are my biggest needs. His is loyalty. We both agree to make sure we do the things we each require. Time passes by and I fall asleep in his arms.

It is about 6:30 when he kisses me to wake me up. I awake with a smile on my face.

chapter 11

Battle of the Exs

January 6, 2007

**No one wants their exes to meet, especially after a
bad break up. But an ex is an ex for a reason.**

"It's time to get ready. You gotta wake up shorty."

I get up and we both get dressed to go out. I put on a sexy long dress. It is chocolate to match my skin tone and it clings to my body in all the right places. It is low cut in the front to show off my cleavage and cut just above my butt in the back. It's not the same dress I wore when I saw Walt, but they are similar. What makes it a sexy dress, is how tight it is and the way the back is cut. It's skintight. Almost like a second skin. On my feet, I wear thigh high gold boots. I look devastatingly beautiful. If I must say so myself.

I walk towards him with one hand on my hip as I switch like it's nobody's business. *"You like papi?"* As I spin around so he can check me out.

He smirks. *"Damn shorty I love. That dress is hugging you in all the right places. And that walk. Damn you look so good."*

"Thank you. I do what I can."

We dine in downtown Charleston. Our meal is excellent and the conversation is wonderful. After dinner Adontis asks me to dance and I accept. He holds me close to his pelvis as he has one of his hands right above my behind and the other hand on my mid back. Soft jazz plays in the background. He sniffs the perfume on my neck as he pulls me closer and closer to him. I have my arms around his neck and I lay my head on his chest. Thankfully my heels give me some extra height otherwise my arms couldn't reach his neck. He smells like heaven on earth.

We enjoy our first dance. His nice strong biceps are wrapped around my body. I've never been held in this way. It feels nice. When the song ends it's bittersweet. As we pull apart, I don't want to let go. Have I finally met a real man?

We leave and head to the movies. After he purchases our tickets; we have about a twenty-minute wait until the movie starts.

"You want anything from the concession stand shorty?"

"No thank you baby."

We enter into the theater and we find our seats.

"I am going to the restroom baby. I will be right back."

"Ok beautiful."

As I walk to the restroom a few men stare at me and try to spit some game. I just ignore them and I don't even entertain their excuse me miss. I even get some stink looks from some females. I don't pay them any attention either. I am use to it. I label them as haters and keep it moving. My motto: Haters make me better!

I don't know why some women have to be like that. When I see a woman looking fly, I am on my grown woman shit. I will tell her, you look nice or I like what you are wearing, etc. I don't have time to be a hater. I'd rather uplift another woman that's on her grown woman shit.

After using the restroom, I return to the theater and find my seat. The lights are still on and the theater is packed. There are no more available seats.

"Wow baby! It has gotten packed in here."

"Yes, it did."

Adontis is sitting to the left of me and he has the aisle seat. The movie still hasn't started and coming from the right of me I hear someone call out my name.

"Tasha?"

I turn to the right to say *"Yeah"* and as I turn the lights begin to dim. Once I turn around, I see a familiar face staring back at me. It is Malcolm. My heart falls to my stomach. Oh, my gosh. I can't believe it. Not him. Not tonight. Not here. Not sitting next to me.

"I guess I see why you ain't been responding to my texts or returning my calls."

Adontis looks at me. *"You know this boy?"*

"Boy? Nah dog I am all man. Ask Tasha."

I can see in Adontis' face that he is ready to blow up. Before he does, I try to calm him down. Clearly, I must know him, considering that he knows my name.

"Baby calm down please. This is Malcolm."

By the look on his face, I can tell he remembers the name. I also realize that I talk too damn much. It was bad enough I told him about him, but why the hell did I also tell him his name. I had a dumb moment, I guess. I could slap myself right now. To make matters worse, I did fail to tell Adontis that Malcolm lives in my state and that I met him. Hell, he didn't ask. I'm not just going to be volunteering that kind of information.

"What up baby. You miss me?"

"Hell no! Now if you can shut up maybe I can enjoy this movie!"

The previews begin and I get close to Adontis. Malcolm decides to put his arm on the back of my chair. I look over at him and he smiles at me.

"Damn baby. You wearing the hell out of that dress."

I just roll my eyes at him and try to ignore him. *"Switch seats with me,"* Adontis says. *"For I have to beat the shit out of this jackass."*

I can't even argue. We switch seats and Adontis puts his arms around me and we enjoy the movie. I can feel Malcolm staring at me and I begin to feel a little uncomfortable. I just try to ignore him.

The movie ends and Adontis and I leave together. Adontis goes to use the restroom and I go to sit and wait in the lobby. While I'm waiting, Malcolm walks up to me. I roll my eyes and begin to turn away. He sits next to me.

"Hold up baby. I just want to talk."

"Firstly, I am not your baby. Secondly, we have nothing else to talk about. Our business with one another ended the night we met."

"May I please have a few minutes of your time?"

I look him up and down. *"You have one minute and thirty seconds is already gone. What?"*

As he talks to me, all I hear is gibberish. Some shit about him and his baby mama not being together anymore. He wants a chance to be with me, etc.

I look at him, *"It's too late. I have a man."*

He stands up. *"That's some bullshit. I've been calling and texting you and you haven't responded. Now you with some other nigga."*

"I don't know what to tell you. I'm not available and when I was you weren't. It is what it is."

"That's some foul shit Tasha. I dumped my girl for you."

"No, you dumped her because you didn't really want to be with her. It's good she's free to find a man that will love and treat her right. It's time you do the same."

"Bullshit."

I sit looking at him with no more words to say. He shakes his head as he is walking away. I spot Rodney walking towards me.

"You dating high school students now Tasha?"

"Not that it's any of your business, but he's not my man! What the hell do you want?"

"You know what I want. I want you. Always have. Always will."

"You stalking me now?"

"That's the little bitch my homies saw you with?"

"That's none of your business. Who I am with or who I do!"

"That's an easy one. You ain't doing anyone. You got those thighs of yours glued shut."

Adontis walks up from the bathroom and I stand up. *"You sure about that Rodney?"*

Rodney looks Adontis up and down. *"Can I help you dawg?"*

"No, you can't! You ready to go ma?"

"Yes papi."

I grab his hand and we walk out of the movie theater. I know I am going to have some explaining to do. What are the chances of me running into both of those fools in the same night? We get to the car; he opens my door and I get in. He gets in and we head back to my place. We are silent for the beginning of the drive. I know what's in his head, but I don't want to deal with it. I look over at him.

"Good movie huh?"

He looks over at me quickly, *"Are you going to tell me what all that was about? And you know what I am talking about."*

Damn he knows me well already; he didn't even give me a chance to pretend like I didn't know what he was talking about. I scratch my head and I begin to tell him what he wants to know.

"Shortly after we started talking, Malcom asked me out. I agreed to go. We went to dinner. Dinner and conversation was good, until his girl started calling him. He turned off his phone. Then he told me he was feeling me and I told him I liked him also."

He is driving and carefully listening to me.

"He wanted to know what the problem was. I told him he had a girl and I couldn't mess with him. He was mad and said he wouldn't break up with her unless he had someone better. I told him goodbye. He called and texted me for a while after, but I never responded. Before tonight I hadn't heard from him in about a month."

He looks over at me. *"Did you kiss him?"*

I look over at him. *"No. He had a girlfriend."*

"And? Your ass went out with him anyway."

"Yes, I did. It was a mistake. You and I had just started talking."

He rolls his eyes at me. *"Why didn't you tell me he lived here. Or that you went out with him?"*

"I didn't think it was important. I am not interested in him." We arrive back at my place and go inside. The conversation doesn't end there. He is full of many more questions.

"What were you and Malcom talking about while I was in the restroom?"

I didn't know he saw us talking. Is he a spy or a ninja? *"He told me he was single now and wanted to get with me."*

He looks me deep in the eyes. *"What you want shorty? I ain't bout playing no games ma. You fine as shit."* He licks his lips, which makes me want to lick them too. *"I see why motherfuckers want you. If you mine, you mine. I ain't sharing shit. I will fuck up a mother fucker over what mines."*

I smile. *"I don't want anybody, but you."*

"Ok real talk?"

It is so funny hearing and learning his slangs. He says stuff I've never heard before.

"Yes baby. Real talk."

"Who was that other mother fucker grilling you?"

"I knew that was coming."

"You damn straight. Who was he Tasha?"

"That was my ex-boyfriend. Rodney."

He looks at me shaking his head. *"Well it must be ex's night. What the hell did he want?"*

"He saw me talking to Malcom and was jealous. He also wants to get back together."

"When did ya'll date?"

"A little over a year ago. He cheated. I caught him. We broke up. He has been trying to get back with me ever since."

"Damn you got all these mother fuckers trying to get with you, and you didn't even give them none!"

"That's it there is no more. But I think he thinks of me as the one who got away."

"Well you better stay away."

"I will. There is only one man that I want."

"You sure bout that?"

"Yes baby."

I walk over and begin to kiss him. My phone rings and it is Rodney. I ignore his call and he calls again. Then I turn my phone off.

"That mother fucker trying to get his ass beat. I think you should change ya number."

"Will that make you happy?"

"It's about making us happy. He seem like a problem."

"You're right. We can do it tomorrow!"

"Alight."

I love a man who takes charge. It turns me on. I know he's right my ex doesn't need access to me. Since he won't just leave me alone, I'm forced to make him, by changing my number.

We both decide to change our clothes. I put on a camisole and matching boy shorts. Then I cover myself up with a silk robe. I find Adontis sitting on the couch watching TV and I sit beside him. He wraps his arms around me and we begin to relax. I am bored very quickly and I decide to mess with him.

I get up from my seat to change positions. I end up sitting on his lap sideways with my back to the arm rest and my legs resting on the sofa. While getting comfy on him my robe comes open and I quickly close it.

"Ooh, let me see!"

I smile and say, *"No."*

I kiss him and he kisses me back as he slides his hands into my robe and up my thigh. I don't move his hand as he feels up my legs and rubs on my thighs. After our passionate kiss I tell him, *"I am going to bed, I'm tired."*

"Where should I sleep?"

"Wherever you'd like."

"I want to sleep with you!"

"Okay, that's fine. But can you handle sleeping next to all of this?"

He smiles at me. *"I'll be ok."*

We get to the bedroom; I take off my robe and I get in bed. He takes off his shirt and pants. *"I usually sleep naked, but is boxers ok with you?"*

I look at his nice body and I wonder how he would look completely naked. I wanna know how its hanging. Does it hang more to the left, to the right or straight down the middle?

I shake the thoughts from my mind, I smile at him and say, *"It is very okay!"*

He is looking at me with a smirk on his face. *"And what does that mean?"*

"Oh, nothing baby. Goodnight."

"Goodnight ma."

I turn off the bedside lamp. As we lay in the dark, I have my back towards his chest. He puts his arms around me and softly kisses my neck. I am still in a playful mood and I decide to wiggle my butt against his manhood. I really wanna know how it's hanging and what he is working with.

"Why you playing? Don't rub all that ass up against me cause if you start a fire, you gotta put it out."

I quietly giggle as I continue to wiggle. *"I have no idea what you are talking about."*
"Ok."

He moves his arms from around me and turns in the opposite direction. After a few minutes, I slide closer to him and then put my butt up against his.

"Are you sleeping?"

He laughs out loud. *"Yes!"*

I start to laugh. In a taunting voice, I say, *"No you're not!"*

I turn and put my arms around him and lay my head up against his back. A few minutes later, I am fast asleep.

January 7, 2007

The next morning, I awake and find Adontis holding me. I slip out the bed to freshen up and go to the kitchen to prepare breakfast. I hear Adontis awake in the bedroom and after he cleans up, he comes to the kitchen. He wraps his arms around me and kisses my neck.

"Damn ma you smell hella good!"

"Well thank you baby."

I turn to face him and I softly kiss his lips. He picks me up and sits me on the island kitchen countertop. He stands in between my legs and I wrap them around him. I put my arms around his neck and we kiss some more. After spending some time making out, we finally separate ourselves and we begin to finish breakfast. Over breakfast we discuss our plans for the day ahead. We decide to go out shopping after I get my cell number changed.

After relaxing for a long while we get dressed and head out the door. We are out for several hours and when we return, we are both really tired. Our day consisted of changing my cell number, browsing the museum, aquarium, shopping in downtown and going to the arcade. We had a lot of fun. We go straight to bed and shortly after we are both asleep.

January 8, 2007

I awake to the smell of bacon, eggs and biscuits. It's Adontis last day with me and he will be leaving tomorrow morning. He walks into the bedroom and serves me breakfast in bed.

I smile when I see him. This is different, I've never had this. A girl could get used to being catered to every now and again.

After eating breakfast, we both get cleaned up. I don't want Adontis to go. I wish that he lived closer. I feel nervous about trying the long-distance dating thing. I already care about him and I like him a lot.

I have real feelings for him. I guess after speaking to someone for hours every single day for over six months you begin to get to know them. I'm falling for him. That scares me shitless. However, as long as he shows me, he's who he told me he was, I'm ok with falling. Because I know he's going to catch me. I can't help but wonder to myself if he is the one. We spend the entire day in bed hugged and snuggled together. My phone begins to ring and it is Carmen. I press the send button.

I answer with, *"Hello."*

"Hey. What you doing? Is he still there?"

"Yes, and we are enjoying our last day together. What's up? What you doing?"

"Nothing. I just called to check on you. See how you was doing. But I guess you busy! So just give me a call later."

"Okay, I will."

I hang up the phone and Adontis ask, *"What you wanna do tonight?'*

"It doesn't matter as long as I am with you."

"Well I am in the mood to go bowling. How you feel about that?"

"I am with it."

"Why don't you invite my future in laws. I think it will be fun."

"Future in laws, huh?"

"Hell yeah. I ain't letting your ass go."

I smile. *"Okay baby we can do that."*

I call up Carmen and Kia and we set up plans for later tonight. Dinner and bowling. While I am discussing plans, and making arrangements with them, Adontis falls asleep with me laying on his chest. When I get off the phone, I notice him asleep. I get my camera and take some pictures of him. Damn, he is even sexy in his sleep.

When he finally awakes, I tell him about the plans that I discussed with my sisters. I also show him the pictures I took of him asleep. We stay in the bed, talk and watch a movie until it is time to get ready to go.

We enjoy dinner then we head to the bowling alley. We have a really good time bowling. We play the men against the women and we also do couples against couples. We share a lot of laughs and Adontis seems to really blend in with my family. We end pretty early because my family has work in the morning and Adontis has to get on the road early.

When we get back to my place, we get in our night clothes and have some dessert. He sits on the couch as I fix our dessert. I sit down next to him and he puts ice cream on my nose. I look at him and smile.

"Why you playing?"

"Oh, don't worry shorty. I am going to get it off."

He kisses the ice cream off my nose. Then he pulls me closer to him and he begins to gently kiss my lips. We begin kissing and he moves to my neck. He starts sucking on my neck. As he continues to kiss me, he starts feeling on me. He slides his hands up my shirt and then he begins to caress and squeeze my breast. Even though I know I should, I don't stop him.

Things get very heated when he sticks his head in my shirt and kisses my breast. It feels so good and I don't want it to stop. By this time, he has a handful of my breast in his mouth. He is squeezing and sucking on my titties. I move my shirt off his head and push him away from me.

"I'm not ready for this Adontis. I'm sorry."

He just nods his head before excusing himself. I hear him go to the bathroom. I get up and go to the bedroom. I turn my fan on high and lay across my bed. I am trying to cool myself down. He has me hot and bothered.

The next time this happens we might go all the way. Now I know I want him as much as he wants me. He has turned me on and I am horny. I feel my pussy throbbing for him. I've never felt this before. My vagina has its own heartbeat as it thirsts to have him in me. He comes into the bedroom and finds me laying across the bed. He lays down next to me.

"Damn I want you! When I get you I ain't gon let you go!"

"Are you mad?"

He looks at me in disbelief. *"I can't believe you asked me that question. Am I mad at you? I could never be mad at you, I love-,"* his voice trails off.

I lay in the bed staring back at him. *"You love what?"*

He just shakes his head. Under his breath he utters, *"Shit."*

"You love what Adontis?"

"You gon make me say it?"

"I don't know what it is."

"I love you Tasha. Damn."

"That's a bad thing?"

"Naw it's an, it's too early to be telling you this shit thing."

"Not if it's how you feel."

"It's how I feel."

I'm speechless.

He says, "Now you probably thinking my ass crazy."

"No."

"Yeah right. This probably gon sound like a line, but this the real ma." He grabs my face and tilts it towards him. *"I ain't gon lie, I ain't never felt like this bout nobody. You special ma. I see it and I feel it. I see a future with you. Nothing ain't ever scare me, but this scares me shitless."*

I look in his eyes and I can see he means what he says. It doesn't seem or feel like he's trying to run game. What he says feels sincere and genuine.

"I love you ma."

"Wow, you love me?"

"Of course, I love you. How could I not? You ain't got to believe me, I promise I'm gon show you."

We start kissing as he holds me tightly in his arms. I begin to wonder, have I actually found real genuine love?

January 9, 2007

I awake early the next morning. I didn't get much sleep after hearing how Adontis felt about me. I can't lie he took me by surprise. I didn't say I love you back. Not because I didn't feel it, but because deep down I am afraid to. Afraid to fall in love with him. Afraid to be this vulnerable with him. If I am being honest with myself, the feelings I have for him, the love; it feels different. Nothing like any of my past relationships. I am just as afraid as he is.

After much thought, I think I need to be open to this love. I feel ready to tell him, but I want it to come out naturally. I get cleaned up and decide to get breakfast started. Shortly after Adontis awakes, we eat breakfast and then say our goodbyes. A very long goodbye. With hugs and long passionate kisses.

"Be careful baby. Call me when you make it home."

"Of course, I will. I love you shorty."

He pulls me in and kisses me once more. A little longer and a little harder.

"You better. I love you too."

He steps back from me. *"That's how you feeling ma? You in love?"*

"Yeah baby. I'm all in with you."

He smiles. *"I love that."* He pulls me in for another kiss.

"Drive safe and call me when you get home."

"I will. Call me when you go to lunch."

"Ok."

"I can't wait to get back to your lips."

chapter 12

New Exposure

January 19, 2007

Venture out into this world and see what it has to offer.

Adontis and I have continued to date. A few weeks have passed and, in a few days, I will be flying into New York to see him. We have continued to speak on the phone every day and we talk via webcam. I have taken some days off from work for my trip and school is closed for the upcoming holiday. I have never been to New York and I am excited to go.

The day comes for my trip and I have Carmen to drop me off at the airport. Before getting ready to board the plane Carmen asks, *"Do you trust him? Do you love him?"*

I look at her and say, *"With my life and more than words could ever tell."*

"Ok! Be careful and call me when you get there. I love you!"

"I won't be gone long. But I will call you and I love you too."

We share a hug and say our goodbyes. I walk away from my sister and board my plane. I use my time wisely and get some studying done while flying to my man. I can't lie, I'm nervous. Now I am on his turf.

After a few hours my plane touches down in New York. Adontis got me a first-class ticket with no layovers. Before I get off the plane, I call my sister and tell her I arrived safely. After I get off the plane, I proceed into the airport. I spot Adontis and he sees me. He walks toward me and when he reaches me, we embrace. He picks me up off the floor and hugs me.

"Ma I been missing you."

"I missed you too baby."

He plants a very passionate kiss on me before letting me free. We go to get my luggage and go to his car. He is driving a BMW SUV. It's black with red leather interior. The car is banging. He takes us to get an early lunch before heading to his house.

It's a bachelor's pad, but not for long. I'm changing that. His place is very modern and very masculine. There isn't a woman's touch anywhere in sight. His house has four bedrooms and three and a half bathrooms. He gives me the tour and it ends in the garage.

"These are my other babies ma."

He has a red Ferrari with white leather interior, a white Bugatti with white leather interior and a blue Cadillac with gold leather interior, which he drove when he came to see me. All of his cars are nice and they all have custom paint jobs.

"Baby they are beautiful. But I'm your only baby." I stand on my tippy toes to lean in for a kiss. He laughs and bends to meet me. *"You have to find another name for them."*

"You know you my baby ma."

"Yeah and I'm not sharing the title."

"Ok ma I got it. I'll figure out something else to call them."

"Yep I'm territorial I don't share."

He smirks, *"Me either."*

"Good."

He leads us back in the house and we discuss my flight and his day so far. He tells me he has some nice things planned for us.

"Ma while you here, I want you to meet my family. I've been telling them all about you and they want to meet you."

"Ok baby. I would like that."

We finish getting me settled before we leave to head to his brother's house. Once we arrive, Adontis rings the doorbell and a tall handsome guy answers. He and Adontis resemble. They do not look exactly alike, but in seeing him I knew it must be his brother. He invites us inside and Adontis introduces us.

"Bro this my baby Tasha. Tasha this is my bro De'Shaun, but we call him Shaun."

We exchange a nice to meet you and sit and talk for a while. A female enters the room and Shaun introduces her as Melanie, his girlfriend. She sits and joins in the conversation and we all have a good time just chatting. Adontis and Shaun excuse themselves and go to the kitchen.

Since I am my mother's child, I have the ability to hear more than one conversation at a time. Melanie is talking to me and I engage in the conversation. Then I begin to listen in on Shaun and Adontis.

I hear Adontis ask, *"So bro what you think? My lady fine right?"*

"Yeah bro, shorty sexy! A she got a sister?"

"Yeah, she is fine as hell too, but she married. Don't make Melanie fuck you up." They both burst out laughing.

"Man, I ain't worried about that. You really in love with this one, huh? You look all sprung and shit."

Adontis laughs, *"Yeah I am in love with her, but I ain't sprung or nothing bro!"*

"Yeah right! Nigga please. Who you think you fooling? Man, she got you on lock. I think you pussy whipped!"

"Damn bro, that's a low blow. That one hurt. But I'm gon get it!"

"Yeah stay positive bro."

After hearing all this I think uh huh ok. Well I guess we will see about that. Melanie and I get up and go to the kitchen. We enter and find both of them laughing.

Melanie ask, *"What's so damn funny?"*

"Oh, nothing shorty."

Adontis puts his arms around me. Shaun asks, *"What ya'll doing today?"*

"I just wanna show Tasha around Harlem. Give her a feel for the city. What, ya'll wanna come?"

"Yeah bro. I'm with it. How bout you shorty?"

"Yeah I'm with it."

We leave and they show me around Harlem. I find it to be nicer than I expected. The town is very culturally rich. I can feel the Harlem Renaissance. The pro African American Movement at that time. It is inspiring. It makes me want to continue to push to achieve my goals. We visit some museums and I enjoy seeing the art of the artist of the 1920's. It's truly beautiful.

We go to dinner. When we're done, Shaun suggest going to a club. We arrive at club Phoenix. When we get there the line is down the street. Adontis takes my hand and we all walk straight to the front. The bouncer doesn't ask for our ID's or use the metal detector on us. I hear a few complaints being shouted at the bouncer as we walk in. Inside the club is packed.

I ask Adontis, *"So you come here often?"*

"Naw not really."

We head over to the bar to order some drinks. I see a couple of guys walk up to Shaun and greet him and Melanie then they greet Adontis. It is with a familiarity. Adontis introduces me. Melanie heads to the bathroom. The first bartender comes over to take our drink orders. She is familiar with Shaun and overly friendly. She greets Adontis and I can tell this isn't their first meeting. He introduces me to her as his girlfriend.

The bartender turns her attention back to Shaun and finishes flirting with him. Shaun flirts back with her. It doesn't seem innocent. Their mannerisms make me think that they are fucking. A second female bartender comes over to speak with Adontis. I see the way she is looking at him and it is as if she wants to eat him. She begins smiling at him and doing the damn most. The bitch is flirting with him. Adontis cuts her off and introduces me to her as his girlfriend. I can tell that she isn't liking seeing me with him.

She looks at me, *"I'm sorry. I didn't know ya'll was together."*

"It's cool," I say. I'll never let a bitch see me sweat.

"What can I get ya'll?"

"Hennessy straight and a cosmopolitan."

"Ok, I'll be right back with your drinks."

When the bartender walks away I'm ready to light Adontis' ass up. This damn sure ain't the way he's going to get my pussy. He got some explaining to do.

"For someone who doesn't come here often, everyone seems to know you. Why is that?"

"Shorty you getting jealous?"

"No, I'm just looking for answers."

I fold my arms across my chest waiting for him to answer me. He smiles at me enjoying the moment.

"You know you sexy when you mad."

"You're avoiding my question."

"No I'm not."

"Then why haven't you answered it yet?"

"What's the question again?"

"You pissing me off."

"Damn, you really mad?"

I begin to walk away from him. He pulls me back by the waist.

"Let me go."

"Hell naw. Mean ass."

"Adontis get off of me."

"Shaun owns this club, damn."

"Why couldn't you just say that from the beginning?"

"Shit I don't know, damn."

The bartender comes back with our drinks. Adontis pays for the drinks and we walk away from the bar. I guess he thinks the conversation is over. The shit isn't. He passes the drink to me. I'm not drinking this shit. I don't trust that bitch. I'll get a drink from another bar in the club. I spot one with male bartenders. I'm headed there next. Before I get my new drink Adontis has some explaining to do. I pull him aside to get some answers.

"Did you fuck that bitch?"

"What bitch? What the hell are you talking about Tasha?"

"The bartender bitch? Don't act like you stupid."

"No Tasha I didn't fuck her. Shit I got blue balls now waiting on your ass."

"Keep fucking with me, they gon be purple next."

"What the fuck does that mean?"

"Why didn't you fuck her?"

"What?"

"Like I said, why didn't you fuck her? She obviously throwing it at you."

"You giving me permission to fuck somebody else?"

"What if I was?"

"Shit your motherfucking crazy ass. Hell no that's a set up. I just met her a few weeks ago when I was here helping Shaun screen applicants. This is only my second time seeing her. I ain't fuck her cause I don't want to. I'm with your crazy ass. I ain't trying to fuck nobody else, but you."

"You better keep that shit that way. I'm not dealing with no side bitches. I'll kill your ass and the side bitch and disappear the bodies."

"Who the fuck says shit like that?"

"You don't got no side bitches, then you ain't got shit to worry about."

He shakes his head.

"I ain't worried."

"Ok. Good."

"It's a whole lot of crazy in this small ass body."

"Yep. I'll be back."

"Where the fuck you going?"

"To get me a new drink."

"What's wrong with the drink in your hand?"

"I'm not drinking shit that comes from some bitch that's trying to fuck my man."

"Alright Tasha. Shit, I'm coming with you. I could use another drink too. You done stressed my ass out."

After getting my drink Adontis and I are walking towards the VIP section to meet Shaun and Melanie. My song comes on and I go running to the dance floor. The DJ gets on the microphone and says, *"This is for the ladies. Let's shake something."* The speakers blast *toot that thing up mami make it roll. Once you pop, lock it for me girl get low. If yo mama gave it to you baby girl let it show...* I start to pop lock and drop it.

Melanie and Shaun get on the dance floor and start dancing. Adontis walks up behind me and starts grindin' up on me. So, I grind him back. I hear Adontis' voice as he says, *"Excuse me dawg."* I look back and notice that the guy grindin' on me is not Adontis.

The guy looks at Adontis. *"Oh, my bad Adontis. This you?"*

"Yeah."

I am in complete shock, *"I thought that was you."*

He takes two handfuls of my ass.

"Well it wasn't. Next time turn around and look before you start shaking all this ass."

"I got it."

January 20, 2007

We dance for a long time before we get tired and decide to find Shaun and Melanie. They are up in VIP. Adontis escorts us up and we sit and relax for a bit. Shaun and Adontis orders us some more drinks. We go back on the dance floor after a few drinks. It is 2:17am when we decide to leave. We get back to Adontis' and I am extremely tired. I take a shower and get in my pjs. Adontis does the same, but separately from me. We both get in the bed.

He starts kissing all over me. I have on some boy shorts and the matching red lingerie. My back is towards him and he keeps kissing on me. He begins to rub on my booty as he tells me he loves me. I turn towards him and kiss him. I know he is trying to get some. I'm not trying to give it up yet. I do know I want to give it to him though, but not until I'm ready. I fall asleep as he holds me in his arms.

chapter 13

Meet The Parents

January 20, 2007

This is an important milestone in any relationship. Especially, when your meeting the man's parents. When a man brings a woman home to Mama and Daddy, he is serious about her.

The next morning when I awake, I go to the bathroom to brush my teeth and wash my face. I come back in the bedroom to find Adontis still asleep. I see his dick print and it looks like he is working with a monster. I sit on top of him anyway and put my kitty kat directly on top of his manhood. He has a morning hard on. With my knees bent back on each side of him, I begin to softly kiss him. I can feel myself getting wet, as I sit on him. I realize I will not be able to hold on to my virginity much longer. I want him and I want to make love to him. I want him to take my virginity.

However, I will just go with the flow. I want my first time to be special and feel natural. As I continue to kiss on him, he wakes up. He rolls me on to my back and kisses me on the cheek. I feel his manhood up against my thigh. He is erect and I can now confirm his ass is packing based on how he feels against my thigh. He goes to the bathroom and when he comes out, I am sitting in the middle of the bed. We decide to go down and cook breakfast together. He tells me that he wants to take me to his store and he wants me to meet his parents.

I feel a little nervous. I'm always anxious at the meet the parent's stage. I'm even more nervous since I love him so much. I know it is a must. I put on a cute sexy red dress. It's not too revealing. Everything is covered and it isn't short. It's more semi-formal. I want to at least make a good first impression. We leave and then go to Fresh. We go inside and he gives me a tour. He sells all kinds of urban name brand clothing, shoes and accessories. He introduces me to his staff and after showing me off. We leave to meet his parents.

We pull up to a huge gate of this grand estate. Adontis punches in a code and the gate opens. There is a long driveway that leads us past a grand fountain. We follow the driveway which begins to curve into an arch as we approach the house. The fountain sits on the inner side of the arch. At the top of the arch is a walkway that leads to the home's front door. This house looks like a castle.

There are two four car garages on each side of the home. I am blown away. I wasn't expecting this. Adontis and I did talk about his family and he told me they were successful. Both of his parents, have money. However, I wasn't expecting all of this.

His mom is a top neurosurgeon and she also teaches courses at the university. We have a little something in common since medicine is also my field. His dad is a very successful attorney with his own practice. They are both published authors in their fields.

As we are walking up to the house, Shaun opens the door and invites us in. We walk inside and we are standing in a large foyer. We follow Shaun to what seems to be the family room. Here comes the big moment. I take a deep breath and exhale. I got this. I'm a charmer. Adontis introduces me to his parents.

"Mom and dad, this is my girlfriend, Tasha."

His mom looks at me with sort of a stink look on her face and instantly I begin to feel uncomfortable. His dad gives me a warm smile. I go to shake their hands and say, *"Nice to meet you."*

His mom doesn't offer or extend her hand. I am taken aback. How rude! So much for my charm. I just look at Adontis for reassurance. He places his hand gently on the small of my back. His dad takes my hand and pulls me into a hug. His wife looks at him out the corner of her eyes likes she wants to slap him.

His dad says, *"It's nice to meet you also, beautiful. We've heard a lot about you."*

The petty in me can't help it, I reply to his dad, *"I see where Adontis gets his good looks from."*

Which is a very true statement. Adontis didn't tell me his dad was fine as hell. They look alike, with a few differences. Adontis' dad's eyes are grey. He has the same curly hair as Adontis. However, it is not fully jet black. He has a patch of gray in the front middle of his head. He has a full beard and goatee, which is colored salt and pepper. He is in shape and his body looks just about as good as Adontis'. If this is what I have to look forward to with Adontis, sign me up. I know women are throwing it at him. Hell, if I didn't have Adontis, I would have been one of those women.

His mother rolls her eyes. I don't really care. I'm not here for her BS. She hasn't even given me a chance. What I can say is that she is actually pretty aside from her ugly attitude. She is about my complexion and she got it together. Her body seems to be together and much like myself she is a curvy woman. I instantly realize Adontis and his daddy have the same type.

"Thank you, sweetheart. Make yourself at home darling."

Adontis takes my hand and leads us to a sofa in the family room. We are sitting across from his parents and the conversation begins. Mr. Lamentez keeps things light and ask the general questions, like how we met and where I'm from etc. I happily answer his questions and try to tell him a little bit about myself. Mrs. Lamentez seems uninterested. It doesn't seem like she is present mentally. I tell them about my career and future plans. Mr. Lamentez shows genuine interest and gives good conversation. Mrs. Lamentez doesn't say anything. I can tell that she doesn't like me. I don't like her either.

We stay there through dinner and I am beyond ready to leave. His mom has been icy and very unwelcoming. I am outside of my element. I don't really know what her problem is. I can tell that she is stuck up and snotty. From the appearance of his parent's estate, it is evident that they are very wealthy. Maybe that is her issue. She thinks I'm a gold digger. If she took the time to get to know me, she'd know I'm anything, but that. I don't want their money. I am not a gold digger and I will not take any shit off of her. I have supported and taken care of myself before their son and I will continue to do so after their son, if he doesn't stick around.

Throughout our entire visit, I have been clinging to Adontis like static. His dad is very outgoing, debonair, kind and sexy. However, I find his mom to be an arrogant asshole. I am sure she will share her dislike of me with him. You better believe I will do the same. Once the painstaking dinner finally ends, we leave. I couldn't be happier. While on the ride back to Adontis' I tell him how I feel.

"I get the impression that your mom doesn't like me very much."

He looks over at me, *"Nah baby it's not like that. She a little overprotective. But I don't care what she thinks. I love you and that's all you need to know."*

"I love you too, but she made me feel unwanted and uncomfortable. And quite frankly I am not interested in being in her presence. I'd rather avoid her as much as possible. I know it's your mom and I would never make you choose. I just want you to know how I feel."

He looks like he's stunned a bit. I'm not the woman to bite my tongue and I don't hold things in. I can't because I'm not built like that. I've told him this and now he is getting to experience it firsthand.

"Wow shorty. I am sorry you feel that way. And I am sorry for how she acted. But I will talk to her. I don't ever want you to feel that way. That's moms, she ain't going nowhere and your ass ain't either."

I only respond with, *"Ok Adontis."*

I don't really have much else to say. I don't expect him to ditch his mom for a woman he hasn't known very long. However, I do expect him to talk to her and try to get this corrected. I'll watch and see what he does. If I see him working on it then I'll know he's serious.

We get back to his place, get cleaned up, change and relax on the sofa. I'm trying to shake it, but his mom really left a sour taste in my mouth. I don't want to take it out on him though, but I'm feeling some kind of way about it. I've got to talk to my girls about this once I get back home.

"Why you sitting all the way over there shorty?"

I look over to him and just shrug. He gets up, walks over to me, and sits next to me. In my mind I'm just replaying the night's events with his mom over in my head. I don't know how a serious relationship with him can work with his mom acting like that. He pulls me from my thoughts when he lifts me into his lap.

"Adontis what are you doing?"

He grabs my face and gently turns it towards him. He's looking me deep in my eyes. It's like he's looking at my soul.

"Look shorty, I love you. I ain't going nowhere and I ain't letting you go nowhere either. That was just moms being moms. She'll be alright. And I said I'm gonna talk to her so don't you worry about it."

"I didn't say anything else about it."

"You didn't have to, its written all over your face. You been acting distant ever since we left."

I turn my face away from him. I don't really know why. Maybe it's the look he's giving me. I think to myself, damn he can read me so well.

I muster out, *"Ok."*

He turns my face back towards him, but he gently holds it there. *"I'm serious shorty. I ain't playing about you."*

The way he is looking at me is making me just want to melt. We are staring each other in the eyes. *"Yes, baby. I believe you and thank you."*

He pulls my face close to him and begins to gently give me pecks on the lips. The pecks turn into him sliding his tongue in my mouth and delivering a very sexually pleasurable kiss. We do a lot of kissing and we fall asleep on the sofa.

chapter 14
Decisions

January 21, 2007

**Life is full of decisions that can lead to many possibilities.
For every action there is a reaction.**

The next morning, I awake in bed alone. After getting cleaned up I find Adontis downstairs preparing breakfast and talking on the phone. When he hears me coming, he quickly ends the call.

"Well who were you talking to this early?"

"No one. Just checking my messages and cooking my shorty breakfast." He leans over to kiss me and I pull away.

"Nice try, but I heard you talking. You wanna try the truth this time."

"Damn you nosy. But since you must know I was finalizing the surprise I have for you tonight."

With my foot in my mouth, *"Oops I am sorry baby!"*

As he smiles, *"Yep you ought to be. Now come on over here and let Daddy taste your lips."*

He pulls me into him and begins kissing my lips. *"I apologize for making an assumption."* He just holds me tighter in his arms. *"It's ok love."* Then he kisses me some more.

After breakfast, we go for a walk, a quick one. It's freezing cold out here, but I wanted to anyway. Fortunately, I packed properly for this trip and I love winter. We come back in and relax. We spend the day hugged and snuggled together, until nightfall and he tells me to get ready. By 7:45 we are both ready to go when the doorbell rings. Adontis opens the door and there is a limo outside and the driver is at the door. He escorts us to the limo and opens the car door.

I look at Adontis in disbelief. *"This is for me?"*

He smiles, *"You are worth it. And so much more. I want to give you the world shorty. Or die trying."*

Once we're in the limo Adontis opens the bottle of champagne and pours two glasses. *"What is all of this for?"*

"This is because I love you and you are so very special to me. I want you to know that and never doubt it."

I begin to kiss him and I don't even notice that we have stopped until the driver opens the door. We are outside of a building that appears to be deserted. Adontis takes my hand and leads me inside. We take an elevator up thirty stories to the very top floor, then we take the stairs to the roof.

He leads me outside and we arrive to a beautiful view of New York. There is a dinner table with everything laid out for fine dining. The table is surrounded by fire pits for warmth and there is soft music playing. He escorts us to the table and we both take a seat. A gentleman comes out to where we are and he introduces himself as Chef Gabriel. He begins to pour our wine and then begins to serve us our five-course meal.

The meal is excellent. It is Italian. Adontis knows that I love Italian food. We enjoy our amazing meal and each other's company. *"Babe I can't believe you went through all of this trouble."*

"Love, for you this isn't any trouble. You deserve it. I have to treat you like the queen that you are."

He has me blushing and I can't stop. *"Thank you so much baby. I appreciate you."* I lean forward and I begin to kiss him.

He hands me a gift-wrapped box and inside I find a diamond tennis bracelet. I remember mentioning to him that I wanted one.

"I heard your hints and clues about this bracelet. I knew I had to get it for you."

"Wow. Thank you, baby."

I get up from my seat and I sit on his lap and kiss him some more. I give him the bracelet and I hold out my arm. He places the bracelet around my wrist.

"It looks beautiful on you shorty."

"What did I do to deserve you?" I lean in and plant another passionate kiss on him.

"Every king needs his queen. You my queen."

We finish the remainder of our courses with me in his lap. Which really is only dessert. I don't want to let this man go. A man who shows he cares and actually listens to me. I've never been in love like this before. Don't get me wrong yes, I loved Walt. He was my first love, but it was puppy love. I was a kid. I didn't know much and I had so much to learn. I still have a lot to learn now, but I've grown and matured since Walt. This is a new type of love. An experience I've never felt. I thought I loved Rodney, but I didn't feel this way about him.

Dinner has commenced so we head back to the limo. We are all over one another in the limo. We arrive back to his place and go inside. When we enter, I find two dozen white roses on the table for me. He has really pulled out the romance. I go upstairs to the bathroom and he goes to the kitchen to make us some drinks.

I come downstairs and find him sitting on the sofa eating cake, drinking Hennessy and listening to soft music. I walk over to his stereo and put on my prearranged playlist, which starts with R. Kelly 12 Play. While upstairs I changed out of my dress. I am standing in a tightly tied white robe. He looks up at me when he hears my musical choice.

"You know that's that let me give you a baby music."

I don't say anything, I just smile and walk over to him. *"Your drink any good?"*

"Yeah it's good. You wanna taste or you gonna drink your wine?" He hands me a champagne glass.

I take the glass from him and sit it on the table. *"Well I think I got something better."*

I untie my robe and drop it to the floor, next to my feet, in white pumps. Beneath I am wearing a white see through corset that straps up the back. The bottom is a crotch less thong with knee high straps. His eyes stretch really big and I can see the shock on his face. I look like a playboy bunny. I sit on top of him and start to suck on his neck. Then I begin to unbutton his shirt.

He places his hands on my butt and begins to squeeze. I take his shirt off and begin to lick up and down on his chest.

"Damn shorty! You sure you a virgin?"

I don't respond to him. I just smile and begin grinding on him. I stand with my back towards him and bend over with my butt in his face. As I begin to unhook my knee-high straps, he continues feeling on my booty. I feel his lips as he starts kissing on my thighs. While I finish unhooking my knee highs, he smacks me on the booty.

I look over my shoulder, as I whisper, *"Ooh daddy."*

I sit on his lap as he unlaces my corset practically tearing it off of me. He starts kissing on my back and feeling on my breast. I turn around to face him. He is smiling from ear to ear.

"Is this for real? Are you really ready ma?"

I think to myself oh my gosh I am nervous as hell. I'm so ready, but so nervous. I hope that he can't tell. Many questions run through my mind. How much will I bleed when he pops my cherry? I don't want it to turn him off and therefore what should have been a special night just becomes a dud. I shake my thoughts from my mind.

I bite down on my bottom lip. *"As ready as I will ever be."*

He smiles. *"Damn you biting that lip again."*

"Yep."

He picks me up and carries me upstairs and lays me on the bed. I'm trying to relax my body and clear my mind. I think he can read how I feel just from looking at my face.

He disturbs me from my thoughts and he says, *"Baby, just relax. I am going to go easy. If you want me to stop just tell me."*

I shake my head at him to reassure him that I'm ok. He begins to kiss and then suck on my breast. He begins kissing all over my body. He is giving me hell of foreplay. I know he is just taking his time because it is my first time, but I am ready for it to be over. Don't get me wrong, I want it and I don't intend to stop until I get it. But the wait is indescribable. Only a woman can know what I am talking about.

I am ready to get a much-needed orgasm. He kisses his way down and starts sucking on my thighs. He pulls my thong off with his teeth. He goes down on me and begins sucking my pussy and licking my clit. It is very pleasurable and I begin to moan and scream out his name. I am getting very wet. He then starts to rub on her with his fingers.

My juices are flowing. Then he slides his finger in, out, in, out. He does this repeatedly then he begins to use two fingers. In, out, in, out, in, out. He does it very slowly. *"Aaaahhhhhh Adontis,"* is what I begin to moan out. It feels good, real damn good. He starts to suck on my lips as he continues to finger me. He has sped up the pace and I'm feeling my body react in ways it never has.

We finally reach the moment when he slides into a condom. I watch him as he slides it on. I wanted to see if he was hung low. Hell, yeah, he is. Shit I need a starter dick. You know maybe four or five inches. His dick size is for a professional. By the looks of what he's working with, this is probably gonna hurt like hell. He enters my walls and I feel him as he eases himself into me. I yell out in pain.

He stops moving in me then he looks up at me, *"Baby do you want me to stop?"*

I can see all over his face, that he really doesn't want to stop. I know he would if I told him to. I've gone this far might as well see this thing through, I think.

"No. Don't stop."

I'm moaning loudly as I try to take the dick that he is giving me. It hurts like hell as he glides in and out of me repeatedly. He takes faster and deeper strokes each time. He continues to glide in and out of me. Deeper and Deeper. Faster and Faster. I continue to moan and it is painful. After several more strokes he goes deeper and I feel it, he breaks my hymen. My cherry is popped and he continues to go in deeper. I'm not sure if I can take it. The pressure hurts and it feels like I need to take a dump and a piss.

"Babe you're in too deep." It feels like he's in my esophagus.

He pulls out some and continues to ride me. We switch positions and enter into doggystyle. He is riding me from the back as he is spanking me on the ass. Surprisingly, I rather enjoy this position. I'm shocking myself. I'm a dirty girl. I smirk to myself. I feel him going in deeper and I'm trying to be a G. I tell myself to just take it. We are on the line between pleasure and pain and I quite like it. He is all the way in me and he is hitting my g spot.

He then asks me to get on top. I've never done this before of course, but hell I'm at my most vulnerable. I don't have anything to lose. I climb on top of him and I position myself properly. He helps to guide me. We get him slid in me, then I begin to ride him. I can take it all. As I take all of him into me, he keeps hitting my g spot and it's a pleasure I never knew existed. As I ride him, he sucks on my tits and plays with my clit. I continue to bounce up and down on him. Every stroke feels like I won the lottery. I begin sucking on his neck as I continue to ride. I begin to feel this sensation running through my body. This is something I've never felt before.

It begins in the pit of my stomach and the only way I can begin to describe it is pleasure. I inadvertently arch my back, my toes curl and I clutch the sheets in between my fingers. I am cumming. I make a sound I've never heard myself make as I scream out in ecstasy.

"Ah ah ah ah ahhhhhhhhhhhhhhh ahhh ahhh ahh ah ah."

This is what an orgasm feels like. He clutches my waist with both hands and begins to make a sound I've never heard him make before either. His voice is deep and it roars out of him. He has cum also, but only right after I finished first. A real man knows a woman cums first.

He pulls me into his arms. *"Damn I love you."* He kisses my lips and he holds me tightly as I lay across his chest. *"Are you ok? I didn't hurt you too bad, did I?"*

I look up at him, *"I love you too baby. And I'm fine."* I lean up and kiss him. *"Did you enjoy it?"*

"Hell, the fuck yes. I probably shouldn't tell you this, but you the best. I love making love to you. And you are so damn tight and right." He licks his lips and kisses my lips again.

I flash him a smile. *"Thank you for being so patient and gentle with me."*

He continues to embrace me and we kiss once again. I'm exhausted and I need sleep. Hell, I put in work too.

"Shit you was worth the wait."

January 22, 2007

I awake in Adontis's arms with a smile on my face. Memories of last night's pleasure run through my mind. I've never been happier. I got the answer to my question. It hangs straight down the middle and baby is hung low!

I get free from his arms and go get in the shower. After last night I know he needs the rest. I have a flight to catch later this afternoon. I hear the bathroom door open and I pull open the shower door to peek. I see Adontis standing naked in all of his glory wearing only a smile. He steps into the shower with me and begins kissing me.

"Did you enjoy last night ma?"

I bite down on my bottom lip. *"You gonna give me some more of what you gave me last night?"*

He doesn't say anything he just kisses me and then he places his hands on my ass. He starts sucking my lips and I suck his back. He kisses down my neck to my breast. Taking a handful of them, he begins to squeeze. Pinching my nipples, he then puts them in his mouth. He is on a full hard and I am already wet. He picks me up and props me against the shower wall and reenters my walls again.

After our love making session ends, we get ready for the airport. The limo is still outside to take us to the airport. We make a pitstop and get some lunch first. After lunch we get back in the limo and we are all over one another. I have got to make up for lost time. I feel like a new woman. I make love to him in the limo on the way to the airport. We have a quickie, but goodie. At the airport, he walks me as far as he can.

"I love you shorty. Damn I don't want you to go."

"I love you too baby. I wish I didn't have to go."

He grabs my face and kisses my lips. *"I love you. Call me when you land."*

"Okay baby, I will. I love you."

I go to my gate and board the plane. While in my seat I can't stop thinking of him. Wow that man. I never expected to feel such pleasure. For the entire flight my mind flashes back to the love he and I made. As soon as my flight lands, I call him. He answers on the first ring.

"Hey shorty."

"Hey baby. I just landed."

"I already miss you. When you coming back to Daddy?"

I smile. *"As soon as I can baby. I have to look at my calendar."*

"I can't wait. Just let me know when so I can get you a ticket. In the meantime, I got to see you soon. I will make a trip down there in a few weeks."

"Ok. I like that. I can't wait to see you again. I am going to find my luggage and my sister. I love you. I will call you later tonight."

"Ok ma. I love you too!"

I see Carmen and we hug. She also brought big mouth Kia with her. They both bombard me with questions about my trip. Then Carmen looks over at Kia and says, *"Uh huh."*

Kia responds, *"Yeah. Um hmmm."*

Confused, I look back and forth at the both of them. *"What are ya'll talking about?"*

Kia looks me up and down. *"Don't try to front. Somebody got their world rocked and we wanna know all about it."*

"Yeah that's right. Spill the juice."

"I have no idea what you hos are talking about."

I grab my luggage and we begin to head out of the airport. We get in the car and head to my house.

"Ok, talk to your big sis. Tell the truth. You got some! It obviously was very good. I can see and smell it on you."

I smile, *"A lady never kisses and tells."*

Kia chimes in, *"The hell with the kissing. We wanna know about the fucking?"*

"Ya'll not gonna drop this huh?"

They both look at each other, then at me. In unison they say, *"Hell no!"*

"Ok. Yeah, I gave it up. It was last night. This morning in the shower. And in the limo on the way to the airport."

By this time, we have pulled into my driveway. We all go inside.

"Your little nasty ass. In the limo?"

I smile, *"What?"*

"Ok and? We wanna know the rest."

"That's all there is to tell."

"Oh, no it isn't. Did you enjoy it? Did he treat you like a lady? Was it everything you thought it would be? Did he still respect you in the morning?"

I smile. *"Oh God, yes! Of course. Much more. Even more than before."*

"Oh Kia, our baby ain't a baby anymore. Last night she became a woman. And in the limo! Oooh you just nasty!"

I start laughing. *"Well he likes me that way."*

My doorbell rings. I go to the door and look through the peep hole. I see a guy holding a gorgeous bouquet of flowers. I open the door.

"Good evening."

"Hello."

"I have a delivery for Tasha Leam."

"That's me."

Kia and Carmen are now standing beside me. The delivery man passes me the vase full of an amazing floral arrangement.

"Thank you."

"You're welcome. Have a lovely day ma'am."

"You as well."

He turns to leave; Carmen closes and locks the door.

Kia smiles, *"Are these from Adontis."*

"I don't know. I guess so. He didn't tell me he was sending anything."

I take the flowers to the family room and sit them on the coffee table. I dig through the bouquet and pull out the card. Since they are so nosy, I just go ahead and read it out loud.

I know you had to leave your flowers from last night here in New York. I thought I'd send you these to brighten up your day. Know I'm missing you and thinking of you each moment of each day. I love you in every way. Take some time to stop and smell the flowers and think of me.

I love you ma,
Daddy

Kia can't wait to speak. *"Oh, you got this brother sprung like a mother. Girl what you do to that man? He is sending you flowers and shit just because."*

I'm blushing uncontrollably. *"I ain't did nothing."*

Carmen chimes in, *"Oh yo ass did something. He daddy now huh?"*

I smirk, *"Hell yeah, he Daddy! Big damn Daddy!"*

"Damn it's like that?"

"Yeah it's like that."

"This looks like an expensive as hell bouquet of flowers. You did something to him. Men don't send this just because unless they did something or they trying to get some. You done gave him some. This man is in love."

"We in love together."

"That's obvious you've been smiling since the airport. I'm happy for you baby sis. I knew I liked him when I met him. As long as he does right by you, he always has my vote."

"And mines too," Kia says.

They stay at my place long enough to hear about the rest of my trip. I even tell them about his stank acting mom and how Adontis handled it. They don't like what they hear. I assure them Adontis has it under control. Once they leave, I take a shower and get ready for bed. I have to call my man first though. I want to thank him for my flowers and I want his voice to be the last one that I hear before I go to sleep. When I grab my phone, I see I have a missed call from Adontis. I dial him back.

"Hey love."

"Hey baby. I love the flowers that you sent me they are so beautiful."

"Not as beautiful as you shorty. I'm glad you like them."

"That's so sweet. You like to make me blush, don't you?"

"Yep. When you happy, I'm happy."

"You make me happy. I am sorry I missed your call. I was in the shower."

"You make me happy too. I wish I was there. I been missing you all day."

"I have been missing you too. I had Carmen and Kia nosy behinds in here grilling me about my trip."

"Oh, did you tell them about last night?"

"I didn't have to, they knew."

"Are you happy about your decision to give it up to me? Do you have any regrets?"

"None at all. And I hope it stays that way."

"Don't worry about that. I promise you it will. I don't want another man to ever get up in my pussy. It's mine!"

Hearing him say this turns me on. I love to hear that he wants me and doesn't want to lose me. *"It definitely is yours. All yours. As long as you act right."*

We talk for a really long time and we both are sleepy, but neither of us want to say goodbye. I realize that it is really late.

"I am sleepy baby."

"Me too. But you gotta get up early in the morning. Get some sleep and I will talk to you tomorrow. I love you!"

"I love you too. Goodnight daddy!"

"Goodnight ma."

chapter 15

Not So Funny Valentine

February 10, 2007

A romantic day to share with the one you love.

It's been about three weeks and Adontis is coming back to see me. He arrives today and will be staying for five days. I spend the morning studying. About two hours before his arrival I get myself ready to see my man.

When he arrives, we spend all of our time together. We start in the bedroom and we don't really come out for air. We order takeout and just enjoy making love and spending time together.

February 14, 2007

The first two days flew by. The second day went much like the first day. We stayed in bed all day and made love. I did get up to cook a late breakfast. At night, we ate dinner, got back in bed, cuddled and made love some more. On the third and fourth days, I had work and school. He stayed at my place and did some work from his laptop until I got back home. We spent the nights with dinner and movies in bed.

Today is the fifth morning. I awake, kiss him on the lips and whisper *"See you when I get off. I love you!"*

He doesn't respond back. He is still asleep. I worked him over time last night. Today is Valentine's day. I arrive at work to find two dozen red long stem roses waiting for me. I grab both cards. The first one reads:

> *To the love of my life.*
> *Happy Valentine's Day.*
> *I made plans for us tonight.*
> *Come straight home.*
> *I love you.*
>   *Daddy!*

I smile. How sweet, but why did he send me two cards? I open the card from the other roses. It reads:

> *Hey baby, I still remember these are*
> *your favorite.*
> *I miss you and I want you back.*
> *I'm coming to claim my prize!*
> *I love you.*
> *See you soon.*
> *Rodney*

I drop the card to the floor in complete shock. Why won't Rodney leave me alone? I call Adontis to thank him for the roses. I race through the rest of the day in hopes to get home and leave before Rodney arrives. I just don't want to deal with the hassle of Adontis seeing him and me having to explain or him thinking I'm doing something I'm not. I rather just avoid it all together. I changed my number, think Rodney would get the damn point.

When I walk through the front door, from the foyer I notice the family room is dark and quiet. I then hear Adontis' voice coming from down the hallway.

"Yeah I definitely want to order that."

I follow the sound and find him in my office sitting at the computer desk on his laptop. He is on the phone and when he sees me, he smiles. I walk over to him and he pulls me to his lap.

He kisses me. *"Hey love."*

I kiss him back. *"Hey baby."*

I realize he is on the phone with one of his suppliers. *"Ok well I'll start out with a few boxes and see if they move. I'm not gon commit to more than that until I see if my customers feeling it."*

I can overhear the guy on the other end of the phone. *"Ok Adontis. I just emailed you the details."*

"Ok. My lady just got home and it's Valentine's Day. I'll look it over and get back with you later this week."

"I look forward to your call for more orders, my friend. Good Evening."

"Goodbye."

I thought that conversation would never end. I know he was handling business, but I'm trying to get gone before Rodney gets here.

"What time did you make plans for?"

"We have time. No rush."

"Well I am going to get ready."

He looks at me questionably, *"What's the rush?"*

"No rush."

"Ok. Well stay right here. I wanna hold you."

In my head I'm thinking, we really don't have time for this. He can hold me later. Rodney could be here any minute. He knows what time I get off work. I reluctantly, stay seated on his lap. He puts his arms around me and kisses me.

"I love you."

"I love you too baby."

Ding dong. Ding dong. Ding dong. Oh, shit I'm thinking. I sigh and walk to the door. I look through the peep hole.

"Oh no," I mutter.

Adontis has followed behind me. *"What's wrong,"* he asks as he walks towards me?

From outside the door, we hear Rodney's voice. *"Open up baby. Let's talk. I know this is one of your favorite holidays."*

"Who the hell is that? Is this why you rushing me to leave? What the fuck goin on Tasha? You fuckin him?"

"Baby no. Hell no! He sent me roses at work today and said he would stop by."

"Baby open up. I just wanna talk. I miss you."

I can see Adontis is pissed. A special moment ruined within moments. *"Tasha who is at the door? Matter fact don't answer that, I'm gonna look for my damn self."* Adontis opens the door. *"This motherfucker again!"*

"Nigga you again! Tasha baby get rid of this buster."

"Rodney, we are over. And have been for a long time now. This is my man. You and I are through."

I look to Adontis and I see the mischief in his eyes. He wraps his arms around me. *"Look here dawg. I see why you can't let go. But you too late. She mines! Every inch of her."* He pulls me in close to him.

Rodney looks pissed. Not that I really care, but I really didn't want him in my business. *"You fucked this nigga? Tasha, damn baby. You told me it was mine."*

I ignore all of what he said. Things between him and I are over. *"Rodney leave."*

Rodney licks his lips. *"Okay Tasha, but this your last chance. I am not chasing after you anymore. You gonna be running after me next time."*

"Goodbye Rodney."

Adontis slams the door in his face. I walk off and go to the bathroom. I get in the shower and try to shake off what I feel. I don't know why, but it seems like he still has some type of hold on me. Damn I still care about Rodney. I don't know why. Even though he hurt me. I didn't want to hurt him. Maybe it was because we were friends first and he was a good friend, but a horrible boyfriend. I don't want him back or anything, but I know he still cares for me. I wish he would just leave me alone and move on to someone else though.

Adontis and I celebrate the holiday. Even though I am with him, I do think about Rodney some. At one time, he was my best friend. I will always love him for what he was to me. We shared some fun memories, but they are just that, memories. I want my future to be with Adontis, he's the one.

We get back to my place and Adontis lays me in the bed and makes love to me. He kisses me all over and I begin to forget all about Rodney.

"You are the one for me. You are the woman I wanna spend the rest of my life with. I love you."

Did he just say what I think he said? That is absolutely what I want. I want to be his wife and the mother of his kids. One day, like years from now, we're not ready for babies yet.

"I love you too baby."

We climax together.

February 15, 2007

The next morning, I awake and kiss him on the lips. He pulls me closer to him and begins sucking on my neck.

"Babe I have to get in the shower so I can get to school."

Without letting me go, *"Ok you'll make it to school."*

"I need to make it to school before my classes end."

"You'll make it. I promise."

"Adontis no! I'm not falling for that again. Babe I gotta get to class." I'm trying to get free. He is back to kissing on my neck and sucking and biting on my ears. He puts his tongue in my ear and begins squeezing on my breast. *"Adontis!"*

He doesn't acknowledge or respond to me calling his name. He continually kisses me in my spot then he slides his fingers down to my pussy. I'm trying to keep my legs closed. Let's be honest with thighs like mine, a man can't get between them easily without my help.

"Open your legs ma," he whispers softly in my ear.

I'm moaning as he is sucking on my titties then moves to kissing me in my spot again. He has gotten me hot. *"Baby I can't. Please let me go! I have to get to school. I have a test to take."* I'm pleading with him now because I know that if he doesn't let loose, I'm going to stay and make love to him.

"Just give me a couple of minutes, I'll make it fast. We can even take it to the shower."

I'm still pleadingly looking at him. He is giving me the let me rock your world look. *"Come on let's go."*

He releases me so that I can get up and we head into the shower. He props me up against the shower wall and glides into me as he interlocks his fingers between mines. He takes long deep strokes in and out of me. As he is riding me the water from the shower is hitting his chest. He lifts my legs across his shoulders as he continues to glide in and out of me. I begin to play with my clit as I'm sucking on his lips. He thrust himself into me faster and faster and faster. My eyes begin to roll back in my head.

I know exactly what is about to happen. With a smile across my face I say, *"I'm cumming!"*

My orgasm burst out of me. He clutches me and squeezes me tight. He begins to make that noise that he makes. We begin to actually shower. I quickly wash my body and go through my morning routine of getting ready. Once I'm finally dressed, I have about fifteen minutes to get to class. He is laying across the bed. I lean over and kiss him.

"I love you baby. Have a safe trip back home. Call me and let me know that you made it home safely."

"I love you too shorty and I will. Since you gave me all of that good loving, now I have to take a nap before my flight."

I chuckle, *"Yeah and I gotta go to class."*

"You ain't wanna send your man home without putting it on him first."

I lean down and kiss his lips again. *"Well you're right. Get some rest and I will call you at lunch."*

"Ok, ma have a good day."

We exchange another kiss and I head out the door to my car. With breaking every speed record and running a few traffic lights, I make it to class just as the professor is about to close the door to begin the exam. I apologize for my tardiness and scramble to my seat quickly. I can say that the love we made was worth it.

chapter 16

Expect The Unexpected

March 7, 2007

**Everything that can go wrong, will go wrong.
Things never happen the way you plan them.**

It has been about two and a half weeks since Adontis and I last made love. My period is late. This has never happened to me so I don't know what to think. I've always been regular. I am afraid to take a test. It may be too early to tell. I decide not to tell my family or friends, but I call Adontis to tell him.

"Hey shorty. What's up?"

I am on the verge of crying and I know he can hear it in my voice.

"Hello."

"What is it? What's wrong ma?"

I don't want to break out crying so I fight back the tears. Having a baby right now would completely deter me from my goals. Especially considering my man is hundreds of miles away.

I respond to him, *"I'm late!"*

"Late for what? You're never late?"

"No, not that kind of late. I missed my period. I haven't had one since before I came to New York."

"Hold up. What you trying to tell me?"

"I think I am pregnant! What you think of that?"

I hear complete silence on his end of the phone. I begin to feel like a complete fool. Did he hang up on me?

"Helloooooooooooooo, are you there?"

"Yeah I'm here. Just in shock. You think you pregnant?"

"Isn't that what I just said!"

His calmness is pissing me off and freaking me out. I don't know how to respond to it.

"Ok that's all good. Did you take a test yet?"

What the hell is wrong with him? Nothing is good about me possibly being pregnant.

"No. I am afraid to. How can you be so calm? I can't have a kid right now. What about my life and career? If I have a baby now, they are both over. I am not ready to be a mother."

"Baby calm down. Just take the test! You might not be. We used protection; you might just be late. You won't know for sure, until you take the test. Take a test and call me back to let me know what's up!"

"But if I am then what?"

"Listen baby, if you are then we just have to get prepared for parenthood. I love you, I ain't going anywhere."

I was not expecting that reaction from him. After talking to him, I feel calmed and relaxed. What I really wanted was the reassurance that he'd be there.

"Ok. I am going to schedule an appointment with my doctor."

"Ok that's fine. Call me when you find out what's up. I love you!"

"I love you too baby!"

After I hang up with Adontis, I call my doctor to set up an appointment. It gets scheduled for later in the week. I don't tell Adontis about the appointment.

March 23, 2007

Adontis has been calling me every day for the last few weeks. I have been ignoring his calls. He leaves me voicemails and send texts. I don't respond to anything. I already went to the doctor and didn't call Adontis after my visit. He has been blowing my phone up every day nonstop. I head home from work and when I arrive, I see an unfamiliar car in my driveway. I pull beside the car and get out. The person in the other car steps out also.

When I see the person, I say, *"Hey! What you doing here?"*

"Well since you haven't been returning my calls or responding to my texts, I came to see why. Talk to me Tasha. What's up?"

I swallow hard. I can see that he is mad and for good reason. I should have called him. He never calls me Tasha. It's always ma or shorty, even baby every now and then.

"I am sorry baby. I've just been busy with school-" He cuts me off.

"Are you pregnant or not?"

I look at him and he is angry. No, he is pissed! I have never seen him this mad and definitely not at me.

"No, I am not."

"You never were? Or you're not anymore?"

"I never was. I just told you I wasn't!"

He looks at me as if he isn't sure if I am lying.

"No Bullshit? Why haven't you called me then? What the hell is going on with you?"

"I don't know. I just found out a few days ago. I was scared I guess."

"Scared of what?"

"Can we go in the house and finish this?"

He looks at me angrily, *"Hell the fuck no! Not til you tell me what's going on. You beating around the bush and I don't like that shit!"*

I look at him sadly. *"I just had a pregnancy scare. I don't want to get pregnant yet, but you don't seem to care."*

He walks up to me and grabs me by my waist, *"Girl what you mean I don't care? I flew my black ass here to see what's going on! I love you enough to stick around and be a man to raise our baby! I am not trying to have a kid right now either. But if you get pregnant, oh fucking well we got a baby. I will be damned if you have an abortion!"*

"I wouldn't abort our baby! That's why I didn't want to be pregnant."

"Ok, but just remember you are never alone! Just don't shut me out like this, shit!" He pulls me into his arms and holds me. *"I love you!"*

"I love you too! I went ahead and got on birth control when I went to the doctor, I don't want any more pregnancy scares."

"Ok shorty that's fine." He kisses me on the forehead and we finally walk into the house.

I look over at him, *"How long are you gonna stay?"*

"Not long. I am going back in the morning."

"You can't stay any longer?"

"No. I gotta get back to work. But I am about to move."

"Move? To where? Why? Why you ain't tell me?"

"To Florida. And I been trying to tell you, but you haven't been answering your phone. I am gonna open up another store. I want to make Florida my home office."

"Oh. Oh yeah. Why Florida?"

"Isn't that where you gon be at after you graduate? You told me that you was going to med school in Jacksonville. I'm in this what you ma. I'm riding with you til the wheels fall off."

I can't help, but to smile. My baby really loves me. *"You was listening huh? Well at least we'll be closer. When I move there, I'll find a place that's not too far from you and school."*

"Well I want to be even closer to you. I want you to move in with me!"

I look at him surprisingly. *"Are you serious? I can't move anywhere right now! I have to finish school. My last semester is this summer. I still have to figure out what I am going to do with my house when I go to med school."*

"I know ma. I'm talking about when the semester ends, after you graduate. Instead of having to look for a place, you move in with me. Forget about the house. You already own it. You can just rent it out or something."

"Don't you think it is a little fast for us to just be living together?"

"I love you. I know with you is where I want to be. I don't need no more time to think about that. I want to wake up to your beautiful face every morning."

I begin to take it all in. I do love him, but living together, it's a big step.

"Stop making excuses. Do you want to move in with me or not?"

He is so damn blunt. This will definitely be different. I've never lived with a man. This is some serious stuff. He ain't giving me no time to think on it or nothing. You only live once right.

"Yes, baby. Let's do it."

We spend the rest of the day together.

March 24, 2007

Early the next morning he gets up to leave. He gets dressed while I am still sleeping. He kisses me and tells me he is leaving and that he loves me.

chapter 17

A New Start

April 20, 2007

**This is always a good way to fix past mistakes. But
we don't get too many of these in life.**

After about a month Adontis has completely moved from Harlem to Jacksonville. Shaun and Melanie moved to Jacksonville also. I fly into Jacksonville early this morning and I will be leaving on Sunday.

Adontis picks me up from the airport. We have breakfast, before he takes us to his Florida store. It isn't opened yet, but it is coming along. He shows me around the space and tells me his vision. Together we brainstorm some ideas that will help with the store.

However, other than seeing my honey the main goal today is for him to show me our new house. I'm excited to see our future home. Adontis completely chose the house without me so, I hope I like it. I can't really blame him, since I was avoiding him. That's water under the bridge though.

We turn into a neighborhood and I see some beautiful upscale looking houses. The homes are not very close to one another. There is some distance between each property. After a few miles and a few turns, to my right I see a beautiful house. I've seen some really pretty ones, since we turned in, but the outside of this house is amazing. I get excited when I realize this house is the one Adontis stops in front of.

The home, like all the others in the subdivision is gated. He stops at the gate and then punches in the code. We travel down a long driveway before pulling directly in front of the house. I can see it is a very large estate. Our house sits on the corner of the street. The home is a lot to take in. It is a two-story home with an attached four car garage and a detached two car garage.

From the outside the house looks like a mansion. The driveway is paved with cobblestone and includes a roundabout for outside parking on the side of the house and one in the front of the house. The detached garage sits on the side of the house at the top of the roundabout. I look over to Adontis and he is grinning from ear to ear as he watches my face.

"Adontis, this is beautiful."

"Wait to you see the inside ma. Our house is on about five and three quarters of an acre."

"This is a lot! And the landscaping is immaculate."

"Yeah it is, but we'll need it. I can't take the credit for the landscaping. I kept the same company the previous owner used. They do great work."

"Yes they do."

He parks in the driveway and we get out of the car. He hands me a set of keys.

"Here are your keys Ma. Go ahead and do the honors."

I smile at him and take the keys from his hands. I'm so excited. I can't contain it. I unlock the door and when we step inside. He leads me in and shows me how to disable the alarm. The home is just as gorgeous on the inside as it is on the outside. There are marble floors throughout the downstairs area and high vaulted ceilings. If I had to guess I'd say about ten to twelve feet high.

"I know ma, its empty in here. Since I made the decision on the house alone. I figured you can do the honors of decorating our home. Only thing we got right now is a bed."

A huge smirk comes across my face. *"Really! Baby this house is beautiful. What is our budget?"*

"Yeah ma really. You ain't got a budget. Do whatever you wanna do."

I give him a mischievous smile. *"Whatever I wanna do?"*

"Yeah ma, don't make it too feminine, though. I'd like it to have some masculinity to it."

Now I'm really smirking. *"Not a problem baby."*

"Good cause here is where we gonna start and raise our family."

I look over to him with a smile, *"One day."* I lean in and kiss him.

"Don't start nothing cause you gon have to finish."

"I never start and don't finish."

He smirks *"Uh huh. Let me give you the tour and we can stop in the bedroom and Christen that room first."*

He shoots me a devilish smile. I smile back at him. *"You ain't saying nothing but a word, let's do it."*

He takes my hand, *"Ok ma. Our home is like 19,800 square feet. We got fifteen bedrooms, eighteen full bathrooms and three half bathrooms. Right now, we in the foyer."*

I'm looking at him in awe. *"Wow that's a lot. This is a lot of space."*

He smirks at me, *"We gon need it."*

I don't know what he means by that, but I guess I'll find out later. *"This is gonna be a lot to clean too."*

"I know. The previous owner also had a house cleaning service. I decided to keep them on once a week to handle things like cleaning the floors, windows, and dusting. And whatever you need them to help with."

"You really thought of it all."

"I tried too. I know you gon have a lot on your plate with med school so I wanted to make sure we had some help."

"Thank you, I appreciate that."

He plants a juicy kiss on me, *"You're welcome ma."*

In the middle of the foyer there are two sets of stairs. The first set of stairs is facing the front door and the other set is facing the opposite way. They each lead straight up before forming a curve. The curve ends when they meet at a balcony. Above the balcony sits a large crystal chandelier on the ceiling. The balcony is midway between the first and second floors. I see from the foyer that the balcony leads to one large staircase that leads the rest of the way to the second floor.

Besides the stairs, four separate pathways lead from the foyer. The first one is a door to the left in the front of the foyer. He escorts me to the door and opens it.

"Ok, ma this is a full bathroom."

The bathroom has a large full body lighted mirror. In addition to the floors the countertops and walls are also marble. There is a separate door inside that leads to the toilet. There is a garden style tub that sits in the middle of the floor.

"Baby this is beautiful. You picked a beautiful house."

"You ain't seen nothing yet ma."

He takes my hand and escorts me out of the bathroom. Back in the foyer we are facing away from the entrance. The bathroom door is to our left. We now have three more doorways that lead from the foyer. Straight back on each side of the stairs is a large open doorway. Before going through the large open doorway, there is a doorway to the left, which is next to the bathroom we just exited and one on the right.

He leads us to the room, which is next to the bathroom. *"Ok ma. This is gonna be a home office. It can be our office. It's big enough for the both of us. You can do your decorating thing in here too."*

"I love it baby."

Back in the foyer he leads me across the hall to the door on the right. He opens the door and it leads to a L shaped hallway. He leads me to the first room on the right. It is a large room with a few windows. He stands behind me and wraps his arms around me and places his hands on my belly.

"I was thinking, once I put some babies in you, this could be a playroom for our kids."

I look back over my shoulder at him and I smile. *"I like that idea."*

He kisses the back of my neck. *"Good."*

We walk down the hallway and there is a second door to our right. He opens the door and leads us in. The space in the room is phenomenal.

"Ok ma, this the second master, which can double as a mother-in-law suite or guest room."

I love the room, but with the way things have gone with his mom, I doubt she will ever be here to use it. I just give him a smile. I don't have a response. He takes us through the room.

"There is a full bathroom and walk in closet."

I can't help, but to look at him in awe. He really went above and beyond. I don't want to ruin the moment, but I have to ask.

"Adontis, can we afford this?"

He looks at me as if I just cursed him. *"We wouldn't be here if we couldn't."*

"I hear you baby, but I'm thinking about the mortgage payment. How much is it? I don't want us in over our heads. Especially with the new store, my school bills and stuff."

He burst out laughing. *"You serious ma?"*

I fold my arms across my chest. *"Yes baby, I am. I don't get what's so funny!"*

"You are ma."

"You didn't answer my question."

"Stay right here. I'll be right back."

A million things are running through my mind. I've never been one to live above my means. I'm not rich, but I do pretty good for myself. However, I'm not doing good enough yet, to afford a mortgage or rent for this house. Adontis pulls me from my thoughts when he walks back into the bedroom with a manilla envelope and passes it to me.

"What is this?"

"Open it and see."

I open the envelope and find the deed along with the sale closing paperwork. The home is deeded to Adontis DeOntay Lamentez. I'm speechless. I flip through the paperwork. It all looks legit. He paid a lot of money for this house. Like eight figures. I almost understand why his mom thought I was a gold digger. With this kind of money, I'm sure he's seen his share.

All I can do is stare at him for a minute while I take it in. Like I knew he had money based off how he's carried himself, gifts he's given me, his home in New York, his cars and his parent's home. However, I didn't know daddy had it like this. Damn.

"You ain't saying nothing ma."

"I don't know what to say."

"Daddy got it, so you got it ma. You don't have to worry about a mortgage payment. Our house paid for. Whenever you ready, we just need to add you to the deed."

I snap my fingers. *"Just like that, you want to add me to the deed? I didn't put any money into this house."*

He pulls me into him and wraps his arms around my waist. *"You think I'm playing when I say we starting our family here?"*

"No. But-"

"There ain't no damn but. I'm all in with you ma. You gon be my wife and we gon build a family together. Unless you got any objections."

I'm flabbergasted. This is the grandest gesture I've ever seen. *"No objections baby."*

I pass him the paperwork back.

"Ok. You ready to finish this tour?"

"Yeah."

He leans down and kisses me. *"Ok shorty, let's go."*

My mind is firing on all cylinders trying to process everything that has just happened. This man has his finances together. He said he wasn't playing about me and he has just put his money where his mouth was. We exit the second master and go down the other leg of the hallway. There is an elevator and a closed door. This damn house has an elevator.

He leads us from the hallway back through the way we came. We are back in the foyer. He steps in the office to put the paperwork back up and I wait for him in the foyer, still in my thoughts a little bit. When he returns, we walk through the large open doorway. We are now in the room that leads straight back from the entrance of the foyer. It is a large open space with a fireplace. This home has a very modern floor plan.

"This is the family room."

"There is so much I can do with this space. I'm so excited to start decorating."

He laughs, *"I know I can see it all over your face."*

I smile at him. *"What's next?"*

There are several different doorways that lead off of the family room. He takes me to the door to the back corner of the right wall. This door leads to the hallway with the elevator. To the left of the hallway door is an open doorway.

"Ok ma let's start with this one." He grabs my hand and leads us through the doorway, which leads to the kitchen. It is also very large.

"Oh my God baby. I love this kitchen!"

"That mean you gon cook for daddy?"

I look at him with a side eye. *"When do I not cook for you?"*

"All the damn time. I be in here all alone. Hungry, no woman to love me or cook for me or nothing."

I take a deep breath. *"Of course, I can't cook for you when we apart. When we're together, I cook. Don't try to act like I don't cook."*

"Yeah ma, you cook. We spend more time apart than together though."

I walk up and put my arms around him, *"That is just until I finish school baby. After classes this summer, I'm here full time. Then you got me all day every day."* I gesture to him to bend down. When he does, I kiss his lips. *"Just a few more months baby. Can you hang on til then?"*

"Yeah I ain't got no other choice."

I let out a long sigh. I don't want to start an argument. I know it's been a little while since we've seen each other. I know he's horny. Hell, so am I. Once I give him some, he'll feel better. The best thing I can do at this moment is change the subject.

"Ok baby, let's finish this tour."

The countertops are covered in a dark marble. The cabinets are all black wood and the appliances are all black stainless steel. In the center of the floor is an island countertop. I'm standing in my very own, chef's kitchen. Off to the left is the eat in kitchen area.

On the back wall behind this area is a doorway with glass French doors which looks like it leads to another hallway. To the left of the eat in area there is another doorway. To the right of where we entered the kitchen there is a closed door. Adontis opens that door and I see that it is the attached garage. It's fully finished and it has working air conditioning and heating along with a workshop and a half bathroom inside.

"You gon be Mr. Fix it now huh?"

"Ma I been Mr. Fix it. I keep you right."

"Yeah babe and I'm overdue for a service."

"And you gon get that service today."

We both laugh as we leave the garage and head towards the doorway by the eat in area of the kitchen. This doorway leads to a large dining room.

"Babe, this house is amazing. This is a lot of space for just the two of us."

"It's two of us for now. Keyword BABIES! I want you to give me lots of babies." He's grinning and rubbing on my belly.

"Really now! How many babies do you want me to give you?"

"At least four. We got the room."

He's positioned himself behind me and he's kissing on my neck while holding me close.

"FOUR BABIES! Don't you think that's a bit much?"

He pulls his lips from my neck. *"Hell naw. We have the room and the finances, why not?"*

"Because I have school and work."

"You know you don't have to work."

I turn to look at him like he is crazy. *"You know I am not busting my ass in school to drop out."*

"I said you didn't have to work. If you want to work, I'll support that. I just want my babies."

"Four is a lot."

"Naw it's not. I'm gon be here in our kids' lives. You ain't in this alone. All I want is my four babies. That's all I'm asking for. Whatever it takes for me to get them you got it."

"Just four huh?"

"Just four ma."

"Adontis."

He starts rubbing on my belly again. *"I speak fertility into your uterus."*

I burst out laughing. *"What the hell Adontis. That's what we doing now?"*

He's still rubbing on me. *"You not gon give me my four babies?"*

I smirk and let out a sigh. *"If four babies is what you want, then four babies is what I'll give you."*

"Don't play with me now. You for real ma?"

"I'm not playing."

"Alright then, promise me my four babies."

I look at him, *"Really?"*

"Hell yeah."

"I promise."

"Naw you got to say that shit."

I sigh and smile at him. *"Adontis I promise to give you four babies."*

"That's what I want to hear. I'm gon hold you to that too."

I offer my hand so we can shake on it.

"I don't want to shake yo damn hand."

I smirk. Slightly offended, I say, *"Well what do you want papi?"*

"Alight you gon get pregnant right now! You better stop."

I ignore his last statement. I know he likes when I speak Spanish to him. So, I do it every once in a while, to keep him on his toes. I'm not bringing out Teresita. That's my Spanish alter ego. I got to keep it spicy. He met her when he came to visit me the last time. I had to make up for not calling him and ignoring him. Needless to say, he left very happy.

"How you wanna confirm this deal then?"

"Let's seal it with a kiss."

"Ok."

He bends down and passionately kisses me.

"We gon practice in a few minutes."

I laugh. *"You so damn nasty."*

"That's how you like me."

We continue our tour. There are four doors off the dining room which includes, just like the kitchen, one doorway on the middle of the back wall with French doors. Then, there is the door we came through, one set of French doors that leads back to the family room and a doorway that leads to another room. He leads us through the doorway of the room we haven't been in yet.

"Ok, ma this is the living room."

The room is large with two beautiful bay windows. I see four sets of doors in this room. The door we came through is now behind us. To the left is another set of French doors which leads to the family room. In front of us in between the bay windows is a door that leads outside to the other cobblestone driveway and detached garage. This is the side of the house.

The last door is to the right of us, which are also French doors. We open the door and there is the hallway I kept seeing while we were in the last few rooms. We step into the hallway and off to the left is a half bathroom. To the right of the bathroom is another elevator. Every time I think it can't get any better, he shows me something to prove me wrong. Across from the elevator is the entrance to a room that sits off to the right of the elevator. He opens the door and leads us to a theater room.

The room seats forty with built in reclining chairs. The seats are in five rows of eight. Just like a regular movie theater the rows have an incline. The room is soundproof with surround sound and a huge movie theater size screen.

We leave the theater room and are now back in the hallway. We turn left then another quick left and we are standing in the hallway with our back towards the half bathroom. He takes me down the hallway and I see the dining room and kitchen are now on our right. Straight ahead at the end of the hall is a door. There is also a door to the left towards the end of the hall. He opens the door that leads straight back first. It is another half bathroom.

Now the last door of the hallway. He opens the door and it leads to an indoor pool and jacuzzi. Inside this room is a side room for changing and a full bathroom.

I'm standing in awe. I can't believe how beautiful this house really is. I begin to envision Adontis and I with a family. Little versions of him and I running around full my thoughts. All I can do is smile. I love him so very much and I begin to see our future together. One that I want. I'm ready to let all of my inhibitions go and jump straight into this life with him. I'm wrapped up in my thoughts when I feel a tap on my shoulder.

"Ma you alright. Where were you just now?"

I look to him and smile. *"In a very happy place."*

He looks at me questionably. *"And where's that?"*

"I was just thinking about us building our family here and I got excited. I see a future for us more amazing than I ever dreamed I'd have."

He smiles. *"I like that. But why is it more amazing than you dreamed."*

I walk up to him. *"Well, that's easy. I've never been this in love before. You were the part of the dream that I couldn't see."*

I place my head against his chest and wrap my arms around him. He pulls me into him, almost as if our bodies are molded together and hugs me tightly. After a few moments, he releases his grip from around me and gently grabs my face. He tilts it up towards him. Looking deeply in his eyes, I feel like I see his soul.

"Me either ma. I love the hell outta you and I ain't wanna be nowhere, but with you."

His lips meet mines and I join him in a passionate kiss. His tongue slides into my mouth and mines slides into his. I begin unbuttoning his shirt. I can't take it anymore I want him.

"I think we need to Christen this jacuzzi right now." I've gotten his shirt open and I've moved down to his pants.

"You ain't saying nothing, but a word." I've pulled his shirt off him. I've gotten his pants unbuttoned and I'm tugging on his boxers. He smirks. *"You ain't playing huh?"*

I smile up at him, *"No the hell I'm not."*

He starts laughing, *"Alright ma, he's yours."* He steps out of his shoes, slides his socks off then out of his pants. I stop for a moment while looking at him. *"What's the matter ma?"*

I bite my bottom lip, *"Nothing. I'm just admiring what's mine."*

I tug on his boxers again, but this time I pull them down and he steps out of them. He catches my bottom lip in between his and starts sucking on my lip.

"You know that turns me on."

I feel an electricity between us as he is sucking on my lips. He pulls away and spins me around. My back now to him. He pulls me into him tightly. I feel him hard for me through my dress. Heat, I feel, as he's kissing on the right side of my neck right behind my ear. Right in my spot.

Kissing leads to sucking and I've begun moaning. He slides his hand up my dress, pushes my panties to the side and finds his way inside of me with his fingers. I'm dripping for him and he hasn't even entered me yet. I begin moaning out his name. He doesn't stop. With his other hand he finds the zipper on the back of my dress.

98

He glides the zipper down. I pull my neck away from his lips and pull my dress over my head and toss it. As soon as it is off me, he finds my bra hooks and unhooks them. I slide my bra off and send it flying somewhere. His fingers are back in me moving rapidly. With his free hand he pulls me back up against him. His lips are back in that same spot. He is palming one of my titties and begins playing with my nipple. Then he moves over to the other titty. He isn't speaking. There is almost this animalistic noise or rather growl that he is making.

I just want him to take me now. I can barely stand at this point and he hasn't even entered me yet. I've put my arms behind me and I hold on to his waist. I need something to grip before I pass out. My head is leaning back into his chest as he continues to kiss my neck, play with my breast, and finger me. I'm moaning his name. At this point, hell I'm ready to beg for it. He has me right where he wants me. He could get anything out of me at this moment if he asked.

He pulls his lips away from my neck, his hands from between my legs and his hands from my breast. I turn and look back at him puzzled. I don't know what the hell is going on, but I want him to finish. I look down and his dick is hard and standing up at attention. He just looks at me and licks his lips. I'm hell of confused.

"Why'd you stop?"

He smiles at me. *"You want this dick, don't you?"*

I look at him with my mouth open. *"What the hell you think? Why are you playing with me?"* He doesn't answer, he just laughs and walks away from me. *"Where the hell are you going?"*

"Follow me and find out." I don't move because I am trying to figure out what the hell is going on. I'm horny and he is playing with me. I see him stop at the jacuzzi and he gets in. *"You coming or what?"* I don't respond I just walk over to him. I'm about to get in and he stops me. *"Don't get in yet."*

I look down at him. *"Why not?"*

He pats the tile on the ground around the edge of the jacuzzi, *"Sit right here ma."* Then he floats to the other side of the jacuzzi and watches me.

I look at him sideways, but I listen. I lower myself down and I sit on the outer edge of the jacuzzi Indian style. I'm just staring at him. I don't know what he is doing, but my kitty kat is drying up and I don't like it.

Quickly he maneuvers in the hot tub. He is right in front of me. I'm staring into his eyes as he is staring into mines. I look down and I see his man hood sticking up out of the hot tub. I lick my lips. He sees me looking, but he doesn't say a word. He just continues to stare at me.

He stretches out his arms and grabs both of my ankles at the same time. He separates my legs from the seated position I was in. He gently allows my legs to dangle over the edge of where I'm sitting into the jacuzzi. He walks in between my legs and begins to kiss on my neck again. I feel his hands glide down my body until he reaches my thong.

He slides it down before backing up, giving himself room to slide it off. He tosses it across the room and comes back in between my legs and he gently slides me closer to him, close to the edge. This time he grabs my ankles and places them on his shoulders. I place my arms on the floor behind me to brace myself. He is kissing my neck again as he works his way down to my breast.

I feel his fingers in me again. It feels as if they never left. I let out a moan as he glides them inside of me. He is teasing me again and I feel invigorated. He pulls his fingers out of me and licks them before he grabs my ankles. He alternates between legs kissing from my feet, up to my ankles and then to my thighs. He spends a little extra time at my thighs sucking on them.

Once he's kissed all of those areas, his lips meet my kitty kat. She's very wet. He begins kissing her with pecks. Pecks lead to him using his tongue. His tongue leads to him sucking. I think I am about to burst. Swiftly, he lifts me off of the edge then lifts me onto his shoulders as he finishes his meal. My head leans back and I close my eyes. He has one hand on my ass holding me up and the other has found its way to my breast. He's pinching my nipples. I have my hands resting or rather gripping his shoulders.

I think I am about to burst. I dig my nails down into him. I feel it in the pit of my stomach, I'm about to cum. I dig my nails into him further. It roars out of me. As I scream out his name.

"ADONTIS!!" I try to take a long deep breath, but he is still kissing her. Causing me to cum again. *"OH ADONTIS!"*

At this point my legs are shaking. I lean forward over him still bracing his shoulders. He's stopped kissing, but he hasn't moved his lips. He leaves them sitting right on her. I stay as steady as I can, so I can get a chance to take a deep breath. I'm trying to compose myself. I'm breathing heavily. I feel his lips pull back and he starts laughing. I think about saying something and I change my mind. He has me right where he wants me. I'm weak as hell right now.

He lowers me down while still holding me and I wrap my legs around his waist. I exhale and lay my head on his shoulder. He's still laughing. *"You like that huh ma? Had that ass shaking and quivering."* I don't say a word. I can't deny it, it's true. Hell, I just caught my breath.

He looks down at me and gently grabs my face lifting it to face him. I look at him to see he's still smirking. *"Ma, are you alright?"*

I take a deep breath then I smile up at him. *"Why you do me like that?"*

He laughs, *"Because I can."*

I don't say a word. I don't have a comeback. Hell, he's right. I bite my bottom lip.

"See you keep doing that shit, that's what had you trembling a few minutes ago."

I've had some time to get myself together, so I go all in. *"Ok."* I lean in and begin to nibble on his lips.

I hear him laughing. He pulls back, *"Ok you asking for it."*

I smile at him. Then I take his lips into mine once again. Sucking and biting on them. I pull back and say, *"Yep, you gon give it to me Daddy?"*

He lifts me then slides into me. He's sucking on my neck and placing kisses all over me. I keep my legs wrapped around him. He leans me up against the side of the jacuzzi wall and begins to deeply stroke. As he's stroking, I'm riding. We are moving perfectly in sync. My lips are on his neck placing kisses all over him. My nails sink into his back as we travel into ecstasy together. I cum then he cums. He stays in me while placing kisses all over me.

"Damn, girl I love you."

I grab his head and hold it in place and I place my lips on him kissing him deeply for a moment. *"I love you baby."* I have my arms wrapped around him and I lay my head against his shoulder. *"Damn I need a nap. You wore my ass out."*

He burst out laughing. *"That's what daddy was supposed to do."*

He continues to hold me as he carries us out of the jacuzzi. He leads us to the changing room and grabs a large towel. He hands it to me. I swing it over my back and wrap it around his back holding it closed with my arms wrapped around his neck.

"We'll come back and get these clothes later. Hell, I ain't even finished giving you the tour yet."

I shake my head. *"Shower then nap."*

He laughs *"Ok ma. Whatever you want."*

He carries us to the elevator across from the theater room. Within seconds of pushing the up button the doors open. We go in and after a few moments, the elevator doors open again. We are in the middle of a large room.

"This is our bedroom ma."

We step off the elevator and onto marble flooring. To our immediate right is a door. He pushes the door open for me to see it is a large walk-in closet. The closet is gorgeous and apparently two stories based on the stairs I see. I guess this house has a third story. I wasn't expecting all of this. I know this sounds crazy because it is just a closet, but it's not just a closet. It looks like an upscale department store. In addition to the marble flooring, there are marble counter tops, cabinets, and drawers. The closet is full of my shoes, handbags, jewelry, and accessories.

"I love it babe."

Being the man he is, there are several shopping bags covering the floor. My man went shopping for me.

"You didn't have to do any of this."

"I know that, but I wanted to."

I'm in awe of him.

"Thank you, daddy. I appreciate all of this and all that you've done."

I plant a luscious kiss on him.

"You welcome shorty. Now this is only your side of the closet. I took the back side. There is another door behind the elevator that leads to my side of the closet."

"This is a lot!"

"Your ass like to shop and you got a lot of shit."

"You right."

"I know I am. I know you wanna get some sleep so we can finish exploring later."

"Ok."

We make it out of the closet and turn right. Ahead of us is a large open empty space. Maybe I can make it a sitting area. To the right of us is the door which leads into the bedroom. Through the door, I can see a hallway and what looks to be a loft.

He turns left and carries me to the next section of the room, which is where the bedroom furniture is. I realize that the entire master suite has marble floors throughout. He ordered the bedroom set that I told him I wanted. My man listens. It is a custom black velvet upholstered double king bed. It is huge. It is surrounded by matching upholstered storage boxes. Now that I know he wants four babies, we need it.

"*Thank you, baby.*"

"*For what ma?*"

"*For listening and just being you.*"

"*You welcome ma. Anything for you shorty.*"

Even with the bedroom furniture there is a lot of space left. He walks past our bed and makes a right which leads us down a hallway to the master bathroom. It is also marble from top to bottom. There are dual sinks, dual lighted mirrored vanity areas, a large garden tub, a large marble stand up shower and three more separate doors. Two of the doors each lead to a private toilet both with a bidet. The third door leads to a linen closet.

"*You really did a great job picking this house. I'm in love with it.*"

He kisses my lips. "*I'm glad you love it.*"

He opens the shower door and I let the towel wrapped around us fall to the floor. Once he steps in, I get down and he turns the shower on. He steps out and gets us some washcloths then comes back in the shower to join me. I'm drained after what he put on me. After we shower, we step out and dry off. He wraps me in his arms.

"*You're so beautiful.*"

I smile at him and kiss him. "*Thank you handsome.*"

He kisses my lips once again. "*Let's take a nap.*"

"*Sounds like a great idea.*"

"*Oh, shit ma, I left your suitcase in the car.*"

"*Oh yeah, I forgot about it too. I don't need clothes to take a nap.*"

"*If you lay in the bed naked, you gon get something stuck in ya.*"

I burst out laughing. "*You done did me dirty today. I need some sleep before you can stick anything in me again.*"

He smiles. "*I can't make any promises.*" He slides into some shorts and into his shoes. "*I'll be back ma; I'm going to get your things.*"

I've finished drying off. I pull the covers back and get in bed. "*Ok baby. Thank you.*"

He leans over me and kisses me. "*I love you.*"

"*I love you too baby. I want to say I appreciate you. Thank you for loving me, finding us a dream home and just for being you.*"

"*You make it so easy to love you. And this house thing, you make it a home.*"

I smile at him. He leans down and kisses me again then heads out the room. A few minutes pass, not many at all and I'm fast asleep. I awake some hours later and Adontis has me wrapped in his arms. I turn to face him and kiss his lips. I wiggle to get free of his grip. I don't know when he got in the bed, but I don't want to wake him. He put in a lot of work; he needs this nap. I'll give him a pass this time. Normally I'd wake his butt up to entertain me. I see my luggage across the room. I get out the bed, go over to it and dig out a robe. I slip into the robe and decide to explore the rest of our home.

I start in the closet and peek at all of the bags Adontis has purchased me. He has good taste. He even purchased a few sexy things for me to wear for him. I think I will put one on later tonight. I discover that my closet also has a hidden safe. After exploring my closet, I head over and peek into his. He talked all that smack about me, but his ass likes to shop too. He has a hidden safe in his closet too. I take the stairs in his closet to the third floor. When I make it upstairs, I'm in a lobby like area. I see that the elevator in our bedroom does go to the third floor. I explore the third floor and notice another room off to the side. I go to the door and it's a vault door. It is cracked open so I peek in and I realize this house also has a damn panic room. This house really has every damn thing.

After I finish touring the upstairs closet and panic room, I take the stairs back down to our bedroom. I walk out of the bedroom and into the hallway. As I walk down the hallway, I see that there are two separate hallways. One right outside of the master bedroom and one towards the front of the house near the stairs. They are both in the shape of a rectangle and they connect on two sides. Each Rectangular hallway has a loft that sits in the middle. There are several open doorways that lead from each loft back to the rectangular hallways. In addition to the lofts and our bedroom; there are thirteen more large bedrooms upstairs. Along with fourteen full bathrooms, a half bathroom, and a very large laundry room.

To the left of the laundry room, I discover a door. I open the door and see another elevator and another set of stairs going up. I thought it was just the rest of the master closet and panic room on the third floor. I guess this house is three stories. I leave the door open and walk up the stairs. I find what appears to be a huge game room or rather a mancave. Adontis has set up televisions and his gaming systems along with his workout equipment. The room has a fully stocked bar as well as a pool table. As I explore the room, I discover that it also has a full bathroom and a walk-in closet.

While standing in the game room, I reflect on the conversation Adontis and I had earlier. I did not know he wanted four kids, but I love him. I'm willing to give them to him. Lord knows this house is big enough to hold a family that size. Apparently, finances aren't an issue. The only thing I have to figure out is school. I don't know how in the hell I'm going to give him four babies and do med school. I do know that I'm all in with him. I'll just have to figure it out. I'm not letting go of my man. I'll keep my promise. I hear a noise and I turn to see Adontis walking in the room behind me. He's wearing a smile and nothing else.

"I see you finished the tour without me."

I smile back at him. *"I'm sorry. Baby you were sleeping so peacefully and you put in a whole lot of work. I wanted to let you get some rest."*

He has walked up to me and put his arms around me. He gently kisses my lips. *"It's ok beautiful. I needed that. After I got your things out the car I went and cleaned up our clothes in the pool room. Then I came back upstairs and you were fast asleep. I just got in the bed behind you and doze off too."*

"You all rested baby?"

"Yeah, I'm good now. I'm hungry as shit though."

I laugh, *"Me too!"*

"Let's get dressed and then get something to eat. I want to stop by my sister house too, so you can meet her."

I let out a long sigh. I knew he had a sister of course and I also knew she lived here in Jacksonville. What I didn't know is that he wanted me to meet her today. We hadn't discussed this at all. I thought it would be just the two of us while I was here this weekend. After meeting his mom, I'm not too excited to meet any more of his family.

"Ok. I guess."

"Ma, why you acting like that?"

"Things didn't go so well with your mom. If your sister's anything like your mom-." I stop speaking. I need to gather my thoughts before I finish speaking.

"What ma? Say it."

"It's just, we've had a really good day. I don't want anything to ruin that."

"Ok ma, I understand what you saying. You gotta give her a chance though. You can't judge her and you ain't even met her yet."

"You're right baby."

"Ok well let's go get dressed. Ya'll gon hit it off, watch."

I roll my eyes, as we head down to our bedroom to get ready. He is walking behind me so he doesn't see it. I don't wanna deal with anymore drama. I guess I'll just feed off of her energy and see how it goes. I don't feel like this, but relationships require compromise. So, I'm not going to put up a fuss.

After dinner, we go to his sister's house. I'm standing right beside him as he rings the doorbell. I'm trying my best to make sure my face doesn't reflect on the outside how I feel on the inside, at this moment.

After a few short moments, the door swings open. On the other side of the door, I see a short female. I'm short, but she's even shorter than me. She looks to be barely over five feet. She has a light-skinned somewhat butterscotch complexion, much like Adontis. Her hair is long and sandy brown. She is very pretty and petite. She looks just like their mom, just smaller and with a lighter complexion.

She greets us both with a smile. *"Hey, ya'll come on in."*

She steps back and allows us to enter. I say, *"Hello, thank you."*

After we get inside, she locks the door and leads us to the living room. Adontis begins the introductions. *"Aisha, this is my baby Tasha. Tasha this is my baby sis Aisha."*

We both exchange a nice to meet you. She offers us something to drink. We sit and start to mingle. Things are going better than I expected. She does seem to be pleasant and sincere. Nothing like their mother. I still have my guard up though. After some time of getting to know one another, I ask Aisha to point me in the direction of her restroom.

Once again, my mother's given gift kicks in. From the restroom, I can hear Adontis talking to his sister.

"What do you think?"

"I like her. She is pretty. She has a nice personality. I think we will get along well. You in love yet?"

He laughs, *"I don't know you might be a bad influence on her. But I am in love. This long-distance shit is killing me. It's hard as hell when we not together. I'm struggling with that shit. I didn't expect it to be this tough. She will be moving here after her graduation this summer and that can't come fast enough."*

"Ok that's cool. Congratulations. My big bro in love. There's a first time for everything, I guess. You don't have much longer til she moves here, so man up."

I am finished in the restroom. I don't leave, flush or wash my hands yet. I want to hear where this conversation is going to go.

Adontis laughs, *"Yeah, but Ma don't like her. Pop been cool about it all though. Ma don't have a reason other than that she with me. But you know me, I do what I want."*

"Oh, yeah Mommy told me. You know me too. I form my own opinion about people. She seems to be okay so far. I see how she looks at you."

"What you mean? How does she look at me?"

"Like a woman head over heels in love. That girl really loves you."

"I love her too sis."

"Yes, I see. She got you smiling n shit. Showing all your damn teeth. I ain't never seen you like this bro. That alone makes me happy. Mommy never like anyone we bring home, if she ain't pick them. That's the way it's always been. That's why I don't bring my men home anymore."

"That's true. You right you know. Hold up, men? What nigga you dating?"

I finish up in the restroom and exit. As I am walking back towards them, I think wow. Well at least I know my instincts were right about his mom. His sister seems cool. Maybe Adontis was right. As I enter back into the room, I sit where I was earlier next to Adontis.

Aisha looks at me and smiles. *"My bro in here grilling me about my man."*

I smile at her. *"Tell him to mind his damn business."*

Aisha starts laughing, *"Exactly sis."*

Adontis looks at Aisha then over to me. He's smiling. *"What the hell, ya'll just gon double team me like that?"*

Aisha and I look at each other, then to Adontis and at the same time, we both say, *"YEP!"*

We burst out laughing as we lean towards each other and give each other a high five. Adontis is sitting looking stunned.

"Ain't this some shit."

We all laugh. *"If you must know bro, my honey's name is Boris."* She pulls out her phone and shows us a picture of him.

I chime in, *"Alright sis get it. He's a cutie."*

Adontis looks at me with a side eye. *"The only man you pose to see is me."* I just smile at him. He turns to Aisha. *"Honey? Oh, hell no!"*

She rolls her eyes, *"Boy please. Anyway, he is twenty-five and doesn't have any kids. He's from here and we been together for a little while. We decided to make things official a few months back. Things are going good."*

We forget Adontis is in the room and begin having a little girl talk for a while. *"Ok that's good. We have to double date sometime then."*

"Yes, sis."

Adontis is sitting there speechless. *"Maybe it wasn't such a good idea bringing you two together."* We look at him and smile.

"Ah honey its ok. We still love you."

I lean over and give him a quick kiss. He just shakes his head. Aisha and I continue to laugh at him for a little while longer. We talk together for hours before leaving Aisha's. Meeting her went better than I ever expected. Before the end of the night, we've exchanged numbers and I realize we have so much in common.

April 21, 2007

It's Saturday morning. Melanie, Aisha and I spend the morning together. While Adontis, Shaun and Boris, do whatever it is that men do. Which really boils down to playing video games. We pamper ourselves the entire day. Which consist of a trip to the nail salon, shopping and brunch.

Aisha opens up to me and shares a little about herself and her boyfriend. She is in fashion school. She plans to be a designer. She shows me pictures of some of her designs and she has some talent. In addition to her fashion classes, she is also majoring in business. In hearing her talk about her plans, I can tell that she is passionate about what she does. I think its dope. I feel the same passion about my career. She tells me, Boris owns his own construction business. So, he does pretty well for himself. She met him on her campus. He was there doing construction work for the university. When he saw her, he couldn't take his eyes off of her. Of course, he had to approach her and the rest is history.

I share with Aisha more about how her brother and I met. I'm surprised at how well we seem to click. She truly seems genuine. I didn't expect to find a friend in her, but I think I did. Her style and taste are similar to mines. We are both over the top. More is more type of ladies. With her help, I pick out a few pieces of furniture for our home and some other décor, which will be delivered. We return in the afternoon to be with our men. We meet them at our place with the furniture in tow.

By the time we get everything in the house and situated where I want it, it's nighttime. We decide to all go to dinner together. We enjoy ourselves and spend the time laughing and telling childhood and other funny life stories. After dinner, we say our goodnights and head home. Adontis and I are riding home and laughing at all the funny moments of the night.

"What you think about Aisha?"

"You was right baby. I really like her. We had a really good time together. She like my sister from another mister. I think we might be partners in crime. Hell, we forgot that Melanie was even there."

"That's funny cause she pretty much said the same thing bout you."

"You know what they say, great minds think alike."

He bursts out in a laugh, *"I wouldn't exactly call ya'll minds great."*

I can't help, but to laugh. He got me with that one. All I can say is, *"Ha ha ha. Very funny. That's one point for you."*

"You ain't really feeling Melanie?"

"No, not really. I mean she your bro girl so I'm cool hanging out with her when we all together. However, once I move here, I don't see us having any kind of real friendship. It's just something about her. I don't know what it is."

"Damn baby. Did you talk to Aisha about it?"

"Naw I mean we was all together and I didn't know how close they was."

"Aisha feels the same way you do. She never like her like that. She just tolerates her cause that's who Shaun with. If you wasn't there Aisha ain't been goin nowhere with Melanie."

"Wow. I guess that kind of explains the side eyes she been giving her."

"Yeah, ma I guess so."

"How'd things go with Boris?"

Long as he does right by my sis, we good. Otherwise, I will bust his ass."

"Damn it's like that?"

"Hell yeah."

"That's so violent."

"I'm a violent motherfucker. I don't play about my women."

"You're women?"

"Yeah, you, my mother and my sister."

"Say that shit then. You was about to see another violent mother fucker."

He smirks, *"You was bout to fuck me up?"*

"You and all your shit."

"Your ass crazy."

"Yep, don't forget it."

"All that crazy in only five feet."

"And five inches. Don't forget that either."

"Your ass still short."

"No, you just abnormally tall."

"You love this abnormally tall motherfucker though."

"I sure do."

He leans in and plants a quick kiss on me.

"And don't you forget that."

"I hear you Mr. Lamentez."

"Do you?"

"I do."

We pull into the driveway. Once inside we put on our nightclothes. For me something tight and sexy. For Adontis just his boxers. We sit on the couch and get snuggled together. I am on the verge of falling asleep. Adontis notices this and stands up and turns off the TV.

"*Come on shorty lets go to bed.*"

I look up at him and hold my hands out. He looks at me and laughs.

"*You a big ass baby,*" he says as he picks me up.

"*But I am your baby.*"

"*Yeah, you most definitely are with your spoiled ass.*"

"*You got me spoiled.*"

"*Yeah, I'm guilty as a motherfucker.*"

When we get upstairs, he takes off my robe and puts me in the bed. I am wearing a brown camisole and the matching boy shorts. He lays in the bed behind me and puts his arms around me. He kisses on my shoulder and then he begins to rub on my booty.

I look over my shoulder. "*What are you doing?*"

He flashes his pearly whites and gives me a devious grin.

I laugh, "*You are so bad.*"

He continues to kiss on me. "*But you like me that way.*"

April 22, 2007

The next morning, I awake and get in the shower. When I get out, he is still sleeping. I slip back in the bed next to him and pull out my books and study for a little while. When I finish, he is still asleep. I turn on the TV and there is nothing on that I want to watch. The next best option is to bother Adontis. I start messing with his lips.

I take my pointer finger and stick it in the middle of his lips. Then I begin to repeatedly and rapidly push down on his bottom lip. I laugh and watch as his lip begins to flop. He pushes my finger off his lips. I put it back and begin again. He has such nice, sexy and plump lips. That's why I'm always sucking on them. I can't resist, but to play with them.

In a sleepy voice, but still very deep, "*Tasha stop! Quit playing!*"

I just laugh and smile. "*But you look so sexy when you sleep. And even sexier when you mad.*"

He cracks one of his eyes open. "*I hope you know I am gonna get you back.*" Then he closes that one eye back.

I get behind him and lay my head on his and whisper in his ear. "*Back? For what? I don't know what you are talking about sonny. You still tired? Did I work you overtime last night?*"

He, once again, cracks open his one eye. "*Don't play dumb like you don't know. And what makes you think, you worked me?*" Once again, he closes that one eye back.

"*Well, sonny boy,*" as I smile at him. "*The fact that I put you to sleep right after and the fact that you still sleeping. All that lets me know that I worked you.*"

As he smiles with both of his eyes closed, "*Maybe you right.*"

He gets up out of bed and goes to the bathroom. With him no longer, there for me to bother, I lay across the bed and try the TV thing again. After a while, I hear the shower water turn off and shortly after he comes into the bedroom wearing only a towel. Out of the corner of my eye, I can see that he is dripping wet as he begins to dry off.

He moves from out of my peripheral vision and I can no longer see him. I hear him getting his clothes out the drawers and assume he's getting dressed. I channel surf for a little while. All of a sudden, I feel a hard pop on my ass. Which makes a loud popping sound. I feel pain shoot up in my butt. I hear him laughing hysterically. I begin to rub my booty to try and soothe the massive pain.

I jump up from the bed, still rubbing my butt. He continues to laugh at me. I give him my famous evil eye. *"I am gonna strangle you."*

I run around the bed to get to him. He jumps on top of the bed and runs away from me and out the door. I run down the stairs after him as he heads to the kitchen. He is still laughing while he is standing on one side of the island kitchen counter. I stand on the other side still rubbing my buns.

Whatever direction I move to chase him, he goes the opposite. Finally, he decides to stop laughing and get serious. While I am still giving him the evil eye, he manages to get a few words out.

"I am sorry ma, but I couldn't resist. The booty was just lying there all nice and plump. You want Daddy to rub it?"

I look at him and cut my eyes. *"And if I let you touch me anytime soon you will know about it."* I walk away from him and out of the kitchen.

He begins to walk out the kitchen to come after me. *"Come on now baby. Let Daddy rub it and make it feel better."*

As he turns the corner out of the kitchen, he walks into my fist. I punch him one good time in the chest. I can tell that the punch stuns him. Maybe it caught him by surprise, but he takes it.

He just laughs at me, *"Ok. We good now?"*

"No! You still can't touch me."

He smiles and says, *"Too late."*

He is already rubbing on my booty. He pulls me in close to him with both his arms now wrapped around me.

"Tell Daddy where it hurts."

I smile. *"Ok can you tell me where he at?"*

A stern look comes across his face. He is shaking his head no. *"Don't play with me woman!"*

"I ain't ready to talk to you yet."

"Aww ma, let it go. You milking this too long. Your cow been done ran out of milk."

He kisses me and continues to rub on my booty. He takes a handful in each hand and begins to squeeze.

I laugh and say, *"Whatever."*

"Ok let daddy kiss it." He spins me around.

I bend over in front of him. *"Get to kissing it then."* He grabs me and spins me again and has me leaning over the couch.

"Ok. I'll kiss it."

Before I know it, he pulls my panties down. I'm shocked because it's not what I expected. I was thinking he'd give me a peck on the cheek and then it'd be over.

"Adontis, what are you doing?"

He doesn't answer me. He has a hand on my back, firmly holding me over the couch, but not hurting me. I feel his lips on my butt cheeks. He begins kissing me all over, from the rooter to the tooter. My mouth drops open. I'm clutching the pillows in ecstasy as I begin moaning. He slides in me and begins to make love to me. We spend my last day just enjoying one another's company.

chapter 18

Love and Pain

May 25, 2007

**These two things always go together. You usually
don't have one without the other.**

It's been about a month since I went to Jacksonville to see our house. We haven't seen each other since. I haven't had time to work on finishing decorating or anything. I figure I can get to the rest of the house room by room, once I get fully moved in. Adontis has been begging to see me. He's also been very busy with getting Fresh up and running. We've talked every day since I left. I've been giving him some phone sex and some sexting, but I know he needs the real thing.

I really just haven't had the time with work, school and final exams. The spring semester ended the week that I went back home. I took on some extra courses this month to get some experience in my field and to boost my resume. My courses and exams are finally over. I finally have a free weekend before my last semester of summer school starts.

I decide to pay Adontis a surprise visit. I mean really, how can I know what my man is doing if I am not there? Plus, we need this time together. I need and want him just as much as he needs me. Aisha and I planned this surprise together. She is graduating college so I'll be here to celebrate with her too on her major accomplishment. Her degree will be in fashion design and business. She's also been interning for the last two years at a fashion company here in Florida.

She has put together a solid business plan. From what she's told me, her next plan after graduation is to start mass producing her designs. She has thousands of sketches and samples of all of her sketches. She is in talks with some companies to decide who she wants to mass produce her clothing. After that she wants to sell them online. Eventually she wants them sold in large department stores. She has named her fashion line after herself. She has already gotten the name trademarked. Her fashion line's name is Aisha Da'Niq. Da'Niqua is her middle name. I'm happy for her. She is following her dreams.

I arrive at our house and I park my rental car in the detached garage. I use my key, go inside the house and punch the code in to the alarm. I don't hear or see any signs of Adontis. I call out his name and I don't get a response. I go to the garage and I see one of his cars is gone.

My plan is to get settled in, cook us a nice dinner and be waiting for him in bed in some sexy lingerie. I get the groceries and my luggage out of the car. I put the groceries away. Then I set the alarm and head upstairs to our bedroom with my suitcase. In the bedroom in a corner is a clothes basket filled with Adontis clothes. At the very top I find a bra and thong.

They are way too small for me. I am a size eight in panties and a double D cup. The thongs are a size six and the bra is a C cup. I can't believe what I am seeing. All I can think is not this shit again. I try to calm myself down. Maybe there's a good reason for this. I'm trying to talk myself down. He ain't doing me like this right?

I hear the alarm sensor chime and it alerts me that the front door has opened. Then the alarm sensor notifies me that the alarm has been disabled. Adontis is home. I'm waiting for him to get upstairs so I can confront his ass about this bra and thong. I stay very still and listen. I hear Adontis', but he sounds muffled. I can't quite make out what he is saying. I sit on the bed, wait and listen as the sound comes my way. He makes it upstairs and steps through the door of the bedroom. I see Adontis' lips locked on this woman's. He has his eyes closed and her back is towards me. Adontis backs the woman towards the bed and she stumbles over me.

The woman calls out, *"What the hell?"* Adontis opens his eyes and sees me. I slap the shit out of him. His face is red in an outline of my hand.

"You Bastard. You mother fucking dirty damn dog," I yell out at him.

The woman looks over at Adontis, *"Who is this Adontis?"*

He completely ignores her question and addresses me. *"It's not what it looks like ma."*

I'm infuriated. I drove all these hours to surprise my man. Only to find him cheating on me.

"Oh really. Is that line pre-programmed in all men's heads at birth? It's not what it looks like huh? You wasn't about to fuck this bitch? In the house we suppose to share in the motherfucking bed we sleep in together! How could you hurt me like this?"

Tears are rolling down my face.

"Baby, I'm sorry. She don't mean nothing to me."

I'm backing away from him. I don't know this man. I don't recognize him.

"Apparently neither do I."

"I didn't sleep with her."

I slap the shit out of him again.

"This ain't her thong and bra?"

I hold up the under garments that I found in the basket. I already know the answer to the question. I can see her breast and butt are too big for them.

"No baby."

"How many hos you got?"

Not aware of the nearby danger the woman decides to open her mouth and comment. *"I didn't know he had a woman. But bitch if you don't want him get the fuck out."*

Instantly I see red. I jump across the bed and grab the chick by her hair. I moved so quickly Adontis didn't stand a chance to try and stop me. He makes his way to me and grabs me by the waist to pull me away from her.

"Ma no!"

I still have her by her hair. She tries to fight back, but I have her in my grip. I'm punching the shit out of her. Adontis plies my hands from her hair and she gets away. She runs down the stairs and then out of the house. He holds me back from going after her and in my hands, I have strands of her hair pulled from the root. I throw the hair in his face.

Normally I wouldn't go for the chick cause my man is who I need to deal with. You think the ho would have some respect and get out. Instead, she calls me a bitch and tries to put me out of my own house. Hell no. It's the quickest way to get that ass beat. And I'd do it again.

"I didn't sleep with her, ma."

"Who's fucking thongs and bra?"

"It's Aisha's!"

"Nigga please. I'm supposed to believe that bullshit."

"It's the truth. Her washer and dryer broke. She washed her clothes here. I found them in the dryer. I called her and she said they was hers. She was supposed to come by and get them today. Call her."

"You know what. It don't really matter. The fact still remains that you was gonna fuck that bitch. In our house and in what was supposed to be our bed."

"Damn ma I'm sorry. She don't mean shit to me. I didn't fuck her though."

"Oh, so you want partial credit! You think because you didn't screw her because I was here to stop it, that you get a mother fucking pass? Apparently, I don't mean shit to you either."

I want to punch the shit out of him. He must have predicted it because as I'm about to swing, he grabs my arms and spins me around with my back against his chest.

"Shorty I'm sorry please calm down."

I'm screaming to the top of my lungs. *"Get the fuck off me!"*

"Ma, I'm gon let you go, just calm down."

I don't say anything, he lets me go and steps back away from me. I shake my head. I really can't believe this bullshit. Suddenly I see red and I think I snap. Before I even know what I'm doing, I'm right in his face. My fists are balled up and I'm swinging on him. The first few punches connect and catch him in his chest. I moved so fast he didn't see it coming. By the time I go to throw the third punch he blocks it then pins me against the wall. He has my wrist in his grasp and raised above my head.

"Let me the fuck go."

"You gotta calm down first."

"Either you fucking let me go or get a knee to your nuts."

His eyeballs stretch in surprise. He's never seen me pissed. Here it is. If he values his family jewels, he better get off me.

"Ok I'm gon let you go."

He lets me go and backs further away from me. This time he looks ready for me if I come running to attack him.

"Whenever you want it, I give it up to you. There is no excuse for this bullshit. Just one time for one month, you couldn't be patient and wait for me! You know I have school and work. I'm busting my ass in school just so I could finish to be here with you. You a selfish motherfucker. It's over. I'm done with your ass."

Tears are rolling down my face again. I throw the house keys at him and run down the steps and out the door. Leaving my suitcase behind. I'm so pissed I don't even care about it right now. He comes after me and catches up to me at the garage as I'm walking in the door. He grabs me by the waist.

"Ma please don't leave like this. I'm begging you. Stay I'll sleep on the couch, at a hotel whatever you want. I need us to work this out. I fucked up I know. Whatever you say I gotta do to make this right, I'll do."

"Get off of me. You want to stay at a hotel so you can go and fuck that bitch?"

"Ma, hell no! That's not what I'm saying. I'll do whatever I gotta do to make this right, just tell me."

"You want to make it right? Unbreak my heart. Rewind this day. Don't cheat on me."

"Ma if I could do that, I'd do it in a heartbeat. Damn, I'm sorry ma. Please come back in the house and let's work this out."

"You can't make this right. Let me the fuck go now," I scream!

He finally releases me. *"Baby please don't leave."*

I tune him out. I unlock the car and climb in. I see his face as I get in the car. He looks at me pleadingly. I don't care. I open the garage door and back out.

Two hearts were broken today.

chapter 19

Bad Break Ups

June 9, 2007

**We've all had them and yet we still don't give up on love.
How much heartache can one woman take?**

It's been two weeks. I have cried my eyes out over Adontis. He has been calling me and I have been ignoring his calls. I decide to wash my hands with him and change my cell number. I'm fucking done. I go club hoppin' with Diamond to take my mind off things. I am throwing back the drinks and dancing hard on the dance floor. I've never drunk this hard. I've also never been hurt this bad; by someone I love so much.

I am dancing by myself. Out of nowhere in my ear, I hear, *"I miss you. You got rid of that buster yet?"*

Of course, it is Rodney. I turn and look at him. *"Yes. No. I don't know."*

My mind is telling me I'm done with Adontis, but my heart still loves him. It yearns for his touch, his kisses, his smile.

"Well can I have this dance?"

I am feeling really buzzed. I don't usually get this tight, but I am trying to forget. Take my mind off of my problems. I begin to wonder, is there something wrong with me? Why am I continually getting cheated on? With Rodney I somewhat understand. Not saying it was right that he cheated, but I wasn't giving him none. With Adontis it just doesn't make any sense. I gave it up to him all the damn time, sometimes several times in a day. He couldn't be patient for a month? Thinking about this just pisses me off even more.

I look to Rodney and say, *"Why the hell not."*

We dance and spend most of the night together. Diamond meets up with a friend and she wants to leave with him. She asks me if I will be ok and I tell her to leave, I will be fine with Rodney. Drunk and feeling tight, I know I shouldn't drive. I ask Rodney to drive me back to his place. He gladly obliges. When we get to his place, he helps me out of the car and leads me inside. He picks me up and carries me upstairs to the bedroom.

"You can sleep in the bed. I will sleep on the couch."

"No. Come to bed with me Rodney."

"Tasha, you drunk."

"No, I am not. Come on."

He pulls the covers back and puts me in the bed. He lays on top of the covers beside me and wraps his arms around me. I get close to him and softly kiss his lips.

He pulls away. *"You know what you doing?"*

"Yes. I want you. The only reason I never gave it up to you was because I was a virgin. Now I'm not."

I pull him towards me. I start kissing and sucking his lips. I know this is a major turn on for him. I know that I am not the same woman he knew two years ago. He has begun kissing me back and I start undressing myself. He helps. He caresses every inch of my body.

We begin making love. Or rather having sex. Is it that I want Rodney or that I want to forget Adontis? I don't know, but at this moment I know I want to have sex with him. I'm horny as hell. I want the chance to see how good he is and what he is working with. He holds my body and loves my body.

He says, *"I love you baby."*

I don't offer a response. I just want to forget Adontis and I want to feel good. I want to feel loved. He kisses all over my body. He's good, really good. In spite of how hard I try; I still feel my mind drift to Adontis. Damn this love won't die. He really does have my heart. In his arms is where I really want to be, but not after what he's done. Rodney slowly guides his way into my body. I feel him deep in me and it feels so good. He rides me and I ride him. We climax together and his sex is so good, he puts me to sleep.

June 10, 2007

I awake the next morning with a slight hangover and fully aware of my surroundings and situation. He awakes and pulls me into his arms.

"Good morning love."

With a look of surprise, *"What happened? What am I doing here?"*

"You don't remember last night?"

"No! Why am I here? What did we do?"

"We made love Tasha. I know you enjoyed it. You had multiple orgasms."

"I was drunk Rodney. I can't be here. I can't do this. I'm sorry." I get out of his bed.

"Tasha, baby I love you."

"I'm sorry."

I look around the room and find my clothes. After getting dressed I spot my purse on the nightstand along with my keys. I slide yesterday's thong inside then grab my keys. Rodney is watching me in disbelief. I can't even look at him right now.

"Tasha."

"I gotta go."

I rush out of the bedroom and proceed to head out of his house. He doesn't call after me or come after me. I'm thankful. I really needed to get out of there. Having sex with Rodney was a mistake. I'm still going through heartbreak. I'm pissed with myself for letting it happen.

On the other hand, I'm glad I got to experience him. He worked me right. He was good as shit. Hung very low, like a damn horse. If I had slept with Rodney when we was together and he became my first, my ass would have been sprung. I'm not now because I'm sprung on Adontis, my heart is still with him.

I arrive home and walk into my house. When I step into the family room and turn on the light, I find Adontis sitting on my sofa. He scares the shit out of me. I guess he pulled a me on me. He must have parked a rental car across the street because there isn't a car in my driveway or garage.

"Tasha where the hell you been all night?"

I guess he forgot that he doesn't have the right to ask me anything.

"Why are you here? Give me my keys and get the fuck out."

"We can't talk about this? I've been calling you trying to talk to you, but you changed your number. I'm here to fix us baby."

"Hell no. There is no us, that's what happens when people break up. Leave my keys on the table and get the fuck out."

I walk out of the room and go up to my bedroom. I head straight for the bathroom. I never expected him to be here. Even though we aren't together right now I don't want him to know I had sex with Rodney. I have got to wash the smell of sex and Rodney off of me. After I've started getting undressed, he walks into the bathroom behind me.

I see him eyeing me and I know he misses all this. Hell, I miss him too. I was with Rodney last night, but it wasn't him. He's the one that has my heart. Shit what the fuck did I just do? He ignores everything I said about us being broken up. Like that makes it less true.

"Where you been all night ma?"

I ignore his question and quickly get in the shower and begin to wash. I don't want him to get close enough to smell me. I smell Rodney all over me. Him smelling him on me is the last thing that I need. He walks over and opens the shower door.

"You not gonna tell me?"

"I don't answer to you. Now would you leave?"

I close the shower door back and continue to wash. He opens the door back.

"Not til we talk and you take me back."

"I'm not taking you back! Leave!"

He looks good as hell and smells so damn good. With him looking like this right now, I would be all over him if I didn't just have sex with Rodney. I would of probably gave it all to him. He is my weakness. He is my drug. I wanna feel his touch so bad. My love for him hasn't died. Seeing him just intensifies it, but I won't tell him this. Especially not now.

"Then we at a damn impasse. I'm not leaving until you do."

"I hope you brought a lot of luggage."

"I am sorry shorty. Yes, I fucked up. But I didn't sleep with her. Yes, I was going to, but I didn't. Doesn't that count for something?"

"No! You would have, had I not been there. Hell, you probably still did."

"Ma I ain't fuck that girl!"

"You wanted to though."

I can see the pain in his eyes. He is hurting from the loss of me. Damn he really does love me. It just makes me even more pissed that he and I are here. We wouldn't be if he didn't make the choices that he made. He is so sincere. I can see it and hear it.

"I know and I'm sorry. It just happened. I was lonely and missing you. She was an ex of mine. I ran into her. We started talking and drinking. I had too much to drink. One thing led to another. I'm sorry. If I could take it back, I would."

Out of the shower, I begin to dry off and get dressed. *"That's not good enough."*

"What do I have to do to make it right?"

"I don't think you can, but give me my space and time."

"Okay ma. I will be down here until you ready. I'll stay at a hotel. Soon as I check in, I'll let you know where I'm at."

He leaves my house, but he doesn't leave my house keys. I lay across my bed. What have I done? What should I do? If I take Adontis back, he can never know about Rodney and me. He took pride in knowing that he was the only man that I had ever been with. Now I have to add Rodney to that list. I thought Adontis and I were done. Seeing him today tells me we ain't done. My heart won't let us be done. I'm fucked.

June 11, 2007

The next day I spend soul searching. I get up early and go to class and work, but I am having difficulty focusing. My life is in shambles and I have got to figure something out. I come to the conclusion that I know I should not have slept with Rodney. He is not where my heart is. Despite it all, my heart is with Adontis. I call Rodney with my number blocked and I tell him I can't be with him. I am going to work it out with Adontis. I love him. He doesn't make it easy to break it off, but I do say goodbye and quickly hang up the phone. The last thing I want to do is give him a chance to make a rebuttal.

June 15, 2007

After making him sweat for five days, I tell Adontis I will give him one last chance. If he messes up again, it's over and I send him back home. Of course, I don't give him none. He will be high and dry for a while. Later in the evening, my doorbell rings. Adontis has been gone for hours and he still has a key. I open the door to find Rodney.

"You told me you loved it. I know you enjoyed it. What's the problem?"

He begins kissing on me. He is a great kisser. He begins feeling on my breast. I kiss him back for a while. I'm shocked to see he still wants me. I guess that's what happens when you got the il na na.

"Rodney, I can't. I started something with you without finishing with Adontis. I can't do this you gotta go."

"No Tasha, you're wrong. You started something with that bitch without finishing with me. But I'll leave. Just remember, I can't wait for you forever."

He kisses my lips again. I kiss him back and he starts sucking on my lips. He has pulled me towards him and I can feel the heat between us. He starts sucking on my bottom lip and at that very moment, he has me.

I slide my hands up his shirt and begin rubbing on his chest. His hand goes up my shirt and he unhooks my bra. At this moment, I get confirmation. I'm not in love with Rodney. I do love him and I do care about him, but that's where it ends. It's all lust. That's what happens when a man gives you multiple orgasms. I just want him to blow my back out.

He unbuttons my jeans and slides his hands in over the top, from the back, and squeezes my ass. He lifts me up from the floor with my butt cheeks in his hands. He carries me over to the dining room table and sits me on top of it. I pull his shirt from over his head and unbutton his pants. I strip him down and I have him naked. He finishes undressing me.

All over my body, he places his lips. Kissing me everywhere. He has my legs spread and he kisses my kitty kat. He licks me all over. Bringing to my remembrance how well he uses his tongue. I rub my hands on his bald head and softly kiss his head. My body feels alive and I don't want to stop. So, I don't. We ride as he glides in and out of me.

He feels all over me and I touch all over him. We end up in my bed and I can't believe I have done this shit again. He makes my body feel so damn good. Everything that feels good, isn't good for you. I feel like I come alive when I am with him. I can't be with him and Adontis. Adontis is where my heart is at.

June 16, 2007

It's around two in the morning and Rodney is laying in the bed next to me sleeping. I really enjoyed what we shared. I can't keep doing this with him. I want to work things out with Adontis so I have got to stop having sex with Rodney.

Rodney is a great lover. He is definitely as good as I thought he was the first time. Actually, he is better. I lay in the bed and fall asleep next to him. We stay in bed together until Rodney awakes later that morning. First thing he does is try to kiss up on me and that is when I wake up.

"Rodney, we need to talk."

He pulls me into his arms. *"Ok baby. We can talk. What's up?"*

I pull away from him. *"I know we shared last night and it was good. But I can't keep going there with you. As good as it was, it was wrong. I am back with Adontis."*

"So. You use to be my girl. And I don't want to let you go."

"Yeah, I use to be your girl. But I am not anymore. I can't keep having sex with you."

"You make me wanna get my shit right. Fuck them other females. If I get you back in my life, I will fly straight. I love you. My fam loves you. Shit my daughter loves you. You are the one."

"Rodney, I can't. We can't. I love him. I gave my body to you. And it was so, so very good. But I have to ask you to leave. And I apologize for leading you on. But you know, I am not that girl."

He gets up out the bed and begins putting his clothes on. *"You making a big mistake. I think I am the man for you. Clearly he ain't taking care of you like I can."*

That's not true, but I don't say another word. Adontis knows how to lay pipe. However, I'm not giving him any right now. It was either my vibrator or Rodney. Rodney caught me at a weak moment. I watch him put his clothes on and walk him downstairs then out of my house.

July 14, 2007

It's birthday time again for me. Adontis and I was supposed to spend it together before I caught him with that ho. I was so pissed that I cancelled all plans with him. He had flowers delivered to my job on Friday. I can't help, but say they are beautiful. However, that don't mean shit. I know I've done some dirt now too. Since I've caught him, I can't help, but to wonder, was this the first time? Has he cheated on me before? Or better yet is he cheating on me now? It's hard as hell to trust again once it's been broken. It's even harder when you have dirt of your own.

Yes, I do miss him and yes, it's my birthday, but I'm still pissed. Still salty. I don't want to spend my birthday with him. I'm enjoying the space. Aside from the fact that I have been horny as hell. I shouldn't have to pleasure myself when I have a man. Oh well. I think I'm gon have to rub one out.

I decided to spend a quiet birthday with my family and friends. No Adontis. Just a nice dinner on today and tomorrow just a little get together. Some seafood, music, cards, cake, family and fun. I meet my family at dinner downtown. I arrive fashionably late. When I arrive to the restaurant, I see my closest friends and family. Including my friends from the Cancun birthday turn up. I also see Adontis sitting next to the one empty seat left. Waiting for me. I roll my eyes. I asked him for space. This is not space.

I wasn't expecting to see him. I thought cancelling the trip he had booked and him losing out on the cost of the trip would have been a clear indication that I didn't want to see his ass. Clearly, he did not take the hint. Aisha and Boris are also in attendance. I greet everyone and head to my seat. Adontis stands and pulls my chair out. He kisses me on the cheek.

"You look beautiful shorty."

I muster out a fake smile and say, *"Thank you."*

I don't need everyone in my business. Diamond knows that we broke up and got back together because we were partying together and Kenya knows too. I had to vent to my friends to keep my sanity. Dinner goes pretty well, except for the fact that I want to slap the shit out of Adontis. I know I need to show that I forgive him for us to move forward, but it's easier said than done.

After dinner we all leave. Boris and Aisha go back to a hotel. I head back home and Adontis follows behind me. He tries to get some affection from me, but I'm not giving him nothing. We get in the house and I don't really feel like talking to him. I know he wants to talk about us, but I'm not for it. It's my birthday and I don't want to be down. I head upstairs to my bedroom. I walk through the doorway and I hear Adontis following behind me with his suitcase in hand. I stop in my tracks causing him to crash into me. I spin to look at him.

"Hold up playa. Where you going?"

"What you mean? We going to sleep right?"

I know I'm pissed because I can feel the attitude, the finger pointing and the neck roll coming. *"Yeah, but you are not sleeping in here with me."*

He looks like he is so frustrated. *"Shorty, you can't be serious."*

"Do I look like I'm joking? It's three other bedrooms in here. Pick one, just not mines."

"Damn, you telling me, I can't even sleep next to you?"

"I'm not about to argue with you tonight."

"I'm not trying to argue with you either. Damn, I came all the way down here to celebrate your birthday with you. You don't even seem like you give a damn."

"I didn't ask you to come."

"You so damn cold. I'll just go ahead and head back home then."

I put my hands up against his chest to stop him. *"It is too late for you to be driving back to Florida. And you been drinking. Just go in one of the other rooms and go to sleep. Damn."*

"You don't give a damn about me. Why you trying to act like you care now?"

I roll my eyes. He is digging his keys out of his pocket.

"Just because I am pissed with you, doesn't mean that I don't still love you or that I don't care about you. If I didn't care about you, I wouldn't care if you left. Hand me your keys."

I reach for his keys and he snatches them away. This is exactly the drama I didn't feel like dealing with. I lean back and fold my arms across my chest.

"What are you fixing to do?"

"I'm leaving. I'll see you whenever."

He turns to walk out the room and I snatch his keys out of his hands. He spins around.

"Tasha, give me my damn keys back!"

121

"No. you can have your keys back tomorrow. Go to bed. Goodnight."

I leave him standing in the hallway and I go in my room and close the door.

"Tasha!"

I ignore him and go off and hide his keys and mines. I hide them in my closet in the pocket of a blazer jacket. I hear his footsteps move away from my door. I open the door and I see him walking towards the bedroom across the hall from mines. I leave the door open and head into the shower.

I get out the shower and I'm wrapped in a towel. I figure Adontis went to sleep since I hadn't heard anything else from him. I stand at the bottom of my bed and begin to dry off. My towel is off and my back is towards the bedroom door. I'm bending over drying my legs and then I walk to my dresser to get my lotion.

July 15, 2007

When I look up, I see Adontis is wide awake. He is sitting up in his bed watching me. I understand. He hasn't had a taste in a long time. He better enjoy the view cause he won't be getting a taste tonight either.

I laugh to myself. I can't believe he is sitting in there watching me like an old perv. I think oh well. I'm not going to say a word to him. He is really about to get pissed though. I pull my covers back and turn off the lights. I get in the bed then dig into my nightstand and find my friend. I turn my vibrator on and I begin to pleasure myself. The house was very quiet before I started so I know Adontis can hear the light buzzing of my vibrator. I don't care.

My eyes are closed and I'm going in. I'm horny as hell. It's after midnight now so it is officially my birthday. I have to get some birthday sex. Even if it's from myself. I'm reaching climax and it's feeling really good. I'm moaning and I have actually forgot that Adontis is in the other room. I'm rubbing my clit harder and faster. I'm about to arrive. The light switch flips on. I open my eyes and see Adontis standing over me butt ass naked.

"Tasha, what the fuck are you doing? You'd rather play with that damn toy than your man?"

I'm pissed he has completely ruined my orgasm. *"Adontis why the hell are you in here?"*

"I'll be damned if I'm going to let you sit here and play with this damn vibrator and you ain't giving me none. If I ain't busing a nut, neither are you. Then you doing this shit with the door wide open so I can hear and see. Not to fucking day."

He moves so quickly; I don't have a chance to stop him. He pulls the covers back and snatches the vibrator out of my hand from between my legs. I don't have a chance to say a word. He takes my vibrator and sends it soaring across the room into the wall.

"What the fuck Adontis!"

I get out of the bed and run over to my vibrator. He is standing looking at me like hell yeah, I did it. I'm looking at my vibrator in distress. I go to pick it up and it has broken into two. There is no power to it, it's just done. He threw it so hard, there's a hole in my wall.

"Don't what the fuck me. You want to get off tonight?" He grabs his manhood, *"You can take this dick or take your ass to sleep."*

I'm so horny and so pissed with him. *"I can't believe you just did that. You gon replace my vibrator and fix my damn wall."*

"I'll fix the wall, but I ain't replacing shit. You don't need no other dick when you got me. What you gon do, you taking this dick or what?"

I want to fight him so bad right now. I'm really ready to square up with him. *"Man get the hell out of my room."*

He shrugs his shoulders. *"Alright. Goodnight."*

I lay in bed pissed. I am so horny right now. I'm not going to give in to Adontis. Him breaking my vibrator was way too much. That's some petty shit. That's alright though, he is still going to buy my vibrator back. I will just use his card when I order a new one. He will see the charge.

I awake the next morning still horny as hell. I roll out of bed and head into the shower. I use the massager in the shower to try and get off. I don't quite get there. Maybe I'm in my own head, but the orgasm I need never comes. Neither do I. I give up on trying. When I get out of the shower, I peek in on Adontis and he is still sleeping. I get dressed, grab his keys and head to his room to wake him up.

"Here are your keys. You can leave now."

He rolls over and pulls the covers back, *"Damn. Happy Birthday to you anyway. Now you kicking me out?"*

He looks so sexy. I'm busy checking out his anatomy. He is standing up at attention, as he always does early in the morning. I don't even acknowledge the happy birthday.

"You said you was ready to leave."

"Yeah, cause you don't want me here."

"Adontis I'm not arguing with you this morning. Leave if you want to leave or stay if you want to stay."

I turn around and walk out of the room and head downstairs. After about forty-five minutes I hear Adontis coming down the stairs. I'm sitting on the sofa eating cereal.

"You ain't cook no breakfast?"

He is looking good and smelling good. I start thinking maybe I should go ahead and get me some. I'm horny and I don't have a vibrator.

"You better get you some cereal."

"I don't want no damn cereal."

I shrug my shoulders. *"It's my birthday! Why you ain't cook breakfast?"*

"It's hard to cook when you being thrown out."

"You are being dramatic as hell. I did not throw you out."

"Hell, yeah you did. You came and woke me up and gave me my keys. That's a clear get the hell out."

"You was ready to go last night, but I took your keys. I gave them back to you so I wouldn't hold you up."

"Ma, I'm not arguing with you. It's your birthday and clearly you don't want me here. I'm gonna slide out. I love you and Happy Birthday."

He bends down and kisses me on the cheek. I just stare back at him. He grabs his suitcase and walks out the door. I lean back against the couch and roll my eyes. He pisses me off so much and I love him so much. Damn I should of took the dick. I'm horny as shit.

I spend the rest of the morning at home alone watching tv. I haven't heard anything from Adontis since he left. I text him to see if he has made it back home yet and its crickets. He doesn't respond. I call him and his phone just rings then goes to voicemail. Clearly, he is ignoring me. Why is it that the people we love most piss us off the most?

Late in the afternoon, I finally get off the couch and head up to my room to get ready. I walk in my bedroom and there is a large teddy bear and a gift bag sitting on my bed. I look in the bag and there are two small boxes inside with a card. I open the card and it reads,

> *Tasha, ma I love the hell out of you.*
> *I know I don't always deserve you, but I love you.*
> *I know that I may not always show you, but you my everything.*
> *Ain't nowhere else I'd rather be than with you.*
> *Ain't no one else for me, but you!*
> *I hope your birthday is filled with as much happiness*
> *as you bring me.*
> *I'm gon do everything in my power to be the man worthy of you.*
> *Let's celebrate you.*
> *The beautiful woman that you are.*
> *Love Adontis*

I'm reading the card and I'm crying. When did I become such a punk? I try to be mad at him then he does something like this. I get my phone and try to call him again. The phone rings, but he doesn't answer. This just reminds me of how he pisses me off. I hang the phone up and send him another text.

> **Tasha:** *Call me ASAP.*

I dig the first box out of the bag and open it. It is diamond stud earrings. They are gorgeous. They match the bracelet that he got me when we were in New York. I open the other box and it is diamond hoop earrings, which also matches the set. They are fire. Damn. He did a good job for my birthday. I would like to thank him and he won't even answer his phone. It's making me feel shitty. I sit at the bottom of my bed and call him again. His phone goes straight to voicemail. I don't know what else to do.

I start getting ready to finish celebrating my birthday and I'm not even in the mood anymore. Everyone is coming over to my house and they will be arriving soon. I pull myself together and put on a smile. My guest start arriving and the party gets going. Everyone is asking where Adontis is and I'm trying to hold it together. I tell them that he headed back home because he had to get back to work. I don't tell anyone otherwise because I'm trying to enjoy the party.

The party is a lot of fun even though my man is gone and is ignoring me. My spirits are lifted when Kia announces to everyone that she is expecting. We are all hoping for a boy, especially Ron. A boy would be perfect. Carmen has all boys and she has gotten off the baby train. This makes six nieces and nephews for me. I pray it is a boy.

The party winds down and everyone leaves. Aisha stays while Boris goes back to their hotel. We have a little bonding time and I'm able to get out all of my frustrations about her brother. She knows all about me catching Adontis with the ho. He told her everything.

"I tried to call and check on you when I found out what happened, but you changed your number."

"Yeah, I did. I'm sorry. I was so pissed with Adontis. I changed my number because I was done with him. I really wasn't thinking about anything else."

"Sis I get it. I want ya'll to make it. I believe ya'll meant to be. I want you to know just because you mad at him or he pisses you off don't ditch me."

I smile. *"You right. That's my fault."*

"I was glad when you finally called me. I know you needed time to cool off and to yourself. I get it."

"Yeah. I did."

"Well, I want you to know that I personally went off on his ass. I made sure he knew he was wrong. If he thought he was gon get a friend in me after telling me the bullshit that he did, he was wrong."

She chose sides and even though he's her brother she chose mines. I'm completely shocked. I realize she is genuine and real. The more I hang with her the more I see she is a real friend to me.

"Thank you. He and I are still rocky right now. We got into it last night and it carried over this morning. It's just, stupid. He left upset with me. I was upset with him. It's a mess. I've been calling him and he won't answer my calls or text. That shit hurts."

"That's bullshit. He is being stubborn."

"Yeah. I don't even know if he made it home safely."

"Let's call his ass."

"You can."

She picks up her phone and gives him a call. The phone rings several times before going to voicemail.

"This yo sister. I'm with Tasha. Let us know you made it home safely."

"We'll see what happens."

"Yeah. Oh, I did mean to tell you, the bra and thong you found was mines. I know it don't make up for the other shit. But hopefully you can put your mind at ease about that."

"Ok well at least that wasn't a lie. It sounded like a lie when he said it."

She burst out laughing. *"Yeah, it does. I don't know why he ain't just leave it in the dryer I was embarrassed enough when he told me I left them there."*

"I know right I would probably die if my brother found any of the sexy shit I be wearing."

"Exactly!"

We both burst out laughing.

"Oh my God. Girl! I just ordered this sexy little thing for Boris' birthday."

She takes her phone out and shows me a picture of some sexy lingerie.

"Oh damn. You definitely gon get it when he sees you in that."

"I damn sure hope so."

We give each other high fives and laugh some more. I really needed this. She has absolutely cheered me up. We stay up and chat for a while longer before deciding to head to bed.

It isn't until late when Adontis finally calls me back. I was just about to drift off to sleep. The party is long over and my birthday is almost over too. I look at his incoming call and turn my phone to silent. I don't want to speak to him. It will be an argument and I am over it. I'm tired and I have work tomorrow. He calls me again so I turn my phone display face down and get in bed. He had all damn day to call me. Fuck him tonight. At least I know he's alive. I'm going to sleep.

chapter 20

Cap & Gown

July 28, 2007

**Any commencement is a special time for a student.
Two commencements down and one more to go.**

It's finally that time. My hard work has paid off. I'm graduating Sum Cum Lade. That's right, I'm at the top of my class. I've worked my ass off to get where I am and I'm not stopping now. The next stop, med school. After I graduate, I'll be moving to Florida with Adontis. I guess we'll see how things go. We have talked since my birthday and things are still rocky as hell. Florida is where I'm going no matter what, that's where the rest of my education is.

My parents would be so proud of me. I really miss them. I wish they were here to see me now. I know that they are in heaven looking down on me. That doesn't stop it from hurting. It still hurts like hell.

I've got my cap and gown; so, I am so ready for today. Carmen has planned a graduation bash for me. The time is here to have a little fun before med school begins. I have enrolled in med school starting next spring. Today, I'm go throw back some drinks and eat some good food.

Adontis and I have still been taking it day by day and trying to work it out. Since having sex with Rodney, I still haven't had sex with Adontis. I am sure he could tell the difference if I did. Plus, it would just be plain nasty. We've talked daily since the day after my birthday. I finally called him back the next night. I had a chance to thank him for my birthday gifts. I'm trying to get on the right track with him. We haven't seen each other since he left though. Hopefully he'll be at my graduation.

Adontis has been working hard though, trying to get back on my good side. I've been getting roses, chocolates, teddy bears, jewelry, money, etc. With his money I replaced my vibrator that he broke. He's been showering me with gifts. He's got to re-earn his right to the

127

booty. If he doesn't get some soon, I think he's going to pop. That's not my problem. Once I feel that he's suffered enough and learned his lesson, I'll give him some.

Enough about him. This is my day. I lay awake in bed and turn over. I don't see Adontis. He was supposed to come down yesterday. I waited up for him for a little while, but he never showed. I tried calling him and his phone went to voicemail. I grab my phone and I don't have any missed calls or text from him. I don't know what to think. I call his cell and his phone is still going straight to voicemail. I know he bet not miss my graduation today.

I roll out of the bed and open my bedroom door. I look across the hall and I see him sleeping in the guest bedroom. Relief comes over me; he's safe and he is here. I chuckle to myself. His ass thinks he is funny. He didn't wake me or anything. I don't know what time he got in last night. Since he drove in from Florida, I can imagine he must be tired. I decide not to disturb him; he needs the rest. I do not want an argument with him today. I head to the kitchen instead.

I'm wearing some brown lace boy shorts and the matching camisole. Shortly before breakfast is ready Adontis walks into the kitchen. He's looking sexy as hell; wearing only his boxer shorts. He looks me up and down like he wants to eat me. Well, let me call it what it is, he's undressing me with his eyeballs. He licks his lips at me, while standing in front of me scratching his head.

"Damn ma you look good. You wearing that for daddy?"

I guess he decided he'd just go in and give it a try. I don't answer him. I just give him a look that says hell no. He doesn't seem to care about how I'm looking at him. He walks up to me and kisses my lips anyway. He slides his tongue into my mouth and it feels like sunshine on a summer's day.

I want to pull away, at least thats what my head says. My heart and my body won't allow it. His lips feel good. Real damn good. It's been months since I've felt my man's touch. While kissing me, he begins rubbing on my booty. I feel him hard through his boxers, on my thigh. It's that morning hard on. He continues to kiss me passionately and I know he wants it. He lifts me up on to the counter, while sliding his hands up my camisole.

I'm still not ready to give him some. I'm still pissed with him. I'm pissed that he cheated on me. Pissed that I slept with Rodney because he cheated. Pissed that I slept with Rodney a second time because I let my hormones take control instead of my mind or heart. He pulls me out of my thoughts when he pulls my camisole off over my head.

"Adontis stop!"

He is begging. *"Come on baby. Damn Tasha. I need you. I really need you."*

He begins kissing on my neck and then down to my breast. He is breathing hard and he sounds like he is in heat. His breath is warm and heavy in my ears. He is turning me on. The animal in him is coming out. That animal brings the freak out of me like only he can.

With my mouth again, I tell him, *"Adontis stop!"*

He moves his lips back to mines. He slides his tongue in my mouth. His touch feels so good. I spread my legs as he comes in between them. With my mouth, I'm telling him no, but my body is saying yes. Hell yes! I want him. I pull away from kissing his lips again. I'm trying to hold off.

"Adontis baby, no!"

He acts as if he doesn't hear me. He moves his hands to my hips. He tugs on my panties and pulls them off. Down on his knees, he pulls me to the edge of the counter by my thighs.

Once again, I say, *"Adontis stop! I'm not ready to give you some."*

Again, he says nothing. Instead, he sticks out his tongue and begins licking. Since he's taken it there, I don't really have much to say. All I can do is moan. I run my fingers through his hair and play with his curls. He begins sucking my clit and I'm in sheer pleasure. I'm unable to speak for a moment. It isn't until I have an orgasm that I'm able to form words again. He pulls down his boxers.

I stop him quickly, while still clutching handfuls of his hair. *"Hold up. What are you doing?"*

With confusion on his face, *"What you mean? What does it look like?"*

"Adontis, I'm not giving you some."

"Why the hell not?"

"I told you no. I told you to stop."

"Yeah, that's what your mouth said, but your body, your pussy, gave me the green light."

"Obviously, yeah it did. I'm horny. She misses you and him. And you broke my vibrator. Hell yeah, my body wants you."

"What's the damn problem then?"

"My mind is still pissed with you."

"You let me eat you, when you knew, that's as far as it would go?"

"My mouth said stop."

"That's some bullshit. You just gonna leave me like this?"

"I didn't get you like that."

I jump down off the counter and pick up my clothes, take it to the laundry room and I go to my room to put on a robe. When I return to the kitchen, he is still standing there, pissed as hell. He gives me a dirty look as he walks out of the kitchen mumbling and cussing. I hear the shower turn on. I guess he's going to put his left and right hand to work.

I finish cooking breakfast and Adontis still hasn't returned. I go to the guest bedroom to find him walking out of the bathroom. He's wrapped in a towel and dripping wet. Damn, he looks good. Seeing him like this, has really made me horny. I want him. While standing in front of me, he pulls off his towel and begins drying off.

I find myself staring at him, the way he was staring at me earlier. He breaks the silence and kicks me out of my daydream or rather fantasy.

"Can I help you with something?"

In my mind, I'm thinking, hell yeah. Let me jump up on it. I snap back to reality and instead, I say, *"I came to tell you that breakfast was ready."*

"I'll be there in a minute."

I stand and stare at him for a few moments before I turn around and walk out the room. Damn he looks good. We sit at the table and have breakfast. I look calm and composed on the outside, but on the inside, I'm thinking about the sex I had with Rodney on this very table. I begin to feel guilty as hell. I'm afraid to tell Adontis what I've done. I'm afraid that he'll leave me. I love him so damn much. I don't wanna lose him. Even though the first time I slept with Rodney we'd been broken up for weeks, I know he'll never forgive me.

We talk a bit over breakfast. My mind keeps flashing to scenes of Rodney and I having sex. Really good sex, but very wrong sex. I'm trying hard to keep my composure. I'm really torn apart. When we're both finished, I'm ecstatic to get up from the table.

I clear the table and Adontis agrees to do the dishes. I head to the bathroom to take a shower. I hear a knock on the bathroom door and then it cracks open. I open the shower door and poke my head out.

"Yes."

"I'm headed out for a minute. I got something I need to do."

I pull the door completely open. I can't believe this shit. What is so important, that he has to do hours before my graduation?

"What the hell do you have to do so, that it can't wait until later?"

"Ma don't trip. Damn. I got some business to tend to. I'll be back in a few hours."

Before I can say anything else, he walks out of the bathroom and closes the door. I turn the water off and head behind him. I'm covered in soap and dripping wet. I'm rushing to catch him so I don't even take the time to grab a towel. I have him in my eyesight, as he's turning the knob to walk out the front door.

"Adontis, where do you think you are going?" He spins around to see me. I'm coming down the stairs and walking towards him. *"What business do you have here in South Carolina? You live in Florida."*

He licks his lips. *"Damn girl. That's sexy as shit. You couldn't grab a towel first though. I don't wanna see all of that, if I ain't getting none of it. That's like showing a filet mignon to a starving man and not letting him eat it."*

I completely ignore what he said. *"You didn't answer my question."*

He smirks as he walks up to me. *"What question? The one about why you acting so pissy? Well, that's cause you horny and you need some dick. If you had let me break you off earlier, we wouldn't be having this conversation; you'd be in bed sleep."*

"Oh ok, so you wanted to have sex with me earlier, so I'd leave you alone? Then you could go and run the streets."

"I really don't feel like this shit. But to answer your question, I don't have sex with you, I make love to you. That's what I wanted to do, until you stopped me. Now I got some place to be. I'll be back in a few."

He turns and heads back to the door.

"I love you."

"Adontis, this is not over."

"Hell, yeah it is."

He opens the door and walks out. I'm not insecure, but I don't know if I can trust him anymore. It's hard to get over being cheated on. Especially when you know you have dirt of your own. A few hours lapse before Adontis returns. He finds me in the bedroom getting dressed. I'm sitting on the bed in my bra and panty moisturizing my body with lotion.

"Hey ma."

"I see you finally decided to return."

"I don't wanna argue with you girl. Damn."

"Whatever Adontis."

He starts laughing. Which really just pisses me off more. *"You really need to get laid. As do I for that matter. Then maybe you can stop all this bitching you been doing."*

I don't say anything, instead I give him the finger.

"Will you? I sure wish you would fuck me. Damn."

I roll my eyes. *"Does it always have to be about sex with you?"*

"It's not always about sex. But in this case, I ain't been getting none for months, so excuse the hell out of me for being horny."

"Yeah, you haven't, but whose fault is that?"

"I don't wanna hear this shit again. You said you forgave me, so I don't wanna hear about it. I'm sick of arguing about it."

I stand up and begin putting my clothes on. *"Whatever. I'm about to head out of here."*

"You mean, we about to head out of here. Keep playing with me. When I get in it. I'm gon punish that ass."

"Whatever." I slide into my heels. *"Let's go."*

I grab my gown and my cap and we head out the door. I think about what he just said. The last time he put that thing on me like that, he had my legs shaking. I could use that right now. I need him to break me off. When he said that my pussy started throbbing at the thought of it. We have a pretty silent ride. I call Carmen to see where she and my family are.

"Hey baby sis. We are on the way. Where are you at?"

"I'm here. I'm about to go and check in. I'll tell Adontis to save ya'll seats. Just call him when ya'll get here so he can tell you where he's seated."

"Ok sis. I love you"

"I love you too."

When Carmen and I hang up, I look over to Adontis and see that he is on the phone. He is talking to Shaun. I've invited Shaun, Aisha, Boris & Melanie to my graduation. They are all coming. I don't really know his parents that well and besides his mom doesn't even like me. I don't need any more drama today. Adontis and I have enough between the two of us.

"I'm going to check in. I'll see you later."

I open the door and get ready to get out. Adontis grabs me by the wrist.

"That's it?"

He caught me off guard. I sink back into my seat and turn towards him.

"What?"

"No kiss, no hug or nothing huh?"

As much as he gets on my nerves, I love the hell out of him. I lean in and lay a kiss on him. We smooch for a little while.

"Ok ma, I'll be waiting."

"See you soon."

I give him another peck then I get out of the car to head inside for graduation. The ceremony begins and it is fabulous. As Sum Cum Lade I have the honor of giving the valedictorian speech to my graduating class. It's a large class and I'm so ready for it to be over with.

Once the ceremony ends, I'm ready to get my party on. With my degree in hand, I head outside to find my family so we can all go to the party. The first person I spot in the crowd is my man. He has a bouquet of roses in his hands. He walks up to me and puts his arms around me.

"Congratulations baby. I'm proud of you." He kisses my lips and hands me the roses.

"Thank you, baby."

His touch has made me wet on the spot. I'm not going to be able to hold out much longer. I need my man to put it on me. I gather my composure. My family spots us and makes it to us. I begin getting hugs and love from every direction as I work my way through the group of family, friends and co-workers. As I'm heading through the crowd, I turn to my left and there is Rodney. First thing that runs through my mind is oh shit. Not today damn!

"Congrats Tasha."

He has a bouquet of roses in his hands and a card.

"Rodney, what are you doing here?"

The last thing I want is for Adontis to see him and for Rodney to begin talking about what we did. I'm taking that shit to my grave. No one else knows Rodney and I had sex and I'd like to keep it that way.

"You know I couldn't miss your special day."

"You shouldn't be here."

"I'm not trying to start nothing. I just wanted to congratulate you and give you these." He passes the roses and card to me. Then he bends over and kisses me on the cheek. He grabs my hand, *"You look damn beautiful. Congratulations baby girl. I love you."*

"Rodney, please not this, not today."

He throws his hands up in defense, as if he is saying, I'm not trying to start anything. *"I'm not here to cause trouble. I'm leaving. I just want you to know, I'm proud of you."*

"Thank you."

He licks his lips and kisses my hand. He stands there and stares at me for a while. It isn't until he begins to walk away, that he lets go of my hand. I'm thinking, wow. He never gives up. I subtly look over my shoulder and I see Adontis staring at me. I know that the shit is going to hit the fan. My family is looking like what the hell. I know everyone that knows my history with Rodney is puzzled. Adontis makes it through the crowd and then next to me. I can see he is about to say something, but Carmen comes over before he can.

"Hey ya'll. Let's head to the party."

I'm so glad she stepped in. *"Ok sounds good sis."*

Adontis doesn't say a word. He just stares at me. We begin walking to the car. After we reach the car and get inside, he cranks it up, but he doesn't put it in gear.

"What the hell was he doing here? You invited that mother fucking bitch?"

"No, I didn't invite him. He came to tell me congratulations."

"How in the hell he know you graduate today?"

"I don't know. I didn't tell him. We do have mutual friends maybe one of them told him." He attempts to grab the roses and card out of my hands. I pull back. *"What are you doing?"*

"Why the hell are you accepting his gifts?"

"Adontis, it's just flowers and a card. Why are you tripping?"

"You need to throw them away!"

"Why would I do that?"

"Why in the hell would you keep them? I bought you roses. You sure in the hell don't need his."

"Why are you acting like you are in a competition with him? I am yours. You already won."

"Maybe that would be believable if his fucking ass wasn't always around. I sure as hell don't feel like I've won. We ain't been on the same page for some time."

"Adontis, I don't wanna argue anymore. Can we just get out of here and head to my party?"

"Tasha, you wanna be with him? Before you answer think long and hard. I want you to be real damn sure."

"Oh, my gosh, Adontis. Really?"

"It's a simple damn question. I'm waiting on an answer. Be sure to think first though. Be honest. Do you want to be with that nigga? I ain't interested in keeping a woman that don't want to be kept."

I shake my head in disbelief. *"I don't want to be with him. I want to be with you."*

"Then the damn roses, got to go."

"I'm keeping the roses."

"I'm throwing them away."

We've been going in circles and nothing has gotten accomplished. By now, I'm all up in his face. I'm so close our lips are almost touching.

"Adontis, stop tripping."

By my robe, he pulls me closer to him. He begins kissing my lips. *"The roses are going damnit."*

He begins unzipping my robe. The sexual tension is through the roof. I climb over to his seat and sit on his lap.

"The roses are staying."

I pull his shirt from over his head. I begin sucking on his lips. He slides his hands under my dress. He leaves his hands there. He begins gripping, rubbing and massaging my booty. I push the button to slide the seat back. I begin to unbuckle his belt, un-button his pants and then I unzip them. With one hand he slides the zipper down on my dress then he slides my dress down off my shoulders.

"The roses are going."

I begin kissing on his chest. *"They're staying."*

He unhooks my bra and begins sucking my titties. *"Damn I want you."*

"I want you too."

"But are you going to let me, have you? I'm not up for a repeat of this morning."

I don't think I can take it anymore. I'm sitting on his lap and he smells so good. His lips taste sweet like caramel. His kisses are sensual and loving. I feel his touch as he is squeezing my ass looking at me waiting for an answer. I give him a devilish grin.

"Yes, baby you can have me." I see a smile come across his face. He releases a breath of relief. *"But now that you've got me, what are you going to do about it?"*

He doesn't say one word. Instead, he reclines his chair back as I slide his dick out of his boxers. He begins sucking on my breast as he slides my thong down. His fingers slip into my pussy. I'm revved up and fully ready to go. I reposition myself so that when I sit on top of him, I'll be gliding him into me.

"I'm not on the pill anymore."

"Ok. That doesn't change anything."

He's grippin on my booty, as I begin to ride. It has gotten hot and steamy in the SUV; the windows are fogged up. I ride him into ecstasy. As I climax, I dig my nails into him and I scream out his name.

When we finish, I say, *"You were right. I needed that."*

He licks his lips and with a smile on his face he says, *"Yeah, so did I. Now we got some place we need to be."*

We slide back into our clothes. *I look over to him and say, "Yep. And I'm keeping the roses."*

"The hell you are."

He rolls the window down and throws Rodney's roses and card out the window as he pulls out of the parking space. I can't believe he threw my stuff out. I'll give him this one though. You got to pick your battles.

"Whatever. Damn. I'm tired."

We arrive to the party about an hour late. Carmen was calling me, but I was obviously too preoccupied at that time. I did text her back after we finished making love that we were on the way. When we walk through the door, everyone starts clapping.

Carmen walks up to me, *"Damn T. Where ya'll been? I thought I needed to put out an APB on you."*

"I'm sorry Carmen. Something came up."

Kia walks up to me, *"Something like what? You got us sitting here waiting and hungry."*

Adontis is standing behind me with his hands on my hips, smiling. I'm blushing. *"Well, if ya'll must know, I was getting some."* Adontis doesn't say anything he just keeps wearing his smile.

Kia looks at me and shakes her head. *"Ya'll some nasty asses."*

Adontis and I burst out laughing. *"Well, we here now. Let's party."*

I'm drinking and dancing. I'm so happy to be where I am. The fact that I just got laid helps too. Adontis comes out to the dance floor and puts his arms around me.

"Hey love. You enjoying yourself?"

"Yeah daddy."

"I can tell. You need to eat something. You shouldn't be drinking on an empty stomach."

"Yeah, I know. I'm gonna eat. Are you ready to eat?"

"Hell yeah."

"Ok. Well, let me go fix you a plate."

I begin to walk off and he pulls me back. He wraps his arms around me and begins kissing me.

"Damn I love you."

"I love you back baby."

I attempt to walk away again, but he won't let me go.

"I'm not ready to let go yet."

I stay in his arms with my arms wrapped around his neck.

"Well, here is where I'll be."

We stay right there, just like that, for a little while. I feel the way I did when I first fell in love with him. I love this man with all of my heart.

Everyone has eaten and we've already had dessert. We've been drinking and dancing all night. It's finally that time, everyone is wanting me to open my gifts and cards. I get a lot of money, roses, balloons and gift cards.

After I open everyone else's gift, Adontis says, *"Now it's my turn. I gave you, your roses earlier, now here's the big one."*

He hands me this massive brown teddy bear. He is wearing a jersey with my school's colors and my last name on the back. On the front, it reads #1. He has on a graduation cap and he holds a degree. The bear is so cute. He knows I collect teddy bears. He's had this one customized for me, which makes him all the more special.

"Aww baby, I love him."

He looks at me and shakes his head. *"Look at the box that's in his hand ma."*

"Oh. Ok."

In the bear's other hand is a pretty wrapped gift box. I grab the box and begin unwrapping it. Everyone is gathering around in suspense. The box is about the size of a small cell phone. I open the box and find a set of keys with a Tinkerbell key chain. I totally love her.

"Adontis, you didn't?"

He starts smiling as he licks his lips. *"I just couldn't help myself."*

I pull the keys from the box for everyone to see. He bought me a car.

"Oh my gosh! Where is it?"

"It's right outside ma."

I run out the door as everyone follows behind. Right in front of the entrance is a purple 2008 Ford Mustang Coupe. It is so hot. It has a black racing strip down the middle and a sunroof top. I jump into his arms.

"Thank you, baby."

I begin kissing him. If he didn't get it earlier, he definitely would have been getting it all tonight.

"I can't believe you."

He's standing biting his bottom lip and he knows that turns me on.

I'm standing directly in front of him, *"I'm ready to go for round two right here and now."*

"Anytime, anyplace. I don't care who is around."

Kia looks at us, *"Hell no. I'm around and I don't wanna see that shit. Ya'll nasty asses need to get a room."*

Adontis starts laughing. *"We don't need a room. We definitely didn't need one earlier. All we need is each other and we got a party."*

"That's right baby."

Kia rolls her eyes and acts as if she is about to gag.

"Whatever Kia. Hate does not look good on you. How you gon talk about us and you walking around here one month pregnant?"

"I'm grown. Your ass isn't."

I smile, *"That's not what Adontis tells me."*

She laughs and throws her hands up in defeat. *"I'm done with ya'll."*

"I pull Adontis to the side. Is this where you went to earlier? The business you had to tend to?"

"Yeah ma. I know we working on us and rebuilding trust, but I didn't want to ruin the surprise."

"I'm sorry baby. You was trying to do something nice for me and I was being a bitch."

"Hold up ma. Hell, yes you was being very difficult, very got damn difficult, but I'm not gon let you talk about the woman I love like that. What's done is done. We working on us, right? You coming home with me to Florida, right?"

"Ok, I hear you. Yes, and yes I'm going home with you."

"Then fuck everything else. I got my woman and I ain't gon never let you go again."

He leans in and kisses me. I wrap my arms around his neck. *"Hold me tight daddy."*

"Don't worry I will."

We continue to party hard, late and throughout the night. I'm tight and feeling right. I know I shouldn't drive. Adontis takes my keys from me. He gives Shaun his keys and we say our goodbyes to everyone.

Ron stops Adontis as we are heading out. *"Get my baby sister home safe."*

"Always."

When we arrive home, Adontis opens my door, lifts me from the car, and carries me inside up to bed. He sits me on the bed. As he is leaning over me from sitting me down, I grab a hold of his lips with my lips. I start sucking.

When I let up for air he says, *"You need to get some rest ma, so you can sober up a bit."*

"No, I need you."

I begin unzipping my dress. He stands watching me with a smile on his face. I stand up on the bed and let my dress fall. I un-hook my bra and let it fall. I haven't been wearing panties since we had sex earlier. I walk to the edge of the bed, then I jump on him. My legs are wrapped around his waist. While holding me up by my butt, he is smiling from ear to ear.

"I love you Adontis."

"I love to hear that. I love you back ma."

"Let's go get in the shower."

"Yeah, I'm gonna punish you."

I think to myself oh shit. Not only is it hot and steamy between us, but now so is the shower. He has me pressed up against the shower door as he's kissing on my neck. My face is pressed up against the glass as he is grabbing on my titties. He's squeezing them and pinching my nipples. We've both worked up a sweat. He begins kissing down my body, as I begin moaning.

He begins kissing me on my lower back, just above my ass. Then he slides his fingers into my kitty kat. He is playing with her as he is kissing on my booty. I'm moaning as I'm in ecstasy. He is giving me the punishment that he promised and I'm enjoying it. The next thing I notice, he spreads my ass cheeks and starts licking. He eats the groceries.

He spins me around and begins kissing on my neck. He picks me up by my ass. He moves his hands around my waist. I wrap my legs around him. He props me up against the shower wall. Then he slides into me. He glides in and out of me as he begins to pleasure me. He takes deep long strides as he thrust himself into me. I begin to scratch him up. In sheer ecstasy, I scream out his name.

chapter 21

Keeping Secrets

August 10, 2007

SECRETS. They can eat away at you. They always catch up to you.

After getting my degree, I headed to Jacksonville to move in with Adontis. I haven't found a job, but I am working at Fresh. Adontis needed my help. Needless to say, I stepped in and helped my man. I've also enrolled in med school. My classes begin in January.

My life in Florida has just begun getting on track. It's been a few weeks since I've been here and my period is late. I haven't had my period in about two months. I had my last period right before I slept with Rodney and I haven't had one since then. I am feeling stressed as hell and I fear that I might be pregnant. I find a doctor and set up an appointment.

When Adontis and I broke up, I stopped taking the pill. I figured I wasn't having sex so I didn't need it. I never planned on sleeping with Rodney, but when I did, I made sure, we used condoms both times. After having sex with Rodney, I waited about five weeks before I slept with Adontis. Adontis and I stopped using condoms back when I first got on the pill. Since we've gotten back together, the plan was to find a doctor here in Florida, then get back on the pill. Now it may be too late. I've done the math and I've thought through the timeline. Based on my calculations, If I am pregnant, it's Rodney's baby. There is no way I can tell Adontis this.

August 13, 2007

Today is the day that I find out, if a big mistake, has led to an even bigger one. The nurse does her job and takes my vitals, urine and blood. I am nervous as hell. I can't be pregnant. I learned my lesson. I'm sitting in the room alone stressing the hell out. The wait seems like an eternity. If I were pregnant and I knew it was Adontis' I wouldn't feel so bad. I'd actually be ok. He is where I want to be.

The doctor comes back with the results. Am I pregnant? If I am, what will I do? I sit back on the examination table and take a deep breath. I have got to relax. I try to reassure myself, I can't be pregnant, right? My luck can't be that bad. I inhale then exhale. The doctor sits on the stool and prepares to give me my results.

As she is looking down at my file she says, *"Ok Ms. Leam, I have your results right here. You're pregnant."*

My face drops. Pregnant rings in my ears like bad dramatic music. I can't believe this. *"Are you sure?"*

"Yes, it shows it right here. I guess these aren't the results you wanted. Well, there are alternatives. Adoption and abortion, depending on how far along you are."

I look off into space. My body is in the room with the doctor, but my mind is gone somewhere far away. I don't know what to do. I can't tell Adontis I am pregnant with another man's baby. I can't do this. My life and my career and Adontis will be gone. I am not even with Rodney. I damn sure don't want to have his baby. I look to my doctor, with tears rolling down my face.

"I want to schedule an abortion if possible."

She hands me some Kleenex and tries to console me.

"I know this is a tough decision Ms. Leam. Remember you have to do what's best for you. We have counseling available to you as well. You don't have to decide today."

I just look at her I don't know what to say. All I think to say is, *"Yes I do. What's next?"*

"Looking at your chart you indicated your last period was June 1st. Do you have a general idea of when you think you became pregnant?"

"Yes, either June 9th or June 15th."

"Ok. Let's do an ultrasound so that I can confirm how far along you are. Once we get that done then we can go from there."

I lay back on the table and the doctor preps me for my ultrasound. The machine is turned on and she puts the gel on my belly. It feels so cold. She puts the device against my belly. I can't bear to look at the monitor. I don't want to see the life that is forming in me.

"You look to be about 8 weeks pregnant."

I shudder at the thought of knowing I am carrying Rodney's baby. I already knew that it had to be his baby, but hearing the confirmation is terrifying as hell. If this was Adontis' baby I know he and I would deal with it together. I feel like a fool. I can't believe I have been so irresponsible and now this is the situation I am in. I can only blame myself. This is a side of me that I would never want my parents to see.

"If you are sure you'd like to proceed with the abortion we can offer you a non-surgical abortion. You are within the ten-week timeline, but we'd have to get you scheduled for it today. I know this is a very tough decision. As I mentioned earlier, we offer pre and post abortion counseling."

"Can you tell me more about how this form of abortion works?"

"Instead of surgery we will give you medication. I'm going to be blunt with you. The first medicine stops the growth of the fetus in your uterus and causes it to detach from your uterus wall. It also ends the development of the fetus growing inside of you. We will then give you another medication, which will cause your uterus to cramp and bleed. This bleeding allows you to expel what was growing inside of you. Your bleeding will be heavier and longer than your normal menstruation. Do you have any other questions?"

"Yes. Will this affect my chances of getting pregnant again in the future? How will I know that the abortion worked?"

"No, this should not affect your future pregnancies. After you have the abortion, we will schedule a follow up appointment with you in which we will run test. This is when we will verify that the abortion was successful."

I tried to be strong, but it hits me; I am about to have an abortion. Tears begin flowing from my eyes. *"Ok. I want to go ahead and schedule the appointment."*

The doctor hands me another Kleenex. *"Ok Ms. Leam. I'm going to leave out and allow you to get dressed. When you head out stop to reception and they will schedule an appointment to get you in to our clinic this week. She will give you the address to where our clinic is located."*

"Oh, so the procedure will not be done here?"

"No ma'am. They will also provide you with information in regard to the procedure as well as the telephone information for our counselors. I wish you the best and I will see you soon."

I begin to dry my eyes. *"Thank you, doctor."*

She walks out the door and I get myself up from the exam table. I finish cleaning the remainder of the gel from my belly and get dressed. I feel like I am in a living hell. I walk out to reception and schedule my appointment for a few days from now. I take all of the information the receptionist gives me and I sit in my car and read it. I've never been this afraid and this alone.

Tears are flowing from my eyes. I can't tell this to anyone. Not even my best friends. I feel so ashamed. After I read the pamphlets, I save the number of the counselor in my phone. I drive over to the nearest gas station and throw away all of the information. I do not want to leave any of this lying around. The last thing I want is for Adontis to stumble upon this.

August 17, 2007

Unluckily for me, today is the day. Over the last past couple of days, I've tried to avoid Adontis as much as I could. I didn't want to look him in the eye knowing what I was about to do. Knowing the great secret that I am keeping from him. Or should I say secrets. In an effort to continue to avoid him, I made my appointment for 8:30 am. I hadn't been able to sleep much so I slip out of the bed at an early 6am. I quietly sneak to the bathroom and get in the shower.

After my shower, I peak my head into the bedroom to see him still fast asleep. I quietly get dressed, grab my shoes, my purse and my keys. I head down the stairs as quietly as I can. I make it out of the house a little after 7am; I get into my car and head down the street. It appears

I did not wake him. By the time, I get done with my appointment he should have already left the house for work. I don't know how I am going to explain to him where I went. On my way to the doctor, I stop by the pharmacy and I pick up some thicker pads. Since apparently, I am going to be bleeding like crazy.

I arrive at the clinic a little after 7:45am. The clinic isn't open yet. There are a few other cars in the parking lot waiting as well. Across the street from the clinic, I see protestors have arrived. They are standing up picketing abortion. I don't need this shit. This decision is hard enough without having to deal with them. The protestors are yelling and screaming anti-abortion phrases and statements. I just tune them out.

It is finally a few minutes past eight. The clinic is finally open. I check my phone, happily, I see Adontis still hasn't called me. That means he isn't awake yet. I go inside the clinic and check in. I fill in all of my paperwork and pay for my procedure. Then I sit in the waiting area. There are a few other people waiting. I'm anxious and afraid. About a half hour passes by before my name is called.

Just as the nurse is calling my name, my phone rings. I look at the display and see Adontis' name. I don't have time to talk to him so I do not answer his call. I just silence the ringer and allow it to continue to ring until he is sent to voicemail. He calls me again and I turn my phone on silent. I can't deal with him right now.

Once I am in the back the nurse goes through her procedures and checks all of my vitals. She gets my weight and temperature. From there I am placed in a room to wait for the doctor. The doctor comes in to administer another ultrasound and walks me through each step. Then the procedure begins.

The procedure goes exactly as the doctor described it. I am given a pill to take. I immediately regret it. I know I just killed my baby. I chose Adontis, over my baby. In exactly twenty four hours from now I have one additional pill to take, which I will take at home. The second pill is what starts the cramps and bleeding. The cramping and bleeding will start within twenty-four hours of taking the second pill.

I'm out of the doctor's office several hours after my arrival. The doctor has given me my instructions and I've scheduled my follow up appointment. I have been told to do or not do the following: do sleep, do drink lots of water, do take vitamins, do not exercise for a few weeks, do not get into any water; like a bath or a pool (also for a few weeks), do not lift anything over ten pounds, and the most difficult one; do not have sex for two to four weeks. I don't know how I am going to keep Adontis off of me for that long.

The doctor also advised me that I may potentially see a milky fluid leaking from my breast due to the abortion. Stimulation to my breast will cause the milk to flow. She advised me not to be alarmed. However, she did inform me that if this occurs that I should wear a tight bra continuously until it dries up. She also warned me that I may experience tenderness of my breast and nipples, but I can take Tylenol if this occurs.

This shit sucks. I sure as hell hope my milk does not come in. I'm trying to hide the pregnancy and abortion from Adontis, not put up a sign pointing to my belly that says, hey baby was here! I'm going to start wearing the tight-fitting bra now. I want to avoid the issue before it has a chance to occur.

I've been shedding tears since the procedure began, during and after. I'm trying to collect myself. I have to call Adontis back and I can't call him in the condition I am in now. I go by the pharmacy to drop off my birth control prescription. While I wait for my prescription, I go to a nearby hotel and check in paying cash. I don't want any bank statement or credit card trail that can lead back to Adontis. Hell, I paid out of pocket for all of my doctor visits and the abortion, in cash. I've also opted for paperless documents. I don't need any mail coming to the house. No paper trails.

The pharmacist said it'd be about an hour or so. I clean up myself and redo my makeup. It is well into the afternoon and Adontis has been blowing my phone up all day. He's been calling and texting. Carmen has been calling and texting as well. Apparently, Adontis reached out to her.

I text my sister and I tell her that I am ok. I ask her not to tell Adontis anything. I inform her that he did not do anything wrong and I am getting ready to call him. She texts me back a million questions of concern. She also tries to call me. I do not answer; instead, I reassure her again via text that I am ok. She tells me she loves me and that she is there if I need to talk. I thank her and tell her I will talk to her later.

Now I'm trying to figure out what I am going to tell this man. I text him back and tell him that I am on the way home. As soon as I send him the text, my phone starts to ring. I mean I barely have a chance to remove my finger from the send button, before he calls me. I contain myself and then I answer the phone.

"Hey baby."

"Hey baby? Tasha where the hell are you? Why the hell you sneak out the house this morning?"

The doctor ordered me to go home and be on bed rest. I have to figure this Adontis thing out first. *"Adontis, I didn't sneak out of the house. You were asleep when I woke up. I couldn't sleep and I had a few errands to run. I didn't want to disturb you I know how tired you were."*

"Bullshit. You don't mind waking me up any other damn time. Where the hell are you at girl?"

"I'm about to head home baby."

"Head home from where?"

"I can't hear you; I think we are losing connection. I'm headed home I'll call you when I get there."

I actually can hear him loud and clear. *"Tasha don't hang up this damn phone girl-."*

I disconnect the line and gather my belongings. I clean the mess I've made and I head to the front desk to check out. Yes, I literally rented a hotel room for like an hour or so. I needed to get myself together. I was a basket case when I checked in. I'm more composed now, but still sad as hell. At least I've had some time to gather my thoughts. I still don't know what explanation I am going to give Adontis when he gets home. I have the drive there to think about it. I pick up my prescription and then head towards home. I haven't eaten all day and I'm beginning to feel like crap. I stop and pick up a bite to eat first.

After about forty-five minutes, I pull in the driveway. I don't bother to park in the garage. I just want to lay down. I gather my purse and my food then I head to the front door. I really still don't know what to tell this man. I walk inside and head upstairs to the bedroom. I begin to undress and slip into some pajamas. Then I get in the bed, plug in my heating pad, place it over my belly, get comfortable and prepare to try to eat my food.

As soon as I am about to take a bite of my sandwich, Adontis steps through the doorway of our bedroom.

"Tasha, where the fuck you been all day?"

He is glaring at me. I know he is pissed and he should be. I'm in the wrong.

"Hey baby."

"Don't give me that shit. Answer my damn question."

"What ques-"

He cuts me off. *"Don't play dumb with me woman. You know what damn question I am talking about."*

"I told you I was running errands. My period is about to come on. I don't feel good because I forgot to eat today." This is all I've came up with so far.

"I don't need to hear all of that shit. What errands were you running Tasha?"

"Just a little here and there."

I can see he is getting more pissed each time I speak.

"Ok so that's what we are going to start doing now? We gon keep secrets and hide shit? You been out fucking someone else?"

I really don't feel like having this argument, but I am at fault. I have to sit here and take this.

"No Adontis we are not keeping secrets. And no, I have not been fucking anyone, but you."

A light bulb comes on in my head and I think of a lie to use. I don't really want to use it, but I'm backed in the corner. I'm in survival mode.

"That's a lie right there. You haven't been fucking me."

I roll my eyes. I toss the covers then my heating pad off me. I get out of the bed and stand up. I go into my closet, open the safe and come out with a large gift bag. The top of the bag is filled with tissue paper. I hand it to him.

"Well, you've ruined it now. Since you had to know, Happy Birthday!"

His birthday is coming up in a few weeks. I hand the gift to him.

"I had to get to the store when they opened to make sure I purchased this before they sold out again. I missed out on it when it first came out. I spoke to a salesman and asked him to please give me a call if they got anymore in stock. I got a call from the salesman that it was back in stock this morning, so I headed out to get this."

He is standing there as if he is feeling dumb. I feel bad for how he is feeling, but it's better that I tell him this than what I was really doing.

"Go ahead, you might as well open it."

I get in the bed and back under my heating pad.

"Aww baby, I'm so sorry. I ruined your surprise." He comes over to me and he kisses me. I feel like shit for making him feel like shit. *"I don't want to open it yet. I want to wait until my birthday."* He hands the bag back to me.

"You might as well open it. It's not like you don't know what it is."

He has his arms around me. *"No, I want to wait."*

"Well then I need to get some rest. I don't feel good."

"Is there anything I can do? Can I get you anything ma?"

"No. I just want to eat and then go to sleep."

"Ok love. Well, I am going to go back to work." He kisses me again. *"I love you."*

"I love you."

He gets up and heads out the door. Now I really feel like shit. I've lost my appetite. My mama use to say, you shouldn't lie because once you start you have to keep telling lies to cover up the previous lies. I didn't fully understand that until now.

August 31, 2007

It's been two weeks and I have my follow up appointment at the doctor today. I have called and talked to the counselors and they have helped me through these last few weeks. They've been very encouraging. I don't know if I would have made it through without their help. Don't get me wrong, I'm still dealing with and regretting my decision, but I'm working on not hating myself for my decision. I'm taking steps in the right direction.

Now the doctors have to make sure everything with the abortion went correctly. This time I made my appointment for after Adontis leaves for work. I get myself up ninety minutes before my appointment, get cleaned up and then out the door. Shortly after arriving to the clinic, I'm called back by a nurse. She of course checks my vitals and everything then places me in a room to wait for my doctor to come in. She gives me a paper shirt and a paper skirt to change in to, to prepare for my exam. About twenty minutes after I'm changed, I hear a knock at the door.

"Come in."

Doctor Tara walks through the door. *"Good morning, Tasha. How are you feeling today?"*

"Good morning. I'm feeling ok today. Better than I have been. I've been an emotional wreck these last couple of weeks. My emotions have been up, then down. I have some days of nausea and a loss of appetite. I ate breakfast today without any nausea and I feel good. The counseling really helped."

"Well, I can say you are looking good. I am glad that the counselors were able to see you through. Continue to use them as long as you need."

"Thank you, I will."

She gets seated on her stool. *"Ok so what we are going to do today is make sure that you are healing properly and that the abortion was a success."* She looks down at my file, *"Your urine and blood came back normal."*

"Thank God."

"Yes, He is good all the time."

"Yes, He is."

"First I want to do another ultrasound. I'm looking to verify that the termination of the pregnancy was successful. Please lay back on the table for me."

She puts on gloves, turns on the ultrasound machine and walks over to me. She lifts up the front of my paper shirt then she applies the ultrasound gel on my belly. The gel is cold. I can't bear to look at the screen. I couldn't look when my baby was forming in me so I sure can't look now, that I've killed my baby. The good spirits that I came in here with are starting to dwindle down. Now that we are doing this ultrasound I am thinking about my baby. Tears flow from my eyes.

Doctor Tara isn't looking at me so she hasn't noticed that I am crying. She walks over to my file and makes some notes. She looks up from my chart and sees me wiping the tears from my cheeks.

She hands me some Kleenex and says, *"It's ok. Let it out."*

She's been so kind and patient with me. I wipe my face and try to compose myself. *"I'm so sorry. I told myself I wouldn't cry again today. I know you are probably saying to yourself, 'This damn girl gets on my nerves. I'm sick of seeing her in here crying.'"* I smile at her and try to perk myself up.

She laughs and smiles at me. *"Not at all sweetie. I can understand where you are and what you are going through. Because I have been in your shoes. I've been young before too. Things sometimes happen that we don't expect and we have to make a tough decision. You in here crying, I can understand. What I don't understand is the ones that come in here all of the time and have no emotion about it. So, if you need to cry, cry."*

She hugs me. It is what I need in this moment. It feels like a mother talking to her daughter and Doctor Tara gives me that. While wiping my tears away I smile at her.

"Thank you."

"You're welcome. We are halfway done. Now I am going to ask you to lay back so that I can take a look at your cervix."

"Ok."

I lean back and the doctor, puts on new gloves, gets her tools and prepares to look at my cervix. I feel the wet lubricant as she begins to ease her tool into my vagina. It is very uncomfortable and cold, but it's part of being a woman.

After she finishes checking, she tells me, *"Ok Tasha you can sit up now if you'd like."*

She removes her gloves and begins making notes in my file again. I'm looking at her for a lifeline. Like ok, what's going on with my body. After she finishes writing, she looks up at me.

"Your ultrasound looked good. The abortion was successful. Your cervix has closed. Which is what we wanted it to do. You are now able to take baths if you'd like. You are also clear to have sexual intercourse when you are ready, but make sure you are ready. Do not rush into it, ok?"

"Yes. I will. Thank you so much."

"You are welcome. Do you have any questions for me?"

"No. I think you answered everything. Thank you again for being so kind."

"You are welcome. You can go ahead and clean yourself up and get dressed we are all done."

She gives me some wipes to clean off my belly and to clean the lube from my vagina. I walk out of the doctor's office relieved that this is over. I am hoping to put this all behind me. I don't ever want to talk about this again. Now that I'm okayed to have sex, I know I am going to have to give Adontis some soon. I have run out of excuses to tell him. I've used: my period is on, I don't feel good, I have a headache, and I have a yeast infection. I am excused out.

I want to do something nice for Adontis and I need to give him some. I decide to cook him his favorite meal so I stop to the grocery store and pick up what I need. I get home and do the household duties, take a nice long bath and then begin to prepare his dinner. I want his meal to be hot and ready when he walks through the door.

I have decided to put on some sexy lingerie because he deserves it. As I am finishing up in the kitchen, I hear him pulling into the garage. I wait for him to walk into the house. When he steps in the kitchen, I walk up to him.

"Hey baby."

I'm standing in front of him in a red all lace teddy. I have on some high heels and I look sexy as hell. I don't know if I am fully emotionally ready for sex, but I feel like I owe it to him. I have been selfish long enough. He is looking at me strangely. Clearly, he wasn't expecting this.

He musters out, *"Hey."*

Then he just walks out the kitchen and towards the stairs like I'm not even standing here. As if I'm not looking like a full course meal he wants to eat. I'm shocked.

"Baby," I call out after him.

He doesn't respond. That was not the reaction I expected. I go upstairs after him. I find him in the bedroom taking off his clothes. He doesn't say anything to me.

"Adontis. What's the matter?"

He looks at me and grumbles, *"Nothing."*

"Clearly it's something. I'm dressed like this and you didn't even acknowledge me."

"I've had a long day. And clearly that ain't for me. I'm so use to you not giving me none why would I expect today to be any different?"

I let out a long sigh. He is right and I don't want to argue. *"You're right baby and I'm sorry. I haven't been feeling good. But I feel better and I want to make up for it."*

"Because you are ready, I should just automatically be ready and willing to give you some?"

I'm trying to keep my cool because I know we are both hot heads; so, someone has to be sensible here if this is going to get resolved.

"No, but I did just sincerely apologize to you and I am trying to fix it."

He has already stepped out of his shoes and now he is stepping out of his pants. He doesn't say a word. I walk up to him and wrap my arms around his neck. He doesn't grab me back.

"Baby, love of my life, can you please accept my apology? I have your dinner waiting for you downstairs come on let's eat."

I jump on him and wrap my legs around him. He knows I don't mind the climb. I kiss his lips, but he doesn't kiss me back. He knows he wants this. He needs to stop fronting.

"I made plans to go out with my boys."

"Can't you cancel your plans with them?"

"And why would I do that?"

"Because you love me and I am deeply sorry."

He is stubborn as hell. I hate when he acts like this. He has never turned me down before. This is different. I jump down off of him. I slide my hands in to his boxers. I figure if I get him excited then I can give him some. When I do, I find a surprise, he already has an erection. That just lets me know, yeah, he may be mad at me, but he is still turned on and horny for me. That's really all I needed to know.

I slide my hands in around the back of his boxers then I tug down on them. He is giving me a look that says what are you doing. I show him. I push him on to the sofa and stand in between his legs. I lean down and kiss him again, but this time I slide my tongue into his mouth. I begin kissing and sucking on his neck, while I am jacking him off. He puts his hands around me and grabs my ass. This is when I know I have him right where I want him. His ass ain't going nowhere tonight.

I squat down in front of him and I begin kissing his dick. Then I start licking. I have to pull out all of the tricks. I've never given head before, but the time is now, I guess. I've always promised maybe one day. Today is the day. I slide his dick into my mouth and I begin sucking. He leans his head back and begins moaning. He grabs a hold of my hair by pulling it up and holding it in a ponytail as I am sucking on him. I'm slurping and spitting on his dick. I peek up at him to see his eyes closed. I continue sucking harder and faster. He is moaning and making new noises I haven't heard him make before. I'm trying hard not to gag on his dick. Me throwing up on his dick would definitely kill the moment.

"Damn Tasha. Oh shit, that feels so damn good."

I just keep sucking. With his other hands he starts feeling on and playing with my titties. I think to myself; I hope milk doesn't come out. I haven't had any at all, but I sure as hell don't want it to start now. I start to run my tongue around the tip of his dick, very quickly in a circular motion. He moans louder. I continue to do that in between sucking him. I pleasure him until the point in which he orgasms. I catch it in my mouth. I'm ready to run to the bathroom and spit it out. I stand up and he pulls me on to his lap. By the way he is looking at me, I can see he is severely turned on.

"Swallow it," he whispers in my ear.

He is holding me tightly and closely. He is kissing and sucking on my neck. I wasn't expecting him to say that. I shake my head no. I can't really talk with a mouth full of cum. He slides his hands in my panties and starts playing with my pussy.

"Swallow it," he whispers to me again.

I shake my head no, again. He pulls my panties off and then sits me on his shoulders with his lips resting on my pussy.

"Swallow it, I said."

He begins licking my pussy. He is sucking my pussy lips and then he begins to suck on my clitoris. He is sucking me in to ecstasy. I begin moaning in pleasure. He gently bites and nibbles on my pussy lips while he is rubbing on my clitoris. I moan out in ecstasy and I forget I have a mouth full of cum. I am orgasming and I inadvertently swallow as I scream out his name.

He looks up at me with a smile then bites his bottom lip. *"Yes, you swallowed."*

I don't say anything. I'm still recovering from my orgasm.

"You ready to take the D ma."

I shake my head, *"Yes."*

He lowers me to the sofa and I lay back as he begins to make love to me. When we finish, he lays in me holding me, until we fall asleep. We wake up a few hours later to eat the meal that I prepared.

I head to the kitchen to warm up our dinner. I meet Adontis in the family room with our meal and drinks. He's dimmed the lights and lit candles all around the room. We sit on the couch and watch a movie while eating dinner. After eating, we snuggle up together. I think to myself; I love this man. I have to do better and be better for him and to him.

chapter 22

His Day

September 7, 2007

> One of the secrets to keeping your man happy is to cater to him.
> As women I know we do it all. Life keeps us busy and once kids are
> added into the mix things can get crazy. However, if you have a good
> man, KEY WORDS GOOD MAN, you have to show him he's appreciated
> every now and then. Most importantly slob the knob ladies. For no
> reason at all. Randomly. On his good and especially on his bad days.
> It will help him get over almost any petty thing you do. Trust me.

It's Adontis' birthday. My baby is now twenty-six. With all that we've been going through I thought that it was important to do something nice for him. I have been a little; well let me call it what it is, I have been a bitch to him over these last few weeks, before we made up. He deserves to feel special on the regular. Even more so on his birthday and for putting up with my shit. He always makes me feel so. Originally, I was just going to cook a nice dinner at home just the two of us. However, I decided to do a little more.

We are going to go out to dinner tonight, in Miami Beach. We will be flying out there for the weekend. I've invited his sister, brother and his best friends, Brandon and Chuck, from New York. They will all attend. It will be a couples' weekend. I wanted to surprise him, but I had to tell Adontis about the trip to Miami Beach so he'd be ready to go and so he wouldn't go into Fresh. However, I decided not to tell him about our guest. That will surprise him because he is thinking it is only going to be us.

I roll out of bed a little after 8am. Adontis is laying snug in the bed. I finished all of our packing last night and Adontis loaded our bags in the car. I head to the bathroom and get in the shower. While in the shower, I am mentally checking to make sure that I've packed everything that we need. I am also going over all of the things that I have planned for our weekend. I have to make sure everyone else's flights get in on time. Aisha is going to pick up his cake and bring it to the restaurant for me.

We have a 1pm flight to catch. Our flight is a little over an hour long. I have sprung for first class seats without any layovers. Our flight will arrive in Miami at 2:15 pm. This will give us enough time to check in and to spend some time alone together, just the two of us.

I rented a beach house for the weekend. The house has five bedrooms with more than enough space for everyone. Since Adontis is clueless to the guest list, I also reserved a regular room for one night. Which is where we will get ready tonight and we will stay there for one night. That way we can get freaky in private. After all, it is my baby's birthday. I have to give him some toe-curling loving. I think he will see Teresita tonight.

To distract him, I will take him out and keep him out long enough for everyone else to get into town. I've given Aisha all the details to get everyone settled in the house. They can get dressed there before heading to the restaurant. Once they've all done that, then he and I can return to our room and get ready. By the time, we arrive to the restaurant our guest should be seated. When I made the reservation, I preordered appetizers and a few bottles, for them to enjoy while they await our arrival.

We arrive in Miami as planned. Once we get checked into our room, Adontis and I spend the afternoon sightseeing and doing some shopping. My treat. It is his birthday after all. I want him to know he is special to me too. I don't want him to spend a dime on this trip. We also enjoy a nice lunch together. Followed by a walk on the beach. It's nice and romantic. Just the two of us. He's been all over me all day and I have been all over him too. I'm so in love with this man.

For tonight, I have asked everyone to wear white and the dress code is semi-formal. Adontis will be in red. I have a very sexy white gown that I'm sure will make his nature rise. We get back to the hotel room after our day of leisure and relax for a bit before getting ready. Adontis is still clueless about the beach house that I rented. I love surprises.

The time comes to get dressed. I am a woman, so of course when it comes to getting dressed, I'm slow as hell. In a short period of time, Adontis is dressed. Per usual he is now waiting for me. I'm putting on my finishing touches when Aisha texts me that they are being seated. I think to myself awesome. My slowness has us about on track. I open the bathroom door and step into the bedroom.

Looking at Adontis I say, *"Hey sexy. Baby you ready?"*

He is wearing a red single button Tuxedo Jacket with the edges of the collar and lapels outlined in black, a black button-down dress shirt with red matching tuxedo pants. On his feet, he has on black shiny dress shoes.

"Yeah ma. Waiting on you," he says with a smirk on his face.

As I smile at him, *"Ok, I'm ready."*

He looks me up and down. *"Um you might want to lose the robe first."*

"Yes, I know. I was just about to."

I remove my robe to expose what I am wearing underneath. My dress has a halter-top strap that ties around the back of my neck with a V-neck cut in the front. The V-neck cut comes down to right above my belly button. It is fitted to show off my cleavage and backless. The dress flows down to the floor in very loose pleats. It has a high split up the front center of the dress. That flows in between my legs up to about mid-thigh.

He is looking me up and down as he bites down on his bottom lip. He looks down at his watch, *"Damn ma. You look gorgeous. What time is that reservation again?"*

He pulls me close to him. He is kissing, rubbing and touching me in places that is prone to make us miss dinner.

"It's now. We have to go. Don't start nothing."

I'm prying his hands off of my booty and attempting to walk towards the door. He pulls me into his arms.

"I'm not even hungry no more. At least not for food. But damn I'm starving to taste you. Feed a starving man ma."

I'm smiling at him it's sexy how hot he is for me right now. If I didn't have everyone waiting on us. I would give him everything he is asking for.

"Baby lets go eat dinner and I'll be your dessert."

"I like my dessert first. I'm ready for you now ma."

He grabs my hand and puts it against his manhood and he is brick hard. I look down and I can see his print through his pants. A very nice, thick, big print. The sight of him is getting me wet and I'm trying to shake it off and stay focused. I take a very deep breath and fan myself with both hands. Now I need to compose myself.

"Adontis. No, we have to go to dinner first. I promise after dinner."

He's giving me the sad puppy dog eyes. I know if I give him some first, we will not make it to dinner.

"You not gon give me none ma? It's my birthday!"

"After dinner baby. Please let's go before we lose our reservation."

He begrudgingly caves in. He looks me up and down like he wants to eat me and then he licks his lips. He repositions his man hood.

"Ok."

The good thing is the restaurant is not very far from our room. I text Aisha to tell her that we are on the way. We arrive to the restaurant within about five minutes. He pulls up front and the valet opens my door. I walk in without him as he gives the keys to the valet and they give him a ticket. I have just enough time to let the hostess in on what's going on. She now knows that the other guests are a surprise. Adontis walks in and the hostess prepares to take us to our private party room. I push Adontis up to walk in front of me as we follow the hostess. He's not having that. I wanted him to be in front since it's his surprise.

"Naw ma. You know better than that. You walk beside me or in front of me. I can't protect you if you behind me."

There's not much to say to that. All I got is, *"Ok."*

I see the private room with our party nearby. They are quietly waiting. I look back at Adontis, as we are walking into the room. I want to see his reaction when he notices them. To my surprise he hasn't seen them because he is busy looking at my ass. When he sees me catch him, he looks up and smiles.

"The ass had me mesmerized ma."

I just shake my head. No words needed. He finally has begun to scan the room and looks at his surroundings and that's when he notices everyone.

"Surprise," they yell out to him.

Everyone stands to greet him with daps, happy birthdays and hugs. He is doing his ear-to-ear grin thing. He thanks everyone as we head to our seats. He pulls out my chair and after I sit, he sits beside me.

"Wow, I can't believe all you here. You got me. I wasn't expecting this. I was just telling Tasha in the car on the way here that we should come back again and do a couples' trip. Thanks for showing up fam that's love. And thank you ma for putting all of this together."

He leans over and kisses me. *"You're welcome baby."*

The server comes and takes our drink order. Shaun pours Adontis and I a glass and does a toast.

"Big bro I love ya to death. I'm happy to be here to celebrate with you and to turn up. I wish you many more happy birthdays. Tasha thank you for extending the invitation to all of us. You did this beautifully. I'm happy my bro found you. To black love, family and friends."

We clank glasses and enjoy our drinks. The remainder of dinner goes by great. Before the end, I disclose to Adontis that I have rented a beach house for all of us to stay together. I also disclose that for the first night Adontis and I will be staying separately in our hotel room.

Adontis is grinning. I know what he has planned. He has had a few drinks and I know he plans to get it. Lucky for him I plan to give it to him. The staff comes out with Adontis' cake and we all sing happy birthday to him. Once we finish, he blows out his candles. I don't tarry too long after the cake. Adontis has been running his hand up my dress all night. He has been rubbing and feeling all over my thighs under the table.

After the bill is paid, Adontis gets up.

"Alight I'm gon go get the car ma."

All I can do is smirk. I know what my man wants. He doesn't have any shame in his game. He's ready. Shaun looks at him smiling.

"Damn, it's like that bro," Shaun asks?

"Yeah, I love ya'll. Thank ya'll for coming out, but we got to go," Adontis says, as he grabs my hand.

Everyone is laughing and making random comments. I'm shocked that he is acting like this. However, it is sexy that he wants me this bad. He really doesn't give a damn who knows.

"Ok guys, I guess I gotta go! Daddy is ready."

"Sis, shittttttttttttt. Yeah, he ready, but are you ready?"

I scoot my chair back and get out of my seat. Adontis has not let my hand go. With a smile, I say, *"If you stay ready you ain't never got to get ready."*

"You better preach!"

We all laugh. Adontis and I tell everyone goodnight and we leave them at the restaurant. Now that we have parted ways from the rest of the group. Its love making time. We get back to the room and both of us are feeling right. Adontis slides his jacket off and sits it on the sofa.

"Damn ma. You're beautiful. I really appreciate all that you did for me shorty."

In my Spanish accent, *"De nada papi."*

He turns his head sideways and looks at me surprised. Then he responds back to me in Spanish. Which turns me on hearing my man speak another language. It's so damn sexy.

"Teresita es que tú?"

"Si, papi," I say with a smile!

I am untying the halter-top straps of my dress. He is unbuttoning and removing his shirt watching me as he is licking his lips. With my forefinger, I beckon him to come over to me. As he walks over to me, I turn away from him. He pushes me up against the wall and slides my panties off.

My face is pressed up on the wall, while his lips are pressed against my neck. He is biting my neck as he slides his hands around the front of my body and he begins squeezing and pinching my nipples. I slide my hands behind me to find his belt buckle. After loosening the buckle, I unbutton his pants.

I slide my hands into his pants then into his boxers. Inside I find that he is risen to the occasion. My dress falls to the floor and I step out of it. I begin to stroke his dick with my hands. He is going from biting to kissing to sucking on my neck, lips and breast. He begins to slide one hand down my body to my pussy. I spread my legs apart for him as he begins to rub on my clitoris. He has me going and I'm dripping wet. He then slides one finger, then two fingers into my pussy. He is stroking me with his fingers and I'm moaning out his name.

"Aye, papi."

He spins me around and lifts me up by my waist. He is wearing a smile. I see the passion in his eyes and it drives me crazy. I wrap my legs around him. We are kissing while I'm rubbing on his chest. He's biting my lips and sucking on me. He glides in me and makes love to me. Each stroke is deeper and deeper. Harder and harder. With one hand gripping on my ass, he takes the other hand and begins playing with my clitoris.

I think I am about to burst. He continues in a circular motion rubbing my clitoris while he is stroking my pussy. I don't know if I can take much more. I'm in ecstasy with him. The way he takes control, commands my body to lose control. I'm trying to hold it and wait for him, but I can't. I squirt all over him. He smiles at me.

"Uh huh. Yeah! Estas tan mojada mami." All I can do is moan in his ears. The pleasure is so great. He is not ready yet. He is grinning at me. *"¿De quién es el coño?"*

I mumble out, *"Es tuyo papi."*

He pumps me even harder. He sensually whispers in my ear. *"No puedo escucharte. ¿Dije de quine de nuevo quién es el coño?"*

I can see he's proud of himself for how he's doing me. I'm proud of him too. Daddy putting in work. He's making my body respond in ways I didn't know was possible. He continues to stroke me and I begin to feel it in the pit of my stomach, I'm orgasming, again. My nails dig into his back. I lean my head back.

"Oh mierda!" There is a lot of heavy breathing between the both of us. ¡I scream out, "Es tuyo papi!"

"Me gusta esa mierda mami."

The more I speak to him in Spanish the harder he goes. He's roaring and making all kinds of sounds. Our bedroom sounds like a damn jungle because all types of animals are coming out of him. I love his animalistic behavior. He's hitting my g spot repeatedly his lips meet mines and he begins biting on my bottom lip. The animal is coming out of him. It's coming out of me too. There goes that feeling, it roars out of me and again, I cum.

I scream out his name, *"ADONTIS!"*

"Damn shorty. Te quiero."

He's still making love to me. He catches my lip in between his and begins kissing me. He slides his tongue in and I slide mine into his. My nails are digging into his back. I can't believe it, I'm about to cum again. I bite down on his lip as another orgasm slips out of me. I need a few moments to catch my breath before I respond.

"Damn daddy. Yo también te quiero."

I can't even keep my languages straight. Hell, I don't even think I'm still on earth. He just took me on an ecstasy ride to Heaven. He smiles as he squeezes me. He's bracing himself, as he cums right in me. I'm glad I'm back on the pill. He does not pull out instantly and I can feel him throbbing in me. While he stays in me, I continue to squeeze my vaginal muscles around his dick. This extends his orgasm. I feel him clutching my waist as it explodes out of him. I lay my head against his chest as he is still holding me up.

"Damn baby, you worked the shit out of me."

He smiles. *"That's what I am supposed to do. Je t'aime."* He kisses me on the lips. This motherfucker just switched languages. Shit we was just in Spain, now he's taking my ass to France. Shit I'm gon follow him there.

"Je t'aime aussi bébé."

He smiles at me, *"Damn girl that's sexy as shit. Daddy like to hear you talk that shit."*

"Je sais."

He plants another kiss on me and then carries me over to the bed. Pulls back the covers and lays me in the bed. He lays right behind me and holds me in his arms.

September 8, 2007

After making love Adontis and I both fall asleep. I awake in his arms and feel his dick hard against my ass. He is rubbing on my clit and his lips are pressed against my neck. I look over to the clock to see it's about 4am. I am tired as hell. The love making session we had tonight went on for almost two hours. We've only been to sleep for about three hours. I look over my shoulder at him like what the hell are you doing. He's smiling back at me.

"Round two."

While wiping my eyes, I'm shaking my head. Hell, I still haven't awakened fully. *"Adontis baby I'm tired. You can't be serious,"* as my voice cracks? Damn I guess with all that screaming I did; I lost my voice.

He pushes his dick up against me harder. *"This feel serious enough to you?"*

I know I am not going to get any sleep anytime soon. I roll over to face him. He is giving me very naughty and dirty looks. This conversation just got serious. Why the hell is he still horny and why is he horny at 4am? His ass should still be asleep. I know I'm tired as hell after how he did me.

In a very sleepy voice with my voice still cracking, I say, *"Baby, I'm tired."*

"And you can go back to sleep as soon as you and I cum again."

He starts kissing on my lips and feeling and rubbing on my titties. He begins to suck on my lips in between kissing me. He slides his tongue in my mouth and I slide mines in his. So much for me getting any sleep. It's his birthday after all. I'm already moist.

He is sucking my tongue as he slides his fingers in my pussy. He is gliding his fingers in and out of me. Slowly. Faster. Faster. Faster. I'm breathing heavily. He rolls onto his back and lifts me up on top of him. I'm kissing him on his neck and his chest as we slide him into me. I begin to ride him. I feel him deep inside of me.

"Damn baby your pussy feels so good."

He is rubbing and sucking on my titties. I didn't want to have this second round, but hell it's worth it. I'm moaning out in ecstasy. He flips me over and gets on top of me. He is going in deeper and deeper and I begin to feel that great feeling. I feel it deep in my belly as it begins to creep out. The excitement of the pleasure that is cumming. A great joy comes over me. I'm moaning louder and louder. As my orgasm comes multiple times in waves.

"Whose pussy is this?"

I'm moaning. Oohs and ahhs escape my mouth. He puts his fingers on my clit and begins rubbing it. *"I said whose pussy is this?"*

When he does that, I don't know what to do. The feeling is indescribable. I have no control over my bodily functions anymore. More waves of orgasms come, each longer and stronger.

As I'm reaching my orgasms' peak, I cry out, *"It's yours daddy. Damn its yours."*

I guess he helped me find my voice, literally. He cums right after me. I feel him squeeze me tightly as he has his release and makes the noise that he makes.

"Damn ma I love you," is all he says.

He slides out of me, we separate. We both need to regain our composure and we both need a cooling down. *"I love you too, Daddy."*

After cooling down, he pulls me close to him. He wraps his arms around me and we drift off to sleep.

We were supposed to have breakfast with our guest this morning, but after round two I knew, we weren't going to make it. I texted Aisha at round 8am when I got up for a potty break and told her that they should go without us, we'd meet them for lunch. It's after twelve noon and I'm still fast asleep. Adontis actually wakes me up.

"*Shorty get up. We got a few hours left until check out.*"

He is fully dressed. I can't lie, the way he put it on me last night, I'm never letting his ass go. I have a big smile on my face when I wake up. Shit he worked me like it was my birthday. It was his birthday, but I got the gift. I laugh to myself and continue to smile as I roll out of bed.

With a grin on his face, "*What you smiling so hard for ma?*"

"*It's a beautiful day; the sun is shining and the birds are chirping.*" As I get out of bed I lean over and give him a kiss. I'm butt naked and he is looking at me like he's a starving man and I'm filet mignon again.

He starts laughing, "*I think it's more like, daddy put it on that ass.*" He smacks me across the ass and smiles.

I smile back at him as I begin to bite my bottom lip. The memory of last night and the early morning events run through my mind. About to give myself a mindgasm. That's a mental orgasm.

"*You was aight,*" I say.

"*Oh, just aight? I need to refresh your memory, huh? We gon miss check out time.*" As I'm laughing, he pulls me in close to him and begins kissing me.

I kiss him then pull back laughing. "*I remember. A refresher is not needed or we will never make it out of this room.*"

"*I don't see the problem.*"

"*Our guest came here to spend time with us.*"

"*They'll understand.*"

I smile at him. I wiggle my way out of his grasp. "*Stop. I'm going in the shower. You can take the bags to the car.*" I begin getting my outfit together and toiletries for the day, packing my other items back up and then I zip my luggage. "*Ok my luggage is good to go.*"

"*Ok ma. I'll get it in the car.*" He walks up behind me and kisses my neck. His arms are wrapped around me while his hands are rubbing on my inner thighs. "*You need some help in the shower?*"

I burst out laughing, "*Stop being nasty. No thank you baby I got it. Matter fact I'm locking you out the bathroom.*"

He smiles, "*Why you wanna do that? I can't watch you shower? I enjoy the view.*"

"*Because we gotta check out. And no, you can't watch.*" I slide his hands from off of my thighs and wiggle from his arms again. I spin to face him. "*I love you and I'm going in the shower. See you when I get out.*" I lean forward and kiss his lips. He squeezes my ass with both hands before giving it a smack.

"*Ok ma.*"

I don't exit the restroom until I am fully dressed. We make it out of the room before check out time, checkout and then head to the beach house. We make it there around 1:30. The crew is chilling waiting for us.

"*Hello everyone. Sorry we are late it's Adontis' fault. And sorry we missed breakfast. I hope you guys enjoyed it.*"

He looks at me in shock that I threw him under the bus. *"It's my fault? How is it my fault ma? I woke you up. You slept in til twelve noon."*

I start laughing and flash a smile. *"If you gon tell a story, tell the whole story. You need me to tell the truth for you baby?"*

He smiles. *"That is the truth. You kept me up all night last night. Then when you finally let me go to sleep you wake me up four o'clock this morning talking about round two."*

I can't stop laughing. *"You are such a liar. That's what you did. I'm the innocent one here."*

Everyone is laughing. Shaun looks at me, *"Tasha, I don't believe him for a second. I know you the good one here."*

"Thank you, Shaun."

Adontis is laughing, *"Bro how you just gon sell me out like that?"*

"Gotta stick up for my sis. Sorry bro. Can't have you slandering her name like that. You trying to sully her reputation. Plus, I'm yo bro, I know yo ass is nasty."

We all start laughing, *"Exactly Shaun. That's what I put up with. But I love him anyway so I think I'll keep him."* I lean in and kiss Adontis on the lips. *"Love you babe."*

We laugh and joke around some more then we head out for lunch, shopping, dinner and clubbing. We make it back to our resort well after 2am. We are all too pooped to party. We head straight to our rooms and to bed.

September 9, 2007

Today is our last day here. Our flights leave out tomorrow and its back to our regular lives. We do breakfast at the house and we spend the morning talking and telling stories and just having a good time. I can see Adontis is happy and that makes me happy. We've been through a lot this year and I hope the worse is behind us because I know we have a bright future ahead of us.

Around noon we get ready to head out for lunch, followed by some sightseeing. When we return to the house, we get in our bathing suits and hit the beach. It feels good out. After laying in the sun for a while we rent some jet skis and get in the water. We have a few races and its nothing, but fun. With hours spent at the beach we retire to the beach house for showers and dinner.

We have a nice candlelit dinner catered at the house and it is romantic. It is outside under the stars and I see all of the couples are enjoying themselves and that makes me happy. This is what this trip is all about. Celebrating my baby's birthday and just having a good time. This trip has been especially good for Adontis and I. We have reconnected in a way that has brought us even closer than before we had our disconnect.

The remainder of the night is spent under the stars. We end up getting back in our bathing suits and get in the hot tub and the pool. We play a few question games. Like how well you know your mate and we all do pretty well. All the couples are booed up and the night begins to end when each couple one by one begins to disappear. Adontis and I are hugged up and making out when Aisha and Boris head into the house.

"Goodnight, guys see you in the morning," she looks over at us and we are in our own world.

I pull back from Adontis, *"Goodnight sis."* They head inside and it's just Adontis and I outside. *"Ok, babe everyone has left, I guess we should head to bed too."*

We are sitting in the hot tub and Adontis unties the top of my bathing suit from around my neck. *"Anytime, anyplace baby."*

I smile at him. *"You so nasty."*

"Yep. And you like me like this." He unties the back of my bathing suit top and it falls in the jacuzzi. He licks his lips and does his ear-to-ear grin. *"Anytime, anyplace."*

He begins sucking on my neck and kissing on my titties. He lays a towel down around the edge of the hot tub, behind where I am standing in the hot tub. While still in the hot tub, he lifts me up out of the jacuzzi and sits me on the towel along the edge with my legs dangling in the water. He places my towel dress around my back, pulls it around the front and closes the Velcro closure.

I'm not sure what he is doing. I begin to get up. I guess he changed his mind and wants to go in. He grabs my hips and stops me from standing. *"What are you doing ma?"* Still grinning at me, *"I didn't tell you to go anywhere."*

He quickly snatches my bathing suit bottom off. He slides me closer to the edge of the hot tub. He gets closer to me and I feel his tongue begin to lick my pussy. He slides his tongue in and out of me rapidly and I'm moaning his name. His tongue slides up to my clitoris and he is making love to her with his tongue. I'm orgasming repeatedly as I scream out his name.

I take off my towel and slip back in the jacuzzi with him. I'm biting my bottom lip and I'm ready to give it to him. I slide my hands in his swim trunks and I can feel him hard as a rock. *"Take em off. I want you naked,"* I say as I tug at his trunks. He slides out of them and walks up on me. He has me pinned against the edge of the jacuzzi. I see from the look in his eyes he is ready to put it on me. He lifts me up against the wall ready to stick it in. I stop him.

Confused he says, *"What's the matter ma?"*

"Nothing. It's my turn." I can tell he is confused and has no idea what I mean. So, I elaborate. *"Your turn to get out of the hot tub and sit on the towel."*

He smiles at me. *"Oh yeah? You ain't saying nothing, but a word."*

He hops out of the hot tub so fast I'm afraid he is going to hurt himself. I walk up in between his legs and begin stroking his dick with my hand. Stroking leads to licking, which leads to sucking and ends in slurping. This time I'm prepared for him to cum and when I know he's cumming I get out of the way and he cums all over the jacuzzi. He hops back in the jacuzzi and finishes me off. When we finish, he slides back into his trunks and I slide back into my towel dress.

We clean up and then go inside and have round two in the shower. We eventually get around to washing and we call it a night then head to bed.

September 10, 2007

Adontis' friends from New York have early afternoon flights. Their flights are at 12:30pm. The rest of our flights aren't until 6pm this evening. We all get up and have breakfast at the house and spend time relaxing. Around eleven, we head to our rooms to get dressed for the day. After getting dressed the men pack the luggage in our rental cars. Brandon, Cassie, Chuck and Liza say their goodbyes to us.

Liza says, *"Tasha it was so nice to finally meet you. We always chat and trip online. Thank you for inviting us. We have got to do this again."*

Cassie, says, *"Yes it was. We've exchanged numbers now too, so we don't need the men to get together."*

I smile, *"You are so right. It was nice to meet you ladies too. Thank you, guys, so much for coming man I had a blast with ya'll and I can't wait to get together again."*

Aisha smiles, *"I knew you guys would love Tasha. I'm glad we all had such a good time. No drama just fun."*

We all hug and we see them out. Adontis says, *"Thank ya'll all so much for coming. This is the best birthday I ever had."* He looks at me and pulls me in his arms. *"Thank you, ma, for putting all of this together."*

Brandon and Chuck exclaim, *"Of course brother. And a big thanks to you Tasha for inviting us. We need more trips like this."*

"Yeah, we do bro. And we gotta make sure it happens," Shaun says.

They finish having their bro moment. Adontis ends with, *"Ya'll have a safe trip and let us know when ya'll get back home safe."*

Brandon says, *"Yeah bro we will, and ya'll do the same."*

The rest of us spend the rest of our day doing some sightseeing and light shopping. Followed by lunch. By the time lunch is over, it's time to head to the airport so that we can catch our flights back home. I'm going to need a vacation, from this vacation, but I had a really good time. Most importantly my baby enjoyed himself and that makes me happy.

chapter 23

ThanksForGiving, Me Hell

November 18, 2007

This day is about being thankful, but what about the things you are not thankful for?

Adontis and I have been able to stay on track since his birthday and things are good. Our sex life is great and I am happy. I haven't thought much about my abortion because I don't want to be depressed. I've pushed it back far in my mind. I know I need to finish dealing with it, but avoidance has been working best so far. I don't want to mess up the good space that Adontis and I are in by reliving or thinking about the abortion I had. I will deal with it, but not today. I want to get through the holidays first.

I have finally finished decorating our house. I spent a whole lot of money to do it, but our home is fully furnished. Never tell me I don't have a budget. I'm over the top and I've went over the top decorating our home, but the shit looks good as hell. Adontis was satisfied with the outcome. He didn't fuss or trip about the amount of money I spent, he just let me do my thing.

Over the last few months, Adontis and I discussed me taking on a more active role within Fresh. This business will be something we can leave our future children.

While I'm out of school I spend most of my free time at Fresh helping Adontis run the business and building it up. Which includes marketing and advertising. I've implemented a new business plan and everything is going well.

Once I get back in school I will still be hands on with the company. I know I will have to find a balance because I am always there. I handle all of the accounting including payroll. I also handle all advertising, hiring, firing and so much more. I don't mind though. He is my man and I'm in this for the long haul with him.

It's the beginning of the holiday season. I've made a deal with Adontis that we'd spend Thanksgiving with his family and Christmas with mine. Unfortunately, his mother is a part of his family. I've been spending the day packing. We have an early flight tomorrow morning. I'm not looking forward to this trip, but Adontis is all smiles. I haven't seen or spoken to his mom since we first met. I've spoken to his dad though. He calls and checks in on us and we call him.

While we are in New York, he is going to take some time to check in on Fresh and see how things are going. I'm going to need a few prayers said for me. I know his mother is going to work on my nerves.

November 19, 2007

After almost three hours, our flight touches down in New York. I try to wear a smile, but I'm not happy. The things we do for love. Adontis and I take a taxi from the airport and head to his parents'. When he moved, Adontis left his Ferrari at his parents' house. He drives it when he comes into town. When we arrive, we notice that Melanie and Shaun are already here. Aisha will be arriving tomorrow morning.

We are spending five long days in New York. I'm dreading it. To make matters worse, we are staying at his parents' house. Adontis put his house up for rent when he moved. I really wanted to stay at a hotel, but Adontis was against it. He wanted to be around all of his family. Thanksgiving will be big. His aunts, uncles, cousins and grandparents will all attend. I'm really meeting the whole family. Listen carefully when I say, I don't want to be here. We finally pull up to his parent's house.

He looks over at me and says, *"Come on now ma. Cheer up. It'll be fun."*

With a fake smile, I look over to him and say, *"Yay."* Under my breath, I say, *"About as fun as having my head cut off."*

"What you say ma?"

"Oh nothing."

When we walk through the door, his mother greets him with a hug. She actually doesn't acknowledge my presence. I take a deep breath and I keep my cool. Again, I say, *"Hello Mrs. Lamentez."*

She looks at me as if talking to me would just kill her. Adontis looks over to her and says, *"Ma, Tasha said hello."*

She rolls her eyes as if to say so. I look over at Adontis. He looks like oh damn this shit ain't gone work. His mother then walks off, without a word to me. I look over to Adontis and point towards the front door.

"Outside now! We need to talk."

He looks at me like really. *"Ma-"*

I cut him off. *"Ma nothing let's go. Outside now."*

He opens the door and we head back outside. Its winter in New York and outside is warmer then inside his parent's house. I'm very agitated and pissed as hell. I didn't fly all these hours to deal with this bullshit. I told Adontis before we came to talk with his mom. He said he did and now this.

"Adontis, I'm trying to make the effort, but your mother is-"

I stop before I call his mother something, I can't take back, like bitch. Even though that's exactly what she is acting like. I don't want to talk about his mother like that; at least not to him.

"I'm going to say this and I'm done talking. My next steps will be action."

"What the hell does that mean?"

"If you would let me finish, I'll tell you."

He looks at me like I'm crazy, *"Watch that smart ass mouth. I'm your man not your child so watch how you talk to me."*

I roll my eyes, but he's right.

"Don't be rolling your eyes at me either. I saw that shit."

"I wasn't trying to hide it, but you're right."

"Damn, did hell just freeze over? You admitted I was right. One point for the men."

I ignore his comments. *"I'm not spending five days up here with her attitude or with being treated that way. She couldn't even say hello to me. You need to talk with your mom again. Even though she's been rude as hell to me since day one, I've never disrespected her. If this is what this week holds, I'll get my black ass back on a plane to my family right now."*

He rubs his hands against his forehead like damn why me. *"Ok ma. I'll talk with her. But your ass ain't going nowhere. I'm gon straighten it out."*

"Adontis I'm so serious right now. You better."

"Ma. I hear you damn! I said I am going to talk to her. Can we go back in the house now?"

We head inside and I go to sit in the family room where I find Melanie, Shaun and Mr. Lamentez watching the game. I greet everyone with a hello. In return, I'm greeted back. I sit on the couch alone. Adontis has gone off to talk with his mom. I wish Aisha was here. She knows her mom is crazy.

I pull out my phone and text Aisha about what has just transpired. She's not really surprised. Her main advice to me is that Adontis is going to have to put a stop to it.

> **Aisha:** *Mom has been doing this shit for years. If he really loves you, he needs to make her respect you. He isn't in high school anymore. That shit is so old.*

> **Tasha:** *That's what I told him.*
> *I said if I'm not going to be respected, I'll be on the next flight out of here. So, he's talking to her now.*

> **Aisha:** *That's good. But don't do nothing drastic. Cause I want you there when I get there.*

> **Tasha:** *And I can't wait for you to get here.*

"Tasha, come here for a minute ma," Adontis yells through the house.
"Ok," I say.

> **Tasha:** *Your brother just called me. Wish me luck. Love you sis. Travel safe.*

> **Aisha:** *You got this. Stay put and I'll see you when I get there. Love you too sis.*

I get up and follow the sound of Adontis' voice to the kitchen.

He looks over to his mom. *"Ma, you got something to say to Tasha?"*

"Hello Tasha. I apologize for earlier. How are you?"

"Apology accepted. I am fine. Thank you."

I really don't care how she is so I don't ask. I know she doesn't really care about how I am. Hell, I don't even think her apology is sincere, but I'll play nice as long as she does. Adontis stands with a smile on his face. He puts his arms around each of us.

"The two most important women to me in this world." He kisses his mom on the cheek. *"I love both of you. Ma, where you want Tasha and I to sleep so we can get settled in?"*

"You can sleep in your old bedroom and she can sleep in the guest bedroom at the end of the hall."

"Ma, really?"

"Don't act like you don't know the rules. Nothing has changed. Ya'll aren't married."

"Ma, you do know we live together!"

"Yes, I do. And don't you think that's enough sin?"

I'm taken aback. I've heard it all. *"Baby that's fine. I just want to get settled in. Can you get my bags and show me where the room is?"*

Adontis looks at his mom in disbelief. She doesn't pay him any attention instead she walks out of the kitchen and heads to the family room with everyone else. I walk to the foyer with Adontis. He grabs our luggage and leads the way to the elevator. We make it up to the guest bedroom where Adontis unloads my luggage from his hands. I walk in behind him and he closes and locks the door.

"I can't believe this shit. Separate rooms. Moms is tripping."

"It's no biggie baby. If my parents were still here, we wouldn't be sharing a room at their house either."

He sits on the bed and pulls me on to his lap. *"I'll be in here tonight with you anyway. It don't really matter."*

"*No, you won't. Your mother already doesn't like me. I don't need her thinking I'm a slut too.*"

"*Well, you do get pretty slutty for me.*"

I start laughing. "*That's supposed to be a secret.*"

He smiles, "*Your secret is safe with me.*"

"*Uh huh. I bet.*" I look up at him and give him a peck on the lips. "*I love you.*"

"*I love you back.*"

While we were talking, he's been feeling and rubbing on my thighs. He decides to start unbuttoning my shirt.

"*Adontis, stop that.*"

Very naughtily, he smiles at me. "*Come on. Right here. Right now.*"

"*Baby don't do this.*" He's unbuttoning my pants and he begins kissing on my breast and unhooking my bra.

"*Don't do what ma? I'm just trying to help you relax. Daddy knows what you need.*"

"*What if someone comes up here?*"

"*Don't worry, I'll make it quick.*"

I try to get up from his lap. "*Oh well then I really can't.*"

He pulls me back. "*Don't worry, you'll be fully satisfied.*"

While I'm sitting back on his lap he begins kissing on my neck and sucking. Sucking leads to nibbling and biting. His hands go down the front of my pants and he starts rubbing my clit. I'm moaning and I begin kissing and sucking on his neck. He kisses his way down to my breast. The sucking and nibbling resumes there. He stands up with me in his hands and lays me on the bed. I take my shirt off and get out of my bra as he pulls my pants and panties off me. My legs are spread wide and he goes headfirst and begins to lick my clit.

He's kissing and sucking on her and taking me on an ecstasy ride. I'm wet and he continues until I orgasm. He flips me over and changes positions. I'm on my knees, with my legs spread and my booty is arched in the air. I look at him over my shoulder and give him a dirty look as he slides into me. He is riding me from the back and pumping hard. I'm using the pillow to mask my moans. He is playing with my clit again as he rides me from behind. He strokes her continually and rapidly and I can't hold it anymore. I cum. He pulls out of me, rolls over on his back and beckons me to get on top. I climb on top of him. I grab his dick tight. I sit on top as I slide him into me.

I begin to ride him. I start slowly as I begin kissing him. His chest, his neck and his lips. As time goes by, I go faster and faster. I begin to sit up on him while I'm riding. He sits up to. I'm bouncing on him with my head laying back. I feel him so deep in me. He is kissing my neck and sucking on me. I begin rubbing on my clit. As I ride him. He's playing with my titties and I ride him harder and faster. He clinches my waist and squeezes me tight as he orgasms and I orgasm with him. I look at him and he is wearing a smile.

"*Damn ma.*"

"*What?*"

"*Girl. You did that shit. Damn I'm still trying to catch my breath.*"

I smile back at him. "*I thought that's how you liked it daddy.*"

"That's definitely how daddy likes it." He leans in and kisses my lips. *"I love you so much girl. Damn I love you."*

"I love you more."

I get off of him and lay beside him in the bed. We lay there and cool off for a moment. He lays behind me and pulls me in his arms. He holds me tight and I fall asleep in his arms.

When l awake, it's about 2pm in the afternoon. Adontis has left the room and I'm alone. Adontis really put in work. I get my towel, washcloth, etc. and head to the bathroom inside the bedroom. Before stepping in the shower, I hear a knock at the door. I slip into my robe and open the door. On the other side, I find Mrs. Lamentez. She looks me up and down. Therefore, I return the favor.

"We've decided to go out to lunch. I told Adontis I'd awake you. We're all getting ready now."

"Ok great, thank you. I was just getting in the shower. I will be right down."

While I'm in the shower I'm thinking about how Adontis just blew my back out. He knows how to work it. Once again, he was right. I needed that. I'm so relaxed. His mom can't even get to me now. Everyone heads out the door and we all pile into Adontis dad's Escalade. Adontis and I sit in the third row and give the second row to Shaun and Melanie. Personally, I'd have preferred if we drove separately. I'm trying to behave so I'll just go with the flow.

While we are riding to the restaurant Adontis is flirting with me. He leans over and whispers in my ear, *"Damn ma. You look so damn sexy. I wanna give you some more of what I gave you earlier."*

I start blushing. *"You need to stop that. You're a bad boy."*

He licks his lips. *"Yeah, I know I am."* He starts rubbing on my thighs. *"You wanna see how bad I really am?"*

I can't stop laughing and giggling. I look up when I hear his mom clear her throat. I find her staring at us from the overhead vanity mirror. I look at him like really, your mom is tripping.

"What's up ma," he says.

"You wanna share with everyone else?"

"Naw not at all. This a private convo, we good."

Shaun starts laughing. He looks back at Adontis. *"Boy, you stupid."*

Mrs. Lamentez says, *"Oh hush up Shaun. Adontis it's rude to whisper."*

"Well, if I didn't whisper, ya'll could hear me. And like I said it's a private conversation." She glares back at Adontis in the mirror. *"Ma come on stop tripping."* I silently sit back and watch. I want to see how this is going to turn out.

"I got your tripping Adontis De'Ontay Lamentez."

He smiles back at her. *"I love you ma."*

She smiles. *"I love you too baby."*

I roll my eyes. She is truly crazy. We spend the rest of the ride with conversations about life. After about five hours out and about we return to the house. We spent some time at Fresh and did some light shopping. We've rented some movies and picked up some takeout for dinner. We are supposed to watch the movies together as a family. This ought to be fun.

I sit on the love seat alone and Adontis comes over to join me. He pulls me from out of my seat and sits in my place then pulls me into his lap. He wraps his arms around me. The movie starts and I can feel his mom staring at me. I decide to give her a show. I tilt my head back and give Adontis a nice kiss on the lips.

"I love you."

"I love you too ma."

When I end the lip lock with Adontis I see her staring directly at me. I flash her a smile and turn my attention to the movie. I feel her give me the stare down for a while longer. I just take Adontis' hands and wrap them around me tighter. If she is going to continue to act the way she acts, I'm going to do whatever I can to piss her off. After the first movie ends, Mr. Lamentez is ready to go to bed. He coaxes his wife to do the same.

"Come on Marilyn baby. Let's go to bed and leave these kids alone."

"I'm not sleepy yet. You go, I'll be up later."

"Come on woman let's go."

He grabs her by the hand and leads her upstairs. I let out a sigh of relief. There's only so much of that woman that I can take at a time. I get cozy on the couch and before the second movie ends, I'm asleep. Adontis lifts me up and carries me to bed. He lays me in my bed and tucks me in.

"Goodnight baby. I'll see you in the morning."

"Don't worry. I'll be back. I'm going in the shower."

"Adontis baby-"

He cuts me off. *"Don't worry. Go back to sleep."*

November 20, 2007

I awake in the middle of the night to go to the little girl's room and I find Adontis holding me in his arms. I slip from out of his arms and from under the covers. I can't believe he's gotten in the bed with me anyway. I don't want any more drama with his mom. When I get back in the bed, I wake him.

"Why are you in the bed with me?"

"Ma what you mean?"

"I mean what I said. You know your mother is crazy. I don't feel like dealing with her crazy cause you in here with me."

"I told you I would be. Go back to sleep and stop fussing." He pulls me into his arms.

"Adontis."

"Shhh." He puts his fingers over my lips. *"Go back to sleep."*

After drifting back to sleep, a few hours later I awake alone. I go looking for Adontis and he is nowhere to be found. I call him on his cell.

"Where the hell are you?"

"Damn. Hello to you too."

"Where the hell are you Adontis?"

"I'm at Fresh."

"Why in the hell did you leave me here alone?"

"I figured you and ma could do some bonding."

I roll my eyes. *"Ah no. Why the hell did you do that?"*

"Ma stop tripping. Ya'll need to spend some time together without me and get to know each other. Enjoy yourself. Besides Aisha will be there soon."

"I don't want to hear that. I'm so pissed with you right now. When are you coming back?"

"Later this afternoon or evening."

"You wrong for this."

"Wrong for what, wanting my mom and girlfriend to get along? Just stop tripping and get to know her."

"I don't wanna hear that."

"Well, I gotta go. I got work to do."

"Adontis."

"Ma, I love you. I'll talk to you later."

Before I can say anything else, he hangs up. I take a deep breath, get cleaned up and head downstairs. I find Mrs. Lamentez and her staff in the kitchen.

"Good morning. Can I help with anything?"

"No, we have it. Thank you."

"Ok. Well, I guess I'll go in the other room."

My voice trails off. Everyone else is gone. Melanie and Shaun went out and Mr. Lamentez is running errands. I pull out my phone to give Aisha a call. The doorbell rings.

"Would you like for me to get that?"

"Yes, please do."

I pull the door open to find Aisha. I'm so happy to see her. I hug her. *"I'm so glad you're finally here."*

"Me too. Where is everyone?"

I tell her everyone's location and she goes in to the kitchen to greet her mom and the staff. Afterward she says, *"Ok T. Since Adontis went and left you lets go out and have some fun."*

"You must have read my mind."

Aisha and I take her bags up to her room. We tell her mom that we're heading out. We hit the town and do what we do best; go shopping. We make it back to her parent's house after 11pm. Time got away from us. We hadn't realized it was this late. When we pull into the driveway is when I check my phone. I see several missed calls from Adontis along with voicemails and text.

I look to Aisha, *"Oh snap, Adontis been calling me. I didn't hear my phone ring."*

She smiles, *"Well serves him right for leaving you."*

We both laugh as we get out of the car. Adontis is heading out of the house and heading my way.

"Tasha, where the hell you been? Why you ain't answer my calls?"

Before I can respond Aisha interjects, *"Hello to you too big bro,"* He looks over to her and doesn't speak. Aisha looks at me with a slight smirk on her face. *"Ok T, well I guess I am going to go in the house and let you two speak."*

I smile at Aisha and say, *"Ok. See you inside."*

"Something funny Tasha?"

"Yeah, you are."

"I'm not laughing and I'm still waiting on you to answer my damn questions."

"Well, Aisha and I went out, we had an early lunch, we went shopping and then we had a late dinner. I didn't answer your calls because I didn't hear my phone ring. Time kind of got away from us."

"How very convenient. I leave you here so you go out and ignore me all day?"

"Adontis, I did not ignore you. I told you I did not hear my phone ring."

"That's some bullshit."

"I don't want to argue with you, I'm tired. I just want to get cleaned up and relax." I open the back door to get my bags out of the car.

"I know all of them damn bags ain't yours."

"You told me to hang with Aisha. Did you think we wouldn't go shopping? I only used one of your credit cards."

He shakes his head. For a moment, he doesn't say anything. He just stands there speechless. He reaches in the car and helps me with my bags.

"How much money did you spend?"

I look at him like he's crazy, then I shrug my shoulders. *"How in the hell should I know? You'll see when you get the statement. Unless you want me to give you all of the receipts."*

He shakes his head, *"Never mind."*

"Ok then."

November 21, 2007

We head into the house. Mr. and Mrs. Lamentez have both gone to bed. Shaun and Melanie are relaxing on the couch. Aisha has gone up to her room to put her things away. Adontis and I take my bags up to my room and head back downstairs. We spend the rest of the night on the card table playing a few games of spades. Adontis and I are on teams against Shaun and Melanie. Aisha chills and watches us play. We play into the wee hours of the night. We finally call it quits after 3am and head to bed. Adontis heads to my room.

"Baby you need to go to your room."

"My room is wherever you are. Don't act like you don't want me next to you."

I stare at him for a moment. *"Adontis I'm serious. I do want you in here with me. I'm trying to respect your mother's wishes."*

"So am I. Don't worry about her wishes, think of my wishes. Hush and come on to bed." He begins to pull the covers back and climbs into bed.

"I'm exhausted I don't feel like fussing with you anymore. Do what you want. I'm going in the shower."

"Ok I will. I'm going to sleep goodnight love."

"Goodnight."

I step out of the shower and find Adontis fast asleep. He looks so peaceful when he sleeps. I dry off, put on my nightclothes and slip in the bed next to him. I snuggle up to him and he puts his arms around me. I love him so much, words can't say.

The next morning, I awake to a knock at my door.

"Rise and shine its breakfast time." I hear Mrs. Lamentez's voice from outside of my room door.

"Ok. I will be down in a few," I respond.

"Ok."

I look over my shoulder to see Adontis still in the bed with me. Now how am I going to get him out of here without being seen? I roll over and gently shake him.

"Good morning sleepy head. Breakfast is ready and your mom is in the hallway making wake up calls."

He flashes a smile to me. *"Good morning beautiful."* He leans over and kisses my lips.

"Did you hear what I said?"

"Yeah, I heard you. We'll be down in a minute."

"What if she knocks on your door?"

"Don't worry about it. I got this. Plus, my door is locked so she can't get in there."

He climbs out of bed and begins putting on some clothes. He grabs his cell and texts his mom.

"Ok it's done. Let's go to breakfast. I'm hungry."

"What did you say to her?"

"Does it matter?"

"Yes, it does."

"I'd be down in a minute. I'm on the toilet."

"She bought that?"

"Yeah, why wouldn't she?"

Down at the breakfast table we all get settled, say the blessing and begin eating. I see Mrs. Lamentez looking at me sideways and I don't know why. Hell, at this point, I don't care. I'm here and I'm not going anywhere. She can hate me or love me. It really doesn't matter. Shortly after we finish breakfast, the doorbell rings. Adontis gets up to answer it. From the foyer, he escorts in an older couple. Aisha gets up and runs to them.

"Grandma and Pops, you guys look so good."

She embraces them both in a great big hug. I take a deep breath not sure of how this will go.

I'm unsure of if this is Adontis' Mom's or Dad's parents, until I hear Mr. Lamentez say, *"Mom. Pop. How are you doing?"*

He walks over and hugs his parents. Mr. Lamentez's mom embraces him in a hug.

"My Baby. You look so good son. Honey doesn't he look good?"

"*Yes dear, my boy does look good. Come give your old man a hug. How you doing son?*"

"*Oh Pop, I can't complain.*"

Mrs. Lamentez is sitting in her chair like a mute. Shaun and Melanie move from their seats and greet the grandparents. Adontis walks over to me and grabs my hand. I don't want to go, but I do. He leads me from my chair to his grandparents.

"*Grandma, Pops, I'd like for you to meet someone. This is my beautiful girlfriend.*" I extend my hand to his grandmother.

"*Oh child, put that hand away.*" She opens her arms and embraces me in a great big hug. "*What's your name beautiful?*"

"*I'm Tasha.*"

"*It's nice to meet you. I'm grandma Abigail, but you can call me Grandma. I see why my grandson loves you.*"

I smile and blush a bit. "*I can see why he loves you too. You have such a beautiful presence and spirit.*"

"*Thank you, sweetheart. This here is my husband, Clarence.*"

He smiles at me, "*You can call me Pops. Come here and let me take a look at the young lady that has Adontis' heart.*"

As I am blushing, I walk over to him. "*It's nice to meet you.*"

"*It's nice to meet you too darling.*" He embraces me in a great big hug. "*Alright now Adontis, don't let this one get away.*"

Adontis does that ear-to-ear grin thing. "*Oh, Pops I'm not.*"

"*You bet not or you gon have to answer to me.*"

"*And me too,*" Grandma chimes in.

"*Yes sir. Yes ma'am.*"

I can't help, but to blush. His grandparents' reception of me was better than I ever thought it would be. Pops walks over and hugs Mrs. Lamentez.

"*Hey baby. How are you doing?*"

"*I'm fine Dad.*"

Grandma puts a hand up from where she stands, "*Hi Marilyn.*"

I think to myself wow. Ah, ha Grandma and Mrs. Lamentez don't get along. What are the odds?

"*Come on and have a seat Mom and Pop. We just finished eating breakfast, but we can have something whipped up for you.*"

Adontis and Shaun go outside to get their grandparents bags from out of their car and they take them up to their room. Everyone has a seat back at the table. Shaun and Adontis returns and we all engage in conversation. Shortly after, their breakfast is served to them. While they enjoy their breakfast, we all continue to talk. Mrs. Lamentez is having Thanksgiving dinner catered. That's totally different than my family's tradition, but I don't say anything. When in Rome…you know the rest.

Grandma says, "*So you're having this dinner catered, Marilyn? Back in my day, we didn't do no catering. All the women folk got together in the kitchen and fixed dinner.*"

I can see Mrs. Lamentez roll her eyes as soon as Grandma opens her mouth to speak. I'm not ashamed to say I'm enjoying watching Grandma torture the hell out of Mrs. Lamentez. Lord knows she's tortured the hell out of me. In the most bougie way, Mrs. Lamentez responds. Her tone has an air of arrogance along with a tone of, or rather a sense that she thinks she is better than Grandma. In other words, she comes off condescending.

"Yes, Abigail I'm having Thanksgiving dinner catered. We are having so many guests; I thought it best to cater."

Grandma looks at Mrs. Lamentez with a look of disbelief. She responds in a very calming tone. *"Well child this here your house so I guess I'll just be a guest. I suppose it will be ok if I don't make my famous sweet potato pie this year."*

Simultaneously Adontis, Mr. Lamentez, Shaun and Aisha all yell, *"No!"*

Aisha goes even further and says, *"Grandma you know I look forward to your pie every Thanksgiving. You have got to make it."* Adontis, Shaun and Mr. Lamentez all shake their heads in agreement.

"Well babies I doubt that Marilyn has the ingredients for my pie. I would need someone to go to the store."

Again, they all say, *"I'll go."*

Grandma laughs her very beautiful genuine laugh and she says, *"It doesn't matter who goes. Let me write out my list."* She digs in her purse and pulls out a pen and paper.

"Tasha and I will go," Adontis says. I look at him as if to say, Oh really, we will!

Aisha speaks again, *"Well I want to go too, but bro you can drive."*

Next thing I know I find myself in Aisha's rental with Adontis, Aisha, Shaun and Melanie heading to the grocery store. Once we make our way out of the mad house known as the grocery store, we head back to the house. Grandma has changed her clothes and has gotten comfortable. She has on her apron and she has begun making lunch. Mrs. Lamentez is nowhere to be found. Adontis inquiries about his mom and Mr. Lamentez tells him she went upstairs to lie down.

Personally, I hope someone gives the chick a valium. She is constantly and consistently wound up. Ever since Grandma has gotten here, she has been surprisingly quiet and not so much in my face. The remainder of the day seems to fly by. We spend the remainder of the day entertaining and being entertained by Adontis' Grandparents.

November 22, 2007

Bright and early, it's now Thanksgiving morning. I roll over onto Adontis' chest. I kiss him on the lips and he doesn't budge. I begin kissing him all over his face.

"Wake up." I kiss him awake from his sleep. *"Good morning baby. Are you awake?"*

"No, I'm trying to sleep."

"Well sleep time is over. Get up."

I pull the covers back and sit on top of him. He is laying in the bed in the nude. He is sleeping on his back with his arms folded up behind his head. I'm bouncing up and down on him as I'm kissing him.

"Wake up baby."

I feel his nature that is already risen. Bouncing on him the way I did was over kill. His anatomy is always ready early in the morning. As I'm bouncing, he opens his eyes.

"Why don't you give me something to be thankful for on this beautiful Thanksgiving Day?"

"You so nasty."

I give him a mischievous grin, *"So, what's the problem?"*

He grins at me and rolls me over onto my back. He strips me of my boy shorts and camisole. He then begins to place kisses all over my body. He works his way down and he has made it to my kitty kat. Kissing, sucking, licking and blowing her. Ecstasy, as he is pleasuring me. I'm moaning and making sensual sounds as he pleases me.

I hear a knock at my door, but I can't muster out anything other than my moans. He is eating the hell out of me and I know I will cum soon. I try to say yes, but no words come out. I don't hear the sound again so I think nothing else of it. I fall back into ecstasy as Adontis continues to do what he does very well.

Several minutes later, I hear someone outside the bedroom door, but I choose to tune it out. I'm about to orgasm and I refuse to not finish. I am reaching the beginning of a glorious peak. Adontis keeps going as I begin cumming. I hear someone clear their throat and I open my eyes and find Mrs. Lamentez staring at me in disgust. I gasp in disbelief. I don't know how long she has been in here. I try to stop Adontis, whose head is under the sheets, he obviously can't hear a thing. I try to push him away.

While still down there, he says, *"No beg for mercy! You wanted to be thankful right. I'm giving you a reason to thank me."* He begins again.

His mom is still standing there. She hasn't left the room and she is staring at us in total shock. Almost as if, she is frozen in time. I'm trying to muster out the words to tell him to stop between moans, but no words come out. It's crazy because even though I know I shouldn't, my body is responding to the pleasure. Hell, I'm not trying to, but damn it's so good. I'm doing my best to fight back orgasming with his mom standing there.

In between moaning, all I can manage is, *"St- ahh! St- ahh! St- ahh!"* It's so faint he can't hear me. Every time I try to form the word stop, he licks or sucks something that steals my speech away.

"You know this is my pussy," he says as he lifts his head up to look at me.

His mom is still staring at me with fire in her eyes. Now that I have been able to catch a breath, I can only stare back at her in disbelief. I don't know what to say to her. My mouth is gaped open, but I'm unable to speak due to the embarrassment that I feel.

Adontis finally sees my face display a look of sheer horror. He gets his head from under the covers and turns around to see what I am looking at. He stares directly into the face of his mother. She looks at him in disgust. His face is moist with my juices all over it. I'm so ashamed I want to sink into the bed and die.

As if her anger has built up to point in which she is on fire; so that it melts her from her previous frozen position. She spins on her heels without saying a word. She walks out of the room and slams the door. Adontis lays there with his mouth wide open.

"Oh shit. Oh shit. Oh shit. Damn. Ma, why didn't you tell me she was there? Shit, how long was she there?"

He is looking at me and I still can't speak. I'm in total shock. He lays his head down in my bosom. I can't believe it. I'm lying in the bed with my hands over my eyes. At this moment, I wish I could shrivel up and die, just for a little while.

"Adontis, you didn't lock the door when you came in here last night?"

"Damn ma. I forgot."

I put my hand over my mouth in disbelief. *"Your mother just caught you eating my pussy. I can't go down there and face her and your family."*

He lays there just shaking his head. *"Shit ma, I know. Damn."*

I'm thinking to myself in all of that I didn't even get to finish my orgasm. Adontis gets out the bed and slips on his pants and shirt. He heads towards the door.

"Where are you going?"

"I gotta go talk to her and apologize."

"And what should I do? I'm not going down there now."

"Yeah, ma you are. Get on some clothes and let's go."

"No, I'm not. Plus, we have two nights left to stay here. I can't face her after what just happened."

"Well, you gon have to, unless you plan on walking out of my life right here and right now."

I shiver at the thought. I slide out of the bed. *"I need to shower first."*

"Ok, I'll see you when you come down."

"Oh hell no. You gotta wait on me baby. I don't wanna walk down there by myself."

"Alright ma. Hurry up."

He sits back on the bed and begins rubbing his temples as if he is trying to rub the stress away. I gather my things and head to the shower. I am unable to even think clearly. I can't believe my man's mom walked in on us. If we were just having intercourse, I think that would have been a little better. Adontis giving me head and his face covered in me, is the worst.

I step out of the bathroom after I'm fully dressed. I don't want anything remotely close to another sexual moment to happen while I'm here. We head downstairs. Everyone is at the dining room table eating breakfast. We are greeted with a good morning from everyone, except his mom. I just want to run out the door full speed to the nearest airport and get the hell out of New York. Adontis tries to ask his mom for a minute of her time, but she cuts him off before he can.

"I'm busy right now."

He doesn't say anything back to her. Adontis coaxes me to take a seat and he does the same. His mom is giving us the nastiest look I've ever seen. I can't lie, I understand why she is pissed. Now she has a real reason to hate me. Sitting at breakfast, I am unable to eat a thing. I know I am going to have to apologize to her.

Although I don't know why in the hell, she would walk into my room uninvited anyway. I know it is her house, but I am a guest here and that is an invasion of privacy. Hell, if she had just given me five more minutes, I would have been able to speak. If you knock and don't get an answer that doesn't mean come in anyway. It's almost like, if you go searching for something, you are bound to find it. She did. Adontis face down with his face in my pussy. I am pulled from my thoughts when I notice that the rest of the family is looking at the three of us. I think that they can sense the tension. Aisha breaks the silence.

"*I'm so glad to be here with my family. I just want to say I love you all.*"

We all respond back with, "*We love you too.*"

Mrs. Lamentez excuses herself and heads to the kitchen. Grandma looks over at me, "*Baby, why are you not eating? You feeling ok?*"

I try to give her a smile "*Oh, I'm not very hungry, but I feel ok.*" What I really want to say is hell no. I just experienced the most embarrassing moment of my fucking life.

"*Ok baby. I'm just checking on you.*"

"*Thank you, I appreciate it.*" I'm trying so hard to keep it together. I don't want them to read on my face what I really feel.

Adontis sits in his chair enjoying his breakfast. Clearly, he has not lost his appetite. He seems to no longer be as disturbed by what just happened. There is light conversation throughout breakfast and I'm a million miles away mentally.

When breakfast is over, Aisha pulls me to the side. "*You ok? What's going on T?*"

"*No, not really. Your mother just walked in on Adontis and I this morning.*"

Her eyeballs stretch and I see just how much she and Adontis really look alike. She has a slight smirk on her face and then she burst out laughing.

"*Are you serious? Get the hell out of here.*"

I am so agitated with her. "*Aisha, this shit is not funny.*"

"*T, I'm sorry to laugh, but damn. I wasn't expecting that. I was more expecting you to say you were pregnant or something. Anything, but that. What did mom see?*"

"*Let's just say Adontis' head was under the covers.*"

"*Awkward. That shits horrible.*"

"*Really Aisha. That's all you got? This ain't the time. What the hell am I gonna do?*"

"*I'm sorry T. I'm back.*" She has cleared the smile from her face. "*Have ya'll talked to her yet?*"

"*Adontis made a failing attempt to when we came downstairs.*"

"*Failing is right. The way she looked at ya'll sis, damn. Well, I'd recommend that you both apologize and then go from there. How'd she catch ya'll?*"

"*Adontis' dumb ass didn't lock the door when he came in my room last night. She knocked, but I didn't answer. I was busy. Next thing I notice I hear a gasp and I look up to see your mom.*"

"*Wow. That's some crazy shit.*"

"*Tell me about it.*"

Adontis comes in the room and grabs me by the hand. Aisha just smirks at him. He rolls his eyes at her.

"Where are you taking me?"

"We gon go talk to mom."

"No, you go first."

"No, we going together."

I reluctantly let him lead me upstairs to his mom. He knocks on the bedroom door and his dad opens it. It's clear that they have been discussing us. His mom tries to leave the bedroom.

His dad grabs her by the wrist and stops her in her tracks, *"Marilyn stay right here."*

She rolls her eyes, but she doesn't leave. While looking away from us she says, *"What? What do you want? Why are you in here?"*

"Ma, we apologize for what you walked in on. We disrespected your wishes and for that, we apologize. It won't happen again. Against Tasha's judgement and request, I crept into her bedroom last night. If you are going to be angry with anyone, it should be me."

"My apologies also Mrs. Lamentez, for disrespecting you and your home. I allowed Adontis to come in the room with me and I am as much to blame as he is."

As we are speaking, she just stands there glaring at us.

"Marilyn baby, can you accept their apologies?"

She rolls her eyes at us both, *"I'll accept it. I can't even look at either of you right now. I need to go."* She breaks free from Mr. Lamentez and walks out the room. Mr. Lamentez is just staring at us.

"I'm sorry Pop. I didn't mean for ma to see that. I thought I locked the door."

His dad just shakes his head. *"Don't be sorry son, be careful. Now I'm going to have to hear about this shit til the end of damn time."*

Across my face comes shock. I thought he would be pissed. He doesn't seem to care that we did what we did in his home.

"I want to apologize to you also Mr. Lamentez. I didn't mean to disrespect your home."

"Sweetheart nothing to apologize to me for. I see you make my son happy and that he loves you. You all are grown and will do what you want no matter what. As long as you all happy, I'm happy. I'm going to head back down."

After he leaves, I look at Adontis. *"This will be a Thanksgiving I'll never forget."*

"You and me both. It's your fault for waking up all horny this morning, talking about give you something to be thankful for. Your nasty ass. My momma warned me about girls like you." He is smiling and grinning.

I stand glaring at him with a half smirk on my face. I want to laugh, but I can't. *"Too soon Adontis, too damn soon to be cracking jokes. I don't know how you can be so cool about this."*

"Ma, why the hell not? I can't change the shit. It happened so I gotta keep it moving. Moms shouldn't have been walking into rooms she wasn't invited into. I sure as hell ain't hear nothing down there between your big ass thighs, them damn earmuffs. She had to find out the worst way possible, her son eats pussy and he found one that he loves to eat."

He pulls me towards him and kisses me. *"I eat you for breakfast, lunch and dinner. Bet it taught her ass a valuable lesson. She won't be walking through anymore closed doors uninvited, even if it's her house."* He starts laughing and leans in to give me a kiss on the lips. *"Let's go back to the rest of the family."*

I'm standing with my mouth gaped open. I can't believe the things he's saying. He pulls me by the wrist. *"You standing in here wit yo mouth wide open. Come on now Tasha lets go downstairs, before I put something in yo mouth. Then we be in trouble all over again."*

I look at him and cut my eyes. *"Shut the hell up. You always got to have a smart-ass mouth."*

He laughs as he leads me downstairs. *"You damn straight."*

When I get downstairs, I realize Carmen has called me several times and texted me. I find a quiet place and call her back. She just wanted to check in on me. I tell her I have had a hell of a morning.

"What happened sis?"

"It is way too much to tell right now. When I get back home and get settled, I will tell you all about it."

"This sounds juicy as hell."

"It is."

"I miss you baby sis. I want you here with me."

"I miss you too Carmen. Adontis and I have gotten serious. You have to share me." I start laughing.

"Yeah, I'm trying not to be selfish. I miss having you around and now this year you're not hear for Thanksgiving. I don't like it."

"Me either, but I had to compromise. I will be home for Christmas."

"Yes, I know, but it's not enough."

I smirk. *"I know. I do miss you guys."*

"We miss you too! Your nephews are asking for you."

"Let me talk to them."

I talk with my nephews and Carmen for a little while longer. I also speak to Kia, Ron and my nieces. I miss the hell out of my family. This is my first holiday not spent with them. I hurry and finish up the conversation with them because I am about to bust out into tears. I miss them so much. Adontis finds me and sees my eyes filling with tears.

"Baby, what's wrong? Is everything ok?"

I don't want him to see me like this. Crying like a baby. I sniffle and try to hold in my tears. *"I'm ok."*

He wipes the tears away from the corners of my eyes. *"Why are you crying ma?"*

"I just miss my family."

"Aww baby."

He puts his arm around me and embraces me. He just holds me and gives me the comfort that I need. I get my emotions in control and he is my rock. He understands. Since I was sixteen years old my family has been my sister and brother and their families. That's all I've had.

"We are just growing or rather extending your family. Adding me and all of my people. Whom you will start to meet soon enough. They will love you as much as I already do."

He just holds me in his arms for a little while and it feels like heaven on earth. We spend the afternoon watching the game as the remainder of Adontis' family members begin to arrive. His parents' home quickly begins to fill with his aunts, uncles and cousins. He is taking me around and introducing me to everyone. It is so many people. His family is huge. I meet his favorite Uncle, Riq. It's short for Tariq. Uncle Riq is sexy as hell. He is Adontis dad's baby brother. Adontis and he resemble a lot and they both look just like Adontis' dad. They look like the same person during different decades of life. Uncle Riq is about twelve years older than Adontis and he is a self-proclaimed lifelong bachelor. He is very blunt and straight to the point. Just like Adontis.

"Unc, this my shorty, my lady love Tasha. Baby this is Uncle Riq."

I've heard a lot of stories of the infamous Uncle Riq. Let's just say if Adontis and I ever have a son, Uncle Riq can only have supervised visits. He was getting Adontis into clubs when he was underage. He took him to his first strip club. They used to party together a lot before Adontis and I got together and he moved to Jacksonville. Riq has always been more like a big brother than an uncle to Adontis. They are very close so I am happy to finally get to meet him.

I smile and say, *"Nice to meet you."* I extend my hand for a handshake. Uncle Riq takes my hand and spends me around to get a full view.

"Nice to meet you too beautiful. Ok nephew this the little sexy chocolate thing that got yo nose open wide as hell."

Adontis burst out laughing. *"Unc you ain't pose to say shit like that in front of her."*

"Why the hell not? You telling me chocolate don't know she got your ass sprung? Boy please she already knows that shit."

I cover my face in embarrassment as I chuckle. Adontis smirks a lil bit. *"She ain't got me sprung Unc."*

Riq gives him the side eye. *"Nephew, who you think you talking to? Do I need to remind you of a certain conversation we had?"*

Adontis eyeballs stretch in disbelief. *"Unc? Man stop!"*

Riq laughs. He has a very infectious laugh everyone around who had been listening to the conversation laughs too. He puts his hands up in surrender.

"Aight Nephew. Unc gon stop. I heard many wonderful things about you Tasha. I'm glad my nephew met a lady like you."

I smile, *"Thank you."*

After that conversation ends, I am just thrilled to finally be off display. Adontis and I have a private moment where we are alone for a few moments. I try to ease my question in.

"What certain conversation did you and Unc have?"

He throws his head back in disbelief and releases a long overly exaggerated sigh. *"Tasha, come on ma. Quit being nosy. That ain't nothing you need to worry bout."*

"You not going to tell me?"

"Naw ma. Come on let me finish introducing you. We bout to eat dinner in a minute."

I don't fight him on changing the subject. I let him take my hand and continue to finish introducing me to his family. I'll take this L. You have to pick your battles. As time begins to go into the evening, we gather in the dining room, where we get seated for dinner. As I stated before, his parents' house is a mansion. The dining room has three very large dining room tables. The room is decorated in autumn colors. The tables are properly set with nice silk linen, silverware, plates, glasses etc.

Adontis pulls out my chair, I sit and he pushes my chair in. He sits to the right of me. To the right of him is Riq and then Shaun followed by Melanie. To the left of me is Aisha followed by their cousins. Our table is filled with cousins, their significant others and Riq.

Riq begins to tease Adontis a little. *"She just brings the gentleman out of you huh nephew?"*

I'm thinking not again I do not want to be center stage anymore today. Adontis smirks. *"Yeah, Unc I gotta take care of my lady."*

"I ain't mad at cha nephew. I taught you well."

They both begin to chuckle. Mr. Lamentez ask for everyone's attention so that he may bless the food. We all get silent. He does a nice blessing. Dinner then begins to be served. As dinner is being served, we all take turns going around the room sharing what we are thankful for. Our dinner is delightful. I really enjoy the time with Adontis' family.

November 23, 2007

I've been waiting all day for Thanksgiving day to come to an end. It has been the most embarrassing day of my life. It did get better because it started hellaciously. Yes, I said hellaciously. It was so bad I had to make up a word for it. The only way to go was up. Meeting Uncle Riq was very interesting. He seems like a cool dude though. I also enjoyed getting to meet the rest of Adontis' family.

We finish the night having fun. The parents have all gone to bed or went home. It's just the younger generation hanging out. We spend the rest of the night having fun and playing games. It is well after 1am when the rest of the cousins leave. Melanie heads off to bed and it is just Adontis, Aisha, Shaun and me. We decide to play a round of spades. We split into teams. Ladies against the men.

Adontis looks at me, *"Ok shorty, let's make this interesting."*

"How so? What are you thinking?"

"Let's make a bet. You choose what you want. I choose what I want."

"Ok. What do you want? What's your wager?"

He smirks at me. *"If I win, I will buy you fourteen pairs of vibrating panties."*

"What the hell?"

Shaun is laughing his ass off. I thought it was starting off good. He was buying me something, but I wasn't expecting him to say vibrating panties.

"Let me finish ma. You have to wear them for one week straight for twenty-four hours a day. You only get a break when bathing, using the toilet or when I take them off. I will pick the week when I want you to wear them. Most importantly they will be remote controlled panties and I will possess the remote the entire time."

Aisha burst out laughing. *"Oh shit. You a nasty ass. T don't take that bet."*

Shaun interjects, *"Aisha mind yo business this between them."*

"Hell no. I got to look out for my sis. T don't do it."

I start smiling, *"Aisha we got this. Ok Adontis I'll accept your bet if you will accept mines."* Aisha throws her hands up in defeat.

"Ok ma, let's hear it."

"When I win you have to be my maid for the week. On call at any time of the day. Naked at all times. Available to do whatever I request. At whatever week of my choosing."

Aisha starts laughing. *"Ok sis, not bad."*

Shaun looks at Adontis with a smirk on his face. *"Damn bruh, we can't lose this shit."*

"Hell, no we ain't losing this bruh." Adontis looks to me smiling. *"Ok shorty. You have a deal. We have two witnesses. Let's seal the deal with a kiss."*

"Ok, baby."

He leans in and gives me a kiss. He slides his tongue in my mouth and pulls my hair. I bite his bottom lip. We pull apart slightly and end our kiss with a peck on the lips.

"Damn. Ya'll do know we still in the room, right? We did not need to see all that shit."

I roll my eyes. *"Shaun shut up."*

"I'm gon shut up T., but that's why ya'll asses gon lose and you gon have to pay up."

Aisha jumps in, *"We ain't losing shit. Adontis we bout to change your name to Bentley."*

"All of this damn talking. Let's play cards."

I smile at Adontis. *"Let the game begin."*

"Ok let's review the house rules. First team to get to five hundred wins. No double or nothing. Loser has to comply with the bet."

"Yeah, yeah, yeah Shaun. We got it. We ready."

"Ready to lose," Adontis says.

"We ain't losing baby."

"We'll see about that. Deal the cards bro. First spade deals."

Adontis deals out the cards and he is the first one to get a spade. I roll my eyes as he does his ear-to-ear grin thing.

"Whatever that don't mean nothing."

"This is the beginning of this L you bout to take. Don't get mad at me when you wearing them panties and I'm pushing the button at the most awkward times."

I cut my eyes at him. *"Just deal man."*

The first round of cards is dealt and my hand is pretty good. If I get hands like this all night, I am confident that I will win. Aisha and I discuss our books and place our bet. The game play goes like this for the first five hands and Aisha and I are in the lead. My confidence is up. We've set them a few times and they are in the negative. Aisha and I are a little past halfway there. I start talking trash. Like I love to do with my competitive ass.

"Oh, oh baby. I'm gon make sure I buy you some lotion. I don't want to see no ashy knees or ankles when you working for me."

Aisha burst out laughing. *"Girl you hell."*

Adontis gives me the side eye. *"It ain't over yet ma. You bout to deal us a bomb ass hand. Matter fact put us down for blind six. Bro it's time to get back in the game."*

Aisha writes their bid down.

"Oh whatever. Ya'll are right where ya'll belong. Behind us." I pass the cards to Adontis to cut. *"Your cut baby."*

He hits the top of the cards and says, *"Run that shit."*

In my mind, I am thinking hell no. Anytime you want to mess up the rotation of the cards don't cut. That's exactly what he did. I pick up my hand and it is garbage. I look at Aisha and shake my head. She shakes her head too. We both know that both of us have nothing. I look over to Adontis to see him skinning and grinning. I know he has a hand.

"Ok Shaun, it's your play."

"Hold the hell up sis. I gotta talk to my partner. Bro can you get me three books?"

"My nigga I can get you four."

Aisha rolls her eyes. We both know what time it is.

"Ok sis. We going ten for two."

I just shake my head. Aisha rolls her eyes and increases their bid. We begin the round and it is a sweep, they make all of the books except one. They are smacking hands and celebrating. This has taken them out of the negative and 101 points behind us. Adontis grins again. They can go blind six again.

"Sis we going blind six."

"Yeah, yeah, yeah."

Aisha rolls her eyes as she writes down their bid. The next hand is dealt. I skip the cut also. Aisha and I bid five. The round is played and she and I get five. They get eight. They are now only thirty points behind us. I'm pissed.

"Ma you getting quiet over there."

I don't say a word, I just give him the finger.

He chuckles. *"Yeah, as soon as I get you home."*

I cross my arms over my chest and roll my eyes.

"You look so damn sexy when you do that. Do that for Daddy one more time."

I ignore him and pick up my cards. Again, our hand is horrible. We bid five and they bid eight. Everyone makes their books and we are tied.

"Oh oh. I'm coming for that fine chocolate ass ma. Your ass getting quiet. You ain't got much to say now huh."

I just ignore him. Shaun is laughing his ass off. *"You too sis your ass quiet as a church mouse."*

Aisha rolls her eyes like only she can. We play the next couple of rounds and we alternate taking the lead. This game is close as hell. We are at what should be the last hand. Aisha and I have 485 and they have 462. We only need fifteen points to win.

We get our hand and the most books we count between the two of us is five. They place their bid and go for eight. Aisha and I do the math. If they get eight, they will win by seven points. Now I'm nervous. If we can't set them, we'll lose. Or rather I lose. This is my kitty kat on the line here.

"You ready for this loss ma?"

"I was just about to ask you the same thing."

We begin to play and Aisha and I take the first five books. I'm feeling good about this. We just need to get one more. Adontis and Shaun win the next five books. The nervousness comes back over me.

"Let me put you out of your misery ma. Ya'll loss."

Adontis drops his last three cards. He is holding the highest three cards in the game. Both jokers and the deuce of diamond. He and Shaun give each other hi fives.

I drop my head down in defeat into my hands. *"Shit."*

Aisha is pissed. *"Damn."* She had all spades too including the fourth highest spade. *"I tried T."*

"I know sis." I exhale.

"I hope you ready ma. Because I sure as hell can't wait."

"Whatever Adontis. I'm going to bed."

"You not going to give Daddy a kiss before you go to bed?"

I look over my shoulder at him and cut my eyes. I walk away and head up to bed.

I get some much-needed rest. I am able to sleep in this morning. Adontis is not in the bed with me. I think Mrs. Lamentez has given up the life of wake-up calls. At least to me. I roll over in the bed and grab my cell phone. It is 11:11 am. I did not mean to sleep this late. I was tired though. I figure Adontis must still be asleep too.

I roll out of bed and head to the shower. It is well after 11:30 am when I step out the shower. I dry off and lay my towel across the bed. I sit on the towel and begin to moisturize my skin. I get myself together and head out my room. I walk to Adontis' room and his door is closed.

I do not knock. Hell, he is my man. There is nothing that he has, that I haven't seen, touched, tasted or swallowed. I open the door and he is laying in the bed still asleep. I leave the door open. I do not want any trouble. I sit on the bed next to him.

"Good morning baby. Wake up."

He opens his eyes. *"Hey ma. Damn you look beautiful."*

I smile. *"Thank you, babe. Now get your butt up."*

"I'm up." He grabs my hand. *"Let me let you feel him."*

I snatch my hand back. *"No. Keep him down until we get home. And get up and get dressed."*

He burst out laughing. *"Close the door first ma."*

"Hell no. I'm not trying to cause any more confusion with your mom."

"You know Daddy sleeps naked."

I smirk. *"Ok. Well, you are up so I will close your door on my way out. I'll be in my room talking to Carmen. Come get me when you're finished."*

"Alight shorty."

He sits up and kisses me. I leave his room and close the door. I get Carmen on the phone and catch up with her. She still wants to know what happened yesterday. I tell her I'll tell her when I see her. She is not happy that she has to wait. I let her know when Adontis and I are flying back home. She reminds me to call her and let her know that we landed safely.

Shortly after Adontis shows up to my room, I finish talking with Carmen and we head downstairs. Everyone is scattered around the house. Melanie is in the kitchen eating and we join her. After a little while Aisha and Shaun trail in. We all eat breakfast and then spend a little time with the parents and grandparents.

Shaun, Melanie, Aisha, Adontis and I decide to head out to do some shopping, have lunch and stop by Fresh. We get back to his parents' house and all spend time together. Mrs. Lamentez hasn't said very much to me since she caught Adontis and I having sex. Hell, she hasn't said much to Adontis either. At least we are getting the cold shoulder together.

We have dinner together as a family. We say our good nights and give out hugs to everyone. His mom is still standoffish, but I hug everyone else, which really is just his dad and grandparents. Adontis, Aisha and I turn in early. We have an early flight to catch in the morning at 10:30 am. I can't wait to get back to the south.

When I get upstairs, I get all of my things packed up. I organize my wardrobe for the next day all I will have to do is shower, get dressed and pack up my essentials after I use them in the morning. After finishing up my stuff, I head to Adontis' room. I have to make sure I get his stuff together too or it will not be together. I know my man. I walk in his room and I leave the door open.

He is sitting on the bed. *"What's up ma?"*

"I came to get you packed up."

"You always taking care of Daddy."

"I always will." I bend down and kiss him on the lips. *"Ok babe, what are you wearing tomorrow?"*

He pulls out his jeans, boots, belt and sweater. He is a label whore. It is all Gucci. He pulls aside a white tee, a pair of boxers and socks. I pack the rest of his things up leaving out his essentials.

"Ok babe you are good to go. I have my alarm set for 7:00. I will make sure I come in here and wake you up."

"Thanks, shorty."

"You're welcome love."

He stands up and pulls me towards him. He lays a very luscious kiss on me. *"Wait til I get you home."*

I smile. *"Goodnight."*

"I love you ma. Goodnight."

"I love you too." I walk out of his room and close the door.

November 24, 2007

My alarm is blaring at me. I roll over to get my phone. I set a pre-alarm that I didn't tell Adontis about. It is 6:46. I'm so ready to get back to the south. After turning off my alarm I get out of bed and slip my robe on. I need to get Adontis up. His ass is just as slow as me early in the morning. I walk in his room leaving the door opened. I learned my damn lesson. He is laying on his back fast asleep.

I lean over and kiss his lips. *"Babe wake up."*

"Alight." He doesn't move. His eyes haven't opened and he is still laying in the bed.

I exhale. He is like a little boy. He does not like to get up early in the morning. I shake him. *"Wake up Adontis."*

"I'm up ma. Go ahead and get ready."

He still has not gotten up out of the bed. I know this man. If I walk out of here and leave him like this, we are going to miss our flight. I pull the covers off of him and put them on the chair next to his bed. I should have known it; he is fully naked. I don't know if I should give him the covers back or close the door. His anatomy is standing up at attention. Prime and ready.

"Get up!"

"Damn ma. What you doing? Give me my covers back."

"Nope. Get up and get ready. You don't need them."

I walk out of the room and close the door. I head to Aisha's room to make sure she is up. I lightly knock on the door.

"Come in."

"Hey sis. I was just making sure you was up."

"Yes T. I'm ready to get back home to my man."

"I know that's right. Well, I'm going back down the hall to fight with your brother. He will not get out of the bed."

She laughs. *"Have fun with that."*

I roll my eyes, *"Thanks for nothing."*

I walk out of her room, close the door and back down to Adontis' room. I'm back in his room and he is still in the bed. He hasn't realized I'm in the room. He is still laying on his back with his eyes closed. He did not get up to get the covers. Instantly I realize he is jacking off in bed. He is moaning as he is pleasuring himself. He is calling out my name.

"Ahhh Tasha."

I don't know if I should be flattered or offended. I quietly close and lock the door. I do not want his mother walking in on this shit.

"Adontis what the hell are you doing?"

He isn't startled or bothered by the fact that I am here. *"You gon come help me finish ma?"* He is gripping himself. *"Come sit on your seat."*

I'm about to lose it. *"Adontis, we have a flight to catch. We don't have time for this. And I promised your mom I wouldn't do this in her house anymore. I meant it."* I walk over to him and pull his hand off of his dick. *"Get up and go get in the shower man."*

That was a mistake. He grips my wrist and pulls me on top of him. *"Daddy will make it quick."* He is pulling my robe off of me. *"I heard you lock the door. Ain't nothing stopping this."*

"I am. Adontis, stop man!"

He is pulling my gown up. *"I know you ain't got no panties on. Take a ride on your favorite seat."* He's starts kissing on my neck and rubbing on my breast.

"No. I'm trying to be respectful and you are making this very hard." I begin to slide off of him.

"You make me very hard." He grabs my hand and wraps it around his dick. *"You feel this? You gon leave your man like this?"*

I feel him throbbing in my hand. I never want a good hard one to go to waste. *"Adontis!"*

"Ma why you got me begging for what's already mines?"

"I'm trying to do the right thing."

He slides two of his fingers in me and starts fingering me. He had me turned on a long time ago. I cream all over his fingers. He sticks his fingers in his mouth and sucks it off. *"We could have been done already. You wasting time."*

My mind is telling me not to do it, but my body slides him into me. I begin to ride him. He is making love to me and I get that much needed orgasm that I didn't get on Thanksgiving Day. It is about 7:45 am when we finish and I am behind schedule.

"Damn baby. I told you I needed you." He kisses my lips. I put my gown and robe back on. Adontis slides into his pajama pants. *"I'm gon make sure ain't nobody out in the hallway."*

"I'm going in the bathroom. Let me know when it is clear."

He walks out of his bedroom and I hear, *"Good Morning Ma."*

"What are you doing? You in there with that fast tail girlfriend of yours?"

He sounds offended. *"Ma don't talk about my lady like that. She should be in her room."*

"Lady? Ha! I just walked past her room. The door is open and she is not in there."

"Ma. I'm serious. Respect her. I love her."

She rolls her eyes. *"Why? Charlene's daughter is interested in you. She is going to be an attorney. Her dad is a judge. She comes from a great family."*

"Ma. I'm not doing this with you. I love Tasha. Her family is great. And if you took the time to get to know her. You would know she brilliant, beautiful, loving and smart. And since you so concerned with status, she going to school to be a doctor. MD."

She is quiet. She has no come back. He finally shut her up. I want to scream out in happiness, but I can't. I'm being so quiet. I cannot get caught again. I think I even forget to breathe.

"Now you can either help me find her or go back to bed."

"Ok son. I'll help you."

"She came in here and woke me up and said she was going to start getting ready. Maybe she went down to get something to drink or eat."

"You really don't know where she is at?"

"Naw, but I'm going to go find her. We have a flight to catch."

"Ok let's go."

The first thought I have is damn he lies well. While I'm still hiding in the bathroom, he texts me.

> **Daddy:** *It's clear. Head to Aisha's room and once we get downstairs I'll call you and you can tell me you are in there.*

> **Tasha:** *Ok*

I quietly walk out of his bathroom. I peak my head around into the hallway from his bedroom. I almost piss on myself. Standing in the middle of the hallway staring back at me is Shaun.

Whispering, *"Ya'll some sneaky asses."* He is smirking at me.

I whisper back, *"Man shut up. I don't have time for this."*

I have a grin on my face. He shakes his head and walks off. I sneak to Aisha's room and lightly knock on the door. She opens the door wrapped in a towel.

"T what the hell. Why you still got the same clothes on?"

I quickly explain the plan to her. She shakes her head. *"Ya'll two."*

My phone rings.

"Ma where you at? We got a flight to catch."

I play along in case his mom is ear hustling our conversation. *"I'm upstairs."*

"Upstairs where?"

"I'm in Aisha's room. Helping her figure out what to wear."

"You see what time it is? You need to be getting ready. We on our way up there."

"We?"

He hangs the phone up and after a few moments there is a knock at Aisha's door. Aisha opens the door to Adontis and their mom.

"Good morning mom. Hey bro."

They both greet her with a good morning.

I am very sour about what I heard his mom say. She is trying to push that broad up on my man. I put that to the side and I say, *"Good Morning Mrs. Lamentez."*

"Morning."

"Ok Aisha, well now that we got your stuff figured out, I'm going to go get ready."

"Ok, sis. I'll see you in a few."

"No kiss for daddy?"

His mom rolls her eyes. I'm thinking why the hell is he trying to start something. *"I'll give you a kiss later. Ok?"*

"Nope."

As I'm walking out of Aisha's room, he pulls me towards him and kisses me. He doesn't keep it PG-13. I follow his lead and kiss him back. He looks at his mom as if to say now what.

I don't say a word. I just walk off. It's 7:57 am when I make it back to my room. I have got to take a shower and get ready in very little time. Adontis has us so behind schedule.

I walk out of my room fully dressed and ready to go a little after nine. My lashes are on and my lips are popping. I have on some thigh high boots over some thick black tights. A short black sweater dress and silver jewelry. I look sexy if I must say so myself. I'm pulling my suitcase and I stop at Adontis' door. I leave my luggage outside the door and I walk in his room.

"Babe, you ready to go?"

"Damn shorty. Don't hurt em. You look beautiful."

He walks over and kisses me. *"Thank you, baby. You looking sexy yourself. Gucci down."*

"Yeah. My sexy gotta match your sexy."

"You did that baby. You ready?"

"Yeah. Aisha ready?"

"Yeah, she texted me. She downstairs waiting on us."

"Alright ma then, let's go."

He grabs his luggage and mines and carries them downstairs. We get our luggage packed in the car and say our goodbyes to his parents, grandparents, Shaun and Melanie. We get to the airport about forty-five minutes before our flight.

Overall, I guess this was a semi good trip. Most of his family made me feel welcomed. All except for his mom. I don't like what I heard her say about me while I was hiding in Adontis' bathroom. I'll just have to keep working on her. I'm trying to be better to her and just maybe she'll come around. My mom is gone, so I'd like to try and have a better relationship with her. Especially if Adontis and I continue down this good path.

chapter 24

When The Bottom Falls Out

December 15, 2007

In life, you can plan, but there is no guarantee that your plans will succeed. What do you do, when they don't?

It's a few weeks until Christmas and I've been feeling depressed. It's been about four months since I aborted my baby. It changed me as a person. I would have been about six months pregnant today. Instead, I am here with no baby and nothing, but regret. My life hasn't been the same since. I still haven't told anyone. Not Carmen. Not Diamond. Not Kenya. Not Rodney.

I'm trying to move on and work past my abortion, but it still hurts like hell. I did what I thought was best for Adontis and I; or rather what was best for me. I couldn't have that baby and Adontis. I'll be damned though. I still regret it. Nothing was worth me killing my baby. Not even the man I love. I think I've started to resent him for it. That's not fair. He didn't do it. That was all me.

I keep seeing mothers with their baby's everywhere I go. It is like a constant reminder that I killed my baby. My maternal instinct is awakened every time I see a baby. I wish I could go back to that moment and do it over again. I said I would never have an abortion and yet I took that drug that took my baby from my womb. Lord forgive me!

To add fuel to the fire Adontis has been coming in late every night and I am already withdrawn from him. I hope he isn't cheating on me, but I really don't know. He tells me he is hanging with his boys and I should trust him, he isn't cheating. I'm afraid to go looking because I can't take finding out the worse. What I do know is something is wrong, we're cracked.

Lately, we seem to argue about everything. We have been intimate a few times, but my heart hasn't been in it lately. The guilt has just been eating away at me. I want to tell him, but

I'm afraid to. I said I'd take this secret to my grave, but why does it feel like it is killing me? This secret may take me to my grave.

Sexy as I am, I'm home alone on a Saturday night. I haven't seen Adontis since earlier today. We spent our morning together at Fresh until he left to go out. Leaving me to run the business and close up at the end of the day.

December 16, 2007

Unfortunately, this has been the new normal. Before he left, he said he'd be in early. It is now after midnight and his ass still isn't home. I am already angry when I call his cell. It goes straight to voicemail pissing me off even more. I don't leave a message.

The time continues to pass: 1:30 am; 2:20 am; 3:30 am; 4:12 am. I begin to worry if he is ok. I have called him at each of these time intervals and received no answer. Just a full voicemail box. My mood changes from angry, to mad, to upset, to concern, to worry. By this time, I don't know what to think. I hope and pray that he is ok. I am scared something could have happened to him.

I sit on the sofa downstairs unable to sleep and I begin pacing the room. I continue to try and call his cell to no avail. At 4:53 in the morning I hear a key turn in the lock. He enters the front door; I run to him and hug him. I am so grateful that he is ok. The happiness quickly passes. I haul off and slap the hell out of him. My new mood, I am pissed. I can see he has been drinking, but he is not drunk. Furiously he looks at me.

"What the hell. What the fuck wrong with you?"

I stare at him and cut my eyes. I refuse to answer him. If looks could kill, he would lay dead before me. I go upstairs to our bedroom and lock the door. I don't want to argue tonight, it's late and I am tired. He comes upstairs behind me and tries to open the door.

"Tasha, open the damn door."

"You not sleeping in here tonight. Go sleep with whoever kept you out til five in the morning."

"You tripping. Open the damn door."

I turn off the lights and walk towards the bedroom part of the room without another word to him. He bangs on the door a few more times and I keep my silence. After a while, I hear him walking away. Once in the bedroom part of our room, I lock that door just in case he takes the elevator. I don't want his ass in bed with me.

Later in the morning, I am ready to chew him out. It's early for us considering the time I actually went to bed. I did not get much sleep. I check the bedrooms upstairs and there's no sign of him. I go downstairs and find him passed out on the couch. I hit him hard across the shoulder.

"Wake the hell up. We gotta talk."

He opens one eye to look at me. *"Damn Tasha, can't you see I am sleeping? Can't this wait?"*

"No, the fuck it can't. Get up and get up now."

He sits up on the couch and starts rubbing his eyes. *"Shit, what's up?"*

His eyes are bloodshot red. It's crazy to me how he acts so nonchalant. Like he didn't just come home at almost 5 am. I roll my eyes at him.

"I am fed up. If you wanted to party to all times of the night, why you ask me to move in with you? I ain't putting up with this shit. There is no reason for you to be out so damn late. If I did this, you would go fool. If partying is what you want, then I will move the fuck out and on from you."

I can see the surprise look on his face as he looks at me. *"You saying I can't hang with my boys? It's either you or them?"*

"That's not what I said. Do you have to stay out all night? Unless you was out fucking something. Is that what you were doing?"

"Tasha, you know damn well, I ain't fucking around on you. I told you I was with my boys and that's it."

"I don't know what you doing. What I do know is you told me you would be home early. I called you several times last night. You didn't answer your damn phone once."

"My battery was dead. And you been acting shitty lately. Actin' like you ain't wanna be bothered with. So, I gave you your space."

"Bullshit. Your boys got cell phones. You never thought, let me call my lady and tell her I'm ok. I'm gonna be late. Something. You left me wondering if you were alive or hurt. Thanks for considering my damn feelings. And you say I been acting shitty? What that got to do with you being out all night. That's apples and oranges. Two different damn things."

"You blowing this out of proportion. I can handle myself. And these ain't no apples and oranges. Your attitude been real fucked up since we got back home. When you act like that, I don't want to be around you."

"Well, that's fine. You handle yourself and I will handle myself and my shitty attitude."

I walk off and go upstairs. He follows behind me.

"What the fuck does that mean?"

I ignore him and his question. I grab my luggage and I begin to pack my things. As I pack them, he unpacks them.

"Where the hell you think, you going?"

"I'm leaving. You want to party and have your fun. You don't want me here."

"How you know what I want?" I act as if I don't hear him speaking to me. I continue to pack my stuff. *"Fine, shit. If you wanna go, leave. But don't try to blame it on me."*

I wasn't looking for this response. I love him and I want him to change. I also feel guilty about the secrets that I am keeping from him. It's eating away at me on the inside, but I know I can't tell him. I shift the focus off of me and place the blame solely on him.

"Don't blame me honey. You don't want a woman. You want a maid. That's not me. I am here cooking your meals, washing your clothes and keeping the house clean. Everything that needs to be done in this house baby, I do. It would be nice to get some appreciation. We don't even go out anymore. The same things you did to get me, you gotta do to keep me."

"That works both ways. You don't do everything you use to do. You damn sure ain't been giving me none lately. But you know what, you wanna go? Then leave. Shit. I am not holding you here."

He walks out of the bedroom and leaves the house, slamming the front door. I don't really want to leave. I love him and I want us fixed. Not heartache and hurt. This is the man I want to spend the rest of my life with. Additionally, I start med school next month. I will have to find me a new place to live that is close to campus. I don't have time for this with the holidays around the corner. I stop packing and sit on the bed. The tears begin to flow and I can't help, but to cry. I really love him.

I take some time to cry it out and then I gather up some of my clothes and pack up my essentials. I am walking out the house when I see Adontis pull back into the driveway. I have my luggage in my hand as he is walking up towards me. He has a beautiful bouquet of long stem roses in his hands. I don't even acknowledge them as we approach one another.

I say, *"I will get the rest of my things after Christmas."*

He grabs my hand. *"Shorty please don't go. I am sorry. I was wrong. I fucked up. I love you and I don't wanna lose you. Can we go inside to talk about this?"*

I snatch my hand away from him. *"What else is there to talk about? You already told me how you really feel. You told me to leave, right?"* I pop the trunk and put my luggage in my car.

"Damn ma. You know that's not what I meant."

"That's what you said."

"Do you love me enough to stay and work this out?"

"I do love you. That's why I am leaving."

"That makes a hell of a lot of sense. You love me, but you leaving me? You walking out on me!"

"Yeah, that's right. I already called Carmen and told her I was coming for Christmas. I am going to my sister's. I wanna give you a break from me. I think you want your space. I'm going to give it to you. Give you a chance to reevaluate your life and us; decide if you really wanna be with me or if you wanna be a bachelor."

"Ma you know I want to be with you. I don't need no damn time to figure that out. Damn Tasha. I love you. Shit."

"Well maybe it's that you don't want to live together. Maybe this was more than you thought it would be."

"Ma don't say that. I know I love you and that I wanna be with you. I don't want nobody else. I bought this house for you. For us."

"I hear you, but I don't believe you."

I grab the handle to open my car door. He grabs my hand and closes the door back.

"Shorty, it's you I want."

"Prove it. Cause that's not how it has felt these last three weeks. Maybe the newness of us has worn off. I don't know, but I know things aren't right. Take this time and make sure you want me." I snatch my hand from his grasp and open my car door again.

"Ma."

"I'm leaving Adontis."

"You gonna come back?"

"Only if you want me to."

"I don't want you to leave, but you still leaving." I get in the car and crank it up. He stands between me and the door.

"Please move so I can close the door."

He slides the roses in the car. *"Are you going to take your flowers?"*

I take the roses from him and put them on the seat next to me. *"Ok, I need to close the door."*

"Can I-," I stare at him very rudely, he pauses and looks at me pleadingly. I'm ready to go and he is stopping me from leaving. *"Shorty, can I at least have a kiss before you leave ma?"*

I roll my eyes. *"No."*

He looks as if he is hurt. He steps out of the way. I close the door and roll the window down. *"You don't forgive me? If you loved me, you would stay."*

I didn't mean to hurt him, but I am hurting right now too. For so many reasons. The worse part of it all, I can't even tell the man I love, what is really hurting me. I have got to deal with this abortion. Just as much as I want to give him time to figure things out. I need to work on myself too.

"I do forgive you, but if you love me, you wouldn't let me go alone."

I back out of the driveway and I hear him call my name, but I don't stop or answer him.

chapter 25

Major Decisions

December 22, 2007

**One wrong move can make you or break you. You must
think wisely before making life changing choices.**

I have been at my sister's house for a week. Being around my family is what I needed. I have been keeping busy by doing a lot of shopping. I've even done some soul searching.

I've spent some time really feeling the loss of my baby. I've taken the time to feel the downs about the choice I made. I've even called the counselors to talk through my feelings. I don't think that I've fully forgiven myself, but I am working on not hating myself. That is a good start. I have to heal me before I can give all of me to Adontis.

The other part of my soul-searching led me to realize, I want my man. I don't want anybody else. I know I did some messed up stuff. I know I didn't always treat him right. I want a chance to fix it though.

Maybe I made a mistake leaving him in Florida. What if he has realized that he doesn't want this relationship or us living together. I will be heartbroken. My mind is constantly racing. I don't know what I'll do if we don't fix this. I know his mother will be happy.

Adontis and I have talked throughout the week. I'm still waiting to find out when he is coming down. Christmas is literally in a few days. No better time than the present to start fixing things, right? I give him a call and his phone just rings until it goes to voicemail. I know he is focused on work, but I am irritated. I want my man here with me.

Since he didn't answer, I shoot him a text.

> **Tasha:** *Hey baby. I'm trying to figure out what day you coming down. Hit me back.*

About thirty minutes passes before he responds back to me.

> **Daddy:** *What up shorty. I ain't gon be able to make it. I got too much going on here at Fresh. It been real busy with you gone.*

I look at my phone in disbelief. He didn't even have the audacity to tell me, he texted this bullshit to me. I am not going to respond to him. I could blow up at him and go off, but what's the point? We just ain't gon work out after all. I want to come first in his life. If I can't come first, I don't want to be in it. It hurts because I still want my man so bad. Despite me wanting to hold on to us. I think it's safe to say, this is the end if he isn't here for Christmas. After about ten minutes, he sends me another text.

> **Daddy:** *You ain't gon say nothin back? I'll see you back at home after Christmas, right?*

I don't have shit else to say. I lay back in my bed. All I can do is cry. This was supposed to be our first Christmas together as a couple and we won't be spending it together. Who in the hell does that? I guess I'm single again for Christmas. He knows how important this holiday is to me, but he still isn't coming. If he thinks I'm coming home to him after Christmas, he is in for a rude awakening. As soon as Christmas is over, I'll be house hunting. I lay in bed until I cry myself to sleep.

Once I wake up from my afternoon nap, I get myself up out of bed and get dressed. I decide to try to spend some time with my family. Before leaving the bedroom, I see I have a few more texts and a few calls from Adontis.

> **Daddy:** *Ma?*

> **Daddy:** *You ain't gon answer me?*

> **Daddy:** *Daddy love you anyway. Text me or call me when you ready to talk.*

He gon be waiting a long time for me to text or call him because I ain't doing it. I'm done! I do my best to put on a happy face. I don't want to bring anyone else down. I don't have an appetite so I don't really eat anything besides some crackers. However, I do have a few drinks to numb the pain.

Carmen, Kia and I have some last-minute shopping to do. We go to a few stores and they all are a mess. We go in and get what we need as fast as we possibly can. The lines are insane. I think everyone had the same idea.

December 23, 2007

After spending over three hours out, we return and it is after midnight. I spilt some juice on my sweatshirt in the car. Its soaking wet and outside is cold. I bring a few bags in with me then I walk straight upstairs to the bedroom to change my shirt.

I enter the room and close the door. I pull my shirt over my head and then reach for the light switch. When the light comes on, I turn around and see Adontis step into the bedroom from out of the bathroom. He walks up to me and pulls me into his arms. As if it is an automatic reflex, I jump on him and wrap my legs around him. Absence does make the heart grow fonder. I forgot that I was even mad at him. Me not speaking to him went out the window when I saw him.

"Damn. I been missing you shorty."

"I thought you couldn't make it?"

"Never. I would never miss spending Christmas with you ma. I was packing when you texted me earlier. Then I went straight to the airport."

"Uh huh. So, you got jokes?"

He smiles, *"I just wanted to give you a lil surprise."*

"I'm pleasantly surprised."

"I see. You finally talking to daddy again."

"What you mean?"

"You ain't talked to me since I texted you earlier and said I wasn't coming. I been texting and calling you all day."

"Yep. I was done."

He looks at me in utter disbelief. *"Done?"*

"Yeah. When I read that you weren't coming-" I pause and tears begin to roll from my eyes.

"Damn ma don't cry." He begins to wipe the tears away.

I close my eyes to try and fight back the tears. *"I told myself that we were over in that moment. Because there is no way that this man really loves me if he won't be here with me. Then to find out via text. That hurt."*

"I apologize ma. I wasn't tryin to hurt you. I was just tryin to surprise you. I love you with all my heart. I damn sure don't wanna hurt you or see you hurting. I need you to know that. In here," he places his hand over my heart, *"and in here,"* as he points to my head.

I shake my head at him, giving him an ok.

"You hear me ma?"

"Yeah, I hear you."

"I missed you the entire time you been gone. It's been lonely as shit in that big ass house without you. You all that matter to me. You my priority."

Hearing this makes me smile. *"I missed you too baby. All I want is to get back to us."*

"Alight. I know we got some shit to talk about and work through, but I'm here. I ain't going nowhere."

He kisses my lips and I kiss him back hard. In this moment I feel how much I really missed him and how much he means to me. I realize without a doubt, he is my soulmate. I want to spend my forever with him. He looks me up and down as he holds me up.

"Damn. This is what I like. I come home to my baby and get a strip show too."

"You came, baby you can get whatever you want."

I start to kiss him some more. Words can't express my joy in seeing him here with me. He smiles and gives me a devilish grin.

"Whatever I want?"

I smile back. *"Whatever, but within reason. You know the bullshit that I ain't gon do. But not now. I gotta finish helping my sisters."*

With a smirk on his face, *"Yeah I know that. What you will do is more than enough."*

"It better be."

He places his hands on my ass and starts to kiss my breast. He unhooks my bra and slides it off of me. He is sucking on my breast and it feels damn good. We haven't had sex in weeks and it is just what I need. I don't bother to try and stop him. Instead, I just enjoy the pleasure. Someone starts loudly pounding on the door.

"Tasha come on bring your ass. Come help us with this stuff." Of course, it is the loudmouth, Kia.

He begrudgingly stops kissing and sucking on me. I yell back at Kia, *"Ok I am coming."* I turn to Adontis, *"Sorry baby. Later."* He puts me down to the floor and I finish changing my clothes.

"But you owe me. Don't forget, it's whatever I want." He kisses me once more.

"I won't forget."

We submerge from the bedroom and head downstairs. He goes to hang with the fellas and I go to the kitchen. Kia says, *"Damn girl. I am sorry. I didn't know he was here. I guess I know what ya'll was doing. Ooh nasty."*

I start blushing. It is no way for me to hide it. *"I didn't know he was here either. He told me he couldn't make it. But I got a pleasant surprise."*

"I'm glad he's here, now your ass can stop moping around."

"I wasn't moping around."

In unison they both say, *"Yeah you were."*

"Wow, my bad I guess."

I really thought I was hiding it. After we finish in the kitchen, I leave with Adontis and go to the hotel suite he has for us. Shortly after we get in the room, I begin to take off my clothes. I am standing in the room butt naked and Adontis is staring at me and looking me up and down. He licks his lips and I lick mine. I step into the bathroom and run the water for a shower. He enters and joins me in the shower.

"You are so beautiful."

He starts kissing me and I kiss him back. We begin to make love. I give him everything he wants. We finish our night lying in bed. He tightly holds me in his arms. It feels good to have his skin touch mine. It's been too long of a time since he has held me like this. In his arms, is where I fall asleep.

I awake late in the morning and just lay in his arms. I am extremely happy to have him here with me. I'm not naïve. I know sex doesn't fix our problems, but it's a start. It certainly makes both of us happy. I turn on the TV to find nothing of interest on. I get up and make my way to the restroom. As I am brushing my teeth and washing my face, he enters the restroom and does the same.

"Good morning baby," I say. *"Did you sleep well?"*

"Like a newborn baby, breastfed for the first time."

All I can do is laugh at him. *"Oh really?"*

"Hells yeah. And speaking of breast-feeding, I think it's time."

"Ooh you so nasty."

He laughs and starts kissing me. *"But you like me that way."*

"Yeah, you right about that."

We leave the bathroom and make our way back to the bed. He lays me down and begins kissing my neck. He works his way down and kisses me all over. He licks me up and down and begins to squeeze my breast. We begin making love. After we finish, we both fall asleep.

It is late into the afternoon when I awake and see that I have some missed calls. They are mostly from Carmen and Kia. I go to take a shower first and decide to call them back while I am drying off.

Carmen answers, *"Hey sis. Where are you?"*

"I am at the hotel."

"You getting ready to see the lights or are you still busy putting it on Mr. Adontis?"

The lights. Another tradition of my family. Every year we go to the County Park to see the Christmas lights. *"Honey, if I was still busy putting it on Adontis, I wouldn't be talking to you. I just got out the shower. We got time."*

"How very nasty and unsettling. TMI. But anyway, see you at my house. Don't be late."

"We will be on time. How about ya'll be ready when we get there. See you soon."

"We'll be ready. See you soon sis."

While only wearing a towel, but completely dry, I sit next to Adontis and softly kiss his lips. *"Baby get up."*

He opens his eyes. *"Yea ma what's up?"*

"You need to get ready to go see the Christmas lights."

He gets out of the bed. *"You coming in the shower with me?"*

"No. I just got out. I'm going to get dressed."

"Naw, I think you still dirty."

"Babe."

He grabs my hand and leads me to the bathroom. He puts it down in the shower. After several hours, we are both ready and we head to Carmen's house. On the way there, I have Adontis stop to a drive thru and get us something to eat. Because I know my family is slow. Let's be honest we worked up a sweat in the hotel room and an appetite.

As usual Carmen is still getting herself and her kids ready. Kia and Ron have not shown up yet. Adontis and I sit on the sofa snuggled together talking and listening to music. Half an hour later, Kia and Ron arrive. As soon as she walks in, I rub her belly and talk to the baby. Since she has started showing, I do this every time I see her. Per usual she fusses with me and I bother her even more. It's how we show our love. Shortly after, everyone is finally ready to go.

Our night consists of seeing the Christmas lights and going out to dinner. We have a really good time. After a long night of laughter everyone heads home and Adontis and I head back to the hotel. Back in our room we put on our pajamas and get in the bed. He puts his arms around me and I tell him I would like to talk.

"Baby, are things going to be different this time? Cause I don't wanna go back to the same situation. I don't mind you hanging with your boys. But not all the time and not to all hours of the night. I won't come second to them or anyone else in your life, but the Father himself."

"You leaving, left me with some time to think. While you was gone, I missed the hell out of you. After a lot of thinking, I realized there needs to be some changes. I ain't wanna lose you. You the best thing in my life. I want you to come back home with me. And I promise to prove it to you. But at the same time, are things gonna be different with you? The crankiness and the bad attitude. Can you work on that?"

I smile at him and kiss him. *"Ok I am glad that you feel that way. I know I haven't been the easiest person to get along with. I will work on being better. I know I have been acting real stink. I apologize baby. I don't want to be without you. I love you."*

He kisses my lips. *"I love you back shorty. This means you coming back home with Daddy?"*

"Yes baby. I'm coming home."

December 24, 2007

It is Christmas eve morning. My honey and I take a nice, hot steamy shower together. There is a lot of kissing, rubbing and touching. That's just by me. He starts at my neck and kisses his way down. Before I know it, he lifts me up by my ass, sits me on his shoulder and then he props me against the shower wall. I exhale. I know what he is about to give to me. I brace myself as he begins to lick.

I feel a tingle run up my spine. I hold my head back and I begin to moan. He is giving it to me in all the right ways. My arms flail around as I'm trying to gather myself. I need something to grip on as I feel my orgasm sneaking up on me. With my eyes closed my arm flail around a little while longer until my hands reach the top of his head. I feel his silky thick curly locks. I slide my fingers into his curls. With a handful of his hair in each hand I take a grip.

My orgasm is here. I feel it in the pit of my stomach the most wonderful sensation. It runs through my body as I scream out in ecstasy and clutch his hair as tight as I can. It takes a moment for me to come back to reality. He had me gone in another dimension. When I look down at him, he is grinning from ear to ear.

"I'm the master of this pussy."

A very true statement. He makes her react like only he can. I bite my bottom lip and laugh out loud. He is lowering me down from his shoulders to his waist. I wrap my legs around him.

"Yes, baby you are." I lean in and begin to kiss his lips.

He is kissing me back as he slides into me. He is smiling at me. *"You a little nasty ass."*

I burst out laughing. *"What did I do?"*

"You ain't wipe my face or lips off. Nothing."

I roll my eyes. *"Hell, I know I taste good. If a chick can't taste herself, something wrong with that pussy. I wouldn't feed you anything I wouldn't eat. Remember that."*

He looks at me, smirks and licks his lips. *"Hell yeah. Tasting like a damn gourmet meal. I like when your ass nasty like that shorty."*

"I know you do. You just as freaky as me."

"I'm not complaining."

I slide my tongue back in his mouth as I begin riding and he begins stroking. Gliding in. Pulling back. Gliding in. Pulling back. He never pulls out. He pulls close to the edge then dives back in. He takes his fingers and begins to rub my clit. Again, I feel that wonderful orgasm sensation. I feel flutters in my tummy as I begin reaching my peak. I scream out his name. I feel his hands grip my hips and I know, he's about to cum too. He gets right to the brink of when he is about to cum and it explodes out of him.

We take a deep breath and exhale. *"Now we actually need to shower."* He laughs out loud.

"Naw it's time for round two."

Everyone will be staying the night at Carmen and Frank's house. Ever since we lost our parents, we make sure to spend as much time together as possible. Especially during the holidays and definitely for Christmas. We are all each other got. It's our job to make sure we stay close. However, that also means three families under one roof. It is a lot of fun. Don't get me wrong though, I wouldn't want to do it every day. Once a year is more than enough.

Ron and Kia are there when we arrive. *"I see you love birds have made it from your love nest,"* Kia says.

"Whateva tramp. Don't hate. Ya'll ready to get started?"

Carmen looks at me. *"Hell yea. We been waiting on ya'll."*

"Ya'll could have started baking without me. Well, we here now. So, shut up and let's get to work."

Kia says, *"Oh feisty! Carmen, she got her claws out honey."*

I smile. *"Whateva. Bite me."*

Carmen jumps in with a smart remark. *"I am sure it is too late. I know Adontis already has. Your ass smiling hard as hell."*

All I can do is laugh. *"And he did it so well."*

Kia frowns up her face in complete disgust. *"Ooh nasty girl."*

"That's what he calls me and it's what I answer to."

Their mouths drop open. Carmen looks at Kia. *"Oh, no she didn't?"*

"Oh yeah, I did."

We all burst out in laughter. Christmas music fills the house and after working hard and sweating in the kitchen the ladies and I join the men. They are playing dominoes and we decide to watch them. I sit on Adontis' lap. He rubs his hand on my upper thigh.

"You gonna be my good luck charm, shorty?"

Before I have a chance to utter a single syllable, Ron responds with his quick wit and charm. *"Dawg, now I know you wanna lose. Ain't nothing good or charming bout her."*

Everyone laughs, including Adontis. I must admit it was funny, but I will not laugh with me being the butt of the joke. I give Adontis the evil eye.

"How you just gonna laugh at me like that?"

With a smirk on his face, he says, *"Ma I ain't laughing. Now ya'll stop laughing at my baby."*

No one listens to him and they all keep on laughing. I decide to play the big baby role and pout. I stick out my bottom lip and I make it quiver as if my feelings are greatly hurt.

I whisper in Adontis' ear, *"I guess you won't get none of my good luck charms tonight."*

I smile and get up from his lap and walk away. He sits in his chair and smiles back at me. *"We will see about that now won't we."*

The kids are sent to bed early. We stay up late and have a few drinks and wrap some last-minute presents. I sneak away and leave Adontis with everyone else. After turning off the lights, I get in bed wearing sweatpants, calf high socks and an oversized t-shirt. Adontis walks in the bedroom before I have a chance to cover up and turns on the lights.

"What the hell you doing?"

I look up to see him. *"What does it look like? I am going to sleep."*

"What the hell you wearing? I can't snuggle up to that."

As I smile at him, I say, *"Good. Goodnight."*

I get out of the bed to turn off the lights. We are standing right next to each other and he turns them back on.

"Come on now shorty. Seriously? What you mad? You don't want Daddy to touch you?"

"Exactly."

He smiles and pulls me towards him. *"Don't be like that shorty. Besides, this will not stop me from touching you. I don't have to see what's under here, to know what's under here."*

He does that from ear to ear grin thing which only deepens his dimples. He starts kissing me softly and I don't want to kiss him back to prove a point, but damn his lips are so soft. I can't help myself. I begin kissing him back and he slides his hands up my t-shirt. He lays me down across the bed and starts kissing on my stomach, starting at my belly ring. He works his way up to my breast and starts kissing them. He takes a handful and then puts them in his mouth. I start quietly moaning.

"Oooh Adontis."

He starts to nibble on my breast. He takes my shirt off and starts kissing on my neck. I begin to unbuckle his belt and unbutton his pants. I pull his pants down to the floor and he pulls my sweats off. I pull his boxers down and he pulls my panties off. I bend my legs as he begins kissing up my feet working his way up to my thighs. He spreads my legs to separate my knees and my thighs. He puts his head in between my thighs and begins kissing my kitty kat. He begins to lick and suck on her and she is already wet. I start to moan louder and louder.

"Ooh Daddy," is all I can manage to say.

He keeps working me and I keep getting louder. I try to mask my moans by putting a pillow over my mouth. He flips me over on to my stomach. I get on my knees and he starts kissing on my lower back. I feel him enter my walls while he smacks my ass. I begin to clutch the sheets in between my fingers. He slowly and gently begins to stroke me. He keeps me close to him with one arm around my waist. He pulls me into him with his hand on my stomach. He smacks my ass with the other. Then he squeezes my breast as I start cumming all over him.

We roll over. I take a handful followed by a mouthful of him. He ain't never got to ask for it. I'm going to give it to him as freely and as much as I can. I tease and stroke him in ways that drive him insane. I feel him squeezing and clutching me as I pleasure him. I get on top of him. It is my turn to ride. We continue to work it out and sweat. We don't stop until we both reach our peaks and we climax together.

chapter 26
Christmas Joy

December 25, 2007

**Every child looks forward to this day. The day we celebrate
the birth of Christ. A day to be thankful that he was born and
willingly died for our sins. Also, a day full of presents and gifts.
The most important gift of all is the gift of eternal life.**

Early the next morning the house is awakened by my oldest nephew, Carmen's son, Andres. It's Christmas and it's time for everyone to open their presents. I reluctantly get up out of the bed, yawn, stretch and put some clothes on. I awake Adontis and he gets dressed and we head to the Christmas tree.

The children are bright eyed, bushy tailed and anxious to open their presents, while the adults just want to go back to bed. Especially me. That work out session Adontis and I had last night has worn me out. The children open their presents and have joyous smiles on their faces. They begin to play with their toys and show one another what they have gotten. Carmen begins to start fixing breakfast. One by one the men begin to open their presents and then the ladies go. I am taking pictures of everything so I go last.

I open the gifts from my brothers and sisters first. Then I open the gifts Adontis has gotten me. There are three of them. One is wrapped in a pretty Tinker Bell Christmas paper. He knows I love her. The others are wrapped in a pretty purple and white Merry Christmas paper.

He has gotten me everything I wanted. I never expected to get any of them. He was listening to my hints. I got the iPod and Mac Book I wanted. He also got me some accessories to go with them. I wasn't expecting either much less both. I am very grateful and I thank him.

"*Thank you, baby. I love them both so much. I didn't know you were paying me any attention.*"

"*I know you didn't. Hell, you left all of the necessary hints. But I got one more gift for you.*"

He goes to the garage and drags in a really big box. It's about the size of a 37-inch non-flat screen TV. The box has the same pretty Christmas themed Tinker Bell wrapping paper with a giant green bow. I look at him surprised.

"*Baby, what is this?*"

"*Open it and see.*"

I look around and see the entire room is in suspense with me. I begin to unwrap the box. I have no idea of what he has on the inside. I try to think about it, but I don't come up with anything. There was nothing else that I asked for. This box is so big. Plus, he was dragging it in the house. It must be heavy.

I push my wondering thoughts out of my mind and I finally unwrap the box. I remove the lid and inside I find a somewhat smaller gift-wrapped box. This one is wrapped in the pretty purple Merry Christmas paper. Adontis lifts it out of the box for me and sits it on the floor. I unwrap it and open it. I find another gift-wrapped box inside.

It is wrapped in the Tinker Bell gift wrap. Everyone is on the edge of their seats in suspense. I can't believe he did this to me. I begin the unwrapping process again and I do it nine more times. Each time the wrapping paper alternates from Tinker Bell to the pretty purple Merry Christmas. I look at Adontis who has a grand smirk on his face. I'm trying not to get irritated. At this point I'm about ready to quit.

"*You really think you funny, don't you?*"

He smirks. "*I love you.*"

Everyone is still sitting around smiling wondering what is inside the box. I unwrap what I hope is the last box. It is about the size of a gift card box. Before opening it, I look to Adontis.

"*There better not be another box in here.*"

He is wearing a smile. "*I guess you gon have to open it and see.*"

I open the box and there is not another box on the inside. This is the last box and inside this box I find air. It is completely empty. I turn it upside down and show everyone nothing is inside. The entire room erupts with laughter.

"*You got to be kidding me. All of that for nothing?*"

He looks just as surprised as me. He stretches his big eyes in surprise. "*Oh, snap shorty. I must have put the wrong box in there.*" He starts checking his pants pockets. "*Yo real gift must be in my pocket.*" He pulls something from out of his pocket.

I roll my eyes at him. "*I can't believe you put me through that for nothing.*"

"*Shorty, it was funny. A little Christmas laughter.*"

"*Whatever.*"

He hands me another box the same size as the last one, the size of a gift card. It is unwrapped. I open the box and inside I find a card. The card reads,

---

SAY YES!

I look over at him. *"Really Adontis? Say yes to what?"*
He smiles at me. *"Flip the card over shorty."*
I flip over the card and it says,

WILL YOU BE MY WIFE?

I begin to shake I can't believe it. I had no clue what was in the box, but I wasn't expecting this. He has caught me completely off guard. My man can keep a secret. I'm astonished. Tears are flowing from my eyes. I look over at Adontis. I want to get him to validate the words on the card. When my eyes meet his, he is on bended knee. My mouth drops open.

He is holding a ring box with a big ass diamond ring in the middle. The band is platinum and thick with diamonds going all the way around it. The ring is very over the top and blinged out. It is sparkling and shining like crazy. It looks like a princess cut diamond ring. If I had to guess I'd say the ring is about thirty-carats. Yes, I said thirty carats. I can spot a diamond anywhere and I know my carats. Just call me Bugs Bunny.

He removes the ring from the box. *"I ain't hearing you say yes yet ma."*

It would have been a beautiful moment, but with the tears I'm crying. I am not looking cute right now.

"Yes Baby! Yes! For the rest of my life, yes!"

He grabs my hand and slides the ring on to my finger. It's a perfect fit. The rock has a nice weight to it. He did his homework. He picks me up into the air and he kisses me. Everyone is standing around clapping and taking pictures. I kiss him and I don't want to stop.

"I love you baby. Thank you. This ring is beautiful."

"You did an amazing job Adontis," Carmen says.

"*Yes, you did,*" Kia chimes in.

Ron daps Adontis up, "*Thank you for your blessing, Ron.*"

"*My brother.*"

December 28, 2007

There has been a whole lot of love making since Adontis proposed to me. I haven't gotten much sleep these last couple of days. It has been worth it. A few weeks ago, I never would have thought Adontis and I would be here. I am happy as hell to be here. I'm going to be the new Mrs. Lamentez. I've called Diamond and Kenya to tell them the good news. Of course, they were both so happy for me. I asked them both to be in my wedding and they've accepted.

Adontis has gotten the blessing of my family. I found out that a few months back he apparently spoke with Ron and got his blessing to propose. My man did things the right way. Today we are flying out of Charleston to get his family's blessing. We are not going to even tell them that we are coming. The plan is to be in and out. Our flight leaves out at 9:02 am.

We take my car to the airport and park it there. Our flight is scheduled to land in New York at 11:05 am. We are going to give them the news and spend the day with them. Our flight back to Charleston leaves at 10:02 pm. The only person that knows is Aisha. She called me to congratulate us. She is in Florida spending the holiday with Boris' family.

At the airport we take a taxi to his parent's house. "*Baby I'm nervous. I don't think your mom is going to like this. Hell, I know she is not.*"

"*Ma, I don't give a damn. You make me happy. Moms can't live my life. I'm a grown ass man. I love you and I am marrying you. She just gonna have to accept the shit.*"

I let out a deep sigh. "*I think the shit is going to hit the fan.*"

"*I ain't worried about it ma. You need to stop worrying about it. We in this shit together. I ain't going nowhere.*"

He pulls me close to him and kisses me. I feel like I'm about to melt in his arms. We pull up to his parent's estate. Adontis punches in the code to the gate and has the driver, drive us up. There are a few cars outside. It looks like they have company. He pays the driver and we get out of the car.

"*Here goes nothing.*" Adontis rings the doorbell and his dad answers.

"*Hey son! Hello Tasha baby!*" He embraces the both of us in a hug. "*I'm so happy to see you kids. The house felt so empty. Come on in. Where is your luggage?*"

We walk in. "*We didn't bring any Pop. We are only here for the day. We are flying back out tonight.*"

"*Tonight, why so soon son?*"

"*We have to get back. We wanted to see ya'll. Where is mom?*"

"*Your mom is in the family room. Let's go ahead in and surprise her.*" I'm thinking oh she is going to be surprised alright. This lady might try to kill me.

"*Who all over here Pop?*"

"Your grandparents, Riq, his lady for the day or whatever you want to call her. Of course, Shaun and Melanie are here. Oh, Charlene and her daughter Charlotte."

I instantly remember the name. I look over at Adontis. "Ma don't start. You ain't got nothing to worry about."

"Baby I'm not worried."

He takes my hand as I follow behind him. I know I have the man, the ring and soon I'll have his last name. Charlotte isn't even competition. I'm only in competition with myself. As we are approaching, Mrs. Lamentez calls out from the great room.

"Honey who is at the door."

Mr. Lamentez doesn't answer yet, he just leads us to the great room. "Just look and see for yourself." He steps aside and allows her to see. I'm standing behind Adontis therefore she can't see me.

"My baby came home. And you came alone, without that-"

He cuts her off. "Ma, don't you dare."

Standing behind Adontis I'm trying to be respectful to her, but she is pissing me off. She has no reason not to like me. If it was for catching Adontis and I having sex I would understand, but she hasn't liked me since day one.

Grandma chimes in, "Marilyn child what is your problem?"

Mrs. Lamentez ignores her.

"I know you hear me talking to you child. Tasha is a lovely lady and she is going to be my granddaughter one day. I am happy to have her."

"Over my dead body. My son will never marry that girl."

Mr. Lamentez shakes his head. "Marilyn stop!"

"I am just trying to tell Adontis he can do better. Son you came just in time. Charlotte is here. Doesn't she look lovely."

I've had enough. I can't take anymore. His mother is so rude. I release Adontis' hand. When I let his hand go, he turns around.

"Baby wait."

He grabs my hand back. This is when his mom and the rest of the room sees me.

"I can't take any more of this Adontis."

I free my hand from his grip, turn around and walk towards the front door. I want out. Out of his mother's house. He comes running behind me. He catches me in the foyer.

"Baby." He grabs my hand and stops me from walking out.

We hear from the great room, "Marilyn you don't know when to shut up. You owe her an apology. You don't have to like her, but you need to respect her. Adontis chose her. That is who he wants to be with. He loves her and she makes him happy."

"Riq, I don't need to hear that." She looks to her husband, "Isaac, why didn't you tell me that girl was with him?"

"Don't put this on me Marilyn. I stepped aside so you could see them. I didn't realize that Adontis was blocking her until you put your foot in your mouth. You have never liked any woman that Adontis has brought home. He is a grown damn man. That is my son and I love him. I love

Tasha too. You are going to fix this." He looks to his parents, "*Please excuse my language Ma and Pop.*"

They both nod an ok to him.

"*I am not doing anything,*" Mrs. Lamentez exclaims!

The great room gets quiet. Tears are rolling down my face. She did hurt me. Because she is his mother I chose to walk away. If she was a bitch in the streets. It would have come to blows.

"*Adontis, let me go. I'm going back home.*"

He pulls me close to him. He is wiping the tears from my face. "*Baby don't cry. Home? Home where?*"

"*Charleston. I can't put up with this disrespect for the rest of my life.*"

"*Baby, we just got back right. I can't lose you ma. If you ready to go, we can go together. Let me just tell my dad we leaving and we getting married. Then we can go. Just promise you'll wait right here.*" I'm just looking at him. "*Ma promise me.*"

I let out a sigh. "*I'll wait.*"

He walks back to the great room. "*Dad, everyone we are going to leave.*"

"*Son don't leave. Marilyn, fix this.*" She doesn't say a word.

Grandma says, "*Son, where is Tasha?*"

"*She is in the foyer waiting on me.*"

Grandma gets up. "*I'm going to go talk to her.*"

"*Wait Grandma, before you do, there is something I want to say.*"

"*Ok baby. What is it?*"

"*Tasha and I came up here today, hoping to spend the day with the family. This was supposed to be a one-day trip with us flying out tonight. Mom you ruined that. More importantly you deeply hurt the woman I love. I love you moms, but I love Tasha too. I need you to accept that and stop treating her this way.*"

He pauses for a response from his mom, but she doesn't say anything. "*Ok. We also came up here to tell everyone that I asked Tasha to marry me on Christmas day. She said yes. Ma she ain't going nowhere.*"

Mrs. Lamentez gets up and walks off. "*I'm not accepting nothing.*"

Mr. Lamentez hugs Adontis. "*That's what I'm talking about son. I'm happy for the both of you. Let me go give my daughter another hug.*"

I'm hearing all of this and I'm trying to compose myself. I can't. Mascara has run down my face and I look a fucking mess. I quietly open the door and step outside. I run to the side of the house. I take my mirror out of my purse and a makeup wipe. My lashes are falling off. I clean my face up and try to get myself together.

I hear the front door open and Mr. Lamentez say, "*Son where is Tasha?*"

My cell begins to ring. I know it is Adontis. I have glue on my lash in one hand and my mirror in the other hand. My phone rings again. I put the lash on and then it rings again. I get my next lash ready then I put it on. My phone hasn't stopped ringing. I dig in my purse and pull it out. I answer the phone.

"*Ma where you at? You promised me you was gonna wait for me.*"

"I needed to fix my make up."

"Where ma? I done checked all of the bathrooms downstairs."

"I'm outside."

"Ma, its cold as shit out there."

"It's colder in there."

"Where you at outside?"

"On the left side of the house by the garage."

"I'm coming."

With the size of his parent's home, it takes a little while for him to reach me. He walks up to me. *"Some people in there want to talk to you. Pop, Unc, Grandma and Pops want to hug and congratulate you."*

"I'm just ready to go babe. Like one of the happiest moments of our lives just got ruined. I'm in a sour mood."

"Baby shake it off. I know my moms hurt your feelings. It was mean as shit. I'm pissed about it. Because you an extension of me. When you hurt ma, I hurt too. I wish I could change it or fix it. But I can't. What I can do is love you. Show you that love and surround you with my family that loves you and wants to show that love to you also."

I'm still hurting, but his efforts do ease my pain. *"Ok baby."*

He pulls me into his arms and kisses me. *"You ready to go back inside ma?"*

"No not really. But let's get it over with."

He leads me back into the house. We head into the great room. His mom still is not in the room.

"I apologize for my wife Tasha. I don't know what her problem is. I love you and I just want to say welcome to the family sweetheart." He grabs me and gives me a great big hug. *"I'm honored to have you as my daughter."*

"Thank you. Mr. Lamentez. I'm honored that you'd have me."

"Call me Pop."

I receive love and kind words from the rest of his family.

Mr. Lamentez looks at Charlene and Charlotte. *"I apologize ladies, meet my daughter, Tasha."*

They both say hello. It seems very begrudged. I say, *"Hello."*

Charlene says, *"I think we are going to go ahead and leave. Please tell Marilyn I will call her later."*

"Yes, I will do." Mr. Lamentez escorts them to the door.

I'm just looking at Adontis like I'm ready to go and he gets the point. Mr. Lamentez comes back to the great room.

"Alright Dad. Tasha and I are going to go ahead and leave."

"Nonsense. My oldest son just got engaged. We have to celebrate. Let us get dressed and we can go get something to eat. We are leaving Marilyn right here."

Adontis looks at me, putting me on the spot. I'm really ready to go, but I don't want to take away from Adontis the chance to celebrate us with his family. At least the ones that want to celebrate.

"Ok baby."

"We'll wait for ya'll down here."

Uncle Riq, his lady, Shaun, Adontis and I wait in the great room while his dad and grandparents get dressed. After about half an hour they are all downstairs. It is finally realized that they never saw the ring.

Grandma brings it up, *"Let us see this ring baby."* I show her the ring. *"My Lord, it's beautiful. And so big. I pray that your marriage will be just as beautiful."*

"Thank you, Grandma."

We all head out and go out to eat. We have a good time and great conversation. His mom not being here makes it drama free. After our early dinner, we go by Fresh, then we go out for ice cream. When we finish, it is time for us to go to the Airport. After a few hours we are back in Charleston. I couldn't be happier. I have got to tell Carmen about this trip. Adontis drives us to Carmen's. I want to be around my family tonight. I am exhausted and I just want to sleep. I won't tell Carmen tonight. We'll be here until the third. We head back to Florida that morning. I have plenty of time to tell her.

We get in the house and everyone is asleep. I walk into the guest bedroom, get my night clothes together and walk in the bathroom. I'm stripping out of my clothes as Adontis walks in behind me. I'm still in my bra and panties when he wraps his arms around me. I'm not in the mood for sex. I just feel stressed.

"Ma, I know it been a long day. It didn't go as we planned and things turned sour. I'm sorry that it went the way it did. I know you hurt. You haven't said much since it all happened. I understand. I want to help you relax. Can you step out of the bathroom for a minute and let me get this together for you?"

"Adontis, I just want to wash and go to sleep."

"Baby, please let me do this for you."

I exhale. *"Ok."*

I walk out of the bathroom and go sit on the bed. He comes in the bedroom and grabs his suitcase. After a little while he comes back in the bedroom with his suitcase. He is in his birthday suit. He grabs my hand and pulls me up from the bed. Then spins me around with my back facing him. He unhooks my bra and then slides it off of me. His hands slide down to my waist. He grabs the top of my panties and pulls them down to my ankles. I step out of them. He leads me to the bathroom and closes the door.

The bathroom lights are off and he has lit and spread candles all around the room. There is a hot bubble bath waiting for me. He turns on soft relaxing music. He leads me over to the garden tub.

"Ok ma. Step in." I step in and he gets in behind me. *"Your bubble bath is filled with Lavender and Jasmine. I want to help you relax."*

I lay in the tub for a while with my head resting against his chest and my eyes closed. He was right. This bath is so relaxing. He begins massaging my neck and shoulders, then my back.

"You are so tense shorty. Daddy going to work it out."

He massages and rubs me into relaxation. When he finishes, he washes me. It's sexy to feel my man touch me so tenderly. It's not sexual, but gentle. Careful. He is caring for me. When he finishes, he gets me out the tub and dries me off and then himself. He lifts me up and then carries me to the bed. He pulls the covers back and lays me down. He covers me up and kisses me on the lips.

"Get some rest ma. I love you."

"Thank you, baby. I love you too."

He walks back into the bathroom to clean up. I drift off to sleep. I don't know for how long, but I feel the covers pull back. Adontis slides in the bed behind me. He pulls me into his arms and holds me close.

chapter 27

Can't Keep A Good Woman Down

June 16, 2008

**What goes around, always comes around.
You have to jump over life's hurtles.**

Three months ago, Kia finally had my nephew. I haven't been able to go home to see him yet and it is driving me crazy. Pictures just aren't enough. I can't wait to hold and kiss and love all over him. We will be going to see him soon. Aside from that, the last six months have been fairly peaceful and quiet.

In spite of the drama, Adontis and I are still happily engaged. We are having a somewhat long engagement. We dated officially, for almost a year before he popped the question. Quite naturally after Christmas and his amazing proposal I came back to Jacksonville with him. We both made promises to one another and we have been keeping them.

I have started interning at the local hospital and I love it. I'm also still working at Fresh. Between both jobs and school, I'm really busy. It's good to work at the store with Adontis because it gives us time together. Fresh is doing great. We've opened a few more stores in Florida and New York. Soon we will be opening up new locations in a third state, Georgia.

He has five chains opened and he is opening a few more in Georgia over the next couple of years. After Georgia we will start looking into opening stores in North Carolina. The first Jacksonville store is his home office. Every now and again he has to do some light traveling for business reasons. I go with him every chance I get. Which really means as long as I don't have to be in class.

Our wedding is in six months. It is scheduled for January. I've always wanted a winter wedding. It will be in my hometown of Charleston, South Carolina. Our lives are really good despite his mom's behavior. Nothing with her has changed. Adontis isn't speaking to her. She isn't speaking to him either. I know it bothers him. I wish I could fix it, but I don't know what to do. The word on the street is she isn't coming to our wedding. His dad has said that he'll be there no matter what.

I'm trying to be a better me so I want to get right with his mom. I am continually working on me. I am doing my best to do everything right. She and I will soon be family. I want the drama to stop. Even though I am not the one with the problem. I am willing to do whatever is necessary to make it stop and to keep my man happy. Even biting my tongue when it comes to his mom. I doubt she will come no matter what I do. We are going to take a trip to visit his parents again in a few months and see if we can change her mind.

Moving forward, I plan to do a lot of traveling to my hometown to make wedding arrangements. I have been working a lot of long hours and going to school when I'm not working. I have not been home very often. Outside of Fresh, Adontis and I manage to make time for one another, no matter what.

After work and school, I get settled back at home. I take a shower and I manage to prepare dinner. My honey is working late tonight. He has inventory to do. I pack dinner up picnic style and head over to Fresh.

I pull up to Fresh and the parking lot is deserted, aside from a few cars. It is after business hours so the store is closed. With the basket in hand, I head to the front of the store. I unlock the door, step in and lock back up. I quietly creep to the back, where the office and stock room are. I hear the sound of a few voices as I approach. I step through the back door and around the corner. I see Adontis and his three store managers. One male and two females. They haven't seen or heard me. Their backs are all towards me. Thankfully it is nothing, but business going on I see. Everything is on the up and up.

Still unaware that I am there, Adontis says, *"Ok team. I think everything here looks good. Thank you for all ya'll do. I couldn't do this without you. Ya'll can head out. I have a few more things to finish up just lock up on your way out."*

The store manager looks to Adontis, *"Ok boss. Sounds good. I'll see you tomorrow."*

The assistant manager and key holder chime in their goodnights. Before they have a chance to spin around to see me, I clear my throat. In unison they spin around. I look to Adontis, then to the managers.

"Hey baby. Hey guys."

They all greet me with a hello. They gather their things, say goodnight and then head out of the store. Adontis hasn't said a word. He's just staring at me.

"Honey, are you ok?"

"Yeah, I'm good shorty. I wasn't expecting to see you here."

"Do you want me to leave?"

"Don't put words in my mouth."

He walks up to me, wraps his arms around me then leans down and kisses me.

"Ok. I knew you was working late, I thought I'd bring you dinner."

I lift up the picnic basket I'm holding. He takes the basket from my hand and sits it on the desk. He takes in a handful of my ass and pulls me in closer to him.

"I thought you was bringing me dessert."

I smirk. *"Is that why you looking at me like that?"*

"Hell yeah! I was waiting to hear the staff leave. While thinking some dirty thoughts of what I wanted to do to you."

"Why you always gotta be so nasty?"

I reach for the basket attempting to unpack dinner. He grabs my hands, holds them up in the air and interlocks his fingers in between mines.

"You like daddy nasty," he says, as he begins kissing on my neck.

"Adontis baby it's late. I figured we'd have dinner and some wine. I'd help you finish up here then we'd head home to bed."

"I have a different idea."

He is still kissing on my neck, which has led him to start sucking on my neck.

"I don't think I wanna know your idea."

He starts laughing. *"Why not? Anytime anyplace."*

I try to free my hands when he catches my lip in between his. He begins sucking and nibbling.

In between nibbles I say, *"You're not hungry?"*

"Yeah. I'm trying to eat you, but you playing."

I laugh out loud. *"Your dinner is going to get cold."*

"That's what the microwave for."

I look at him and just shake my head. This wasn't what I had in mind. I decide to just give up on the fight. He's not going to give up.

"Ok."

"That's what daddy wants to hear."

He does his ear to ear grin and shows off his beautiful dimples. He moves the basket to a chair then lifts me on to his desk. He pulls up my dress and pulls it over my head. I'm sitting on the desk and I open my legs for him to come in between. I begin to unbutton his shirt as I kiss down his chest. I reach his pants, unbuckle his belt and then unbutton them. Tugging on his boxers I slide them down. He grabs the bottle of wine, opens it and drinks from the bottle. He gestures the bottle towards me and I take a sip. His lips have reached mines while his hands undo my bra then trail off to my thong. He pushes it to the side and slides his fingers inside. I begin to moan as he awakens the hunger in me for him.

He holds my thong to the side as he slides in me and begins to ride. I begin moaning as he is hitting my g spot with every stroke. He kisses trails of hickeys down my neck to my breast. He pulls out and spins me around. Bending me over the desk he rips my thong off. Naughtily I look over my shoulder at him. He places a hand over my belly pulling me close to him as he slides in me again.

I'm moaning out his name as I feel him deep in me. His other hand is squeezing on my breast, while his lips are kissing on my neck. I turn to face him and he moves his lips to mines. I begin to feel me reach my peak. My nails dig into the arm, he's wrapped around me. I begin moaning louder and faster as an orgasm burst from me. He strokes me a few more times. Before clutching my hips between his hands. He cums all in me.

He stays in me for a few moments as he kisses down my neck. *"Damn shorty."*

I look back at him, *"What?"*

He pulls out of me and just shakes his head. *"You do something to me. Damn. I love you ma."*

"I love you too daddy." I smile and kiss him. *"You ready to eat now?"*

"Hell yeah. I worked up an appetite."

"Yes, you did."

We slide back in our clothes; I warm dinner and we eat. Afterwards I help him finish up at the store and we leave for home.

June 17, 2008

I arrive at work early this morning. As soon as I get in, I check in with my supervisor and then get to work. I usually work a split shift. This way I can go to work early in the morning. Leave and go to school during the late morning. Then come back to work in the evening.

Since it is summertime, I have just finished my classes and I did not enroll into summer school. I will be enrolling in classes in the fall. However, I will take next spring's semester off. There is no way I can get married, handle school and other things. I probably should take the year off, but I don't want to get too far behind.

After making some of my rounds I begin to feel a little faint. I am having hot flashes and something just doesn't feel right. I end up rushing to the bathroom. I barely make it into the stall before it erupts out of me. I'm vomiting.

After I get it all out, I go to my supervisor and tell her I'm not feeling well. I don't want to get checked out at my job. I don't want my coworkers in my personal business. I leave and I go to my personal doctor. To my OB. I think I know what's wrong, but I'm hoping it's not the case.

I arrive at my doctor's office and I have a long wait because I don't have an appointment. The nurse finally calls me back so the doctor can see me. I tell the nurse that I haven't been feeling well lately and that I just threw up. She takes blood and urine samples. I am left alone for a while and after some time the nurse returns with my doctor.

After greeting each other, she sits on her stool. *"I know what's wrong with you Tasha. You have been feeling sick because you are pregnant."*

Pregnant rings in my ears over and over again. All I can think to myself is not again. Damn. I can be a spokesperson against birth control. It sure as hell doesn't work. Either that or I am fertile as hell. Every time my life gets on track. I get pregnant. I don't want a baby before marriage, but I damn sure will not abort another baby. I look at her and ask her what I asked her the last time.

"Are you sure?"

"Yes, I am sure. Like always there are other options. I know how hard it was for you the last time. Maybe you can call someone."

"No! I am not doing that again. I just want to keep what happened the last time between you and me. I will be ok."

The doctor and I establish my due date and she prescribes me prenatal vitamins. I schedule my next appointment and I go to my car. I lay my head against the head rest and I take a deep breath and exhale. I crank up my car and I go to the pharmacy and then home.

I get into the bed and I fall asleep. I feel a soft and gentle kiss on my lips. I open my eyes and I see Adontis.

He asks, *"Baby you feeling ok? You are never sleep, or home for that matter, this early."*

"No. I left work early and went to the doctor."

He sits on the bed next to me. *"Why didn't you call me ma?"*

"I decided to wait for you to get home."

"You still should of called me. What's wrong with daddy's shorty? What the doctor say?"

I sit up to face him so I can look him in the eyes when I tell him the news. *"Nothing much of anything. She just wrote me this prescription and told me I was pregnant."*

His big eyeballs stretch and his mouth drops open. *"Pregnant?"*

"Yes. A little over two months."

"Wowwwwwwww." He places his hands on my stomach and kisses my belly. *"I am going to be a daddy?"*

I flash him a smile. *"Yeah. Duh. Obviously."*

"Well, how you feel ma?"

"I feel better. I am glad to know why I have been so tired lately."

"Yeah, that's good, but that's not what I meant. How do you feel about being pregnant?"

"Ok, I guess. I was shocked when I found out. Like I've been on the pill to prevent this. But here I am pregnant. But I am happy about it, I guess. How do you feel?"

"I love you. I'm very happy. You know I been wanting you to have my babies for a while. This one down three to go. We ain't plan this, but it's all good. You need me to do anything?"

I just smile at him. *"No baby. I am fine. The doctor just said I need to get some rest. What you mean for a while we were supposed to wait until after we were married?"*

"Well last year when you thought you was pregnant, even though it was unexpected, I was kind of happy. I started getting use to the thought of being a Daddy and having another little me or a little you running around. Then when I found out you weren't, I was kind of disappointed."

I lay back down in the bed. *"Wow. I didn't know that. Well, your wish has now come true."*

He kisses me again and lays beside me. *"Yes, it has. When the time comes, I can't wait to tell everybody. What about our wedding?"*

I let out a long sigh. *"I don't know baby."*

"Well, we got three options. Move the wedding up. Move the wedding back. Get married on the original date."

"I don't like those choices."

"Well baby it don't matter to me. I'll marry you whenever and wherever."

"Our wedding is seven months away. I'll be nine months then. Our baby is due on our wedding day. I guess we gotta push it back."

"Okay. That's fine with me. If we push it back, we can go to the courthouse and get married before our baby gets here. Then have a ceremony later after our baby is born. Plus, that will give us more time to convince mom to come to our wedding."

"Yeah, I guess it will. Wait, you want to get married at a courthouse?"

"I just wanna marry you. I don't care where. And I want you with my last name before the baby gets here."

"Ok. Well, let me think on it and we'll go from there."

"Alight ma."

"The one thing I know is I'm done with birth control pills. The shit doesn't seem to work. We were better off using the pull-out method."

"Hell, no ma. That shit don't work either. Do you know how hard it is for me to pull out? Shit you probably got pregnant that time when you picked up your refill late. I ain't never pulled out in time."

"Really and you're just now telling me this? Adontis, you doing too much. You might be right though, I forgot about that."

"Hell yes. We been in the moment. Your pussy so damn good. You have to get on something or your ass will get pregnant again for sure by February. That's fine with me, but you might want a break."

I look at him sideways. "Hell no. I'll talk with my doctor after our baby is born and see what the best option is."

"You betta. I love you ma. Get some rest." He wraps me in his arms and I fall back to sleep.

chapter 28
Twenty-Three

July 10, 2008

**The age I will be when I become a mom and get married. I look
forward to this being the happiest year of my life yet.**

My birthday is coming up. I'm ready to have a good time. Tomorrow Adontis and I will
be flying into Charleston. We will be celebrating with my closest family and friends including
Aisha and Boris. They are flying in with us.

Shaun is in Miami and he won't be able to make it. Miami will be the home of a Phoenix
night club. His grand opening is next weekend. He's been down there for a few months.
Melanie has traveled back and forth to see him when she could. I didn't invite her to my
birthday weekend. If Shaun isn't coming, she doesn't need to.

I plan to spend time with my family Friday night followed by a nice dinner Saturday and
a small gathering at Carmen's with games Sunday night. We haven't told anyone about my
pregnancy yet. I'm not quite ready to share the news. I know the suspicions will be flying
around when everyone sees I'm not drinking. I don't know how I will play that off for three
days. I'll have to think of something.

Next Monday we have an early morning flight out to Turks and Caicos Island. Just Adontis
and I. He didn't want to tell me, but he had to so I'd pack accordingly and to take off from
work. We'll be there for an entire week. It's a lovely vacation before our baby arrives. Soon it
will be all mommy and daddy duties for the both of us. I'm going to have to pack some sexy
lingerie as well as swim wear. I won't be able to fit any of my sexy stuff as my pregnancy
progresses. Adontis better enjoy it while he can.

Adontis walks in the bedroom while I'm wrapping up packing. *"Hey love."* He leans in and
plants a kiss on me. Then he leans in and kisses my belly. *"Hey daddy's baby."*

"*Hey daddy.*" He is rubbing my belly. I'm shaking my head in disbelief. "*You are so over the top.*"

"*You damn straight. My love is carrying our love.*" I smile at him. He pulls me in and kisses me again. "*Yep, just let me have my moment. Don't fight it.*"

I don't. "*You got it baby.*"

July 11, 2008

Adontis, Aisha, Boris and I arrive in Charleston early this Friday morning. All of my family is still at work. I check in with Carmen and let her know we've arrived safely. We get a rental car and head to Carmen's. Carmen has already gotten the guest bedrooms together for the four of us. I let us in and show Boris and Aisha to their rooms and we all get settled in. Adontis and I are alone in our bedroom.

"*Your baby is hungry.*"

He walks up and puts his arms around me. "*Oh yeah. Which one?*"

"*Both of us.*"

He burst out laughing. "*Ok shorty. Let's get ya'll fed.*" He calls out to Aisha, "*A sis, ya'll wanna go get something to eat.*"

She hollers back, "*Absolutely.*"

We leave and head out for breakfast. After we eat, we hit the mall and shop a little bit before going back to my sisters. We get back late in the afternoon. We relax in front of the tv. I fall asleep, until Carmen arrives with my nephews. My face lights up when I see each of them. They are now nine, five and three. Carmen leaves the boys downstairs with us then goes upstairs to get settled.

I get a chance to play with the boys a bit and I couldn't be happier. A few hours later Kia and Ron show up with their kids. My two nieces who are also five and three and my newborn nephew who will be four months in a few days. I practically run to Kia to get him from her hands.

"*Auntie's Baby!*"

Kia looks at me and sarcastically says, "*Damn Tasha, how are you too?*"

Ron chimes in, "*Right!*"

I smile, "*My bad ya'll I've been waiting so long to meet him. Pass him here Kia.*"

"*Well, you shouldn't of moved so far away.*"

I give him a stink look, "*Really Ron. You know what, it ain't about you. It's about me and my nieces and nephews.*"

He laughs, "*Whatever girl.*" He gives me a hug and then walks over to Adontis. They dap one another up. "*What's up bro?*"

"*Nothing much big bro?*"

I roll my eyes and take my nephew from Kia. I head back to the sofa and sit next to Adontis. We spend the night just watching movies and order takeout. It is very relaxing and exactly what I need.

July 12, 2008

My morning starts out with me running to the toilet. They call it morning sickness, but it's more like anytime sickness. After throwing up I brush my teeth and return to the bedroom. I notice Adontis hasn't budged he's still fast asleep in bed. I grab my phone and look at the clock. It's a little past four in the morning. I climb back in the bed and that's when he stirs. His eyes crack open and he looks at me.

"You good ma?"

"Yeah baby. Go back to sleep."

I don't have to tell him twice. He plants a kiss on me and then envelops me into his arms. Before I know it, he's asleep again. It's not long before I join him.

Within a few hours I awake again. We start our morning with breakfast as a family. Afterwards we head to the fun park for arcade games and outdoor games. I usually ride in the go karts, but with being pregnant, I won't. My baby is too important. I suggest to Adontis that we play golf. He, Aisha, Boris and I play miniature golf. The rest of the guys do go karts with the three oldest kids. Carmen and Kia sit out with the rest of the kids. We stay there through lunch time and grab a bite to eat there before heading back to Carmen's.

We have a few hours to relax before getting ready to head to dinner. We head to our rooms. Carmen puts her two younger boys down for a nap. A sitter will be coming over to watch them, while we are out. In the bedroom I begin to undress. I'm tired. I head to the bathroom and step in the shower. Adontis comes in after me.

"You need some help shorty?"

I know what his help entails and all I want is to take a nap. I smile at him. *"Absolutely not. I know where your mind is."*

He grins at me as he undresses and steps in the shower behind me. *"Ma, what you mean?"*

"It means I'm tired and I just want to take a nap. No sex."

"You act like I don't have no self-control."

I burst out laughing, *"You don't!"*

He looks offended. *"Ma that's cold. I ain't gon bother you. I'm gon shower and then lay down til its time to get ready."*

"Ok. Good."

He stays to his word; we finish our shower and slip into bed. He lays on his back and turns the tv on. I lay across his chest.

"What you doing shorty?"

I look up at him. *"What you mean? I'm laying down to take a nap."*

"Ok, but why you laying on me?"

"Oh! I can't lay on you now?"

"Nope," he says, as he smirks!

Now I'm offended. I sit up to look at him, like you can't be serious. *"It's like that?"*

"Yep," he says with a smile.

I roll my eyes. He's being an ass and I didn't see it coming. I don't say another word. I move away from him and get on my side of the bed.

He starts laughing, *"I was just playing with you ma!"*

I don't find it funny. I don't respond or acknowledge what he said.

"Tasha!"

I'm silent.

He sits up, throws the covers back and rolls over to me. He leans over me, *"Ma, I know you hear me. I'm just messing with you."*

My eyes are closed and I still don't respond to him.

"Now, you just being stubborn."

I still don't say a word or open my eyes.

"Ok."

I hear him scooting away from me. I feel his hands slide up under my body as he scoops me up into his arms then he lays me on top of him. Finally, I break my silence.

"What are you doing?"

I begin to maneuver to get off of him. He wraps his arms around me before I can go anywhere.

"Why you been ignoring me?"

I sigh. *"Adontis let me go to sleep."*

"Go to sleep. But I ain't letting you go. You gon sleep right here in daddy's arms."

I roll my eyes.

"I don't care if you roll your damn eyes."

With one hand he pulls the covers over us. He begins rubbing my outer thigh, which he knows soothes me. I don't feel like fussing with him anymore. I don't say another thing. I lay there on his broad chiseled chest and relax into him. I enjoy the comfort of his arms gently wrapped around me. He continues to rub me down as I drift off to sleep.

I feel his hands patting me on the butt. *"Shorty get up, it's time to get ready."*

I sit up from his chest, where I leave a small puddle of drool. I wipe it off with my hands. He laughs. *"You was tired huh?"*

I yawn, while rubbing my eyes. *"Yes, I was."*

He leans in and plants his lips to mines right in the middle of my yawn. He pulls me into a passionate kiss as he slides his tongue in my mouth.

I pull back. *"What are you doing?"*

He looks at me confused. *"What you mean?"*

"I was just in a deep sleep, with drool and all. I know I got morning breath."

He laughs. *"Girl please. You all mines. You taste good to me."* He pulls me towards him and begins kissing me again. I don't fight it. It's pointless anyway. *"I'm gon stop now, or we ain't gon make it to dinner."*

I laugh. *"Then you better stop. Me and the baby hungry."*

He plants soft pecks on my lips while rubbing my belly. *"Daddy gon stop. Let's get ready then so I can feed my babies."* He throws the covers back and we get up to begin getting ready.

We hear a knock at the door. *"Tasha, ya'll up,"* Carmen asks?

"Yes," I answer back.

"Ok."

Tonight, I am wearing a hot pink mini dress. It poofs out around the belly and waist area and it has pockets on the sides. I chose this dress because it helps to conceal my belly since I am showing a little. Naked, I look like I'm bloated. I'm still sexy. My dress is sleeveless, strapless and zips up the back.

It's comes down about mid-thigh. I have on some strap up heels that tie up my legs. I've accessorized with the diamond earrings and the tennis bracelet that Adontis bought me. I walk out the bathroom once I'm fully dressed. Adontis is laying across the bed watching sports center.

"Damn ma don't hurt em. You look beautiful baby."

"Thanks, baby." I'm running my hand across my stomach area as I mouth to him, *"Do I look pregnant?"*

"You look beautiful shorty."

"Oh my God, so I do?"

"Ma calm down. No, you don't." He wraps me in his arms. *"Let's see if everyone is ready."*

Tonight's dinner is at the restaurant where Adontis and I shared our first date. It's a really nice restaurant and the food is great. I'm going to eat until my heart is content tonight. We have a reservation for sixteen. The list is: Carmen, Frank, Ron, Kia, Aisha, Boris, Diamond, Eliah, Kenya, Deon, Shena (my cousin), Byron (my cousin), Janet, Rita, Adontis and I.

I wish I could drink so bad right now, but I can't. The only reason I can think of is that I have a headache, but I don't know if that will work. I guess we'll see. We all arrive around the same time and get seated. Kenya and Diamond introduces everyone to their men. I know all about them, but this is my first time meeting them. One side of the table has a long bench and the other has individual chairs.

"Baby I want to sit on the bench."

"Ok ma. Slide in and I'll come after you."

I slide about midway in. After sliding in Adontis follows. I lean into him and whisper in his ear, *"You always cum after me daddy."*

His eyeballs stretch and I know I caught him off guard. He licks his lips and starts laughing showing off his dimples. He leans in and whispers back to me. *"Your ass is so nasty."*

We have tuned everyone else out and begin whispering back and forth to one another. I smile at him. *"Did I say something wrong?"*

"Nope. That's what I'm supposed to do."

I bite on my bottom lip. *"You gon do that for me tonight too?"*

"You betta stop that, for I take you in the bathroom right now."

The thought runs through my mind as I smile at him. *"Don't threaten me with a good time."*

We are completely wrapped up in one another, when Shena clears her throat. *"Ummm ya'll know we here with ya'll right?"* Everyone is staring at the both of us.

Adontis smirks. I smile. *"Yes cuz, we know. Sorry everyone."*

Shena just shakes her head and laughs.

Everyone has taken their seats. Adontis is to the right of me. Kenya and Deon are to my left. With Shena to the head of the table on Deon's left. Aisha is to the right of Adontis with Boris followed by Rita. Byron is to the right of Rita at the opposite head of the table from Shena. Across from me is Carmen with Frank to her left. Ron to her right and Kia to his right. To the left of Frank is Diamond and Eliah. To the left of them is Janet and across from her is Rita.

Everyone begins ordering drinks, and I only order water. I feel several eyes on me. Diamond looks at me, *"You ordering water Tasha?"*

I feel the eyes of everyone that was thinking what Diamond asked staring at me. Adontis is quiet as a church mouse. He ain't provide no back up at all. *"Yes. I have a slight headache and I want to get some food in me first to see if it goes away."*

No one says another word. They just stare at me questionably.

"Ok ma. I'll order a water with you too," Adontis finally speaks up. He gets some side eye looks too. Including me. He leans in and whispers to me. *"Why you looking at me like that shorty."*

"I was wondering how long you was gon leave me there drowning in that question."

"Ma. Come on now. I wasn't expecting that. Daddy got your back, always."

"Uh huh."

"Don't play with me girl." He tilts my chin up to his so we are staring each other in the eyes. *"I always got you. Forever shorty."* He leans in and kisses me while rubbing my belly. *"Don't you ever question that and don't ever forget it. I love you shorty."*

"I love you too daddy."

Kenya says, *"Aww, ya'll are just so stinking cute together."*

"Thank you."

"No, no thank you. We here to eat, we don't want to see all of that," Kia says as she smirks.

I laugh. *"You such a hater."*

Everyone chuckles for a bit. I'm just glad that the alcohol talk is over for now. Adontis is chatting with Ron. I turn to Kenya and begin chatting with her a bit. We catch up and she tells me what she has going on in her life. She is moving to Charlotte, North Carolina to be with her man. Things are heating up between them.

We order our meals and the conversations go well throughout the night. The remainder of dinner goes well and I avoid alcohol. Adontis got a chance to chat with Deon a bit and I think they are going to be cool. Deon is a real estate broker and Adontis wants to look at some properties in North Carolina soon to open up some stores.

The cake comes out and they sing happy birthday to me. We eat and enjoy the cake. I thank everyone for coming and for my birthday cards. I read them out loud to everyone. After a great dinner and conversation, we say our goodnights until tomorrow for game night. Back at Carmen's, Adontis and I get settled in for bed. I stand in front of Adontis with my back to him.

"Baby, can you unzip this?"

"Hell yeah. I been wanting to get you naked since you put this dress on."

"Oh really?"

"Yep. Well naked, but you can leave the heels on."

He slides my zipper down and pulls me into him as he begins kissing on the back of my neck. I feel his hand slide to my bra as he unhooks it. I step out of my dress, slide my bra and thong off.

"You got me naked daddy, what you gon do?"

He looks me up and down and smiles. *"Lay on your belly across the bed ma."*

I look at him questionably.

"You heard me, go ahead and do it."

I like when he talks sternly to me like that. I don't say another word I just look at him for a moment while I bite my bottom lip. Then I lay across the bed. I hear him behind me, but I don't know what he is doing. My head is resting on my hands and my legs are folded up in the air crossed at the ankles. I do hear him unbuckling his belt and unzipping his pants. I hear what I assume is his clothes falling to the floor. Then I hear another zipper, which sounds like it could be his suitcase. After a few more moments I hear him walking further away from me.

"Stay right there shorty. I'll be right back."

Before I have a chance to respond he has slipped out of the bedroom. I don't know what he is up to, but I know he never fails to satisfy me. After several minutes he returns. I hear something else fall to the floor. He hits the light switch and I can see what seems to be candlelight bouncing off the walls in front of me. I don't know when he packed candles. He must have snuck them in his suitcase after I finished packing it.

I hear him walking towards me, finally. He climbs onto the bed on top of me. I feel his man hood resting on my ass running up my back. His hands rest on the bed above each of my shoulders, holding him up over me. He leans in and kisses me on my neck as he begins to kiss his way down my spine.

"You ready for what daddy bout to give you?"

I look over my shoulder at him. *"Born ready!"*

He laughs, *"Ok shorty, I hear you."*

He gets off of me and the bed. I feel something warm being poured down my back. Adontis' hands meet my back as he begins to sensually massage me. It is massage oil. He starts at my neck and shoulders. He's kissing me as he is rubbing me down. While he's working his way down my back, his lips are on my neck. He's nibbling and sucking on me.

He continues working his way down my body, placing his lips and tongue all over me as he goes. He's made his way to my lower back and booty. His touches are orgasmic. I want to touch myself, or rather I want him to touch me, the way he has me feeling. I've been moaning since he started and I continue a little louder with each touch.

He begins palming my ass cheeks as he is massaging them, while planting kisses all over my butt. He reaches down to my thighs and continues massaging me down to my toes, leaving kisses everywhere his hands go. He begins kissing back up my body until he reaches my lips.

"Damn you taste so good."

He gets up and rolls me over to my back. Starting at my shoulders down to my arms and breast he massages me. He gently rubs and massages my belly, while kissing my stomach. He spreads my legs and begins massaging my inner thighs down both of my legs to my feet. He has massaged every inch of me and I want him in me now. Overall, the massage last about forty minutes. I beckon him to enter in between my legs. He complies and slips in between my thighs. Placing kisses on me until he reaches my lips.

"Thank you, baby. I really enjoyed that."

"You deserve it shorty."

I catch his lip in between mines and nibble on it then I begin kissing him. He kisses down my body to my breast, belly, thighs, legs, ankles and toes. He begins to work his way back up. After he kisses my thighs, he takes a detour to my kitty kat. I've been dripping wet since the massage. He lifts my legs over his shoulders and begins to make love to her with his mouth.

I'm feeling sheer ecstasy. My toes start to curl. I'm clutching the sheets in between my fingers as I'm moaning out his name. After making me cum, he lifts his head up and looks at me with a smile. He licks all of me from around his lips and continues to kiss his way back up to me.

With my legs still on his shoulders he has reached my lips and he begins kissing. He positions himself and he slides into me. I grab my ankles as he begins to make love to me. He glides in and out of me with long deep thrust. His lips are on mines as we make love. He is hitting my g spot and I orgasm again. His lips have moved to my neck as he nibbles me there. I release one of my ankles and let it rest on his shoulder. With my free hand I cover my mouth to mask my screams of ecstasy. He pulls my hand from my face.

"I want to hear you and I want to see all of you."

I moan as quietly as I can. *"Oh Adontis, ahhhhhh baby. Oh my God, I'm fucking cumming!"*

He smiles, *"That's right cum for daddy."*

Sweat beads have formed on his forehead. He is putting in work. With my free hand I wipe the sweat away. He pulls out of me and rolls over pulling me on top of him. He licks his lips.

"You gon show daddy, how you ride it?"

July 13, 2008

I smile at him as I slide him into me and begin to ride. We continue to make love through the night, changing positions several more times before reaching our peaks. When we finish, I'm lying on Adontis' chest and worn out. I've scratched up his back a bit. My nails went into his skin several times.

"It's not even officially my birthday yet and that's how you do me?"

He smirks. *"Yep. I love you ma."*

I kiss his lips again. *"I love you back daddy."*

Adontis and I sleep late into the morning. When I awake, I'm still on his chest and he is fast asleep. Normally I'd bug him, but Daddy worked me hard last night he needs his rest. I pull the covers back to get out of bed and when I move, Adontis awakes.

"Good morning, Daddy. I was trying not to wake you."

He wraps his arms around me. *"That's a first. What time is it ma?"*

I reach over to grab his phone. *"Baby its almost noon."*

"Damn. I don't ever sleep this late."

"You put some work in last night baby, you had to recuperate."

"Yeah ma, you right. Where you been trying to sneak off to."

"I was just heading to the bathroom to pee then shower. You coming with me?"

"Yep, let's go."

He gets up and we head to the bathroom. When we finally come out the bedroom it is almost one o'clock. Everyone is downstairs. Ron, Kia and the kids are over too. They are all looking at us when we enter the family room. Aisha is looking at us while shaking her head.

"Nice of ya'll to finally join us damn."

I laugh. *"We had a long night."*

"A long loud night."

I look over to Adontis, embarrassed. *"Sorry."*

"Uh huh." She laughs and shakes her head.

Carmen says, *"Now that ya'll are back to the world of the living, we saved ya'll some breakfast. Tasha you may want to cook some fresh eggs."*

"Oh ok. Well, thank you." I look to Adontis, *"Baby you gon come keep me company?"*

"Yeah ma."

After I cook some eggs and warm everything else, Adontis and I eat. We begin the day of games and we start with spades. There are a couple spades games going on. The guest list is the same as last night. As everyone else begins to arrive, we finish up the card game and move on to Taboo. The game night is a fun success. We end the night around 10pm. Everyone heads home or to bed after we say our goodnights. Adontis, Aisha, Boris and I all have early flights in the morning. Everyone else has to get to work. I had so much fun.

July 14, 2008

We get up early for our flights. Adontis and my flight leaves at 8am. Aisha and Boris' leaves at 8:15am. We scramble out of bed and get ourselves ready at 6 am. Before going to bed last night, I washed and dried Adontis' and my dirty clothes. I also got us packed and ready for today. We say our goodbyes and thank Carmen for hosting us then head off to the airport. After returning our rental car we all check in then go through security. We say our goodbyes then head to our gates.

Our flight is a little over five hours with a forty-five-minute layover in Charlotte, North Carolina. Since I've been pregnant all I want to do is sleep, eat and have sex. I intend to do two of the three while on this flight. Maybe I'll do the third while on our layover. Thankfully there isn't a time zone difference so there shouldn't be any jet lag. Our plane lands on the island a little after 2pm. I send messages to Carmen, Kia and Aisha letting them know we've arrived safely. After we get our luggage, we head outside.

"Baby this is beautiful. We could make a baby here, if we didn't already."

He laughs at me. *"Yeah, its gorgeous, but it doesn't even begin to capture a fraction of your beauty ma."* He leans in and kisses me.

"Oh, you trying to get some right now?"

He smirks. *"You know I always want you, but I'm just stating facts. We gon practice for the next one while we here though."*

"Anytime anyplace."

Once outside the airport Adontis has a limo waiting for us. We get inside and take the limo to our hotel. I don't see any of the scenery because Adontis and I have a quickie in the limo. Adontis and I were so preoccupied with getting freaky I hadn't paid any attention to the weather. Upon getting out of the limo at the hotel, I actually notice the weather and the scenery. Of course, our hotel is right on the beach. The weather is a warm and sunny eighty-seven degrees with cool winds blowing. It feels amazing here. The staff greets us outside. The bellhops get our luggage and check us in to our room.

"Baby, this is so amazing. Thank you."

"You're welcome ma."

We are led up to our suite by the staff along with our luggage. There aren't any words to describe the beauty of this island or this hotel. Adontis tips the staff and they give him our room keys and leave.

"Ok ma what you want to do first?" I look at him with a smile. He just laughs and shakes his head. *"Lately, it's been one of three things. You been sleeping all day on the plane. We just made love in the limo. By process of elimination, I'd say you want to eat."*

"Ding, ding, ding, ding, ding. You are correct. Let me tell you what you've won."

He burst out laughing. *"You are too much."*

"Yep, I'm a handful, but you got two hands."

He smiles. *"Tell daddy what he won."*

"Well, you've won yourself a hungry pregnant woman, that loves the hell out you. And appreciates all that you do to make her happy, to provide and to take care of our family."

He smiles again, this time from ear to ear. I smile back at him. I could just drown in the pool of his dimples.

"Thank you, ma. I appreciate you telling me that. You know I appreciate you too." He leans in and kisses me then he grabs my hand. *"Now come on let's go so daddy can feed you."*

We stop at the front desk to get ideas of where we should eat and then head out to the limo. Adontis has rented the limo for our entire stay. Our driver takes us to a restaurant that serves Caribbean food. The food is amazing. I eat myself happy.

After lunch we head to do one of my favorite things. We're going shopping. We hit up some clothing stores and jewelry stores. The highlight of the trip for me is when we go to the baby store. Looking at baby clothes and furniture makes my pregnancy feel so real.

I look to Adontis, *"We should buy something for our baby."*

He smiles, *"Ma, we don't know if we're having a girl or boy yet."*

"I know. We can buy something pink and something blue. That way we're covered on both ends."

"Ok ma. Whatever you want, I'm wit it."

He takes my hand and we walk through the store browsing baby clothes. Adontis says, *"This is it ma. I like this."* He's come across a onesie. He grabs one in pink and one in blue. It says, I'm cute, mom is beautiful, dad got lucky.

I smile *"This is cute. You got lucky in more than one way."*

He laughs, *"Yep and I want to get lucky tonight too."*

"Hell, me too."

We browse a little while longer before heading to the register. Afterwards, we head back to the limo then back to our hotel. We shower and make love. We're both hungry afterwards, but I am also tired and I don't want to go anywhere. We order room service and spend the rest of the night in bed.

July 15, 2008

It is the best day of the year again. The day a queen was born. Yes, it is my birthday. I awake lying on top of Adontis' chest and wrapped in his arms. He is already awake.

"Good morning. Happy Birthday Beautiful."

I smile, *"Thank you. You call me beautiful like it is my name."*

"It is. You're gorgeous." I can't help, but to blush, as he kisses my lips. I sit up and sit on top of him and kiss him some more.

"Thank you, babe. You know you are sexy yourself." I bite down on my bottom lip and give him a naughty look.

"You know it's yours whenever you want it. He always ready for you."

I smile and begin kissing him as we start to make love. After some time, we finish and head to the shower. He wraps his arms around me.

"Ok ma, for this morning we going to the spa. I planned a couple's massage. Followed by a mani & pedi for you. Once we get dressed, we can head down to our massage."

"Baby, that sounds wonderful."

"Yeah, daddy gotta take care of you." He leans in and kisses me. He places his hands on my belly. *"And you too."*

After making love again in the shower, we get dressed. I check my phone and I have many happy birthday text messages, voicemails and missed calls. I take time to check and respond to them all before we head to the spa.

He has set up a private room for just the two of us. Inside is a large room with two massage tables and a large dining table. A breakfast spread is waiting for us. He escorts me to the table and I fix our plates. He then escorts me out to the beachfront balcony, where we sit and enjoy our meal.

"It's gorgeous out here. Are you enjoying yourself out here ma?"

He couldn't be more correct. The beauty of this place is unexplainable. *"I absolutely am. No one has ever done anything like this for me. Thank you, baby. I appreciate this so much."*

I get up from my seat and lean in to kiss him. He grabs my hand and leads me around the table and pulls me in to his lap. He wraps his arms around me with his hands resting on my belly.

"Ma, you deserve this. I want you to know that I love you and I appreciate everything you do for me. I know I fucked up last year and I almost lost you. I appreciate you giving me and us another chance. And now we're expecting our first baby. I always want to see you happy. I hope I always make you happy."

How do I respond to that, when in my head all I hear is, but I fucked up more? Hearing him own up to his mistake makes me feel even more guilty about mines. I want to tell him. I want to clear the air. I want him to know it all. He is my best friend. The problem is I don't think, he'd forgive me. I'd lose him.

He looks at me questionably. *"Ma, are you ok?"*

After being wrapped up in my thoughts, I force a smile. *"You make me happy baby. All I need is you. Nothing else."* That is the truth. I push the negative out of my head and focus on the positive. *"What's in the past is done, it's dead and forgiven. Now it's about you and I and our baby to be."*

He smiles. *"Thank you, baby. I can definitely get with that."* He kisses my lips again. *"I love you ma, so damn much."*

"I love you more."

He smiles. *"Impossible!"* I'm just smiling back at him. *"Are you ready to get this massage started?"*

"Absolutely."

We stand and head back into the room. He intercoms to the staff that we are ready to begin our massage. Wrapped in towels we lay across the massage table awaiting our masseuses. Adontis and I engage in small talk and it leads to conversations about our upcoming wedding. I can't wait to marry my love. Unfortunately, I still don't know what date. With my surprise pregnancy, I still have to decide if I want to push it back or not.

I'm not going to let it stress me out though. Our massage is very relaxing. It's different from the one Adontis gave me the other night. His was very sexual and pleasurable. His touch always turns me on. I revel in the relaxation as the masseuse rubs away all of the stress I have been carrying. I don't know how long it lasted, but it was a piece of heaven on earth. It was so relaxing I apparently fell asleep. Adontis awakes me with a gentle touch.

"Ma, get up."

I open my eyes to see him standing in front of me in a robe. He is holding a robe for me to slip in to. I sit up and climb off of the table as he helps me into my robe. He leads us through a door to another room where there are two pedicure chairs. He helps me into my chair and gets in the chair beside me. We turn the massager on in the chairs and just relax.

"You have made this day so special baby. Thank you."

"Ma you deserve the world. And I'm going to give it to you. Or die trying."

I lean in and kiss him. *"Thank you, baby, but I don't need the world. All I need is you."*

"You got me ma and I ain't going nowhere."

"I'm going to hold you to that."

He smiles, *"You can hold me to whatever you like."*

I finish my pedi and I get my nails done. Afterwards we head back to our room to get dressed. He takes me shopping again today. We have lunch while we are out shopping and when we finish, we end up back at the hotel. I'm too pooped to do anything else. All I want is a nap. I strip down to my underwear and climb into bed. Adontis tucks me in.

"Since you are taking a nap, I'm going to head to the gym and get in a run. Do you need anything before I head out?"

"Just a kiss."

"That I can handle."

He plants a kiss on me, then goes to change his clothes and heads out. I awake a few hours later, to a peaceful room. Adontis dimmed the lights before he left and closed the curtains. I reach for my phone and the time says 6:02 pm. The sun will be setting soon. After unlocking my phone, I see I have a message from Adontis.

> **Daddy:** *If you reading this, get ready for dinner my love. See you soon. I love you!*

> **Tasha:** *I'm heading to the shower. See you when you get here daddy. I love you more!*

I roll out of bed and head to the bathroom. While showering, I hear the bathroom door open. I peek my head out to see Adontis.

"Hey beautiful." He walks over and kisses me.

"Hey baby. Don't you look sexy."

He smiles. *"This all for you shorty."*

"I'll take it."

He laughs, *"You a trip."*

"Yep. I guess I need to hurry up and get out the shower. You look like you ready for me."

"This your day ma. Take your time. I just wanted to tell you about the next surprise I had for you."

"I love surprises. Well, only the good ones."

"I know you do. I ain't want you to come out swinging so I thought I better warn you first."

I laugh out loud. *"Okay. What does that mean?"*

"I have two ladies here in our suite."

Before he has a chance to finish, I'm looking at him sideways, like what the hell. I know he always wanted to have a threesome, but hell, he should have done that before me. He missed his window. He done put a ring on this. I ain't going for that shit.

"Don't look at me like that, ma. Let me finish."

He knows I don't do that threesome shit. I'm strictly dickly. I don't know where this is going. *"Ok finish."*

"These ladies are here to do your hair and makeup." Relief and excitement come across my face. *"See I knew I needed to warn your crazy ass before you walked out to see them, then you wanna kick my ass. I ain't got time for that shit. I'm a one-woman man."*

"Correction, you are an only Tasha's man."

He smiles, *"You right ma. I'm only yours."*

"It better stay that damn way."

His eyeballs stretch, *"You woke up feisty huh?"*

I laugh. *"It's the baby."*

He smirks. *"Don't blame that on my baby."* He leans in and kisses me. *"I'm going to let you finish washing. I brought your robe in here for you. Do you need anything else?"*

"Just to say thank you."

"You're welcome. I'm going to get things finished up for dinner. The ladies are in the living room. They are going to wait on you. If you need me, I have my cell phone."

"Ok."

He heads out the bathroom and I finish showering. I can't believe he has gone all out for me. This man is showing me that he is everything that I need. It's not the material things. Don't get me wrong, they are great, but his heart and love for me, is everything. The thought and planning he put into this trip and into tonight alone tells me how much he loves me. I can't wait to become his wife and to have his babies. Tears begin to roll from my eyes as I think on how much love we have for one another. I take a deep breath and get myself together. This baby has me emotional as hell.

I step out of the bathroom after showering and begin to dry off then moisturize my skin. When I'm done, I slip into a night gown, then into my robe. I walk out of the bedroom and into the living room of the suite and I see the two ladies that Adontis has told me about. I greet them and we introduce ourselves. They have a workstation area setup. I get seated and they both get started. The hairstylist will just be curling my hair. She begins to comb and section off my hair and then the curling begins.

Before the make-up artist begins, she asks me a few questions about what I'm wearing and if l want a subtle or dramatic look. Of course, I go with dramatic. We talk through my look and what colors I'd like. We decide on a hot pink, matte lipstick. A silver glittery eyeshadow with bold black eyeliner. As she begins to wrap it up, she finishes with adding fake eyelashes.

Once both ladies are finished, the stylist pulls out a mirror and I am wowed. My hair is parted in the middle. Down my back flows body wave curls. My edges are slicked down and I'm serving sexy.

"Oh my God. I look amazing. Thank you."

"You're welcome."

"We know you have to get dressed so, we're going to pack up here and hang around for a few moments after in case you need any touch ups to hair or make up."

"Thank you, ladies, so much. You've been great."

I head to the bedroom to get ready. While in the bedroom, I text Adontis.

> **Tasha:** *My hair and make-up are done. The ladies did a fantastic job.*

Finally, I begin to get dressed. Tonight's attire is a turquoise and hot pink floral print halter dress. It is backless and has a low plunge neckline. It is fitted right under my breast down to my upper torso area. Then it flares out around the mid belly area, all the way down past my ankles. It is very flowy with high splits up each thigh. The dress still hides my baby pouch. To avoid messing up my hair and makeup, I step into the dress. I pull it up and then tie it around my neck. I put on my diamonds, earrings, necklace and bracelets.

I step out of the bedroom and thank the ladies again for their services and tell them that my hair and make-up are still good. They are both smiling at me.

"Yes, you look beautiful."

"Yes, you do."

"Thank you so much ladies. I appreciate everything."

"You're welcome. Oh, and Happy Birthday."

"Thank you."

"You're welcome. The two of you make a beautiful couple. Reminds me of my husband and I."

I smile. *"You ladies have been great."*

They've already packed up all of their belongings so they head out. I step back into the bedroom to finish getting ready. I have no idea where Adontis is. On my feet I slip into strappy hot pink open toe stilettos. The straps go all the way up to my thighs. I shoot Adontis another text.

> **Tasha:** *Hey baby, I'm ready.*

I sit on the bed and wait for my honey. After a few moments, the doorknob turns and he walks through the door.

"Oh my God!" He's standing in the doorway with his hand still on the knob. He licks his lips. *"You are stunning ma. Damn, have you seen yourself?"*

I smile as I stand to walk towards him. *"Thank you, daddy."* When I reach him, he takes my hand, spins me right into his arms and plants a kiss on me.

He doesn't let me go. He just holds me in his arms. *"You're welcome. You ready to go ma?"*

"Ready."

"Good because if we stay in here any longer, we gon miss dinner."

"I'm sorry, I know it took me a while to get ready."

"Nah ma. It's your day, we on your time. If we miss dinner, it will be because I'm making love to you." He licks his lips and smiles. *"I want you out this dress. Shit, I'll slip in through one of these slits and slide the panties to the side."*

I burst out laughing. *"You are so nasty."*

"You like me like that."

"Nope, you got to feed me first Daddy. The ba-"

He cuts me off. *"You not gon keep blaming your greediness on my baby."*

I laugh again. He knows me so well. *"It's the truth."*

He looks at me questionably. *"I don't buy it."* He plants another kiss on me before unwrapping his arms from around me. He grabs my hand and we lock fingers.

"Let's go beautiful."

Adontis leads us out and down to the limo. We take a ride for a little while before coming to a stop. We get out of the limo and we're on the beach. He lifts me into his arms and carries me across the sand.

"I didn't know you was going to where these sexy ass heels tonight and I can't have my baby falling so daddy is going to carry you."

I smile, *"I'm ok with that."*

"I knew you would be because these heels gon stay on."

He is looking at me very naughtily. All I can do is laugh out loud. There are tiki torches that have lit the path. We arrive in front of a table under the stars. Our table is also surrounded by tiki torches in the shape of a heart. The wind is blowing and we have a beautiful beach front view. Adontis sits me in a chair. There is a large bouquet of roses waiting in the other chair. He hands them to me.

"Happy birthday beautiful."

"These are beautiful. This is so beautiful. Thank you." He leans down and kisses me before taking the seat next to me. *"How did I get so lucky?"*

"I'm the lucky one. We have a chef that will be preparing our meals and on the table is the menu."

A waiter steps forward, introduces himself and takes our drink order. Adontis orders some liquor and I order a non-alcoholic Bahama mama. This way at least I can pretend like I'm having a drink.

"You aiming for the man of the year award, baby you got it."

He smiles. *"Naw I'm just aiming for the love of Tasha's life award."*

"Baby you already got that when I fell in love with you."

I lean in for a kiss and he plants his luscious thick lips on mines. Before trailing over to my neck and planting a few more kisses.

"You're so beautiful. Now you have this pregnancy glow. Damn baby." He grabs my hand and just holds it. *"I love you ma."*

"I love you Daddy."

We share another kiss. We stay in the moment for a little while. *"Ok ma, you know what you want to eat?"*

"Nope. Do you?"

He laughs, *"Of course you don't. I was thinking about getting the Porterhouse steak with the lobster mac and cheese."*

"That sounds delicious. You should get it so I can eat it too."

He looks at me with a brow raised. *"I had no intentions in sharing."*

"You not gon share with your wife and baby?"

He shakes his head in disbelief. *"Whatever I have ma is yours."*

I smile. The server returns with our drinks. *"Are you ready to order?"*

Adontis looks to me, *"Ma you know what you want?"*

"Yes."

"Ok baby, go ahead and order."

"I'll have the fried shrimp and flounder with a side of mash potatoes and gravy and French fries."

The server takes down my order then Adontis'. After we've both ordered he clears the menus from the table and excuses himself. A few moments later he and another server return with appetizers. There are cheese sticks with marinara sauce, fried hot wings and chicken fingers with honey mustard sauce. Adontis watches me as a smile comes across my face. They sit the food down on the table along with plates, napkins and silverware.

Our server says, *"The chef is preparing your meals now."* He sits a buzzer on the table. *"I will be back to check on you. However, if you need me before then please just press this button on the buzzer."*

We both say, *"Thank you."*

After the server walks away, I look at the appetizers and they look delicious. Adontis and I join hands as he says the blessing. When he finishes, I dig in. He's smiling at me as he is shaking his head.

"Baby you so damn greedy."

I can't help, but to burst out laughing. *"I'm hungry."*

"I know ma. I know you. That's why I pre-ordered appetizers. I can't lie I'm hungry too."

"Yes, you do, thank you."

Appetizers and conversation are amazing. We chat some more about our upcoming wedding and the date. Dinner comes out and the food looks amazing. We both indulge in our meals and Adontis feeds me some of his. I also feed him some of mines. I eat all of my food and I'm stuffed. I look down at my belly and see it poking out a little more than it was earlier. Adontis wraps his arms around me and begins rubbing my belly.

"You good ma?"

"Yes baby. I'm so full."

He laughs. *"You ought to be, you ate every damn thing."*

I chuckle. *"I was hungry."*

"I see that. You have to make room for dessert."

"Baby, I can't eat another bite right now or I might burst."

"Alright ma we don't want that." He buzzes our server and when he arrives Adontis ask him to put our dessert in a takeout container.

"This night has really been amazing, babe. A wonderful dinner under the stars with the love of my life. I couldn't have asked for a better way to spend my birthday."

"Ma, it ain't over yet." Our server arrives with our dessert packaged in a carryout bag. Adontis thanks him and tips him.

"You have more planned?"

"Absolutely. I haven't even given you your gift yet."

"Baby you've given me so much already. I don't need anything more than you."

"That's great, but I want to give you my gift anyway. I'm going to take your roses to the limo. I will be right back."

I admire the beautiful scenery in complete joy. Adontis returns smiling after a short while.

"Ok love. On to the next part of our night."

Adontis scoops me up from my seat and I grab the dessert bag. He carries me as he takes us down the beach. After walking for a little while, we reach a secluded area. It's very quiet except for the sounds of the waves on the beach. Most of the surrounding area is somewhat dark except for a few tiki torches. He stops in front of two large blankets with a few pillows, a cooler, and a gift bag. He bends down and sits me on the blanket on the beach. He slips out of his shoes and sits behind me on the blanket. I'm sitting in between his legs and his arms are wrapped around me.

His lips are pressed up to my ears. His touch is running chills up my spine. When he begins to speak, I feel his lips repeatedly graze my ear with each word. His voice is just as sexy as he is. Being in such a romantic spot with the man I love has me aroused. I keep my composure as well as I can and listen to what he says.

"I took some time to think about what would be a good gift for you ma. I wanted to give you something special. Something that couldn't be purchased from a store. This is what I came up with. I hope you like it ma."

He reaches for the gift bag and hands it to me. I don't have a clue what it is. I dig into the bag and pull the tissue paper out. I pull out the bag a book. Tears instantly begin to form in my eyes. The book's cover reads:

Soul food
A book of poems

By: Tasha Leam

I flip through the pages. Adontis gently wipes the tears from my face.

"I know you've talked about wanting to publish your poems. I went and got your poems copyrighted for you. Then I talked with some publishers. I found you a publisher offering you an amazing book deal.

You just have to sign off on it and you're a published author ma. I've gotten my cousin Kenny, who is an attorney, to look over the contract and he says the offer is good. Everything is in your name; you own the rights to everything ma."

The tears continue uncontrollably and Adontis continues to wipe them away.

"Adontis, baby you're amazing. This is the most thoughtful gift I've ever received. I love it."

I turn around and begin kissing him, sliding my tongue into his mouth as he slides his into mines.

"You're welcome beautiful. That means you're ready for publishing?"

"Oh yes! Absolutely!"

He smirks at me, *"Ok ma, I'll change our flight. When we leave here, we'll fly into New York for a few days. You can meet with everyone and decide what you want to do. I support whatever choice you make ma. If there is anything you want to change, the layout or the cover or whatever, of course you can. This is all yours."*

"Oh my God! I'm so excited, you're amazing baby. Did you choose the layout and the cover photo?"

I'm flipping through the book looking at the poems that are in there. I can't believe I'm seeing one of my dreams come alive. This gift means more to me than anything that I've ever received.

"Yeah, I did. You don't like it?"

"No, I love it! I wouldn't change a thing." After flipping through the book, I come to the back cover. There is a gorgeous photo of me with a brief description about me. *"You're truly amazing baby."*

I turn to Adontis and he is smiling from ear to ear showing me his beautiful dimples. My man is, words really can't describe. He is remarkable. I think of the lowest place we've been and to see where we are now makes joy overflow. I lean in and begin kissing him. Daddy is going to get it tonight; I don't care how tired I am. I hike my dress up and sit on my knees. I position myself on top of him with my knees on each side of his legs.

I begin kissing him as I start unbuttoning his shirt. I start at his juicy lips. I begin with a few quick pecks that leads to me sucking on his lips. In between sucks I nibble on them as well. I've gotten his shirt unbuttoned and I'm sliding him out of it. While I'm rubbing on his chest, he is caressing my breast. He begins pinching my nipples in between rubs. His other hand, he slides it in between my legs. She is already wet when he reaches her. I didn't tell him, but now he knows, I'm not wearing any panties. He laughs when he realizes this.

"Oh, you just decided to leave my dessert unwrapped tonight huh?"

I burst out laughing. *"Yeah, easy access."*

"Uh huh."

He bites down on his bottom lip as he grins at me. My lips move down to his neck and he moves his lips to mines. We're both kissing and sucking on each other. He's nibbling on my neck and blowing in my ear. My hands have reached his pants and I quickly unbutton them then slide my hands in through his boxers. I grab him and begin to stroke him up and down.

He is ready. I kiss down his chest placing kisses all over him. I reach his manhood, grab a handful and begin kissing some more. I begin kissing the head. I start licking around the tip, just to tease him a bit. I move further down to kiss on his balls. Which leads to me sucking on them while jacking him off with my hands.

He moans out, *"Oh shit Tasha! Damn baby!"*

I don't say a word or stop. I just look up to peek at him while I continue. I move back to his dick and before I can continue, he stops me. At first, I'm confused as hell.

"Hold up ma."

"What's wrong, why you stop me?"

"Nothing is wrong. Turn around and sit on your knees."

I don't know what he is doing, but I don't question it. After hiking my dress up, I just do it. Once I'm on my knees he lifts me and sits me on top of his chest. I let go of my dress once he sits me down. My booty is in his face and my pussy is resting on his chest. She is wet and is just leaking on him. I shake my booty and begin gyrating on him. He begins to smack me on the ass.

"You know daddy likes that shit." He lifts up the back of my dress then starts rubbing on my ass. *"This is a hell of a view."* I feel him lean in and begin kissing my cheeks. *"Alright ma, you can finish."* He spreads my cheeks and puts his face in between.

As I lean forward, he pulls the bottom half of me towards his face. We're in the sixty-nine position. He begins kissing, sucking, licking and gently biting all over me. I take him into my mouth and begin sucking and stroking him with one hand. Taking him in and out. With my free hand I'm playing with his balls. He is moaning and I'm moaning. We both make each other cum. I lay right where I am on top of him. My head resting on his lower stomach right above his pelvis. My booty resting right in his face. He gives me a booty rub, while I give him a few minutes to recover.

"Alright daddy you have got to finish this."

I sit up and spin around to face him, while sitting on his stomach. He is still laying back with his hands behind his head.

Smiling back at me he says, *"You ready?"*

"I was born ready."

He laughs, *"It's yours ma. He always ready for you."*

I reach my hand backwards to feel for his manhood and I find him surprisingly sticking straight up, hard and ready. He wasn't lying. I slide down to position myself and then I slide him into me. I press my hands down into his chest as I begin to ride him. I feel him deep in me as he continually hits my g-spot. We begin kissing and he lets me ride for a while before taking control. He puts us in several different positions and makes me have several orgasms before he cums.

July 16, 2008

Things got intense during our love making and at one point he took my dress off. He wanted the heels to stay on though. Now we've slipped under the covers naked as he holds me in his arms. Adontis digs in the cooler and passes me a bottle of water and grabs himself a Gatorade. He begins laughing when he hears me fidgeting with the dessert bag.

"It's dessert time. And the baby is hungry."

He laughs even more. *"You gon stop lying on my baby."*

"You don't believe me baby?"

He shakes his head, *"Nah."*

I laugh as I dig the dessert from out of the bag. I open it and I see it is a six-layer chocolate cake with chocolate icing and decadent chocolate shavings.

"This looks delicious."

"He laughs, you are greedy as hell. If you this greedy this early on, damn, I'm scared to see how much worse it gets."

I start laughing. *"Adontis don't do me like that."*

He smiles, *"I'm just teasing you ma. You know you are forever my baby. Greedy and all."* He grabs a fork out the bag. *"Let daddy feed you."*

I lean against his chest as he feeds me my cake. I realize he is so right when I catch myself dancing where I'm seated. All in excitement for cake. My ass is greedy. He reaches over and digs in the cooler again and pulls out a bottle of white milk and passes it to me.

"Oh my god, are you trying to make me have another orgasm? You really thought of everything." He knows I'm a milk junkie. Nothing goes better with chocolate then ice-cold white milk.

"That's right. Daddy got you."

I take the fork from his hands, *"You have to eat some cake too. It is amazing."*

"You gon feed it to me?"

"I wouldn't have it any other way."

While in between his legs I turn sideways and begin to feed him some cake. *"Damn ma this is good as shit."* As I'm feeding him, he's rubbing my belly.

"I told you."

We finish both slices of cake and I'm full all over again. *"I wish I saved some for later, but it was so good."*

"Good because the rest of the cake is back in our room."

"You know how to make a girl smile."

We lay on the beach just looking up at the stars. We are cuddled up just talking and listening to the waves on the beach. I don't know when, but at some point, I fall asleep.

I hear Adontis' voice, *"Ma, get up and get dressed so we can head back to our hotel."*

Once my eyes are opened, I look down and see a pool of drool on his chest. This seems to be happening a lot lately. I wipe it away with my hand.

"What time is it baby?"

He picks up his phone and checks the display. *"It's 4:37 ma. I called the limo driver and he is back and waiting for us."*

I'm yawning and stretching. *"Oh man sorry, I fell asleep on you baby."*

He licks his lips. *"You good ma. Hell, I fell asleep too. You put that thing on me."*

I start laughing. *"I had an amazing birthday. Thank you, baby."*

"You're welcome beautiful."

I sit up and plant a kiss on him before slipping into my dress. I pass him his boxers and he slips them on while seated. He stands and begins to get dressed. While he is dressing, I'm taking off my heels. Once he is dressed, he helps me up and we begin to fold up the blankets and put them in our empty takeout bag. We stack the pillows on top of the cooler and then Adontis picks me up into his arms.

"Alright ma. I'm going to carry you back to the limo and then I'll come back to get this stuff."

"I took off my heels, so I can walk baby."

"Are you sure ma?"

"Yes."

After about twenty minutes we are back to our hotel. We both begin to strip out of our clothes. I head for the bathroom and run the shower.

"Are you going to join me daddy?"

He smiles, *"Yep."*

We slip into the shower and make love again. By the time we finish and get washed up it's a little after 6am and the sun is out. Adontis puts the do not disturb sign on the door. We both slip in the bed. I lay across his chest as he wraps me in his arms. Quickly I drift off to sleep.

I awake a little after noon. Adontis is still fast asleep. I order room service for us and let him rest until it arrives. I check in with my sisters, Carmen, Aisha and Kia. They are all at work so I communicate with them via text. I send them pictures of our trip so far. We have a good time catching up.

When I hear a knock at the door, I quietly slip out the bed to answer it. Room service has arrived with our food. I wheel the cart into the bedroom and climb on top of Adontis. I begin placing kisses all over his face. He awakes with a smile. While still laying down and with me still on top of him he stretches and yawns.

"Good morning beautiful." He looks to the clock to see the time. *"Oh, shit good afternoon."*

I laugh. *"I ordered us some lunch, cause we slept through breakfast."*

"Yeah, last night was an amazing night." He sits up and kisses me then my belly. *"Let's eat ma."*

"Lunch in bed?"

"Works for me."

I lean over and pull the cart closer. *"I kept it simple and just ordered us burgers and fries. That good for you baby?"*

"Yeah ma."

I lift the plates off the cart and sit them on the bed next to us. I stay seated on his lap and we have lunch while he tells me about what we have planned for the day.

"Ok ma we have a tour that will be here to pick us up at three. That gives us a little time to eat, relax and get ready."

"Where is it taking us?"

"He pulls out his phone. It's supposed to be a safari like tour that will lead us to the beach. The tour ends with dinner."

"Sounds fun. My favorite way to end the night, with dinner."

He starts laughing. We finish our lunch and relax for a little while before getting ready. We head down at about a quarter to three to wait for our tour pickup. Our tour takes us through the evening. We arrive back at the hotel a little after 8pm. The tour and dinner have been amazing, but I'm ready to get back to the room and eat some cake. We slip in our pjs and I cut us some cake. We snuggle on the sofa and watch a little tv. A night to relax is just what I need.

July 17, 2008

Adontis wakes me early. We are both on the couch. *"Good morning beautiful."*

My eyes open and I turn to kiss him. *"Good morning baby."*

"We have another tour planned this morning. I ordered us some breakfast it should be here soon. We need to start getting ready."

"Ok what are we doing today?"

"A day cruise with snorkeling with a lunch picnic on the beach."

"Ooooh. I can put on a bathing suit."

"Yeah. I gotta make sure you cover up all of my stuff."

"How about you make sure you cover up all of my stuff."

"Naw don't try to use my words against me. I don't want all my titties and ass out now ma."

I look at him with a smirk. *"I hear you."* I get up to head to the bathroom.

"Tasha, I'm not playing now."

"I said, I heard you baby."

"Alight."

We step in the shower to get cleaned up. When we're getting out there's a knock at the door. Adontis slips into his robe and heads for the door. He wheels in breakfast. We sit down and have breakfast. Once we finish, we begin to get ready. I slip into a two-piece bathing suit. The top is halter styled and the bottom is high wasted. It holds in my little pregnancy belly.

I spin so he can see me. *"This work for you?"*

"You still got my titties out." He walks up to me and kisses my breast. He spins me around. *"And you showing off this voluptuous ass."*

"Adontis there's only so much I can do about that. They're naturally big. I'm pregnant and you keep sucking them."

"Oh, you want me to stop sucking them?"

"That is not what I'm saying."

"What you saying then?"

"I'm just saying, they growing. Pregnancy is making them grow and having you sucking on them makes them grow too. They gon look like this in whatever bathing suit I put on."

"Where yo cover up at?"

I laugh, *"You are doing the most. It's right here."* I pick up my cover up and tie it around my waist.

"That covers all this ass. Nothing to cover up my titties?"

I give him a side eye. *"No."*

He shakes his head then starts scratching his head. *"Alight ma."*

"You worried bout me. You got all your chest and abs out. Why don't you put a shirt on!"

He laughs. *"Really?"*

"Yes."

He slips on a t-shirt. *"Ok you ready?"*

"Yes." I grab our beach bag with our towels and sunscreen. We head down to wait for our pick-up. Our tour is amazing. It last for about four hours. We arrive back at our hotel get cleaned up and head out for dinner and dancing.

July 18, 2008

We have an amazing time out and arrive back to our room late. I opt to have another piece of birthday cake and a glass of milk. Before cutting a slice, I get undressed and slip into some lingerie. Adontis is in the bathroom. I hear him peeing so I head to the kitchen. Adontis has been drinking all day and all night. He is tight, not quite drunk. His drink of choice is Crown Royal. He has been drinking them straight and mixed. I'm going to have to get him to sleep so he can sleep it off.

I walk back in the room with my cake and some water for him. When I sit in bed, I see Adontis is across the room getting undressed. I'm sitting in bed enjoying the show and my dessert. He is moving super slow and I know he needs to crash. I'll make sure I get him in bed before I go to sleep.

"Baby you want some?"

"Chocolate! Yeah, I want some." I sit my cake on the nightstand and slide out of bed. He walks up to me and stops me placing his hands on my waist. *"Where you going ma?"*

"I'm going to cut you a piece of cake. Or did you want some of mines?"

He smiles. *"I want some of yours."*

I chuckle, *"Ok."*

I turn around to pull the covers back and to get back in bed. I sit in the bed; grab my cake and I take another bite. I look up, to Adontis. He is standing in front of me completely naked. He is on a full hard and staring at me like I'm a meal. At that moment I get it. He was calling me chocolate. When he said he wanted some, he wasn't referring to the cake. I'm staring at him with a smirk on my face. Daddy looks good. He steps closer to me and pulls the covers back.

He spreads my legs and slides my thong off. He begins kissing me in between my knees. I almost drop my damn cake. I sit the plate back on the nightstand. More important matters are at hand. Adontis makes love to me and puts me to sleep. I forgot all about my cake.

I awake a little after 10am and Adontis is laying on my chest with his hand resting on my belly. He is resting so peacefully. I just look at him. As I admire how sexy he looks asleep. I run my fingers through his curls. My man. Damn I love him. The best decision I ever made was giving him my address and letting him come down to meet me. I felt like things were going to change, but I didn't know that he'd change my life like this. I grab my phone and check in with the sisters. It's still a workday so I text them just to check in on the family and update them on Adontis and I. After a little while, Adontis wakes up.

"Good morning daddy."

He sits up and licks his lips. *"Good morning ma."* He plants his lips on mines and then on my belly. *"Good morning, Daddy's baby."*

We get up, get ready and head out to eat. We spend the day in a museum and an art gallery. We purchase some souvenirs for our family and some things for us. We spend the rest of the day sightseeing, being tourist and shopping. We wind the night down with us having dinner in our room on the balcony. We spend another night under the stars. We end the night making love on the balcony.

July 19, 2008

After the love we made, we lay together looking at the stars. We begin talking about our life and our plans together. Once we've laid here for a while, we decide to head back into our room. Adontis lifts me up and puts me in the bed. He locks up the room and slips in bed with me. We share a bit more pillow talk before drifting off to sleep.

We start the morning with breakfast before getting ready to head out. *"Ok ma, today, I'm taking you horseback riding on the beach. Before you say anything, I planned this before we knew we were pregnant."* I drift off into my own thoughts for a while. It is such a turn on to hear how geeked he is about our baby. I know he is going to be an amazing dad. *"Ma, where your mind at?"*

"I'm here baby." He looks at me with a side eye. *"I was just thinking about how much I love your excitement for our baby. It's a beautiful thing to see this side of you. I know how you love me, but to see your excitement about our baby, it's sexy. You're already in daddy mode."*

He smiles, *"You damn right. All I want is you ma and a house full of our babies."*

"I hear you Daddy. You got it."

He leans in and kisses me. *"Back to today's plan, I spoke with Doctor Tara and asked if it was safe for you to ride. With you being an experienced rider, she gave an ok as long as it's just walking."*

My face lights up. *"Really! Oh my God baby I love it."* I wrap my arms around him.

He smiles, *"I knew you would. But you will be taking it slow. A couple of steps and pictures, then your ass coming down. I've informed the staff and they'll be near you the entire time. I also have a photographer coming to take some pictures of us. These are memories I want to remember forever. And I want to share it with our children. Starting with this one."* He places his hand on my belly.

I bite my bottom lip smiling up at him. *"Baby, this is great. I won't argue with any of that."*

"You better not. Daddy will spank that ass."

I burst out laughing. *"Well in that case, maybe I will."*

He smirks, *"Yo lil nasty ass."*

"Only for you daddy. That's how you like me."

"You damn right. Better be only for me. I don't want to have to kill a mother fucker."

"Ooh ok baby, bring that back down. You already know that." I lean in for a kiss. He doesn't bend down to kiss me back. *"You just gon leave me down here hanging?"*

He laughs. *"Never ma."* He leans down and wraps me in his arms. He kisses me passionately after sliding his tongue into my mouth. There is nothing, but heat between us. *"Ok ma, we better stop before we miss everything."*

I smile, *"You started this."*

"You the one that asked for a kiss."

"I was gon do a quick one."

"Nope, that's what you thought."

I laugh, *"Whatever. Let's get ready."*

Horseback riding is a wonderful experience. I did take it very easy, since I am pregnant. Adontis made sure of it. I don't think I stayed on the horse more than five minutes. The photographer captured our moments while with the horses. We also took some photos together without the horses. It was more like a full photo shoot. Our photos will be delivered to our hotel tomorrow. I can't wait to see them. It's been a beautiful day. Very romantic.

After the shoot, we head back to our room to get cleaned up. Our afternoon is spent in the casino and we do a little bit of gambling. He stays with me while I play the slot machines. I bet small so I lose small and win small. I'm totally ok with that because I don't like to lose money. When I finish, he plays poker and I stay by his side. He wins a few grand. My baby has a poker face. After his wins he decides to cash out. We leave the casino and head out to dinner.

Dinner is followed by a walk on the beach. Hand in hand we talk and take in the beauty of our surroundings. It's a beautiful way to end our night before heading back to our room. Once we're back at the room we get settled in and I slip into some lingerie. We end the night on the sofa and not before long we are making love.

July 20, 2008

Today is our last day here. We have a flight out in the morning to New York. I roll out of bed and begin getting our things packed. Adontis is still in bed asleep. We traveled with an extra piece of luggage to transport all of our purchases home in. I start by packing all of them up first. I move on to mines leaving out clothes for today and tomorrow. When I'm ready to pack Adontis' things, I go to wake him up.

I climb on top of him. *"Hey love. Wake up."*

He peeks open an eye and looks at me. *"Yeah ma, what's up?"* He closes his eye back.

"I'm getting everything packed up and I need to know what you wearing today and tomorrow." He doesn't respond he just lays there, arms folded behind his head and sleeping. I start placing kisses on his lips. *"Adontis."* Still silence. *"I know you hear me talking to you."* More silence.

I get off of him and I peel the covers back. As usual, he's standing up at attention. I kneel on the bed next to him and grab a hold of his manhood. I begin massaging him in between my hands. I hear him begin to moan. I begin to lick on him and I look up to see him peeking down at me. When I see him, I stop. He looks at me questionably.

"Ma why you stop?"

"I just needed you to wake up. Now you can answer my question."

I begin to climb over him to get out of the bed. He grabs a hold of me by the waist and stops me.

"Ma, where you think you going?"

"To finish packing. What you wearing today and tomorrow so I can get you packed up?"

"Ma?"

"What?"

"You know this can't go down like this."

"Like what?"

"That's enough talking."

He flips me over onto my back and climbs on top of me. I'm lying there with my legs closed. I begin giggling.

"What are you doing Adontis?"

"You know what I'm doing.

"I'm trying to pack."

He grabs his manhood, *"And I'm trying to unpack."*

I burst out laughing, *"You are being so nasty."*

"That's how you like me."

I roll my eyes. *"Adontis."*

"Ra'Quel Tasha Leam." I just stare up at him. *"You asked for this. I was sleep."*

"I just wanted you to get up to answer my question."

"Daddy up." He leans down and kisses my lips, kissing down my body. *"You ain't giving daddy none?"*

I smile, *"It's yours daddy."*

"You damn right." He leans in and begins kissing me. *"Damn you taste good."*

After making love we roll out of bed and order breakfast then head to shower. Shortly after we're out of the shower breakfast arrives. We sit at the table in our robes and enjoy breakfast. When we finish, we head back to the bedroom to get dressed. Then I finally get the answer to my question. I get Adontis' non-essentials packed up and we head out.

Our day is spent visiting some tourist attractions and sightseeing. In between we grab a light snack. Our night is spent at a dinner theater show. It turns out to be a wonderful end to a phenomenal trip. We get back to the hotel and check the front desk for our pictures. They have arrived. Back in our room we get comfortable and spend the rest of our night looking at our pictures and relaxing.

July 21, 2008

We get up and get ready. I walk through the suite and make sure we have everything. I've packed all of our remaining things and we head out to the airport. While at the airport, we grab something to eat. Turks and Caicos has been wonderful. My man did an amazing job.

Our flight is a little over three hours long. We land in New York City. Adontis has booked us a hotel for a couple of days. He's also booked another limo. The limo driver takes us to our hotel where we check in and drop off our luggage. We leave and head off to a lunch meeting with Kenny. Adontis gave me a copy of the contract, I looked it over on the plane. Kenny goes over everything with me line by line. I'm able to ask him all the questions that I have and he answers them.

Overall, the meeting goes well. Based on what transpires, I decide to sign with the publishing company. We enjoy the rest of our lunch and I look forward to what our relationship holds. We leave our lunch meeting and head to the publishing company. We further discuss the offer and I sign off on the deal. My book will have a special dedication page. It will be dedicated to both of my parents Ronald Leam and Leeyah Leam and to the love of my life and the inspiration for my love, Adontis.

I couldn't be happier. We all celebrate in the meeting room. Once we leave the meeting room Adontis and I head back to our hotel and get cleaned up. We are both ready to get back home. He contacts the airport and he is able to get us a flight out tomorrow night.

"Ok ma we'll just leave tomorrow night and check out then for the next day."

"Ok baby. I am ready to get back home."

"I know you are ma. Me too."

I sit on top of his lap. *"Thank you, baby, for everything you've done for me. You are amazing."*

"You're welcome beautiful." He plants a kiss on me. *"Let's get ready before we don't make it out of this room."*

We're going out to celebrate tonight with Kenny, his wife Tina, Brandon, Cassie, Chuck and Liza. We go to an upscale restaurant and enjoy a nice dinner. It's nice to catch up with friends. We have a really good night with great conversations. We get back to our hotel and crash. We've been ripping and running all day.

July 22, 2008

We start our day with a late breakfast followed by a little sightseeing and shopping. We stay out through a late lunch and come back to the hotel. Back at the hotel we get everything packed up and then relax for a bit. The time comes to catch our flight so we head out to the limo and off to the airport.

We land in Jacksonville in a little under three hours. I contact our sisters to let them know we are home safely. We head to our car and home. We're both exhausted. Adontis pulls the car in the garage and we head up to bed. He'll get our luggage tomorrow. I had so much fun on my birthday trip, but I'm happy to be home.

chapter 29

Depression

August 22, 2008

Depression will eat away at you if you let it. Never allow yourself to be depressed. No matter what, enjoy yourself and live life to the fullest.

It's been a little over two months since I found out I was pregnant. I still haven't changed our wedding date. I haven't been able to reserve the church and reception hall for the same date. This is getting frustrating and I don't know what to do. We still haven't told anyone about my pregnancy yet. I have a doctor's appointment today and Adontis is taking me.

Tomorrow he and I are flying out to see our families. We'll stop in Charleston for a few days and then off to New York to see his parents. We'll tell them then about our soon to be family member. I'm over the moon about this. Not even his mom can bring me down.

My book has been published and it will soon be released. I'm excited. We are in the car heading to the doctor's office on this rainy and gloomy day. While riding in the far-right lane, we get stopped at a red light. Adontis looks over at me and rubs my belly.

"I can't wait for my boy to get here."

"Or my girl," I say with a smile.

The light turns green and Adontis is still rubbing my stomach. *"Baby the light is green. We gonna be late."*

He just smiles at me. I can see his love for me and our baby all over his face. He moves his hands from my belly and his foot from the brakes. He begins to gently push the gas. As he proceeds to take off, I see movement in my peripheral. After I turn to look, I try to turn my body to brace myself and protect my baby.

"OH MY GOD, ADON-!"

The car is pounded by a massive eighteen-wheeler. The truck crashes into Tasha's side of the car. Adontis hits his head on the driver's side window as it breaks. Glass shatters everywhere as his airbag deploys into his chest. The impact of the crash is so hard that their car goes spinning across several lanes.

The car inevitably stops, when it impacts another vehicle. Also, on Tasha's side of the car. Tasha and Adontis are now several lanes over and facing the opposite direction. Other drivers have to slam on their brakes and swerve to avoid hitting them.

A woman who witnesses the accident pulls over to check on them and to call 911. She reaches the car and sees Adontis and thinks he is unconscious, but he opens his eyes and looks around. He is briefly stunned by the accident. Suddenly he collects himself and realizes where he is.

He turns over and looks at Tasha. She has glass fragments and particles in her arms, legs and on one side of her neck. She is also bleeding badly from somewhere and her air bag failed to deploy. Adontis unhooks his seatbelt and calls out Tasha's name. She doesn't answer him. He starts screaming her name. She doesn't make a movement or a sound.

The police, fire department and EMS arrive. The paramedic checks Tasha for a pulse. While Adontis tells them, she is pregnant and not responding. He is about to lose his mind. They are trying to keep him calm and get him away from the scene. He refuses to listen to them.

Adontis starts again with yelling out her name. "Tasha, baby! Ma hang on baby! Tasha!" The paramedic is checking her wrist, but he hasn't felt a pulse. Adontis sees this and tears form in his eyes and he is crying out to God. "Jesus. I know I don't always do right. I know I mess up a lot. Please protect her and our baby. Please save them. I cannot lose her. She is the love of my life. She about to be my wife."

The paramedic yells out, "We have a pulse, but it's faint. We have got to move fast."

Adontis catches his breath and begins to thank God. Tasha has lost a lot of blood. After putting her in a neck brace, they cut open the car using the jaws of life. They carefully lift her out and on to a backboard then on to a stretcher. They roll her to the ambulance and get her strapped in. Adontis rides along.

At the hospital, they rush Tasha to the emergency room. Adontis tries to come in with her, but they tell him he can't. He won't even let the doctors examine him. He tells them to focus on Tasha. His stress is through the roof. He calls Aisha and Carmen. Aisha arrives at the hospital fairly quick and finds him there pacing. Aisha hugs him and he is crying. She tries to console him and find out what exactly happened.

Several hours later Carmen and Ron arrive. They caught flights into town. Aisha tells them what she knows so far, which isn't much of anything. Tasha has been in the emergency room for some time now. Adontis is sitting in the waiting room and then he gets up and starts pacing again.

Ron is on the phone with Kia when the doctor finally comes out with a minister. Ron puts Kia on speaker phone so she can listen in. Everyone begins to freak out. Not sure of what this all means. They all gather around the doctor. He introduces himself to everyone and then the minister. The doctor begins to speak and everyone gets silent.

"We could only save one-"

Before he can finish Ron cuts him off. This is oh too familiar to him and Carmen. They lost their parents in an accident and by the time they were notified there wasn't anything they could do. There was no goodbye to be said because their parents were already gone. He can't take the loss of his baby sister especially not in the same manner as the loss of their parents. Something in him snaps.

"What the fuck you talking bout one? Man tell me what going on with my sister!"

The doctor steps back a little. Ron is scaring the shit out of him. Carmen looks as if she might just break. Kia is on the phone trying to keep Ron calm and Carmen together. Adontis is teary eyed. Fear is gripping him in this moment. Aisha is trying to console him.

The doctor had already established a rapport with Adontis. He looks over to Adontis for an ok, to continue to divulge information. Through watery eyes, Adontis gives the green light.

"Doctor tell us what is going on."

"Well from what I can see, Ms. Leam was approximately four and a half months pregnant."

Everyone gasps, except Adontis. Carmen looks at Adontis, she looks pissed and sad.

"Tasha having a baby?"

Kia yells out, "Was? What the hell that mean?"

Adontis is frustrated and his main concern is Tasha right now. He just heard that someone died. He already loved his baby, but he can't lose Tasha. He puts his hands on his head in disbelief. He is trying to clear his thoughts. He is afraid of what he is about to hear.

He responds, "Ya'll let's hear what the doc gotta say, we can talk about that in a minute. Go ahead doc."

"I'm sorry Mr. Lamentez, but the baby died on impact. Tasha is stabilized. One of you can go in and see her. If you need to talk, Rev. John is here."

Adontis lets out a sigh of relief. Then feels a pang of guilt. He is thankful Tasha survived, but they lost their baby. Tasha's family stands around in shock.

"I gotta go see her. I'll answer ya'll questions when I come back."

Adontis follows the doctor to go see Tasha. He walks in alone and closes the door behind him. On their walk the doctor advised him that she is doped up on medicine and asleep. Bandages run up her arm and it is in a sling. She has some stitches on her leg and on her arm. The glass cut her several times. He stands beside her and kisses her gently.

"I am so sorry baby. I love you so much."

He just sits in the room with her.

After some time, I awake in a hospital room. I don't know how long I've been out. Instantly flashes of the accident play in my memory. I briefly relive the event before I realize that Adontis is in the room with me. He jumps up from his seat and comes to my side. When I see him, I smile. I see cuts all over his face and he has a few bruises. I am in a lot of pain. My body aches everywhere.

Even though I feel like crap, the first words out of my mouth are, *"How is our baby? I don't feel her anymore."*

He looks down at the floor. Then he looks up at me teary eyed. *"Our baby didn't make it. The doctor says our baby died on impact."*

The only thing I can do is cry. I wasn't ready to be a mother, but I wanted my baby. I lost two babies in less than one year. He grabs my hand and comforts me, but he doesn't know of all my sadness. Only of one of them. He tells me some people want to come in and see me. He kisses me and leaves the room. When he leaves, Carmen enters the room. She sits and talks with me and keeps me company. Our other family members alternate coming in and out to check on me.

While they are with me the police officers are taking Adontis' statement. The other driver fell asleep at the wheel. He was taken into police custody for negligence. He fell asleep while he was driving. Which caused him to run a red light. Aisha convinces Adontis to go get checked out by the doctors. He gets a few stitches and some pain medication. After a long while I send Carmen to go get Adontis. It has gotten late and visiting hours are about over. He comes in the room.

"Hey ma, how you feeling?"

"Like shit. I just want you in here with me."

"Okay. I'm here. I ain't gon leave you. Just let me go and tell Aisha to take everyone back to the house and let them get settled in."

One by one everyone comes back in to see me and say their goodbyes.

Carmen kisses me on the forehead. *"Get some rest baby. I'll be back to see you tomorrow. I love you."*

"I love you, too."

August 23, 2008

The next morning when I awake, I find Carmen in the room with me. *"Hey sis. How are you feeling?"*

"Hey sis. Like I've been hit by a Mack truck. Where is Adontis?"

"Yeah, you kind of were. He went home to get cleaned up and to get you a change of clothes. I told him I would sit with you."

"Thank you."

"You know you are welcome. Are you up for a chat?"

I shrug my shoulders. I know where this conversation is going to go. *"I guess."*

"Why didn't you tell me sis?"

"We hadn't told anyone yet. I just wanted to wait until after yesterday's appointment. We were going to find out the sex of the baby. Then we were going to spread the news. We were planning on flying into Charleston today, to tell you guys. Then we were going to go tell his family. I've been a little stressed lately so I needed to hear everything was good first."

"Ok. I understand. What are you stressing for? I'm your sister. I want to always be here for you. But you got to tell me when you need me."

"I know. Dealing with so much. Adontis' mom not coming to the wedding. I know it is bothering him. I was trying to figure this wedding thing out. Since finding out I was pregnant I knew my original date wouldn't work. Our baby was due on our wedding day."

Tears flood my eyes uncontrollably. Saying it out loud makes it all the more of a reality. Carmen comes over to console me. I let the tears flow for a bit before talking again.

"Our solution was to push the date back until after I had the baby. We couldn't get the dates to line up for the church and the reception hall though."

"Sis you know I would have stepped in to help. Why are you trying to do everything yourself? You are not superwoman. Besides even superheroes need help sometime."

"I know sis. I didn't want to stress you. You have a full plate too. You have your kids, your husband and your patients. You don't need to add my stuff to the plate too."

"That is what I am here for. I always got you. You just gotta tell me, when you need me."

"I know Carmen. I know."

Adontis walks through the door. *"Hey love. Hey sis."*

Together, we both say, *"Hey."*

He leans in and gives me a kiss. *"How are you feeling today ma?"*

"I've been better. The meds they got me on help, but don't take away the pain. I missed you while you were gone."

"I missed you too ma. Has the doctor been in to check on you yet?"

"No not since I've been up."

Carmen interjects, *"The nurse stopped in earlier when you were sleeping. They wanted us to buzz them when you woke up."*

"Oh ok." I hit the call button for the nurse's station. Adontis sits in the other chair next to me. The nurse walks in a few moments later.

"Good morning Ms. Leam. How are you feeling today?"

"I've been better."

"On a scale of one to ten where is your pain level right now."

"It's going up. It is around a six. I am experiencing some discomfort. My right arm hurts like hell."

"Ok well let me change out your IV, it's time for some more pain meds and an ice pack."

The nurse steps out and returns shortly. She changes out my IV bag and gives me the medicine. Then she slides the ice pack into my sling.

"Leave this ice pack on for about thirty minutes. Once the meds start to work, I want you to buzz me. The doctor wants me to get you out of bed and get you walking today."

"Ok. I will. Can I take a shower?"

"Yes, you can. Let's get you walking first and then you can have a shower."

"Thank you."

"You're welcome Ms. Leam. I'll be back to check on you. Don't forget to buzz me when your pain eases."

"Got it."

Carmen and Adontis stay and keep me company. Once the medicine kicks in I call the nurse back to my room. She comes in and gets me ready to take my walk. The nurse begins to sit my bed up and puts the side rail down. Adontis walks over with my house shoes and robe. I sit up and Adontis slides my shoes on my feet. The nurse gets me up and standing. Adontis and Carmen help me into my robe and Carmen ties it around me. I feel a shooting pain run up the right side of my leg. I squeeze Adontis' hand. I cringe at the pain.

"*I got you ma.*" Carmen opens the room door and Adontis and the nurse lead me out the room down the hall for a walk.

"*Ok, Ms. Leam. We have you.*"

We take a short walk and it hurts. My legs, back, arm; hell, my whole right side feels jacked up. The meds do help though. I can't wait until I am feeling one hundred percent again. I thank God that I was able to walk away from that accident. I'm blessed.

We make it back to my room. Adontis and Carmen assist me in taking a shower. It feels so good to be able to wash my body. There is a knock at the room door. Adontis steps out to answer it. It is Aisha. She has brought Ron to check on me.

Adontis tells her I'm showering and they can come in, in a minute. Once I am all cleaned up Carmen helps me into my gown and back into my sling. I get back in the bed and everyone begins to come in leaving the door opened. Shaun walks in the room after a few minutes.

"*I came straight from the airport. Sis you, ok? Bro you good?*"

"*I'm getting there.*" He walks over, gives me a hug and makes his rounds greeting and hugging everyone in the room.

"*I'm aight just worried bout Tasha.*"

We sit in the room and talk for a while. There is a knock on the opened door.

"*Come in.*"

Doctor Tara walks in. "*You have a full house. Good afternoon everyone.*" Everyone greets her back. "*I just came in to check in on you and talk to you Tasha. How are you feeling?*"

"*I am happy to see you. I am doing ok.*"

Adontis ask that everyone step out for a minute. I stop him. "*Baby they can stay.*

Excuse me where are my manners? Doctor Tara, these are my sisters Carmen and Aisha. Of course, you already know Adontis and last, but not least my brothers Ron and Shaun."

Doctor Tara flashes a smile to everyone "*It's nice to meet you all. I wish it were on better terms.*"

They all respond with, "*Nice to meet you too.*"

"*Ok Tasha, I've looked at your chart and your vitals. Everything looks normal. You are going to be experiencing the pain for a little while, but I have written you a prescription for when you go home.*" She hands the prescription to Adontis. "*You can go ahead and drop that off today. Mr. Lamentez.*"

"*Ok, I'll do that.*"

"*The prescription is for tomorrow. I'm going to go ahead and discharge you tomorrow, Tasha. I want to see you for a checkup in two weeks. Call my office and schedule an appointment. Make sure you keep your arm elevated even while you are sleeping. I want you to also ice this arm three to five times a day. I need you back at one hundred percent."*

"Ok doc. I will. Thank you for checking in on me."

"Of course. I am on call tonight so I will be here if you need anything. Otherwise, see you in two weeks. The nurse will have your discharge papers tomorrow and my directions for your recovery."

I smile. *"Got it thanks again."*

"It was nice meeting you sisters and brothers. I'll see you next time Mr. Lamentez." They give Doctor Tara a wave goodbye.

"Thank you, see you doc," Adontis says as Doctor Tara leaves my room.

August 24, 2008

Finally, today is checkout day. Mr. Lamentez has called and checked on me every day since he heard about the accident. Adontis' grandparents, family members, friends and my family members also call or text to check in on me. It is greatly appreciated.

Ron headed back to his wife and their kids on yesterday afternoon. Carmen is flying back home today. I've enjoyed the time I've been able to spend with them. I miss living close to them. On the way home, Adontis stops and we pick up my prescription. When we get home, I sit up with him, Carmen and Aisha for a little while before I head to bed. My meds make me drowsy.

We haven't divulged to anyone else about the miscarriage yet. We plan to tell his parents the next time we go for a visit. Before Carmen leaves for the airport, she comes in and says her goodbye. Aisha takes her to the airport and Adontis stays with me. He lays in the bed next to me watching tv. I chat with everyone via text until I drift off into a deep sleep.

September 7, 2008

The first two weeks flew by. My family has continued calling to check in on me daily. That is, the ones that know what is going on with me. I've had a few doctors' appointments and everything is healing up well. Per the doctor's orders, I take an additional three weeks off from work. Not from Fresh though. With help from Adontis I still make sure the accounting and payroll things are done. I work from our home office.

Today is Adontis' birthday. I can't really do for him what I would like. I ordered his gift online and had it delivered weeks ago. I'm not in a celebratory mood and neither is he. Aisha picks up the cake and takeout that I ordered. Aisha, Boris, Shaun and Melanie celebrate with us. I also invited both of his parents. I wanted it to be a family thing. It's a simple dinner to celebrate him. I want to do something nice for him when I am feeling better.

Mr. Lamentez comes to celebrate, Mrs. Lamentez refused to come. We finally tell his dad about the miscarriage and it saddens him. His mom missed out on knowing since she wouldn't come. I guess we'll try to tell her next time. He shows us support and stays through the weekend. It gives him a chance to spend some time with all of his kids. Adontis takes him to Fresh and they hang out a lot while he is here. I don't spend much time with them. I'm not up to it.

September 14, 2008

My classes started around the time of the car accident. I didn't have any time to get myself together. I needed to be in my classes, so I went to them. Even with my arm in a sling and on pain meds. Adontis has been, I don't even know if there is a word to describe it. He has taken care of my every need and want. He has been driving me to school and carrying my books to my classes.

I am physically present in my classes, but mentally I am so far away. I have to tape record my lecture notes because I can't write. I do my best to get by in my labs using my left hand. My professors have given me some leniency. Fortunately, my reputation proceeded me here due to my outstanding grades, transcript and past professors.

When I am not in class, I am at home in bed feeling depressed. Adontis has noticed changes in my behavior. I keep to myself and I have shut him out. Again, like with the abortion. I haven't been eating and in all of my spare time all I do is sleep. I know he is trying to be there for me, but I am having trouble dealing with the guilt.

I also failed two of my first exams this semester. I don't fail that's not me. I don't even want to think about what that is going to do to my GPA. I put it out of my mind and don't think about it. I couldn't even bring myself to tell Adontis that I failed. He has been transcribing my notes so that I can study. Helping me in every way possible and I have just been checked out.

I am just lying in the bed under the covers with my eyes closed. Someone enters the room and I hear, *"Hey baby sis. How are you feeling?"* I peek from under the covers to see Carmen. She sits on the bed next to me.

"I am ok, but what are you doing here?"

"Then why are you laying up here all depressed? Yes, you lost your baby, but it's not the end of the world. I know it hurts. You have to move forward in life. Adontis loves you and he is worried about you. He called me and asked me to come. He has been so concerned for you. He told me that you failed two exams this semester. That's not you sis. You are beautiful, smart and intelligent. He feels like you have checked out. All he knew to do, was to call me. Here I am. What is going on?"

I had no clue that Adontis knew that I failed my exams. He must have been going through my school things. I begin to cry. I can't hold this in anymore. *"It's all my fault. Where is Adontis now?"*

Carmen looks at me confused. *"He left to give us some time to talk. How is this your fault?"*

"All I did was complain about how much I didn't want a baby. I killed my baby. I aborted my baby, Carmen."

Carmen has a puzzled look on her face. *"What are you talking about? The doctor said the baby died from the accident."*

Tears are rolling down my face. I let out a loud sigh. *"No, not that baby. My first baby."*

There is a breath of relief. I finally said it out loud. I've admitted it. Carmen has a super stunned look on her face. I know she doesn't mean for it to show, but I totally caught her off guard.

"What first baby T?"

I bow my head in shame. *"I got pregnant fifteen months ago. I had an abortion. I never told Adontis. I never told anyone. Me losing this baby is payback for aborting my first baby."*

I can see she's trying to hold in her shock. *"Wow. That's a heavy load to carry all by yourself Tasha. Why didn't you come to me and talk to me? I'll always have your back. No matter what."*

I begin to sob even harder. *"I didn't tell anyone. I was ashamed. I didn't want to be judged."*

She looks hurt. *"I would never judge you."*

"I guess I was wrong for not telling you. I tried to put it all behind me and now this."

"Well, why did you have an abortion? I thought Adontis wants kids?"

"Because it was all wrong. Wrong timing. Wrong place. Wrong man."

She just looks at me more stunned than the last time. I keep dropping bombs on her. *"And what does that mean?"*

"Adontis and I were going through some things. We broke up for a few weeks. I got drunk one night and I slept with another man." My sister's face displays complete and utter shock. *"It was Rodney."* Carmen really liked him until he screwed me over. She thought he would have been the one. She doesn't say anything though she just continues to let me talk.

"I enjoyed it the first night. Then when I got home that morning Adontis was at my house, begging to get back together. After some days, I decided to get back with Adontis. I called things off with Rodney right after that. But you know him. He doesn't give up easily. He came over to my place and I told him nothing else was gonna happen with us. He started to kiss on me and we had sex again."

"Damn, Tasha. That's deep. I didn't know you was going through all this. I would of been there for you."

"I should of let you. Because it was so hard. The first time I gave myself a pass, but the second time. Man-." I just shake my head. *"Adontis and I were back together and I cheated on him. I felt like a ho. I don't sleep around. I didn't want anyone to know. I just wanted to forget it ever happened. And I kind of did. Until I turned up pregnant. Since I had, had sex with Rodney I was not about to turn around and have sex with Adontis. I made Adontis wait a while first. I was hoping it would be Adontis. When the doctor told me how far I was there was only one person it could be. Rodney's ass.*

Adontis doesn't know I cheated. He takes pride in being the only man I have ever been with. I knew he would never accept otherwise and he definitely wouldn't accept another man's baby, especially Rodney's. They hate each other. I felt alone and ashamed. I figured an abortion was what was best for me. After I did it, I realized it was the biggest mistake of my life. I have tried to get past it. And when I got pregnant this time, I wasn't ashamed I was proud. Happy for a second chance to be a mom."

"Damn. That's a whole hell of a lot to go through. Especially by yourself T. I am your sister. I love you and always will. Nothing will change that or stop me from having your back. Stop carrying things by yourself. I don't care if it feels embarrassing. I will never judge you. You made a mistake. You have got to forgive yourself so you can move on. We learn from our mistakes. Forgive Tasha. So, you can get on with your life."

Carmen hugs me and we share tears together. *"That's it. You have got to get the pain out so you can continue to move forward in life. I love you."*

"I love you too. Thank you for being here and listening to me."

She smiles. *"Always. When you hurt baby sis, I hurt too. We didn't have to be twins for our bond to be as strong as it is. I am glad I can help. Anything for you. I love you so much."*

"I love you too."

chapter 30
No Happy Holiday

November 25, 2008

**When a time of happiness turns sour. Being with family
for the holidays doesn't always bring happiness.**

It's been several months since I've lost my baby. I am still dealing with the loss. I am actually working through it though. Talking to Carmen and telling her my secret has been a big relief. I love my sister so much. She is helping me get through this. I'm going through the grieving process instead of ignoring it. Time is helping and healing. I even wrote a poem for my baby.

My Baby (pt 2)

I loved you
Though I never got to meet you
I carried you
Though I never got to hold you
I felt you
Though I never got to touch you
In my womb
Is where you lied
And in my womb
Is where you died
On that day
I felt my soul cry

Scream
Yell out why
Did my baby
Have to die
Never the chance to grow
Never the chance to know
No longer wanting to be told
If you
Were a boy or a girl
Because it would crush my soul
Unable to gain control
I broke and fell apart
Once again
Another piece of my heart
Now gone

I have focused back on school. My body has healed and physically I feel great. I was able to convince my professors to let me retake the exams I failed and I aced them. I am happy to be back on the right track.

In spite of the major debacle from last Christmas, Adontis still wants his mom at the wedding. I want him happy so I'm supporting him. I guess I kind of have to. He has been my cheerleader through this miscarriage. Plus, I understand him wanting his mom at our wedding. If my parents were here, I'd do everything in my power to have them at my wedding. I can't blame him for trying.

Mrs. Lamentez still hasn't said boo to him since she found out we were getting married. Adontis and I have only communicated with his dad. Once again, Adontis wants to go up to New York for Thanksgiving. I guess I have to go. Adontis won't accept me staying in a hotel. He wants me around the family. I know we are getting married in a few months, but I don't feel welcomed. At least not by his mom.

Adontis' dad has extended the invitation directly to us for the holiday. I think it will be awkward as hell. I will definitely need a couple of drinks to relax my nerves, every single damn day that I'm there. I'll pack some Hennessey. I don't want to speak to his mom. I don't want to hear a half ass apology from her either. I'm at the point where we can agree to disagree. Or better yet, we can agree that we don't like each other and keep it cordial for the sake of family.

Since I have to get back to school, we are not staying as long as we did last year. Thank God! I have also made it very clear to Adontis, there will be no sex in his parent's house. Been there done that, got the t-shirt and burned it. I tried to use sex to convince him to get a hotel room, but he still wasn't down with that. I guess I'll be subject to dealing with his mom.

I'll go, put on a smile and try my best to make this family thing work. After all, when I marry him, I'll be marrying his family too in a sense. His mom needs to know, I ain't going nowhere. Mrs. Lamentez is just going to have to make room for another Mrs. Lamentez. I'm in our bedroom packing up Adontis' and my last-minute things. Adontis walks into the bedroom and wraps his arms around me.

"Hey shorty."

I continue packing. *"Hey love. How was work?"*

"It was long ma. Dealing with these damn employees calling out and shit. I'm gon be firing some mother fuckers real soon. I had enough of this shit. How the hell you the manager and never want to show up to work. I'm in there doing all the shit I been told him to do. But I ain't letting shit stress me. I got enough shit to worry about. How was your day shorty?"

I turn and kiss his lips. *"Clearly better than yours."* I begin undressing him and I pull his shirt over his head.

"Oh, you want Daddy like that?"

He is smiling and grinning. I cut his grin short. *"No stinky,"* as I smirk at him. *"I want Daddy to get in the tub. You smell like you had a long day too."*

He is grinning and shaking his head. *"Damn ma, that's cold."*

While laughing, *"I love you anyway. But seriously you need to hit that tub. I have your bath water ready. Let's go."*

I'm leading him to the bathroom. He smacks me across the ass. *"You must be plan on joining me."*

"No Adontis I got too much to do."

We've reached the bathroom. He spins me around and begins kissing my lips. I unbutton his pants and let them fall off of him. He thinks he is about to get some. He is so mistaken. I slide his boxers down and they fall to the floor. I pull out of the full-on tongue kiss that he is trying to start.

"The tub is all yours." I give him a peck on the lips and begin to walk out of the bathroom. He pulls me back. *"Ma, you ain't giving me none for real?"*

I pry his hands from around me. *"No Adontis I still have a lot to do before we leave."*

He folds his arms across his chest. *"I can't believe you doing me like this."*

"Wash."

I spin around and head out of the bathroom. I finish packing and cooking dinner while Adontis is bathing. We have dinner once he is out and dressed.

November 26, 2008

Adontis and I finish dinner then clean up the kitchen and head to bed. He tries to get some again, but I'm trying to get some sleep. It's bad, but I gotta say I leave him hanging. I'm tired. I'll get him next time. I'm in a good and deep sleep. I feel Adontis' dick poking me. Right in the ass. I want to sleep. I ease away from him. He scoots closer. I ease some more and he scoots closer.

I don't have anywhere else to go. If I scoot again, I'm going to be on the floor. I feel him scoot back. I'm thinking about time. Bruh, take the hint. Not tonight. He pulls me backwards, into his arms. Running from him is not working. I feel his dick in my back. I try to scoot away some. He has me in a Kung Fu grip. I feel his fingers slide down my side then he begins rubbing my thighs. My plan is to keep my thighs closed.

He tries to slide his hands in and I have my legs clutched closed. He can't get in. He does something with his legs. Somehow, he gets one of his legs in between mines and the next thing I know my legs are spread wide open. This dude really is a ninja or a magician. His fingers are in between my thighs and he is now playing with my kitty kat. I can't fake the sleeping thing anymore. Time to speak up. I crack my eyes open. The clock reads 3:17am. We have a 10am flight.

"Adontis, would you stop!"

He doesn't speak. This man has gone mute. What the hell. He moves his lips to my spot. He starts kissing and sucking on my neck. My nasty ass wants to sleep, but he has me aroused. He begins kissing on me. I shake my head. I can't believe this shit. I roll on to my side and climb on top of him. Might as well.

The alarm is sounding off. Its 7:27am. I hit the snooze button several times. Not only did Adontis wanna get it on, but he wanted to have a marathon. When we finished it was after 5am. I have the wonderful displeasure of waking him up.

It takes a lot of fussing, but I get Adontis up and out of bed. I make up the bed, get myself ready and we make it to the airport on time. Our flight is only a few hours. Since I didn't get much sleep last night, I catch a nap on the plane.

It seems like as soon as we board, we are deboarding the plane. New York, we have arrived. Adontis and I have talked about the awkwardness of seeing his mom. Yet we are still doing it. Yay me. As usual we take a cab to his parent's place. Once through the gate we get out of the car and ring the doorbell. Adontis texted his dad on the way over, therefore he is expecting us.

Mr. Lamentez opens the door and greets the both of us with a great big hug. *"Hey kids."*

I say, *"Hello,"* and hug him back.

"Come on in out of that cold." He helps Adontis with our luggage. *"How was your flight?"*

I don't say much. I just let Adontis answer. *"It was good Dad. Where everyone at?"*

"Your mother and Melanie went out to the store. Shaun, Riq and I are in the parlor shooting pool. I got your room ready. Ya'll can go settle in and meet us in the parlor."

"Ok Pops. Tasha in the same guest room as last time?"

"I figured ya'll may as well stay in your room together."

I have to interject. *"Mr. Lamentez if it's not too much trouble I would rather stay in a guest room. I want to respect Mrs. Lamentez's home."*

"Baby this my home too, but I understand. The guest room you stayed in last time is available and ready for you."

"Thank you."

Adontis leads us upstairs. I get settled in my room, but not too settled. The morning after Thanksgiving I'm outta here. I'm not even gonna unpack. Adontis walks in my room. *"Ma, you ready to head back downstairs."*

"No, not really."

He gives me a side eye. *"Ma. You ain't did nothing wrong."* He grabs my hand, *"Come on let's head downstairs."*

I roll my eyes and then follow him down the stairs. We spend the afternoon in the parlor. I have a few drinks. It has calmed my nerves. I shoot a little pool with the guys and just relax. It is stress free without his mom here. We head out for dinner around 4pm. It is late in the evening once we return. Shortly after we arrive the doorbell rings. Adontis goes to answer.

He returns to the family room with Aisha. She walks in and greets everyone. I'm happy for some more moral support. We all relax together until everyone decides to go to bed. Mrs. Lamentez and Melanie haven't returned yet. That is fine with me. Adontis pulls me aside before I can head upstairs.

"Ma, let's go for a ride."

"A ride?"

"Yeah ma. Literally and figuratively."

I start laughing. *"You are so damn nasty. A ride to where?"*

He grabs his keys out of the drawer. *"Does it matter? You with Daddy. We gon hop in the Ferrari and take a ride."*

I shrug my shoulders. *"Ok baby. Why not."*

We grab our coats, Adontis sets the alarm and locks the door behind us.

November 27, 2008

Knowing Adontis, he wants to get a little freaky sneaky. It's after midnight and we just wanna have fun. We decide to get it in at Fresh. Why not, we've Christened all of the other ones. It's after hours and no one will be there. Besides a hotel would be boring. Maybe we can roleplay a little. We just want to get a little kinky. Maybe Teresita will show up.

We are stripping out of our clothes as we are entering the store. We leave the lights off because it's more fun that way. Adontis took his shirt off while he was unlocking the door. Once inside he locks the door behind us. I am down to my bra and panties very quickly. I leave on my thigh high boots. I only had on a dress. He goes to punch in the alarm code while unbuttoning his pants. I come over to give him a little motivation. I slide his pants and boxers down and begin licking and sucking on his dick.

The alarm doesn't disable. It just begins to beep rapidly. He tries the code again. The alarm goes off and begins to echo loudly throughout the store. It is a hell of a distraction. I stop giving him head. Let's be real I can't focus. My head game is great. My hand eye coordination is on point. However, with this alarm going off I don't know which way is up.

The store phone rings. Adontis pulls up his pants and boxers. We try to find the phone in the dark. The alarm is blaring and the phone is ringing. The alarm is loud as hell. It is starting to give me a headache. I finally spot it and pass him the phone. He answers and it is the alarm company. He tells them who he is and they ask for the account password. He gives them a password. They tell him the password he has given is incorrect.

Adontis looks confused as hell. He set up the alarm and the password with them himself. He doesn't know how in the hell it could be wrong. While he is talking to the alarm company his cell phone rings. I answer his cell and it is the store manager. He hears the alarm going off in the background.

"Hey Adontis-"

I cut him off. *"Damian this is Tasha. Adontis is on the phone with the alarm company right now. We are at the store and set the alarm off. What is the account password and the alarm pin number so Adontis can give it to them?"*

"Ya'll at the store this time of night? What ya'll doing there this la…" His voice trails off. *"Ya'll nasty asses."*

I ignore the hell out of him. *"Damian, I don't have time for this. What is the code man?"*

He burst out laughing. *"Ya'll so damn nasty."*

I roll my eyes. I'm trying not to cuss him out. *"The code man!"*

Still laughing he says, *"The pin is 7369. The account password is Kingdom."*

I roll my eyes. *"Bye!"*

I hang up on him. I enter the code into the alarm and the alarm finally stops blaring. I look to Adontis.

"Baby that was Damian. The password is Kingdom."

Adontis gives the password to the company. They tell him something and I hear him say, *"Ok. Thank you. Goodbye."*

"I'm gon have a talk with Damian ass tomorrow. He changed the damn passwords and ain't tell me. They dispatched the cops since I ain't know the password. They gon call them back and let them know everything is good here. But since they already coming, they still gon come check shit out. Shit. I don't fuck with the police. They gon be here any minute."

"Oh shit. I have to find my dress. I threw it somewhere when we walked in."

"Alight ma. Let's look for it."

I begin to start searching then we hear a knock at the front door. I run behind the counter. There is nowhere else to hide. I would have to pass the front door and windows to get to a dressing room or to the stock room. I am stuck hiding behind the counter. I never found my dress and let's face it, I'm not appropriate. I look around me to see if there is any item of clothing I could slip into. Adontis turns on the lights then walks up to the door and unlocks it. He puts on his I don't hate the police face.

"Good evening."

"We received a call that the alarm at this location was going off."

"Yeah. I'm the owner of this store. My manager changed the alarm code without informing me. I've spoken to my alarm company and everything is good now."

"What were you doing here at this time of night?"

"I need a reason to come to my store?"

"We'll ask the questions. What's your name?"

"Lamentez."

"Mr. Lamantayyy, can we come in and take a look around, make sure everything is ok?"

I am about to die behind the counter. I wish these cops would leave. Kick rocks. We good here damn. There is a rack next to me with some clothes hanging up. I manage to quietly slide a man's 2XL basketball jersey off of a hanger. I slip it on over my head while still crouching down. This should cover all my parts.

"It's Lamentez! And everything is ok."

"You say you are the owner?"

"I am!"

"Do you have ID to prove that?"

"Yeah." He reaches in his back pocket to pull out his wallet. It is not there. "I had it a few minutes ago. It must have dropped out."

Adontis glances back to see if he sees his wallet on the floor. The cops take that opportunity to step into his store. I look around the floor near me and the alarm where I was giving Adontis head and see his wallet. I think to myself, damn. I crawl over and pick it up.

"Dropped out where son?"

I begin to get concerned. Adontis doesn't like that shit. He doesn't want some random man especially a white cop calling him son. It does something to him triggers some anger in him. I don't want it to escalate. These cops are obviously looking for a reason to mess with him. I don't want any problems. They ain't killing my damn man. I am clothed now so I can come out. I get up from behind the counter and begin to walk towards them. I have my hands in the air clutching Adontis' wallet. Hell, they ain't killing me neither.

"Baby, your wallet is right here."

"So, you are not alone, huh son?"

Adontis lets out a frustrated sigh. I know they are pissing him off. I just want him to keep his cool. Let's get through this moment and back to our lives.

"Baby its ok. I have your wallet here."

I reach Adontis and the officers and step in front of Adontis. This way I am between he and them.

"Who are you ma'am?"

"I am his fiancé."

I open up Adontis' wallet and hand the officer his ID. I see the cop glance at my left hand. He sees the ring on my finger and I can see it stuns him.

"What is your name Miss? Do you have an ID?"

"I am Tasha Leam. No, officer I didn't bring my purse."

"That is an awfully big ring on your finger." He looks to Adontis, "What are you some kind of a rapper?"

To myself, I'm thinking no this motherfucker didn't. Adontis just stands and looks at him like he is stupid. I figure I better give the answer. I won't acknowledge his statement about my ring. It's none of his business.

"No, he's not a rapper."

"I think he can speak for himself Miss."

Adontis puts his arms up above his head and rest his arms there. *"My lady just told you I wasn't a rapper."*

"Well, how do you own this store?"

Adontis looks at him like he is stupid. *"What the hell is that supposed to mean?"*

All kinds of things are running through my head. I just want them to leave. The officer steps back a little and looks at us, then he looks down at Adontis' license.

"This license is from Florida."

Adontis says, *"Yeah and what's your point?"*

"Don't get smart son. What you doing all the way up here with a Florida license. You know living here in New York you need to have a New York license."

I feel Adontis' rage burning through the back of my skull. *"Baby. It's ok."*

I'm trying to keep him calm before he explodes. Adontis clasps his hands together above his head and sucks his teeth.

"That's why I don't live here in New York."

"You own this store here, but you don't live here?"

"Man, that's what I said. Can you just go run my license so we can get this shit over with! Damn."

I lean back into him. I want to remind him that I am here. I need him to calm down. He is about to blow up. His mom already hates me. She doesn't need any more reasons. Adontis in handcuffs would be another reason to hate me.

"Son you need to calm down."

"Man, I am calm. Ya'll just here fucking with me. For no damn reason. You got my ID and shit. Run the shit so you can see I'm good and leave me the fuck alone. Damn."

I take a deep breath. I feel Adontis leaning into me. I want to hold his hands, but I don't want to make any sudden movements. My hands are still up in the air and Adontis still has his arms on his head. The officer passes Adontis' license to his partner. His partner goes to their car to check it. The officer is just staring at Adontis and Adontis is staring right back at him. It takes a few minutes before the other officer returns with Adontis' ID.

"That your car outside there, son?"

"Yeah man it is. Why?"

"I told you we will ask the questions." I know it is taking everything in Adontis for him to hold it together. *"That's a mighty fancy car boy."*

Oh shit. He said it. *"Boy!"*

Instantly I notice, his tone has changed. I know this is his breaking point. He is about to go off and there ain't shit I can do about it. When he reaches this point, I can't stop it.

"Listen, I am not your son and I damn sure am not your boy. I am a grown ass damn man. Now you have been disrespecting me since you got here. First you walked into my damn store uninvited. You were told by my alarm company that everything checked out. You have insulted my intelligence, my woman and my race. I have been patient with your asses. Enough is fucking enough. I personally know Mayor Withington. My attorney is Debra Hainsworth. I am sure you

have heard of her. I have your names and your badge numbers; you will be hearing about this shit. Finish running my shit and get the fuck on."

I know now is not the time. However, he has me hot and bothered. It is amazing how he turns his street side off and on. The professional in him just came out. The educated side. To look at him one wouldn't think he had an educated side. He looks like a street nigga. However, my man graduated high school at sixteen. His undergrad was completed when he was nineteen and his masters at twenty-two.

"Are you threatening an officer?"

"I did not threaten you. Stop bullshitting. I do not have shit else to say. My attorney will finish this conversation for me."

I'm about to lose it. I can't calm him down. He is pissed and justifiably so. The other officer walks back in the store. He hands Adontis his license back, but I grab it. I don't want any problems and besides I still have his wallet. Adontis doesn't even reach for it. No sudden movements. The officer that ran Adontis' license whispers something to the other officer. They whisper back and forth for a few moments.

The officer who was running Adontis license says, *"Everything has checked out. You're good to go."*

Adontis still doesn't say a word. I think that it is best that way. I speak for the both of us. *"Ok."*

I pull open the door for them so they can understand I'm ready for them to get the hell out. They walk out the door. I get the keys from Adontis and lock the door back. I don't bother to fuss with him for his attitude towards the cops. That's not what he needs. He needs to know he has my support and that I got his back. I spin around and face him. I gesture for him to lean down towards me. I wrap my arms around his neck as I kiss him on the lips.

"It's over baby. Are you ok?"

"Those racist mother fuckers. I ain't his mother fucking son. Those bitches are in for some shit. First thing Monday morning I'm having them dealt with." He deeply exhales.

"I know baby. I know." I continue to embrace him.

"I'm gon fucking cuss Damian ass out."

He picks up his phone and dials him. He really goes off on him. The call only lasts a few minutes before Adontis hangs up on him. Of course, the mood is gone. I get Adontis calmed down then we head back to his parents. The house is dark and quiet. I guess everyone is asleep. I go to Adontis' room and lay with him for a while with the door open. I just want to give him comfort and let him vent as much as he needs to. I stay there until he falls asleep. It's after 3am, but I get up and head to my room.

There is thankfully no Thanksgiving wakeup call from Mrs. Lamentez this year. Dinner is going to be catered again this year. However, the guest list won't be nearly as large. Adontis' grandparents have decided to spend Thanksgiving with Adontis' aunt. The news of how Adontis' mother acted last time I was here spread throughout his family. All of Adontis' dad's side of the family will not be in attendance. Everything feels so divided. I can't help, but to feel like I caused it.

The majority of Adontis' mother's side lives on the west coast. I will not meet them until the wedding, but they RSVP'd unlike his mother. I don't want to be here. I've decided to stay in my room until Adontis awakes and comes to get me. I take a shower get dressed then get back in my bed. There is a knock at my door.

"Come in."

The door opens and Aisha walks in. *"Hey sis. What are you still doing in bed?"*

"Girl, avoiding your mother. Just as I assume, she is avoiding me."

"Oh, my goodness. Girl. I can't. Mom needs to apologize and get off of her high horse. Shit." She rolls her eyes and lays across the bottom of the bed.

"Yeah. Well, let me ask you this. Why is she so acceptant of Melanie?"

She rolls her eyes again. *"Well, Melanie is the one she chose for Shaun. She's, her pick. Melanie can do no wrong in her eyes and she can control Melanie. Her family has status as my mother likes to call it. Which is bullshit. Her mom was on drugs and her dad paid to have it covered up. Melanie hoed around in high school before Shaun. Melanie is so far up mom's ass, til it ain't funny. Mom being able to control Melanie also lets her control, Shaun. She can't control my ass and we bump heads all of the time.*

She can't control Adontis either. She is taking that out on you and that shit ain't fair. Her pick for Adontis is Charlotte and she is a damn hoe. She loose as hell. You know my brother. He don't want no woman that done been with everyone else. The worst part is that if she actually took the time to get to know you, she would realize that you are everything she ever wanted in a daughter in law."

"Wow. Damn Aisha. You just gave me all the damn tea."

She starts laughing. *"Well sis you ain't thirsty no more."*

"You right about that. I just don't know what else to do with your mom. She is putting a major stress on Adontis and my relationship. I don't ever want to tell him he has to choose between she and me. I just want her to treat me with the respect that she wants."

"Nothing else you can do sis. Just continue to be you. Hell, she'll come around sooner or later. If she don't, then she gon miss out on a whole lot."

"Yeah, you right. Well, let me wet your pallet about my night last night."

"Oh shit. What did you and my brother do now?"

I shake my head. *"It started off really good. We wanted to get a little freaky sneaky. But of course, I wasn't going to do it here. Adontis had an idea. We'd go to Fresh to get it in."*

"Ya'll nasty. Ya'll asses always up to something."

I laugh. *"For my baby, I'll be that. Long story short we trying to get it in soon as we walk through the door. Adontis puts in the code to the alarm and the shit doesn't work. I'm half naked he's half naked. We set the alarm off. It is ringing loud as hell."*

Aisha is laughing her ass off. I just shake my head.

"Girl, the alarm company calls the store. Damian calls Adontis' cell while Adontis is on the phone with the alarm company. Damian changed all the codes and didn't tell Adontis. I get the password and code from him. I give Adontis the password and I punch the code into the alarm pad. The cops come out and are racist as hell. Asking all kinds of inappropriate questions."

I give her the rest of the details. *"Sis it was a nightmare."*

"Damn T. Ya'll always got some shit going on."

"Who you telling. Adontis ain't getting it no more in New York. While we here our sex life will be non-existent."

"Ya'll two stay doing the most."

"I know girl. It wasn't supposed to be all that."

She is laughing and shaking her head. *"Yeah, I bet. You ready to get out of bed yet sis? You know I got your back."*

"I know you do. But no."

She starts laughing and gets up out of the bed. She is pulling me out of the bed. *"Come on let's go see what Adontis is doing."*

"Isn't he still in bed sleeping?"

"Naw when I passed by his room the door was open, but he wasn't in there."

"Why the hell he ain't come talk to me?"

She shrugs her shoulders. *"Let's go."*

She pulls me out the room and we head downstairs. When we pass by Adontis' room, it is still empty. We get downstairs and find Shaun and Melanie having breakfast. The table is set for everyone, but we are missing a few. There is a fruit tray full of strawberries, grapes, apples and pineapples. Sitting on a warmer is a long pan filled with scrambled eggs, bacon, biscuits, sausage and pancakes. In three different pitchers there is chilled apple juice, orange juice and water.

"Hey ya'll. Have ya'll seen Adontis this morning?"

"Naw I ain't seen him," Melanie says.

Shaun chimes in, *"He went upstairs to talk to moms."*

"Oh."

I look at Aisha. I'm thinking here we go. What a way to start off Thanksgiving. At least she didn't catch Adontis and I in bed together again. I pull Aisha to the side.

"Can you go see what's going on with him and your moms?"

"Really T?"

"Yes, Aisha. Please!"

"Alight sis, for you."

Aisha heads back upstairs and I sit down at the table with Shaun and Melanie. I don't have an appetite. I really want to get today over with so I can get back home. We chat for a little while then Mr. Lamentez comes downstairs. He greets all of us with a warm good morning. He pulls out his chair and begins fixing his plate.

"Tasha, come on sweetheart, fix yourself a plate."

I don't want to be rude, but I really don't want to eat anything. My stomach is in knots. I do not really want to be here. I do not want to see his mother.

"Yes, Mr. Lamentez I will. Thank you."

"I hope I am not overstepping. When I told you that you can call me dad, I meant it. You are a part of this family."

I smile. *"Thank you. I will."*

I put some fruit on my plate and nibble on it nervously awaiting Aisha's return. I'm so nervous. I don't know how things are going upstairs. I feel like I am in the twilight zone. Everything down here seems so calm cool and collected. Aisha steps into the dining room.

"Excuse me, I just need to borrow Tasha for a moment."

I stand up and walk out of the dining room with her. She leads us to the family room. *"Ok Aisha. What is going on? What did you find out?"*

"Ok T give me a second. Mom has lost her mind. She is on some she isn't coming down to celebrate Thanksgiving because she isn't thankful."

I'm taken aback. Hell, I'm offended. *"This is ridiculous. Her antics are not going to stop our wedding. I'm just ready to go home. I've had enough."*

"I know. So has Adontis, Dad and I. Adontis asked me to get you and bring you upstairs."

"For what? She ain't wanna talk to me."

"Maybe she don't, but he wants you to get a chance to say whatever you want to say."

"And your mom knows I'm coming up there?"

"Yeah T. He said it right in front of her."

"Only if you come with me."

"T this ya'll business."

"I thought you had my back?"

"I always do."

"Please come up with me."

She sighs. *"Ok, T. Let's go."*

We get upstairs and as we approach their parents' bedroom; I can hear Adontis and Mrs. Lamentez arguing. Aisha doesn't knock she just opens the door. I'm nervous as hell. I don't know what the woman may try to do to me. Adontis is sitting on a sofa and his mom is sitting across from him on a chaise. Adontis stands when I walk into the room. He leans in and kisses me on the cheek.

"Good morning shorty."

"Good morning."

He grabs my hand and leads me to sit next to him. Aisha sits on the armchair. Mrs. Lamentez looks at me and rolls her eyes. I just shake my head. The nastiness never stops.

"Shorty, I know you got some things that we talked about that you want to say. Go ahead and say it. Mom it's your turn to listen." She looks at him as if she is offended.

"Everything I have to say, I mean with the most respect. Even though you've never given any to me. From the first day you met me, you didn't like me. Not because I did anything to you, but because you didn't want to." She is rolling her eyes, but I don't care I got a lot to say.

"I'm definitely not perfect. But I love Adontis. I do my best to show him and to care for him. In your mind you think I'm some piece of trash. However, I am an educated black woman. I graduated at the top of my class in high school and undergrad. I'm in med school studying to be a doctor. I will graduate at the top again. I bust my tail to work hard, study and to care for your son. In every aspect I aspire to be a great wife and one day a mother, to your future grandchildren.

I hope you can get yourself together and get over your issues with me because my parents are gone. Our kids will never have them in their lives. I want our kids to have a relationship with the only grandparents they have on this earth. But I will not bring my future kids around you, when you have so much hatred towards me. I will not allow that poison around my children." Her eyeballs stretch and now I see where Adontis gets it from. Adontis is shaking his head in agreement with me.

"Seeing as to the fact that my parents died when I was young, I looked forward to having a new mother figure in my life one day. I always thought that it would be my future mother-in-law. But you never gave me a try. Never took the chance to get to know me, as a person. Adontis and I both want you at our wedding. I don't want to bring drama to this family. I'm here because I want to mend it. Wipe the slate clean. I'm asking that you give me a chance. Get to know me and allow me to get to know you. Let's begin to start acting like the family we will be in a few months." I look to Adontis, *"Baby that's all I have to say."*

"I want to add something, shorty."

"Ok baby."

"Ma, you got in your head that you want me to be with Charlotte. That's never going to happen. For whatever reason you like her and she a ho." He looks at me, *"Shorty I hope you don't get offended, but I feel like I need to say this. If I piss you off just cuss me out later."*

I'm thinking what the hell is he about to say. Aisha looks at me strangely. I look at her and shrug my shoulders. I don't know what is about to fly out of Adontis' mouth, but I'm concerned.

"Ma, Tasha said it earlier. You act like she trash. And that's where you wrong. My baby saved herself for me."

I'm about to die inside. I can't believe he just said this shit to his mother. I look over at him like what the hell is wrong with you. Aisha gives him the same look. Mrs. Lamentez actually looks shocked.

"We all adults here. Ma you already know Tasha and I have sex. Ain't no need to act like this a big deal. Yeah, you found out the worst way possible, but you know. What I want you to understand though, is that Tasha is a lady. She ain't no ho. She ain't been around, like your friend Charlotte. You always wanted me with a decent woman, from a good family, honest, faithful and a virgin. Well Ma, that is Tasha. I took her virginity."

"Oh my God. Adontis!" Now I'm really embarrassed. I just want to run out of the room.

"Shorty, I'm sorry. Ma you can say whatever you wanna say. The floor yours."

"I don't have anything to say. I want to be left alone."

"After everything we just said, all you can say is you wanna be left alone?"

"That is what I said."

"You not coming to your first-born son's wedding?"

She folds her arm across her chest. *"I said I want to be left alone and I meant it."*

Aisha stands up, *"Ma I got something to say and you can be mad at me. I don't care."* She looks at her like what. *"You being selfish. If you don't show up to this wedding, you are going to regret it and break your son's heart."* Aisha gets up and walks out the room.

I stand and so does Adontis. *"I hope you change your mind about the wedding and me."*

"Ma me too. I really want to share my wedding day with you. If you don't come, we'll never be the same again, but I'll get over it. However, whether you change your mind or not, until you show Tasha the respect that she deserves, we won't be back here again. We flying out first thing tomorrow morning."

She doesn't say a word. Adontis grabs my hand and walks me out the bedroom. *"That conversation was heavy as hell. It still doesn't seem like we got through to her. That is the sad part. You had to just broadcast my virginity?"*

"Ma, I apologized before I said it. I felt like she needed to know. She got this preconceived notion of you. And it ain't based on no facts. She just want me with Charlotte, who has every quality she don't want in a daughter in law. I wanted her to know that the woman that I found, already meets the criteria she wants in a daughter in law and so much more." He leans in and kisses me. *"I'm hungry as shit. Let's eat."*

We head to the dining room and join everyone else. We fill them in on everything. Mr. Lamentez shakes his head. *"I don't know what's wrong with that woman. She has lost it."*

"Pops she pretty much kicked us out."

"She'll be alright. Ain't nobody studying her and her foolishness. She wants to spend the holiday alone. That's her problem. I'm going to celebrate with my children. As a matter of fact, we can just go to my sister house for dinner and leave her here. I'm gon call her now and see what time she is starting."

After breakfast we relax for a little while. As the time draws near, we all begin to get ready to head to Aunt Julissa house. She has welcomed all of us with open arms. This is awkward as hell. When in Rome, I guess. We spend a great deal of time at Aunt Julissa's house. Adontis' family welcomes me. It is a breath of fresh air after being at his parents. I have a chance to meet some new family members and to spend time with everyone I met last year.

It is a really good time. Dinner is great and it is a nice ending to an otherwise rocky day. When we get back to Adontis' parents' house, Mrs. Lamentez is downstairs in the family room. Charlene has come over and they are mingling. Mr. Lamentez, Aisha, Adontis and I all head upstairs. Melanie joins Mrs. Lamentez and Charlene. Shaun heads to the kitchen. When we get upstairs, we all say goodnight. Adontis follows me to my room and closes the door.

"No sir. Get out."

"I just want to catch up with you ma. I ain't gon try nothing."

I give him the side eye. *"Ok, I'm gon change my clothes then you can open the door back."*

He throws his hands up in defense. *"Alight ma, damn."* He walks over and leans against the wall across from me.

"I don't need no more problems."

"Alight. Before I went and talked to moms, I called my lawyer and the mayor this morning about those racist ass cops. They gon be dealt with."

I snap my fingers, *"Just like that?"*

"Just like that ma. I ain't no bum ass nigga. I want their asses fired. I'm going to do whatever I got to, to make it happen."

"Ok, baby. You know you got my support on whatever you need."

"Yeah, shorty I know."

I've finished changing my clothes so I climb into bed. He walks over, leans down and kisses me.

"Your turn. Talk to daddy. You alight ma? This been a long day."

"Yes, it has and yeah I'm ok. I had a good time at Aunt Julissa's. This stuff with your mom, I'm just over it. I gave everything I could. It's up to her to want to be a part of my life. If she don't then ain't shit I can do."

"Yeah ma. It is what it is at this point. I want her at the wedding, but I can't make her come and I ain't stressing no more over the shit."

"Yeah."

He climbs in the bed beside me. *"Adontis stop."*

"Ma, I ain't doing nothing, shit."

"Then go open the door."

"Alight."

I let out a sigh. *"What wrong ma?"*

"I just remembered I need to go pack your stuff up too."

"Naw I'm ready to go."

"That's a first."

"Yep, time to get back home."

He gets up and opens the door and comes and lays back in the bed beside me. He pulls me into his arms. *"Come on let daddy rock you to sleep. Then I'll get up and go to bed."*

I give him a side eye again. *"Adontis!"*

"What?"

"Promise me, you won't fall asleep in here."

"I won't ma. I even kept all my clothes on."

November 28, 2008

I wake up to my alarm blaring. I'm tucked tightly under the covers and Adontis is gone. I roll out of bed to go awake him. Finally, I can go back home. I walk to his room and he's rolling out of bed.

"What, you're actually up?"

"Yeah ma. I'm ready to get home." He walks over and kisses my lips. *"Good morning shorty."*

"Good morning baby. Since you are already up, I'm going to go get ready."

"Alight ma."

He heads to the restroom and I head to my room. It doesn't take us very long to get ready. Once we are both ready, we make our rounds to tell everyone goodbye, including his mom. She doesn't say very much, but oh well. We tried. We leave for the airport I'm so ready to get back home.

chapter 31

Christmas, Again!!!!

December 23, 2008

Sometimes plans change and sometimes it's for the better.

Adontis and I want to start a new tradition. We're settled in our home and it is fully furnished. We decide to host Christmas for both of our families. We've invited my siblings and their families, Adontis' siblings and his parents also. I'm doing my best to get this family together. Our wedding is near and it's kind of a now or never thing.

Everyone accepts our extended invitation except for Mrs. Lamentez. She doesn't respond or acknowledge it. We don't get a reply at all. Adontis and I both agreed this would be our last attempt to reach out to her. If she doesn't come then we will just let it go. I hate how much it hurts him because I know how much he loves her. I can't say the same because she's never given me a chance to know her.

We spend our morning getting the house ready for our families. We only have a few last-minute things to do. My family and Adontis's dad will actually stay at our house. Since Aisha and Shaun live nearby, they won't. Once we finish up all of the last-minute things, we have a few minutes to relax before pick-ups at the airport.

"You like a damn kid ma."

"What you mean?"

"I can see the excitement all over your face."

"Baby, I'm just happy to be able to bring our families together for the holiday. It's just really nice. I wish your mom would of came too. I know she don't like me. And I can't lie, I care and the shit hurts, but I know she loves you. I just want to see you happy for the holiday."

"Ma. I love moms too, but you, my wife. And you make me happy. She made her choice and shit is what it is." He pulls me into his arms and wraps them around me. *"You all I need*

shorty. Don't you ever forget that." He places his thick full lips on me and begins to kiss me passionately.

"I love you daddy."

"I love you too ma."

I fix us a quick lunch and we relax and watch a movie until the time for our family to arrive. Adontis leaves for the pick-ups. He rented a fifteen-passenger van. That way there is enough room for everyone. I head to the kitchen to get dinner started. We're going to have a fried seafood night. The menu is fried shrimp, flounder and scallops. I've made a pot of grits and a pot of jambalaya. Something for everybody. For the kids I have chicken fingers and macaroni and cheese. I'm ready to play hostess.

Adontis returns almost an hour and a half later. Everyone is in tow. I walk from the kitchen to go greet my family. When I step through the doorway, I'm in shock. Adontis' mom is standing in my family room. I need a moment to gather myself, my mind and thoughts. I don't get one. I'm bombarded with love and hugs from all of my family.

Which is followed by his dad. His mom is standing off to the side. I don't know what to do. Is she here to try and kill me? She walks up towards me and all I see is her arms outstretched. Immediately I step back. I don't know what to do with that. I'm not with the fake shit. Everyone is kind of watching and they are shocked. She stops in her tracks. Maybe she is reading the if you touch me I will cold clock the shit out of you look on my face.

"Tasha, can I please talk to you in private?"

I look to Adontis for a rescue. He doesn't offer one. Where is Aisha when I need her. Mrs. Lamentez and I have never had a one-on-one conversation. I don't know why she is trying to start now. This all seems bizarre to me. I don't know what to do. I walk up to Adontis and grab his hand.

"Yes, we can talk in private."

"I'd like for it to be just you and I."

The first thing I hear running through my head is oh shit, she is going to kill me. She has come here to off me. End this marriage permanently before it even starts. I get myself together and shake the thoughts and images of my thoughts from my head. I have got to keep my cool.

"Ok. That's fine. We can speak in the living room."

Since this is her first time in our home, I gesture to her which direction to go. I look back to everyone else.

"Family make yourselves at home. Adontis will show you to your rooms. Carmen can you keep an eye out on dinner in the kitchen please?"

"Yeah T, I got it."

I follow behind her to the living room and close the French doors behind me. Again, I gesture to her to take a seat. Once she does, I sit on another sofa across the room. I don't know what this is about. My guard has a guard up. A dead silence comes over the room for a few minutes. It's beginning to feel awkward. I don't really have anything to say until I hear why she wants to have this talk.

"Tasha, I want to start off by apologizing to you."

I'm sitting looking like Adontis my eyeballs are stretched in shock. Hell, I almost fall out of my seat when I hear what she says.

"The way I've treated you has been not only ugly, but I've been cruel, mean and disrespectful. For that I am very sorry."

I'm not one to bite my tongue and I think she at least knows this much about me. *"I hear what you are saying and I even appreciate that you are saying it. But no disrespect I need clarity. Where is this apology coming from? Is it even genuine? I never expected to get one from you. I just learned to come to terms with not expecting a relationship with you."*

"I deserve that. Let me say this, this apology is absolutely genuine. No scheme or hidden agenda. Ultimately, what I want is a chance to be in your life and to build a relationship with you."

"I hear what you are selling, but I'm skeptical about buying it. This is absolutely a complete three-sixty turn around. I know you're saying its genuine. How can I believe that? What has sparked this change?"

"I understand what you are saying. Several things have caused this change. First, I came to the realization that I was mad at you because I felt like you were taking my son away from me. He moved away just to be close to you."

"I would never do that. In spite of how you've been, I've never asked him to choose."

"I know. That's how I felt and I was wrong. Although I was acting like that, you continually tried to mend things. It took me a while to see that. My husband has been on me about making this right too. The last time I saw you and you poured your heart out to me. I remained stern on the outside, but I heard what you said."

Tears begin to roll from her eyes. Hell, I had forgotten that she too was human.

"I felt your hurt and pain. In that moment, I knew then that I needed to fix us. I saw you for the woman you are. Not the woman I made you up to be in my mind. My mother-in-law and I don't have a relationship. I used to want one with her, but so much bitterness has festered it is beyond repair. I don't want that with my daughter in law. With you Tasha, I want to be the mother-in-law that I once wanted and the second mom that you need. Time to break this generational curse."

Her words have straight punked the hell out of me. Now I'm in tears. She has gotten up and moved to the sofa and sat next to me.

"After hearing what you said I prayed on how to fix it, or rather what to say to you. How to begin. I didn't know how to do it. I didn't even know if you'd receive it. When I received your invitation for this holiday, I knew I would not get a better chance. I'm asking that you please forgive me for every single mean and hurtful thing I've ever said and done to you. I'm truly sorry. Starting today I want to start building our relationship. I want to be that second mom that you want and need. At whatever pace you want it to go. If you'll have me."

Her arms are outstretched to me and I meet her in the middle. We embrace in a long overdue hug. *"Thank you. I accept your apology."* We sit in a tearful embrace for a few moments.

"There is one more thing I'd like to say. I'm just learning that a few months back you experienced a miscarriage from that car accident. I feel like a fool because I was so busy fussing

with you and arguing with you. I missed the chance to be there for you. I promise to you that will never happen again. I am here. Anytime you need me and you are always welcome in my home."

"Thank you." I'm astonished. This is all I've ever wanted from her. Now I finally have it. With a tearful smile, I look to her, *"This means I can count you in for the wedding?"*

"I wouldn't miss it for the world."

Adontis steps into the room and walks over and wraps his arms around us. *"This is all I ever wanted. I don't need a thing else for Christmas."* He kisses his mom on the cheek and then plants a kiss on me. *"Dinner is ready ladies."* He helps both of us from our seats and we head to the dining room and they take their seats.

Once in the dining room I see that Shaun and Melanie have arrived. Aisha is also here and she has brought Boris. He's finally meeting her parents. I greet each of them with hugs. Then I head to Carmen in the kitchen to relieve her and return to my hosting duty.

The rest of the night goes beautifully. This was a day I wanted, but I never thought I'd get. A Christmas miracle.

Everyone fed, my kitchen cleaned and my family repaired. Everyone has turned in for the night. It was a good day. I'm lying in bed next to my love. He has me wrapped in his arms and we are sharing kisses.

"Ma, I'm so damn happy. This all I ever wanted was for you and moms to be on good terms."

"I know babe. I wanted it too and now we got it."

He's begun kissing all over my neck. *"You know you getting this pipe tonight, right?"*

I burst out laughing. *"Adontis. Man, go to sleep. We have a house full."*

"Why you laughing? Yeah, we do. So, what! We in our house. In our bed and the door is definitely locked this time."

"Cause your ass is so nasty." I lean in and give him a peck on the lips. *"Baby, go to sleep."*

"You like me like that. I'm going to sleep alright." He climbs on top of me and starts kissing me. He is butt naked and standing up at attention. He slides his hands down in between my legs. *"How you gon tell me to go to sleep and your ass dripping wet?"*

I smirk at him, *"Because I'm sleepy."*

"Daddy gon put you to sleep, with a smile on your face."

I start laughing. *"Uh huh. Put me to sleep then."* I wrap my legs around him.

December 24, 2008

It is finally Christmas Eve. Time for new traditions. We spend time with our family just relaxing and enjoying everyone's company. After breakfast, the ladies all get in the kitchen and we do some baking. I have some time to bond with Adontis' mom and it is amazing. On one hand I'm thrilled to see and meet this side of her. On the other hand, I'm praying that it's real. The last thing I want to do is get hurt. Baby steps with her until we begin to build a relationship.

I do see she is trying and as long as I feel she is really giving getting to know me a chance, I'm open to getting to know her. She teaches me some of her family recipes that Adontis loves and it turns out to be an amazing experience. The more time we spend together, the more I begin to feel like things between us is genuine.

After all the baking is done, we spend the remainder of Christmas Eve having a game night. Adontis' parents turn in for bed and the kids are sent up to bed too. The rest of us do what we love best. We have a game of pool going, spades and drinks. It's turning into a fun family night.

I'm playing cards with my bro against Shaun and Adontis. Carmen and Kia are playing together against Aisha and Boris. Frank was shooting pool, but now he's passed out on the couch snoring. His belly full and a few drinks and that's all it takes. Hell, all it takes is him sitting down and he is out. Per usual we tease him for a while. Melanie is sitting on the sideline watching the card games.

Shaun says to Adontis, *"Bro, you make Tasha pay up for the bet she loss last time?"*

Adontis burst out laughing. I look at Shaun and very disrespectfully cut my eyes. Like my bro is sitting here at this table. He don't need to be hearing about my freakiness. What the hell is wrong with him. He could ask Adontis that anytime besides now.

Adontis smirks at me then says, *"Naw I haven't made her pay up yet. But it will be soon."*

"Sis what bet did you make?"

"Let's just not talk about it."

Ron is looking at me questionably. *"Why not?"*

"Cause I just don't want to talk about it"

"Well, I'll tell you," Shaun says.

"No, the hell you won't. Adontis, get your brother."

Adontis is smiling. *"Bro chill man."*

Shaun throws his hands up in defeat. Ron looks agitated and then he says, *"Ok. How bout this fellas, a new bet?"*

"Interesting," Shaun says. *"What's the stakes?"*

I'm thinking where is this going? Adontis is smiling. Ron says, *"Let's make a two-part bet. A bet between baby sis and Adontis and one between Shaun and me. If we win, whatever bet my lil sis loss last time is cancelled out. Shaun, you lose, you gotta shave your eyebrows off and keep them shaved for a month and you can't draw it in or tattoo or use fake hair or none of that shit. Bald brows my nigga."*

I burst out laughing. *"Wait a minute he can't come to my wedding without no damn eyebrows."* Ron is laughing hard as hell.

"After your wedding, immediately after brows shaved," Ron says. *"I'll bring my clippers."*

Shaun is shaking his head. *"Ok. When ya'll loose, you gotta shave your head bald and facial hair for a month."*

"Alright," Ron says.

"Adontis, what you want bro?"

He is busy laughing. *"Damn I don't know. Hold up let me think for a bit."* There is a brief silence and all eyes are on Adontis. The other card table has paused their game to listen in.

"Ok. Come here ma." I lean over towards him to hear what he wants to say. As I'm leaning towards him, he's staring at my titties.

I have to call him out for it. He is making it so obvious. *"Really Adontis?"*

He looks shocked that I'm calling him out. *"What you leaning them all in my face, shit what you expect me to do?"*

I exhale into a laugh. *"You know, you get on my nerves. I'm leaning over cause you asked me to. Now what?"*

He places a few kisses on my neck. Ron says, *"Oh hell no Tasha. No fraternizing with the enemy."* He pulls Adontis away from me. Adontis laughs out loud.

"Damn bro, why you blocking?"

Ron looks at him with his arms folded across his chest, like he's a tough guy. Then he cracks a smile. *"You the enemy right now my nigga."*

"Baby you holding up the game. Give me your wager."

"Ok ma come here."

I give him a side eye. *"No cause you playing."*

"I'm gon be good. Come here."

I lean in again and feel his lips close to my ear as he whispers to me. He isn't even trying and he's getting me hot. Hell, what can I say he turns me on. Feeling his breath on my neck as his lips graze across my ear is doing something to me. I think I need to go check my panties. He leans back in his chair and I lean back in mines.

Out loud he says, *"Ma, you accept that?"*

"Huh?" I didn't hear a word he said. I was wrapped up in dirty thoughts. *"What did you say?"*

Now he is giving me the side eye. *"Tasha you ain't heard a word I said?"*

"No. Tell me again."

He leans in and whispers again, *"I win, tonight we make a baby."*

All I can do is freeze. I wasn't expecting that. I respond, but I don't whisper. *"Are you serious? That's what you want?"*

"That's all I want ma. We got a deal or what?"

I don't think I'm really mentally ready for another pregnancy. However, I'm playing with my bro and we usually win. Worst case scenario we lose and I have to give my man some and make a baby. That's not too bad. Plus, the chance to cancel out my old bet with those panties and to see Shaun without eyebrows is totally worth the risk.

"Deal."

December 25, 2008

"Seal it with a kiss then ma."

I lean over to kiss him and Ron pulls him away again. *"Hell, no Tasha, he the enemy right now. Ya'll can shake on it."*

Adontis shakes his head. *"Man, you blocking."*

Ron looks at him, *"That's my damn job. This my baby sister."*

Adontis and I shake hands and so does Shaun and Ron. We begin a new game of spades. We are going to five hundred. The game begins and Adontis and Shaun take the lead after the first hand. They maintain the lead for the majority of the first half of the game. We are trailing close behind. There is nothing, but trash talk being exchanged throughout the entire game. Ron and Shaun focus on who is going to be bald soon.

When the score reaches 379 for Adontis and Shaun, my bro and I have 304. We're still trailing and things aren't looking so good. We haven't gotten set on anything; we just haven't been getting good hands. All we need is to set them with one good hand and take the lead. It's Adontis deal. He shuffles the cards before handing them to me to cut. I need a change so I decide to run it. In spades world it means I will not cut the cards. I pass the cards back to him.

"Deal."

He looks at me with a smirk. *"Oh, you think that's gon help? You are bout to pay up tonight ma."*

I roll my eyes, *"Whatever."*

"Don't try to threaten my baby sis. It ain't over til it's over."

Adontis smirks again and then begins dealing the cards. I leave my cards on the table until he finishes dealing. Ron picks up his cards as they are being dealt. I can tell from his facial expression and the utter silence; my bro has a good hand. All I need is to have one to match his.

I look over to Shaun and he's not talking smack this time. That means his hand must be trash. When Adontis finishes dealing I pick up my cards. I'm cutting two suits, hearts and diamonds off the rip. Leaving me with a two-suit hand full of spades ranging from medium high to low. My clubs run down from ace, king, queen and then some low ones. I just need my bro to have the big jokers and maybe an ace or two. I see Adontis shaking his head. I know that's good news for me. His hand is trash too.

"Alright, its ya'll bid."

Ron looks at me, *"What you got T?"*

I count up my books. *"At least six bro."*

Ron smiles, *"Ten for two. Get your head in the game T."*

"I'm in it bro." I write down our bid. I see Shaun shaking his head. I look to Adontis, *"What ya'll going?"*

He looks at Shaun hoping he has something to offer, but he doesn't. *"Board. Shit."*

Winning this hand will make Ron and I winners of the game. Ron plays first and starts with the Ace of hearts followed by the Ace of diamonds. He wins both books. He learns that I am cutting both suits. He plays his kings in both suits and wins both books. That's four books for us already. The card table is quiet. He follows that up with both jokers and wins both books. We're up to six books now.

Ron throws out his lowest spade, a three. Shaun throws out a heart, that means he's out. I smile at him. I throw out the highest spade still left in the game. The deuce of diamond. Our book again.

Since I won the last book, I lead with the deuce of spades; Adontis plays the ten of spades, Ron throws out a low diamond and Shaun throws out a heart. We're at eight books.

I play the Ace of spades and finally I see Adontis drop the Queen of spades. This means he's out of spades and we're one book away from nine. I run down my clubs, Ace through Queen and win all three. We're at twelve books now. I threw off my low clubs when Ron was winning with his aces and kings. My last card is the Jack of spades. Shaun played the king of spades on Ron's second joker. I'm the only one left with spades. It's our book. We just ran a Boston on them. Ron and I jump up and are hi fiving. Shaun is shaking his head in disappointment.

"Shit!"

Ron is grinning. *"I'll make sure I bring my clippers to the wedding for you Shaun."*

"That's some bullshit. We was winning the entire game and ya'll come back in the end."

"We can thank you for that Adontis." I lean in to kiss him and he pulls away.

"I don't want to kiss you. Shit we just loss."

"At least you get to keep your brows my nigga."

"Word bro."

I walk over and sit on Adontis' lap. I whisper to him, *"Maybe tonight I'll let you practice on giving me a baby."*

He smiles. *"I'll take that."*

"Can your woman get a kiss now?"

He leans in and kisses me. Ron walks away. *"Enough of that shit."*

There's a lot of talking and we are in a bit of an uproar, but in a good way. Shaun calls it a night and he and Melanie leave. Ron and Adontis shoot pool and I sit in on the other game. We stay up for a little bit longer before we all decide to call it a night. Frank slept through it all. Carmen finally gets him up and off to bed. In bed with my man. I give him the practice I promised and we make love. Intensely and very passionately before drifting off to sleep. Merry Christmas.

The kids wake up early so by default the entire house is up early. Carmen and I head to the kitchen and begin breakfast. Everyone is in a festive mood and with great cheer. The kids are opening their gifts and the adults are watching. Christmas music fills the house. By the time breakfast is ready Shaun, Melanie, Aisha and Boris arrive.

We gather in the dining room and eat all together. It's amazing. During breakfast, the adults begin to exchange gifts and everything goes beautifully. The gifts are all lovely and thoughtful. Adontis' mom and dad gifted me a pair of diamond earrings to wear on our wedding day. My something new. They're absolutely beautiful. We gifted his parents a cruise to the Bahamas, but not until after our wedding. Adontis pulls out his gift for me and it is five tickets to see Beyoncé in concert in New York City. Exactly what I needed.

"That's for you to have a girl's trip ma. All expenses paid. Your hotel suite is already booked. When you ready I'll book the flights for everyone. All you got to do is just get your girls together and go."

"Thank you, babe. I love it."

I lean in and plant a kiss on him. I keep it PG-13, since we have his parents and kids around. He'll get an X-rated thank you later tonight. I hope all of the girls are available to go. I can't stop smiling.

Kia looks at me, *"Alright now Tasha, I'm ready to see B."*

"Of course, ladies. We'll discuss this later." I have no intention on bringing Melanie. We ain't friends. Sorry, not sorry. I look to Adontis, *"Ok babe, it's my turn."*

He looks at me with a smile. *"I have everything I need right here ma."* He wraps his arms around me.

"A little something extra won't hurt then."

I hand him his gift. He opens his gift and he has five tickets to NBA All Star Weekend in Phoenix next year. I low key want to go with him, but I know he wants to go with the guys so, I'll let him.

He does his ear to ear grin thing when he sees the tickets. *"Ma!"* That's all he manages to get out before planting a kiss on me.

"I guess you can get your crew together and have a good time. But not too good of a time."

He smiles, *"Thank you shorty."*

The rest of Christmas goes wonderful. Time is spent with family and good food. I couldn't ask for anything more.

December 26, 2008

Today is the last day that our family will be here. We all get ready and pile up in the van once Aisha, Boris, Shaun and Melanie arrive. We start with going out for breakfast. Breakfast is followed up with shopping. My mission is to find my concert outfit. We hit up a couple of malls and have a really good time all out together. Before heading home, we stop to have dinner. When we get back to the house it's late. With everyone's flights leaving out early tomorrow we all say our goodnights and turn in.

December 27, 2008

We all get up early this morning and get ready. I get up earlier than everyone to get breakfast ready for them. We don't have time to all sit down to eat, but they can take it with them and eat on the way to the airport. Once everyone is ready, we all pile up in the van and head to the airport.

We say our goodbyes and share lots of hugs. Once everyone has headed off to their gates to board, I have a moment to reflect. This has been the best Christmas I've had in a really long time. I couldn't be happier. It's nice to see that sometimes the best made intentions go perfectly.

chapter 32

Ladies Night

January 5, 2009

Every woman needs a night out with her girls.

Adontis and I have continued to get ready for our wedding. I have left Florida and I am staying in South Carolina at my sisters until the wedding. Adontis is still in Florida working. We have about two weeks left until our wedding and I am ecstatic. Things are going great between us. Since Christmas his mom has stayed in contact with me and we talk on the regular. A change has come. Hell has frozen over. I'm so thankful that she and I are on the right track. I look forward to continually building my relationship with her.

I have some last-minute running around to do. Adontis and I, or rather I, haven't decided on which hotel we should stay at on our wedding night. We booked a few different locations months ago. I hadn't had a chance to come look at them personally and see which one I like the best. Whichever ones I don't choose, I'll cancel the reservations. I made sure that I only booked rooms that allowed for cancellations without penalties. Carmen, Kia and I drive around to each of the hotels so that I can check them out.

We arrive at the third hotel and I find it to be gorgeous. It is in downtown Charleston. It is a magnificent hotel and I am sold on it. I let my sisters know and then we each call one of the other hotels and cancel the reservations. I'm ready!

January 10, 2009

I have told my sister that I don't want a bachelorette party. Instead, we decide to go out to a club and have a lady's night. Everyone meets up at Diamond's house and we are picked

279

up in a party bus. Everyone consist of my bridesmaids and the people who are closest to me. Carmen and Kia do not ride in the party bus because they are at the venue to greet everyone as they arrive. Kenya will also meet us at the venue because she is driving into town today.

We all get in and head out to celebrate my last night of freedom. When we get to the club, it is packed. Everyone gets off the party bus and goes inside, before me. I get off the bus and walk into the club. Once inside I see another set of closed double doors and I hear music blasting.

I proceed to open the doors. I step inside to see what looks like a classy upscale club. The club is filled with my friends and family. A few haters sprinkled in here and there. I am in total shock. The room is decorated in purple, silver, and white, my wedding colors. I walk into the room on a purple plush carpet.

Carmen has turned this club into a party. More specifically, a bachelorette party to envy. Everything is upscale. No paper or plastic anything. There are glass purple plates on silver chargers. There are also purple margarita glasses. The tables are pre-set and everything is downright gorgeous. I say hello to everyone and Carmen directs me to my table.

There is an open bar with several bartenders. All men and they are only wearing a bow tie and boxers. I just look around the room and observe. I can't believe she went through all of this for me. There is a full dessert table with gorgeous cupcakes that look like they were made for a queen. The cupcakes are iced with butter cream icing and they have white chocolate shavings on top. There are two chocolate fountains and plenty of fruit. Strawberries and pineapples. There are also pretzels. I am very impressed. I love everything that I see. There are no games being played. Everyone is mingling and having a good time.

Everyone eats and that special moment comes along. I know what time it is when I hear the music change. I know what's going on. Carmen did not listen to me. This is a real bachelorette party. To keep from self-incrimination, let's just say, there were several male dancers and I behaved like a complete angel.

Side note: Ladies ya'll know how these shows go down. I can't be telling on us. For the ladies that don't know, you need to go experience it at least once.

After the exotic dancers perform, they get cleaned up and come back out to mingle with the ladies. It is really late and everyone is drinking and still having a good time. I begin dancing with one of the dancers. His stage name is Amore and we have a good time. It's all innocent. Aisha left early because she got into a fight with Boris and it ruined her night. She said she didn't want to ruin my night so she'd tell me what happened later. I'm disappointed she didn't really get to enjoy herself. However, the rest of my girls and I had an amazing time.

Some of the dancers invite some of the ladies out to breakfast and they agree to go. Amore personally invites me too and I accept. I probably shouldn't go, but I am just a little buzzed so let's blame it on the alcohol. Got me feeling loose. I tell Carmen and Kia I am leaving with the dancers, Diamond, Janet, Rita and Kenya. They both look at me as if I have completely lost my mind.

January 11, 2009

Carmen says, *"Do you want Adontis to kill you?"*

"He is in Florida. Lighten up, there is nothing wrong with a little innocent breakfast. Besides it's a group thing."

"Ok then, call Adontis and tell him where you are going."

I look at them and cut my eyes. *"I'll see you back at the house."*

"I don't think you should do this."

"I will be fine. See ya."

Carmen just shakes her head. I walk away and leave with Amore and the others. We go to Denny's and we enjoy ourselves. We are all having good conversation and having fun. Amore is flirting with me and I know he wants to get me into bed. His mannerism and actions infer so. I have been doing a lot of drinking, but I am not drunk. I am in my right mind.

I do find him to be very attractive and he has a very nice body. Under different circumstances I would give him a try. Like me being single and him not being a dancer. After we finish breakfast, he tells me he wants to take me back to his hotel room. I see where he is trying to take things so I need to pump the breaks. I decline and he offers to drive me to Diamond's to get my car. Again, I decline. I came with my girls and I'm leaving with them.

Kenya and the ladies are still being flirty with the dancers. I'm feeling a little warm so I tell them I'm going outside to wait on them. I don't know if it's the man or the alcohol, but I need to cool down. Amore offers to join me. I accept and we head out just talking and walking. He walks with me to Kenya's car. When we stop, he pulls me towards him and kisses me. I pull away from him and I don't kiss him back. I already messed up one time. I learned my damn lesson. I'm not doing that shit again.

"You do realize I'm the bride, right?"

"You ain't married yet sexy."

"No, I'm not, but that doesn't change anything."

He begins licking his lips. *"Can I just taste your pussy? Eating ain't cheating right?"*

I damn near almost pass out when I hear this. *"Yeah, it is cheating. I really enjoyed your performance and company, but that's as far as this is going to go."*

He is smiling at me and I can't lie the brother is fine as hell. He is absolutely my type.

"Ok, sexy. If you change your mind," he passes me a room key. *"Come see me I'm staying at the Radisson. I'll be here for a few more days."*

I smile at him and push the key away. Temptation is a hell of a thing. *"I won't. But thanks for the good time."*

"Can I get a good-bye hug?"

I think on it for a second, *"Yeah you can."* I lean in and give him a one-handed hug. The good old-fashioned church hug.

"Have a good night sexy."

"You too Amore."

Kenya and the other ladies step outside and are saying their goodbyes to the guys. It's not long before she unlocks the car door and we all pile in to leave. We are all talking about the nights events and comparing notes. When we make it to Diamond's we all say goodnight and head to our cars. Diamond heads into her house. I get in my car, lock the doors, crank up and drive away. My cell phone rings and it's Carmen. I answer my phone.

"Hello."

"Where the hell are you?"

"On my way to your house. Girl you won't-"

She cuts me off and says, *"The hell with that. Adontis is not in Florida. He is here at my house and he wants to know where you are. I told him you went back to Diamond's. But it's 4:40 in the morning."*

My heart starts to beat so rapidly it feels as if it is coming through my chest. I am already speeding, but I go even faster and start looking out for cops. I did not cheat on him, but I know my man he will be pissed to know that I went to breakfast with another man. My sister has been home for twenty minutes when I pull in the driveway. As soon as I walk through the door, I see Adontis standing in the foyer. It looks like he's been waiting for me.

"Where you been?"

"Hey baby. I didn't know you was here."

He glares at me. *"The hell with all that. Where you been? It's after five in the damn morning."*

"I was at Diamond's. I left my car there earlier. I was gonna stay the night, but her man called her. She left and I headed here. Then, I had to stop and get some gas."

"Why were you riding by yourself?"

"Because I drove by myself." I think, damn he is asking me a lot of questions.

"Uh huh. Ok."

"And what does that mean?"

"Nothing. I'm glad you made it back safely. It's late and I'm tired. I'm going to bed."

He heads upstairs. Carmen enters the room and walks up to me. She lightly, but sternly whispers, *"You fucking up."*

"I know. I got it. That will never happen again."

"It betta not T."

I go upstairs to the bedroom then into the bathroom. After I shower, I get in bed next to Adontis. I try to cuddle up to him, but he is not having it.

"Damn, Tasha move. I'm tryin' to sleep."

I'm horny as hell and my man is pissed with me. I start rubbing up on his man hood. Hell, I'm trying to get me some tonight. I did the right thing and I didn't screw the stripper. Since my man is here, I should be able to get some. I start kissing him on his neck.

"Tasha, stop. Damn!"

"Make me stop daddy."

He pushes my hands off him and rolls over on to his stomach. As long as I've known this man, he's never slept on his stomach. I'm baffled, he really isn't going to give me none. Technically I could take it, but I shouldn't have to beg for what's mine. His attitude has turned me off anyway. I roll away from him and drift off to sleep.

Late in the afternoon, I awake. Adontis is not in the room with me. I have a slight hang over and I feel like it is going to be a long day. I brush my teeth and wash my face. I find Adontis in the living room chilling with Frank and Ron.

I say, *"Hello,"* to everyone.

Adontis doesn't say anything. He doesn't even acknowledge that I am in the room. I feel really guilty. I didn't really do anything, but I shouldn't have been there. I turn around on my heels and walk back to the bedroom. I ponder telling Adontis, but he would blow a fuse if he found out. I decide to take it to my grave. Along with all that stuff that happened with Rodney.

Shortly after I get back to the bedroom Adontis enters. I reluctantly glance up from my phone at him. I'm not sure if he can read the guilt on my face. I look back to my phone pretending to be preoccupied with it. Then he does what I fear most. He starts asking questions.

"Did you cheat on me last night?"

My heart starts to pound. I can't believe he asked me that question. I am starting to perspire. I have to keep a cool head. I look up at him. Not really sure on how to answer his questions. Technically no, but I was out with another man that kissed me. I try to buy myself some time to think.

With a tone of aggravation and complete disbelief, I say, *"What?"*

"Damn. I didn't stutter. Did you fuck some nigga last night?"

I get up and walk over to him. Time for me to sell this. *"Is that what you think of me? I can't believe you said that. You think I am some kind of a ho?"*

"Then what the hell kept you out til five in the damn morning? Ain't nothing open that late, but legs. Was yours?"

My mind is going a million miles per minute. He just dropped a major bomb on me. *"I am not even going to dignify that with an answer. Who the hell do you think you are?"*

Our voices have risen and they continue to rise. *"I am the damn man you are about to marry. But not if you fucked around on me. To make matters worse you got your sister lying and covering for you. Tell me the damn truth. Did you have sex with somebody else,"* he yells out?

I yell back at him, *"Hell no! Only person I was trying to have sex with was you and you didn't give me none."*

He just looks at me as if he is sizing me up. I stare back at him and we engage in a brief staring match in complete silence.

"I damn sure didn't. You on punishment. I promise you, if I find out otherwise all hell gonna break loose."

"Punishment? Who are you playing with?"

"I ain't playing with your ass!"

He walks out the room and I fall back on to the bed. I am so glad it is finally over. I exhale. What the hell is this punishment shit? That's new. I hope he doesn't think he isn't going to give me none. The next time I will take it. I'm not asking and I'm not begging.

chapter 33

Whats Done in the Dark

January 21, 2009

It always comes to the light.

It is three days before our wedding. Adontis has been distant from me. Since our last argument, he has gone back to Jacksonville. We've talked on the phone and he will be back in the Carolina today until our wedding. We haven't been intimate in over a week and I miss that part of our relationship. Hell, I'm horny. I never even got the chance to take it. When he gets here today, I'm taking it. Hell, he should be horny too.

I am at the airport waiting for Adontis. When I spot him, I run to him and I wrap my arms around him. I genuinely miss my man. I try to kiss him and he turns his head away from me and pulls away. Embarrassed, I back away from him. We are both silent. We go to get his luggage and we make our way to the car. Once we are in private, I say something to him.

"Now you not talking to me?"

He doesn't respond. We are barely off the grounds of the airport. I pull the car over and look at him.

"Adontis?"

He still doesn't respond to me. He is looking straight ahead as if he doesn't hear me. I don't know what the problem is, but he is pissing me off. I hate to be ignored.

"Would you please at least look at me?" He looks over to me. *"Do you want to marry me? I didn't do anything and I will be damned if I take anymore shit off of you. What is your problem?"*

I guess I got him fired up. His lips begin to part and words finally come out. *"Your ass lying to me is my problem. You coming in at five in the morning is nothing? Back when I did it you almost had a coronary."*

Agitated as hell, I sigh. *"Not back down this road. I thought this was settled. And baby when you did it, it was a normal thing for you. It was the night of my bachelorette party. Of course, I will be out late."*

"Hell no, it's not settled. I don't know if I can trust you."

I just want to scream. *"This is the last time I will say this. I did not cheat on you. But if you keep accusing me, I will not marry you."*

"Well, maybe we shouldn't get married."

"What the hell. You wait until now to say this shit?"

"Hell yes. I ain't never had this issue with you til now. Something up with your story about that night. I know you too damn well and I know you are lying to me bout something. You think I don't fucking know when you lying? I ain't going into a marriage where I'm being misled and lied to. So, it is off. The fucking wedding is off."

I exhale and stare at him in complete shock. He doesn't say anything else to me. He is looking straight forward and not paying me any attention. I want to fight him so bad right now. Like really square up on his ass. After staying in park for a little while, I get back on the road. I drop Adontis off at the hotel where we were supposed to stay at.

I need to clear my head. I go driving around thinking about all of my problems. I don't know what to do, I made a mistake. If I tell him he will be pissed that I even went. Somehow, I feel like he already knows. But how? I ride around for a little while and arrive back at the hotel. After getting a room key, I go up to the room. I find him on the phone booking a flight back to Florida.

"Can you please get off the phone so I can talk to you?"

"You ready to tell me the truth?"

With tears flowing down my eyes I say, *"Yes."*

He already called off the wedding I have nothing else to lose. He cancels the flight he is in the process of booking and hangs up the phone. He is staring at me waiting for me to speak. I really don't want to.

"Tasha!"

"Ok this is it. I didn't cheat on you and that's the truth. But I was with another man. He kissed me. But I didn't kiss him back." I can see how pissed he is.

"I knew it! I fucking knew it! Who the fuck was kissing on you? And where the hell you been at? Don't give me some shit about Diamond or some damn gas station."

Tears are streaming down my cheeks. I can't believe I am here in this situation days before my wedding. *"His name is Amore. He was one of the dancers at my bachelorette party. He asked me out to breakfast after the party. I went with him and nothing happened. Until I got back to the car and he kissed me."*

"Wow. A damn stripper? You threw away what we had for a stripper. I guess you wasn't going to tell me huh. I hope it was fucking worth it. Why the fuck was you even with him?"

I sit down beside him and the tears are flowing. *"I made a terrible mistake. I was just enjoying my last night of freedom. A group of us girls just went out with the dancers for breakfast. I didn't plan for any of this to happen. I didn't want to hurt you. I am sorry baby."*

285

"*Well, now you have many more nights of freedom to look forward to. It's too late for hurting me.*"

He pulls out his phone and dials a number. "*I need to book a flight to Jacksonville, Florida. I'll take whatever. The first flight you have out of here would be great.*"

I am looking at him in disbelief. He isn't paying me the slightest bit of attention. I guess he's done. I want to fight for us, but I don't know how. He is a strong-willed person. Once he makes up his mind about something, he sticks with it. Without another word to me, he gets up, grabs all of his luggage and walks out of the room.

I know I messed up, but that's some cold-hearted shit. This man kissed me I didn't kiss him back or give any participation. If this is how he acts behind a kiss, one that I didn't even want, I hate to see his reaction to what happened with Rodney. This just further confirms that if he knew about what happened with Rodney and I he'd be done for sure. He is so damn prideful.

I know he doesn't define me, but I don't see my life without him. He is an extension of me and him leaving feels like I just lost a limb. I don't want to move on from him. I want to move with him. It feels like I can't breathe and the walls are closing in on me.

For a while, I break. I mourn. There is something about coming to terms with the finality of losing the one you love. Putting a period on our love story hurts and scares me. I don't know where to go from here. This stings. It's a pain I've never felt and I don't know how to make it stop. I slide to the floor sobbing in a puddle of tears. Eventually I get off the floor and get into the bed. I turn my phone off and ignore the calls and text. None of them are from Adontis and I'm not in the mood to talk or to start telling everyone the wedding is off. I continue to sob until I cry myself to sleep.

January 22, 2009

I slept the entire day and night away. I didn't even eat because I didn't have an appetite. I awake the next morning still alone. I turn on my phone and I have no voicemails or messages from Adontis. I call his phone and it goes straight to voicemail. I guess he went back home. I'm going to have to start making the 'The Wedding is Off' phone calls. I get out of the bed to take a shower and get cleaned up.

While in the bathroom, I hear a noise in the bedroom. I get out the shower to tell room service I don't want any housekeeping. I enter the room and find Adontis. I stand before him dripping wet in a towel. He stands and stares at me and I stare back. I don't really know what to say. I'm happy to see him, but I don't know what this visit is for. My only thought is to try to keep fighting.

"*Baby I am so sorry. Please forgive me.*" He doesn't say anything at first, he just looks at me. After a long silence. He says, "*I forgive you. Just this one damn time.*"

I run to him and wrap my arms around him.

"*This your last and only time. You forgave me for my mistake the least I can do is forgive you too. We both made mistakes, but no more.*"

"Yes, baby."

I want to ask him so bad; how did he find out. He was too sure that I was lying. I know someone had to tell him something, but I refrain. Eventually, I'll find out. When I do it will be my mission for the big pay back. I lay my head against his chest and cry. He grabs my chin and kisses my lips. I kiss him back hard. I really missed the touch of his lips. He picks me up off the floor and I wrap my legs around his waist. He pulls my towel off of me and it falls to the floor. This is just what I wanted. I have been so horny for so long.

He speaks to me softly, *"Ma I love you."*

He lays me on the bed and spreads my legs. He climbs on top of me and he kisses my lips. He begins kissing all over my body. He starts caressing my breast. With both hands, he begins squeezing them and pushing them together. He gets a mouthful of them and starts nibbling on my nipples.

I start moaning. He begins to kiss down my stomach. He makes his way to my thighs. He sucks on my thighs and starts to nibble on them. I lay there enjoying the pleasure. He kisses my kitty kat. He is moving very slowly and then he starts to lick her. I begin moaning his name as I run my fingers through his hair entangling them in his curls.

He starts to suck and nibble on my kitty kat. He has me wetter than a slip n slide. I can't hold it in and I cum in his face. He still licks and sucks on me. I am calling out his name and I have gotten loud. He slides his finger in me and plays with my kitty. My heart is beating extremely fast. He is working me in a way he never has before.

I begin to kiss him all over. I stroke his dick and I begin to suck on him. I like it, but he loves it. He cums all over me and I don't mind it. I am in love with him. I am enjoying pleasuring him. He flips me on to my stomach and I get on my knees. He begins to hit it from the back and smack me on the ass.

"Whose pussy is this?"

I am too busy moaning I do not answer him. He pops me on the ass again, but a little harder.

"I said whose pussy is this?"

"It's yours daddy. It's all yours."

I'm gripping the bed. He continues to smack me on the booty and I continue to moan and scream his name. He flips me back on my back and he re-enters my walls. He begins to ride me and I sink my nails into his back. We roll over and I climb on top of him and start to ride him.

As I ride him, my titties start to bounce in his face and he begins playing and sucking on them. I continue to bounce up and down on him and it feels so good. I bite down on his shoulder to keep from screaming out. We both climax together as he cums inside me. He doesn't even try to pull out. Those days are long over. I'm all his, so no complaints here.

chapter 34

Trust

January 23, 2009

Is something you must earn. Once you lose it, it's hard to get it back.

It is the day before our wedding and we will be having our rehearsal followed by our rehearsal dinner. As the day gets closer and closer it feels like a dream come true. There is no greater feeling than marrying the person you love, knowing they love you just as much.

After Adontis and I made love yesterday we took a nap. However, after that nap we went out to an early dinner and spent the entire day together just the two of us. No cares or worries. We've gotten back on track and I'm grateful for that.

We spend the day with our family going over the plans for tomorrow until its time to go to the church. We spend some time rehearsing our wedding and I feel the butterflies in my stomach. It's surreal. Tomorrow, I will become his wife. My siblings and his siblings attend. I'm thrilled both of his parents are also here and his mom and I are still doing really well.

Once rehearsal is finished, we head to the restaurant for dinner. We enjoy dinner with our family and bridal party. Shortly after dinner ends, Adontis and the men get ready to leave for his bachelor party. I don't want him to go. I know it's selfish, but hell I'm honest. I know what goes on at these parties. Before leaving, he walks me to my car and talks to me.

"I will see you tomorrow my love."

While smiling at him, I say, *"Yes you will baby. I love you."*

We exchange an exotic and passionate kiss. *"I love you back shorty."*

He leaves with the fellas for what I assume will be a wild night of debauchery.

Adontis is in the partying mood. Him and the guys get to the beach house they have rented and get liquored up. They have all types of liquor and alcohol. The music is blasting on the stereo. The men are getting loud and begin to holler out, "Where the females at? I wanna see asses and titties shaking everywhere."

Shaun gets on the phone and makes a call to find out the location of the strippers. Shortly after the strippers arrive and the men get buck wild. There are about fifteen strippers and Shaun tells Adontis to pick the ones he wants first.

With one of his eyebrows raised and a Kool-Aid smile on his face, Adontis responds, "Naw, I shouldn't. But I will."

He picks three girls and they begin dancing for him. Shaun passes him a large stack of ones. He makes it rain singles on them. One of the girls sits on top of his lap and gives him a lap dance. She is grinding on his dick and making his nature rise. He begins grabbing and squeezing on her breast and ass.

chapter 35

Anticipation

January 23, 2009

**Enjoying life and looking toward a new life. Anticipate the
good things in life because they don't always last forever.**

I am back in my hotel room. I am checking to make sure I have everything together. I make sure my lingerie is packed. I begin thinking about Adontis and I miss him. I can't wait to be Mrs. Adontis DeOntay Lamentez. I think about him and how much I love him.

Carmen comes in the room. *"Hey baby sis. Shouldn't you be getting some rest?"*

"Yeah. But I am too excited and nervous to sleep."

"Yeah. Well, it's only normal, but it's getting late. You need to get your rest. I will finish everything up."

I don't put up a fight. I know she is right. We hug and exchange an I love you. I go to bed and toss and turn for a while until I finally I fall asleep.

chapter 36

Woman's Intuition

January 24, 2009

A woman's intuition is a very important thing. It never fails.

The strippers continue to dance for Adontis. One of the strippers' whispers into his ear, "I want you. I can feel you hard for me."

He looks at her and smiles. She continues to dance for him. Shaun comes over to his brother and whispers to him. "You gon hit that? This your last night to have fun. You can have your threesome fantasy." Shaun hands him a box of condoms. "Knock her off bro."

Adontis smiles and scratches his head. He wouldn't mind blowing her back out. Then he thinks of Tasha. He loves her and only her, but his dick is hard and Tasha is not around.

It is as if she is reading his mind. The stripper, Sexual Chocolate, grabs his hands and pulls him up from his chair. She leads him upstairs to one of the bedrooms and closes the door. Adontis goes to sit on the bed. She locks the door then begins to dance over to him.

As she is dancing towards him, she is removing items of clothing. When she makes it to him, she is completely naked. He is grabbing on her and she begins to unbuckle his belt. She unbuttons his pants and slides his shirt off.

Tasha jumps up out of her sleep in a hot sweat. She looks at the bedside clock. The display reads 1:46am. She has a feeling that something just is not right. Tasha searches for her cell phone. When she finds it, she dials up Adontis.

Adontis is busy with his hands all over Sexual Chocolate. Her hands are all over him. She is pulling his dick out when he hears his phone ringing. It is Tasha's ring tone. He pushes the stripper off of him and pulls his pants up. He grabs his shirt and slips it on while he is heading to the bathroom. He buttons his pants up then answers.

"Hey ma. What you still doing up?"

"You ok baby? I woke up with a bad feeling, like something was wrong. Everything ok?"

He thinks, damn. He was about to fuck up. He shakes the thought from his head. "Everything good, you ok?"

"I'm fine. I just had a bad feeling. Are you sure everything is good?"

"Well stay in bed, I'm on the way."

"It's late you should be getting rest."

"And I will, once I come to check on my wife. I will see you when I get there. Goodbye."

Adontis doesn't give her a chance to respond back before hanging up the phone. He walks out of the bathroom and Sexual Chocolate is laying across the bed playing with herself waiting for him.

She sensually says, "You want something nice and wet just for you?"

He looks at her smiling. "Hell yeah. I'm goin go get it." He leaves her on the bed and walks out of the bedroom. He doesn't tell anyone he is leaving. He is going to see Tasha.

When he reaches Tasha's suite, he knocks on the door and Carmen answers. He walks in without being invited. "What you doing here? You know it's bad-"

He cuts her off and says, "Yeah, yeah sis. Where my wife at?"

She points him in the direction of Tasha's room. He opens the door and sees her laying snuggly under the covers. He slips out of his shoes and gets in the bed with her. She is completely naked. Her silhouette is intoxicating. He has his chest against her back and he wraps her into his arms. He holds her tightly and close to him.

While kissing on her neck he says, "I love you ma. Damn girl I love you."

chapter 37

Sex Me

January 24, 2009

Who doesn't appreciate some good lovin'? It's better than a stiff drink.

With a smile, I turn around to face Adontis. *"I love you too daddy."* I begin to kiss him as he kisses me back. Just that quickly, I notice that he is aroused.

He pulls away from me, *"Shorty go to sleep and get your rest."*

"Maybe I want you to put me to sleep."

"Anytime, anyplace."

"Yes daddy, fuck me to sleep."

He does his ear to ear grin thing. I pull his face towards mines resting my fingers in his dimples and I kiss him very sexually. He moves his lips from mines and onto my neck while he gently runs his fingers down my spine. He traces the outline of my nipples with his fingertips placing kisses down my neck. When his lips reach my breast, he takes two handfuls squeezing them together into his mouth.

I'm moaning out his name. He continues to kiss down my body until he reaches my kitty kat. He begins kissing and sucking on her like only he can. He kisses and licks until I reach an orgasm. I clutch his arm as I feel the release.

Now it is my turn. I push him on to his back and take him in to my hands. I begin kissing and sucking on his balls as I am jacking him off. I allow my lips to gently glide their way to his tip. I begin to gently lick around the tip.

"Oh shit, Tasha. Damn ma," he says sensually. *"This your dick ma. Do him like you want. Shit."*

I grin as I hear how satisfied I am making him. I begin to get rougher and rougher with him as time goes on. Kissing and sucking on him while I'm playing with his balls. I take all of him into me. My saliva is all over him and I'm about ready to make him cum. I go harder and faster until I feel him clutch my arm and make the beautiful sound he makes.

I catch it in my mouth. I stand and I'm ready to go spit it out. He grabs me and stops me. *"Swallow it."*

I look at him, like not again. I shake my head no.

"Swallow it for Daddy."

I can't believe he is asking for this again. He is holding on to me waiting for me to swallow. I stop holding it and I swallow it. I open my mouth to show him. He pulls me even tighter into him and slides his tongue in my mouth. He is being a little rough with me and he knows I like that.

He has his hand wrapped around my neck as he is kissing me. He lifts me up and slides into me. He gets in a squatted position and begins hopping us around the room. We begin sliding him in and out of me. He is biting and nibbling on every inch of my body. I'm about to lose it. He has never done this to me before.

We ride each other all over the room. My orgasms come multiple times in waves. Every time I make love to him, it gets better and better. I don't know how in the hell he'll top this. I've placed hickeys all over his neck and chest. I didn't mean too, but damn he worked me right. We continue to ride until he cums again, in me.

I know he is tired. Daddy put in work. He carries us back to the bed and lays me down. He climbs in behind me and holds me for a while. I fall asleep quickly.

He whispers in my ear, *"I love you Mrs. Lamentez. But daddy leaving. I'm going back to the fellas."*

In a sleepy voice, I say, *"Ok. I love you baby."*

He leans over and kisses my lips one last time before leaving. He gets out of the bed and gets dressed. I quickly fall back asleep.

chapter 38

Temptation

January 24, 2009

**Temptation a sure way to mess up your life. It's
hard to avoid, but best to do so.**

It's about 4:49 in the morning when Adontis returns to the rental house. His boys are still partying, but the strippers are getting ready to leave.

Shaun sees him and says, "Damn bro. Where you been? You missed it all."

"Naw, I didn't. I was with my wife."

"You left the boys to go get some? All this pussy right here. Come on bro. Damn."

Adontis is wearing a smirk on his face. "Bro you drunk. Time for all of us to turn in."

The strippers leave and so do all of the fellas except for the groomsmen. The men turn in drunk and happy. Adontis heads up to his room and opens the door. When he walks in, he finds Unc passed out in the bed with a naked Sexual Chocolate. He laughs it off. He and Unc look alike so he guesses she figured she still got what she wanted.

He heads to Unc's room and happily gets in his bed. He thinks about the night's events.

chapter 39

Finally

January 24, 2009

It's great to feel like your life is complete. Finally, I have this feeling.

The ladies in my bridal party are as follows: Carmen and Kia are both my matrons of honor. Aisha and Kenya are both my maids of honor. Aisha is my sister from another mister. We've grown so close and she is now one of my best friends. When I'm not with Adontis, I am usually with her. Diamond, Rita and Janet are my bridesmaids.

My oldest nephew Andres is the junior groom and Adontis' cousin, Natina is the junior bride. Andres is ten and Natina just turned eleven. Our flower girl and ring bearer are my niece Remi and my nephew Anthony. Remi is six and Anthony will be six in a few months.

Adontis' best men are Shaun and Riq. His other groomsmen are Brandon, Chuck, Kenny, Deon and Boris. I completely allowed him to choose his own groomsmen. He's known all of the guys all of his life, except for Deon and Boris. Adontis wanted Ron as a groomsman, but he knew I wanted my brother to walk me down the aisle.

Since they first met at my birthday, he and Deon have become really cool. They've discussed and done some business ventures together. Whenever he, Kenya, Adontis and I are in each other's city we get together and hang out.

Boris and Aisha have remained strong. They seem to have gotten through the argument they had the night of my bachelorette party. Adontis has opened up to getting to know him and they've built a friendship. As long as he treats Aisha right, he has Adontis and my blessing.

My big day has arrived. It's our wedding day. I awake early in the morning. I lay in the bed and smile as I think of Adontis. I love him so much and I know he loves me. In spite of our past problems, I am really and truly happy. I am anxious, nervous and excited all at once.

I get out of the bed and awake my bridesmaids and then I get into the shower. It takes a while, but we are all finally ready to head to the church. We head out the door and to the limo. Get me to the church on time. I have my man waiting on me. I've booked several hair stylists, nail techs and makeup techs for any last-minute touch ups needed. I want my girls to look and feel their best.

chapter 40

Taking A Plunge

January 24, 2009

Take off the training wheels and go for it. You only live once.

Adontis awakes and lays in his bed. He thinks about Tasha. He never thought that he would find a woman like her. He changed from the player that he used to be, all for her. Hell, before her, he was a ho and he knows it. His resume of women runs pretty long. Having her as his bride, makes him proud. He gets out the bed and showers. He wakes up the fellas, they get dressed and head to the church.

When the men reach the church, they go in and begin putting on their tuxedos. The men are dressed in all white tuxedos and white shiny shoes. The best men have on silver vests and the other groomsmen have on purple vests. Adontis is in white on white. His vest is white and he has on a white top hat.

He looks handsome, debonair even. After the men get dressed the barber shows up for any needed haircuts or line ups. The camera men are inside and they take all necessary photos and video.

chapter 41

Setbacks

January 24, 2009

Every time you think you have made it. There is always something that changes. Sometimes you take a step forward and two steps backward.

The girls and I have arrived at the church. We go into a room and begin getting ready. All of the stylist, make-up artist and nail techs are present and they get to work. My makeup gets done first. The makeup artist starts with arching my eyebrows. She puts a blend of purple and silver eye shadow on me before applying my fake eyelashes. Her name is Natasha. I've missed her so much, since I've moved to Florida. Whenever I come home, I get her to do my makeup. She is the best. On to my lips, she glides on a sparkly translucent purple lip gloss. I look like a doll baby.

After my makeup is finished my stylist touches up my hair. Once she finishes, my sisters help me get into my dress. It is sleeveless and low cut to show off some cleavage. Just a little sample for Adontis. A preview of what he is getting tonight. It has a six-foot-long train with a thick strip of purple down the middle of the back that runs to the edge of the train. The purple strip along the back and down the train is lined with purple diamond studs.

The rest of the dress is white. Yeah, I'm bold. I haven't been a complete ho; I've just had some ho-ish moments. I laugh to myself as I think on this. The back of the dress is backless. It cuts a few inches above my butt. I look at myself in the mirror and I am about to cry.

Carmen sees me and she says, *"You betta not. Save those tears for when you see Adontis."*

Aisha chimes in, *"Exactly. You look beautiful sis. I'm thrilled my brother found you. I couldn't have picked a better woman for him. I love you and I am so honored to officially have you as a part of my family."*

I smile. I am so happy. *"Aisha thank you so much. I love you too. T&A forever."* She walks over and we embrace in a heartfelt hug.

"Forever sis. Now I'm going to get out of here before you have me in tears. I'm going to peek in on Adontis and make sure his butt is in line."

"Thanks sis." I give her a kiss on the cheek. *"Pass that on to Adontis for me, please."*

"Ok. I will."

"And this." I pass her a gift bag. *"Tell him to open it privately and I love him and I can't wait to marry him."*

She smiles. *"Ok."* She hugs me again before leaving.

Carmen gets my veil and she puts it on my head. It is a silver tiara with purple diamond studs. I wish my parents could be here to see me. This is the happiest day of my life and yet a very sad day also. My daddy won't be here to walk me down the aisle.

There is a knock at the door and Carmen yells out, *"Who is it?"*

"It's Ron." She opens the door and lets him in. He sees me and says, *"Wow. Baby girl you look so gorgeous. I wish Momma and Daddy were here to see you. They'd be so proud of you."*

I blush. He looks like he is about to tear up. That's not usual it takes a lot to make him cry.

"Thank you, bubba. I wish they were too."

I look over to Carmen who has begun the water works. When I see her, the tears begin to fall. Ron has to be the strong one and comfort us and eventually we get the tears to stop. Natasha steps back in and touches up both of our makeup.

Mr. and Mrs. Lamentez step in to greet me and they both embrace me in a great big hug. Everything seems perfect. Mrs. Lamentez and I are doing great. Mrs. Lamentez is crying tears of joy.

"You look beautiful Tasha. We just wanted to come in and love on you. We love you and we'll see you soon."

I smile, *"Thank you Mrs. Lamentez, you do too. And I love the both of you."*

"Enough of that, its time you call me mom."

It is almost time for the ceremony to begin. Adontis takes a deep breath and smiles. He grabs his hat and puts it on. There is a knock at the door.

"Come in," Adontis says.

He sees his sister walk into the room looking beautiful wearing a gorgeous smile. *"Hey bro. How are you doing? Are you ready for this?"*

He smiles, *"You look beautiful. Yes, I'm ready."*

"Good. If you think I look beautiful, wait to you see Tasha."

He smirks at the thought of what Tasha looks like. *"I know she looks phenomenal."*

"She absolutely does. I just came in to check in on you and to give you this from Tasha." *She leans in and kisses him on the cheek.* *"She says she loves you and she can't wait to be your wife."*

He smirks. *"Oh yeah, I have something for her. She'll get it later."*

"I don't want to know. There is one more thing." She passes him the gift bag in her hand. "This is also from Tasha. It's for your eyes only."

"Ok. Thank you, sis." He hugs her and she walks off and talks with the other groomsmen and stops when she reaches Boris. Adontis steps into another room and privately opens the gift from his soon to be wife. First, he pulls out a note card. The card reads:

1/24/2009
To my best friend, my lover, my husband!
I never knew that love could be like this.
I never knew I could fall so hard
But yet feel no fear
Because I know
You'll catch me
No matter how
Or where I fall
You'll always be there
My heart I've given to you
My love for you is true
And on this day
Today
I get to marry you
Until the end of this world
For my life
I commit
To you
To forever and to always love you
And give you many babies too
Adontis
Daddy
I love you

A smile comes across his face. Tasha's words are an instant reminder of why he loves her so much. Her words are loving and thoughtful. Her sincerity further confirms her love for him. He never thought he would ever get married. He did not even want to get married until he met Tasha. She really changed him for the better.

He digs into the gift bag and pulls out a gift box. On the top of the box is a note card with a message. It reads:

A gift for you
Wear this today my love.

He opens the box and finds a gold diamond encrusted Rolex watch. He removes the watch and finds an inscription on the back. It says:

> *To my husband and best friend*
> *Adontis*
> *I love you beyond words and beyond this world*
> *I pray that we'll have lifetimes*
> *together and time*
> *will always be on our side.*
> *Love Always,*
> *your wife Tasha*
> *1-24-09*

He is grinning and exposing his dimples even more than when his face is in a relaxed state. He never expected any of this. Tasha really surprised him. He slips the watch on and feels honored to wear it. His lady has great taste. He digs in the bag and pulls out the final item. It's a manila envelope. Approximately six by nine inches. He opens the envelope and finds a photo of Tasha. Not just any photo, it is risqué. She is wearing black fishnets and red stiletto heels. She has on a white button-down shirt buttoned once midway down.

She is showing off her beautiful body and cleavage. Adontis can't help it, but this picture of his wife is getting a rise out of him. He is ready for her right here and now. Now he knows why this was for his eyes only. He peeks in the envelope and sees another note. The note reads:

> *I have a blown-up copy of this photo waiting for you at home.*
> *In the meantime, enjoy this view.*
> *If you think you're horny now*
> *Wait until tonight*
> *Daddy*
> *I can't wait to get my hands on you*
> *And make love to you*
> *As your wife.*
> *I love you Daddy.*
> *See you soon*

Adontis can't help, but to grin. He is ready for the ceremony to begin. He wants to see Tasha. Get his hands on her. Touch her. There's a knock at the door and Adontis goes to open it. He finds Shaun on the other end. Shaun walks in and closes the door behind himself.

Shaun looks at him, "You ready for this big bro? It's not too late to run. Just give me the word, I'll get the car started right now."

Adontis smiles at him and says, "Why in the hell would you say that bruh? I'm nervous as hell already."

"I'm sorry bro. I just wanna make sure you know you got options and shit."

"You need to stop that. I'm here, I love Tasha and I'm gon marry her."

"I love Tasha for you too bro, but you ain't got to get married. Today is officially the day that your life ends. I just want you to know that."

Adontis puts his hands over his face. "You stressing me out bro."

"Ok. My bad. I'm done. I just know you gon be on lock down. We ain't gon be able to kick it like we use to. I'm gon miss that, that's all."

"Come on now bro. We still gon kick it. You my best damn friend. Ain't nothing gon change that. Not even marriage. I'm just getting married and you just getting another sister. That's it. You acting like I'm dying or something."

"What's the difference? Death; marriage; they bout the same thing to me. I ain't never doing this shit."

"I'm not changing my mind. If you want to be a part of this, come on."

"Alright bro, I'm with you."

They both walk towards the sanctuary.

"About time."

"Well, I might change my mind if Carmen would give me some. She acting like she can't cause she married."

Adontis looks to him in complete shock. "We in a church. You know you going to hell, right?"

He shrugs his shoulders, "That's a chance I might take for Carmen. She need some young meat."

Adontis shakes his head in disbelief. "You dumb as hell."

"I'm just saying and I get to walk with her. Hell yeah. Make this a double wedding."

"My nigga. She already married."

"She don't really love him. I'm telling you all I need is just one-time wit her."

They walk into the church and take their places. The church is packed and people are continuing to come in.

"You going straight to hell."

"I'll be happy."

"If Melanie don't kill you first."

"She be alight. She ain't Carmen."

Adontis looks at him in shock. "My nigga."

"I'm just keepin' it real wit you bro. I ain't giving my last name to Melanie. But I'll do it for Carmen. They can be sisters and sisters-in-law."

The groomsmen and bridesmaids begin to line up and get ready to walk into the church.

He burst out laughing. "You dumb as hell bro. We'll finish this conversation later."

Carmen and Kia kiss me on the cheek and go to take their places in line. I think to myself. I have something old. Something new. Something borrowed. Something blue. The wedding party walks in and Ron and I get ready.

"I love you baby sis."

Ron kisses me on the cheek and pulls my veil down. My flower girl goes down the aisle and then it is my turn to walk. I walk into Ki-Ci and JoJo's song. All My Life. When Adontis sees me, I can see the major smirk on his face. When I see him, I try to fight back the tears. Through all the mess he and I have been through. I am extremely happy to be here. Ready to become his wife. Ready to start a family and continue to build a future together. When Ron escorts me to the front of the church, everyone is seated and the pastor speaks. We've asked Pops to perform our wedding ceremony. He agreed after we agreed to premarital counseling with him. We did about twelve hours of counseling with him during our engagement.

"Who giveth this woman away?"

"I do, Ron A. Leam Jr."

Adontis takes my hands and Ron goes to his seat. Pops begins the ceremony and tears escape my eyes. I tried to fight them back, but I have no success.

"Is there anyone here who sees just cause why this man and this woman should not be joined together? Let him speak now or forever hold his peace!"

"I do!"

Everyone gasps. I can't believe what I am hearing. I recognize the voice. I am pissed beyond words that this person would do this on my wedding day. Adontis spins around to see who has interrupted our wedding. I exhale hard and spin around. He is standing midway down the aisle along with four other men. His two brothers, cousin and best friend.

"Tasha baby, you can't marry him. It's gotta be me. I love you. Remember the love we shared?"

Adontis looks at me and says, *"What the hell is he doing here Tasha?"*

I look back at him then at Adontis. Then I look back to him again. He is walking towards me. Everyone is watching this play out.

"Tasha don't marry him baby. Marry me."

He gets down on his knee and pulls out a beautiful diamond ring. *"Let me make you, my wife. Just say yes."*

Adontis is about to attack him. Ron jumps up and holds Adontis back. *"Bro this your wedding day, don't let this nigga ruin it. I'll bust his ass though."*

"No, I'm gonna bust some ass," Uncle Riq says. Shaun grabs a hold of him and stops him.

He ignores everyone and is still on one knee, he says, *"Tasha say yes!"*

I'm in silence. Hell, I think I've gone mute. The room is spinning and I don't know what to do. I didn't see this coming at all. Why me? I should faint and maybe that would just end everything. I really don't want to make my wedding even more of a spectacle.

Adontis yells out, *"Tasha?"*

I utter out...

Printed in the United States
by Baker & Taylor Publisher Services